GRAVEYARD SHIFT

GRAVEYARD

SHIFT

MICHAEL F. HASPIL

A TOM DOHERTY ASSOCIATES BOOK **TOR** NEW YORK

GRAVEYARD SHIFT

Copyright © 2017 by Michael F. Haspil

A Tor Book
Published by Tom Doherty Associates
175 Fifth Avenue
New York, NY 10010

www.tor-forge.com

Tor® is a registered trademark of Macmillan Publishing Group, LLC.

The Library of Congress Cataloging-in-Publication Data is available upon request.

ISBN 978-0-7653-7962-7 (hardcover)
ISBN 978-1-4668-6922-6 (ebook)

Our books may be purchased in bulk for promotional, educational, or business use. Please contact your local bookseller or the Macmillan Corporate and Premium Sales Department at 1-800-221-7945, extension 5442, or by email at MacmillanSpecialMarkets@macmillan.com.

First Edition: July 2017

Printed in the United States of America

0 9 8 7 6 5 4 3 2 1

For my wife, Penny.

And to M. & M. for getting me out of São Paulo in one piece.

ACKNOWLEDGMENTS

During the long and circuitous route this book has taken to publication, I had the pleasure of inflicting it upon numerous souls generous enough to read its varied incarnations. I apologize in advance to anyone I've accidentally left off this list. Rest assured that your contribution helped make this novel what it is today. To Mark Davis, whose mid shift screenplay scene conversations inspired Gail's unfortunate fate and planted the seed of what would grow into this story (hopefully, the South will rise again in "Southern Blood"— coming to a drive-in near you). To Bree Ervin, who was the first volunteer to read an embarrassingly raw early draft and patiently provide feedback, thank you. To my parents, Frantz and Liliane, for encouraging a love of books and always ensuring I was well read. To my siblings, Nicky and Thierry, for putting up with my insane rants and providing geographical feedback regarding the greater Miami area. To the myriad other readers, some of whom subjected themselves to multiple drafts: Taylor Sims, Anita Romero, Jessica West-Fields, Naomi Brown, Laura Paulini, Jennifer Powelson, Connie Doyle, Thomas Transue, Brian Kotek, Dave and Rochelle Tisinai, John Riden, Lisa Louden, Carissa Cline, Bobby Veazey, Kathryn Veazey, Susan Boucher, Kenny Boucher, Michael Rothman, Teya Hajek, Jeanne Stein, Vickilynn Rivera, Tim Baptist, and Jennifer Meadows. To Michael Stackpole for his classes at Gen Con and

"The Secrets" newsletter, and Graham McNeill for convincing me I could actually do this thing. To Mario Acevedo, thanks for the awesome blurb, brother. To all the great folks at Pikes Peak Writers and the Rocky Mountain Fiction Writers. To all the Veterans of the Long War who helped support this project. The Emperor Protects. To my critique group, the Highlands Ranch Fiction Writers, a.k.a. "Because Magic" (Lisa Hawker, Vicki Pierce, Claire Fishback, Marc Graham, Laura Main, Nicole Greene, Chris Scena, Deirdre Byerly, Lynn Bisesi, and Chloe Hawker) I couldn't have done this without you, and I'm still working on that race of atomic supermen to help us conquer the world. Special thanks to my editor, Moshe Feder, my copyeditor, Terry McGarry (who saved my bacon several times in this novel), Diana Pho, and the entire team at Tor who toiled to get this book through all the wickets and bring it to market.

Supreme thanks to my inimitable agent, Sara Megibow, who has more patience than the communion of saints. This is but the first step toward world domination!

Wer mit Ungeheuern kämpft, mag zusehn, dass er nicht dabei zum Ungeheuer wird. Und wenn du lange in einen Abgrund blickst, blickt der Abgrund auch in dich hinein.

He who fights with monsters should see to it that he himself does not become a monster. And if you gaze long into an abyss, the abyss gazes also into you.

—Friedrich Nietzsche, *Jenseits von Gut und Böse*
(Beyond Good and Evil), Aphorism 146

GRAVEYARD
SHIFT

1

Wednesday, August 11, 8:45 A.M.

No sign of forced entry.

Detective Alex Romer took in that detail as an afterthought. He pulled on the sky-blue Tyvek booties and crossed into the air-conditioned crime scene, his footsteps making muffled sounds on the Florida Tile flooring. People here had dollars, which meant they had influence, which meant scrutiny and associated headaches. Which told Alex he was making a start on ruining the new day.

This was Coral Gables, an affluent suburb of Miami, and it was too early to be investigating a murder. The house was just big enough that it might garner envy from most people, but it didn't stand out in this neighborhood. A large central stairway dominated the foyer and wound its way upward. Alex thought there should have been skylights and massive picture windows framed by tall palms to offer a carefully calculated peep show of privacy. Hidden conspicuous wealth was an oxymoron.

The entire entrance should have been drowning in sunlight. Most vampires didn't like that.

The place smelled pungent.

Garlic. Concentrated. Way beyond what anyone would use for cooking. And something else. Vinegar with a hint of baking soda.

Bright artificial light streamed from the next room, where people murmured in concerned voices. The forensic services unit had brought in portable lights and set up before they'd thought to call him. That was odd. They were moving very quickly, which complicated things. Now he'd have to explain everything to these kids like it was Day One.

With a grimace, he set off for the lighted room. As he stepped toward it, an impressive oil painting came into view. It was the ninth trump of the Major Arcana of the Tarot, The Hermit, holding his lantern aloft as a beacon encircled by encroaching gloom. The painting depicted the scene as if the lantern's powerful beams were actively battling the darkness—not simply traversing it, but piercing it, lancing it . . . laying waste to it.

It was more than just a masterly rendition; it was a symbol. It was the sigil of the Lightbearer Society. Since the Reveal, the Lightbearer Society had purportedly been helping both established vampires and the newly turned integrate into mundane society. "The Reveal," that's what everyone called it. The global event when vampires had flung aside their cloaks of secrecy and darkness to brave the scrutiny of the proverbial light. It was just the Reveal. The Lightbearers were dirty as hell and had money and influence to spare. Headaches free of charge.

Shit.

Well, now he knew why everyone was Johnny-on-the-spot this morning. That's why they hadn't waited for him to arrive.

A voice interrupted his thoughts. "When you're done admiring the art, we could use your help with the vic. You know, anytime that's convenient for you."

Alex took in the man who'd spoken. Detective. Wearing a cheap suit off the rack. The suit implied professionalism, but Alex knew better. Still, it was more professional than the loose khakis and light green camp shirt he wore.

"You're Nocturn Affairs, right?" The man barely hid the scorn in his voice.

Alex raised his eyebrows as if to say, "What do you think?" He held up his badge and ID.

"Nocturn." There was that word. Since the vampires weren't going away anytime soon, the politically correct folks wanted the V-word to become a no-no now. They'd come up with "nocturn." A lazy truncation of *Homo nocturnus*. Alex didn't like it. The word sanitized the reality. It was a kind of lie. He supposed that in some people's eyes that made him a bigot. But he'd been in the business far too long to change his ways now, and despite all the Lightbearer Society's propaganda, he knew vampires for what they were—ruthless and bloodthirsty.

"What've we got?" Alex asked.

"Female. Apparent age mid-thirties. She's one of yours. Got herself decapitated."

That was all the city needed right now. Tensions ready to bubble over and a high-profile vampire murder. Everyone would go ballistic.

There was a bit too much activity in the house right now. Alex needed to clear it out.

"Think I can get some time alone?" Alex asked.

One of the forensic techs, who was prepping a doorjamb to lift prints, addressed the cheap-suited detective. "Perez. Your scene. Your call."

Perez hesitated.

"Ten minutes," Alex said.

"Take five, guys," Perez said.

The tech nodded and walked outside, sweeping up the rest of his team in his wake.

Alex looked at the doorjamb the tech had been working. They'd find nothing here. He formed a theory of events and knelt down. He felt the edge of a rug that led into the room. It was still damp.

He sniffed. Garlic and vinegar. Bingo, here was the source of that scent.

"You think you might take a look for yourself?" Perez prodded. "After all, you came all the way down here."

Alex allowed himself a small laugh, answering sarcasm with sarcasm. "Yeah, what could it hurt, right?"

He stood and walked into the room, stepping over and around dried blood splatter. The pattern spoke volumes. There wasn't nearly as much blood as one would presume from a decapitation, but Alex had been expecting that. Vampire physiology released blood rather reluctantly.

The room itself was more of a pass-through with a doorway at the other end leading farther into the house. A glorified short hallway. Choke point. There were two small tables against each wall at the midpoint. One still held a fancy white vase. Blue filigree swirled around it. Its partner hadn't been so lucky, and shards of no doubt rare porcelain littered the tiles and the rug.

An investigator from the county coroner's office leaned over a woman's headless body. The woman had been fit. She was a vampire, after all. She was wearing a red power–suit jacket-and-skirt combination with designer boots to match.

"Cause of death?"

"Don't be a wise-ass. It's too early for your bullshit," the investigator answered without looking up.

"Rivera, always a pleasure. Where's her head?"

Rivera tilted his head in the direction of a covered mound a few feet away.

"Mind if I have a look?"

"Well, that's why we got your happy ass down here, isn't it?"

Alex stepped over the body, crouched down, and lifted the covering from the head.

He looked into the face of an until recently attractive redhead, her skin already turning waxy.

"Does she look familiar to you?" Alex asked.

"Yeah. Can't quite place it though."

"Maybe Lelith? She's kind of dead ringer, right? Pun intended," Alex said.

Lelith was the spokesperson for and figurehead of the Lightbearer Society. Very smart, very hot, and Alex bet she landed somewhere near the evil end of the whole good-bad scale.

"Now that you mention it, yeah," Rivera agreed.

This woman wasn't Lelith, but she sure looked like her. Alex was betting that was why they'd killed her, and more importantly, he guessed that was why she'd been here in the first place. Decoy.

He looked at the severing cut. Two strikes, three at most. Whatever had done it had been razor sharp.

"Machete?" Alex guessed.

"Yeah, or something like it. What makes you think that?" Rivera answered.

"It's what I would have used. Common enough. Doesn't mess around. They were scared. Couldn't take chances. Had to do it quick."

"They?" Perez asked from the doorway. "Multiple people did this. If I were to guess, I'd say three or four. You smelled that stink coming in, right? You think anyone cooks with garlic that concentrated? Especially her?"

"Hard to smell anything over your aftershave," Rivera said.

Alex let the covering drop back over the severed head, stood, and gestured toward the far door.

"All bullshit aside, Rivera, you were in here before me. Let me run through it for you. They let her walk in and get far into the house. House like this is sure to have an alarm. So they disabled it and reset it so she could turn it off. Make her think nothing's wrong. That tells us it was planned. But they killed the wrong lady, so that tells us it was a target of opportunity."

"Wait. What? How is she the wrong lady?" Perez asked.

"They were going after Lelith. When we check, we'll find this house belongs to the Lightbearer Society. That's what the painting out there tells us. Lelith's their grand pooh-bah. You know, from all the PSAs about 'Truth Not Myth.'"

"Yeah, yeah, the whole superhelpful, 'I'm a nocturn and I do blah blah blah' people," Perez said. The Lightbearers ran commercials day and night to improve the overall vampire image. Not that they really needed to; the last several decades of pop culture had done enough of that while vampires were still in the myth category.

"You got it. Technically, we probably need to inform Lelith her life is in danger. Make it all official-like. But she knows, that's why she sent this youngblood. Hmm . . ."

Alex drifted off, caught up in his own speculations. That didn't quite add up. If Lelith knew it was a trap, why not send enforcers in her place or a strike team? It didn't make sense to let the double get killed. He was missing something.

Alex continued, "they let her walk in. Past here. She should have seen it coming, smelled them or heard them, but she didn't. So we know she was a youngblood. An oldblood like Lelith would never have fallen for it. So, she sees something through there, scares her enough to try and run for it. Again, an oldblood wouldn't have run and even a youngblood wouldn't run from just one or two people. So we know there were more than that." Alex stopped to see if the two other men were following his reasoning. They showed no sign either way. He continued to run through his idea of the crime.

"So she runs through here. Perfect choke point. One way in, but no way out. Because someone is standing right over there." Alex pointed to where Perez stood framed in the doorway.

"They hit her with some O.C.—that garlic Mace. That's what you'll find when you get the carpet analyzed. Homemade, but industrial strength, is my bet. Anyway, they hit her with the Mace. But they can't take any chances. If it really is Lelith, she can still tear them apart and be none the worse for wear. That's when he hit her from behind."

"Who?" Rivera asked.

"Whoever cut off her head. Strong, too. He came up behind, grabbed her by the hair. And then . . ." Alex pantomimed the action. "One. Two. Quick. Room's not quite wide enough for someone that big to fully swing a sword at speed. But with a machete, not all that hard."

"Sounds like you could have done it yourself," Perez said.

Alex ignored him. The man didn't know how right he was. Alex had done it hundreds of times. For nearly three-quarters of a century he had been part of a secret program. The code names changed more often than he bothered to track. The operators all called it UMBRA, the original name from the aftermath of World War II, when it had begun. Project UMBRA. The name stuck. Alex had been part of a deadly hunter-killer squad the OSS, the CIA, and finally the National Security Agency employed to "neutralize" vampires. Once, that would have sounded crazy to civilians, but that was before Hemo-Synth, before the Reveal. That was before the Supreme Court had given thousands of vampires sanctuary and citizenship and the NSA suddenly had a genocidal embarrassment on their hands they wanted to erase. UMBRA went away in a hurry. So now, Alex worked vice, and occasionally, homicide.

Rivera interrupted. "That's not how it went down. Blood spatter is all wrong." He pointed at the severed neck. "This wound was post-mortem."

"That's 'cause you're expecting arterial blood flow. Vampires don't have that."

"Shit." Rivera leaned back from the body and nodded in acknowledgment. "You guys really need your own ME."

"Yeah, I know. We need a lot. Let's hope the whole bureau thing comes through, huh?"

Rivera ignored him. Instead, the man went over his notes, scratched out whole portions, and began making corrections.

"Not your fault, Rivera. How many of these have you worked?" Alex said.

"First one." Rivera continued scrawling down notes.

It had only been two years since the Reveal. Alex could only think of three other local cases during that time where a vampire had been the victim. And one of those was all the way up in Osceola, so it hardly counted as local.

Perez stepped over the body and squeezed past Alex. "There's something you need to see."

Alex followed him deeper into the house. A crime-scene investigator took a series of pictures in the next room. Another bank of portable lights glared at a wall.

"We'll be out of your hair in a sec," Rivera told the man.

Alex looked at the subject of the photographs, a grouping of straight lines spray-painted in red across the bone-colored wall.

Two parallel vertical lines bisected by a single horizontal. Superimposed upon them were two Vs, one upright and one inverted—like a rudimentary Masonic symbol.

It was the calling card of Abraham, a notorious serial killer who'd left a bloody swath of vampire victims across Europe and three American cities.

Complications aplenty.

Shitstorms galore.

Day ruined.

No one had figured out how Abraham overcame the vampires. Now Alex had a pretty good idea. Abraham wasn't just one guy.

"So, the Nocturn Killer has come to Miami?" Perez used the name the press had given the murderer.

Alex's phone rang, the ring tone way too upbeat for the circumstances.

He didn't need to deal with this today. The Lightbearers would have their people on it. Alex had problems of his own.

"No. See the false start on the paint line there?" Alex pointed to the top of one of the lines, where it was clear the painter had started again. "Who called this in? Money says it was an anonymous tip.

Probably the killers themselves. They throw this up to muddy the waters and stir everyone up. I'm pretty sure it's a copycat."

He was pretty sure it *wasn't* a copycat.

"Was this symbol ever released to the public?" Perez asked.

Alex's phone, oblivious to the situation, continued jauntily whistling the main melody of the Bangles' "Walk Like an Egyptian."

Instead of answering Perez's question, Alex answered his phone. The voice on the other end sounded panicked. Alex took the information and hung up.

"What gives?" Perez asked.

"Looks like this one is all yours. Nocturn Affairs will try and get another liaison officer down here. Between you and me, I wouldn't hold your breath," Alex said.

"So where are you headed?"

"Brownsville. Possible vampire in a blood frenzy."

"Another one? Better you than me," Perez said.

"It isn't likely. Sun's up. But, you know how it is," Alex said.

"Yeah. Well, hope it's a BS call for your sake."

It wasn't.

Alex manhandled the dark blue Explorer into a parking lot on the western end of the shopping plaza. In front of him, half a dozen cruisers formed a makeshift cordon, roughly twenty-five yards from the entrance of a small market and its shattered front window.

A gaggle of uniforms took cover behind their cars—a jumble of green-and-white Miami-Dade Police cruisers mixed in with the City of Miami Police's blue-and-white livery. They pointed trunk guns—AR-15s and Mini-14s—and pistols at the doors. Off to the side, several cops held the press and other looky-loos at bay.

It was the standard goat rope whenever a vampire might be involved. The odds were low that there really was a bloodsucker around, since the sun was already beating down with full late-summer fury and it wasn't even midmorning. While it was true that sunlight wasn't as deadly to vampires as the myths implied, at the very least it made most of them severely uncomfortable, and some suffered third-degree burns with only slight exposure.

Alex parked the SUV and killed the cherry lights. He stepped out into what felt like an impossible hundred-and-fifty-percent humidity with heat to match. It wasn't as oppressive as Kemet at this time of year, but Kemet's was a blistering, drier heat.

Egypt, he reminded himself again. That was what they called it now. It had been more than two thousand years since the Greeks had renamed his homeland after a mispronunciation of a misunderstanding, and it felt almost as long since he'd been there. Re beamed overhead, charging Menkaure's body with His invigorating light. The power coursed through him, raw and unchecked. As long as Re held vigil overhead, Menkaure was nearly invincible. It was darkness that held weakness for him.

Alex ran a hand over his dark, bald, cool head, wiping away a thin sheen of moisture, due solely to humidity, since he didn't sweat. He wasn't a vampire, but his body, like a vampire's matched the ambient temperature, in this case that of the air-conditioned interior of his SUV. He suppressed the urge to slam its door. Charged up as he was now, if he did, it might never open again.

"Who's the primary?" He projected his voice, and with it, his authority, but it took an effort to keep the annoyance out of it.

One of the Dade cops muttered, "Guess the nocturn squad finally decided to show up. Took your sweet-ass time."

Alex ignored the man and walked nearer to the line of police cars.

Ah, irony.

Once, Menkaure had been the Morning and the Evening Star, He of the Sedge and the Bee, Pharaoh of the Two Lands. Few men would have dared to speak to him without awe in their voices. Now, he walked the Path of Asar as penance, and though all of humanity owed him innumerable debts, he found naught but scorn in their tone.

Alex asked his question again, louder this time. "Who's the primary?"

A middle-aged man with salt-and-pepper hair stepped forward. He wore the taupe uniform of the Miami-Dade Police and had a paunch that pushed his gun belt low.

"Right here," he said. "I've got men watching the back of the store. It's not coming out of there."

"It?" Alex asked.

"Yeah, the vampire. I mean, the um, nocturn."

"I'm fine with 'vampire.' Are you sure? Seems a bit early." Alex pointed at the sun.

"Yeah, we're sure," the cop answered. "We've got four officers down on account of going in there and trying to deal with it—him. Couldn't make an ID. He's probably an undocumented nocturn. We think he's in a blood frenzy. I'd just as soon not take chances."

"What's the deal with Miami PD responding?"

"New rules. Overwhelming force, plus they were close enough to augment. The way things are going, orders are we're supposed to show the city no one's sitting anything out."

Alex shook his head in disagreement. This was all wrong. The leaders were making things worse. They should have been doing business as usual, telling everyone there was nothing to get worked up over. Instead, they were ignoring the storm surge that preceded the hurricane.

A younger cop spoke up. Alex made him for a boot—a rookie—instantly.

"He threw two officers right out the front window. At least twenty yards. The other guys barely made it out."

Twenty yards? More like twenty feet. Maybe. With a running start and if the wind was right.

"Did they get bitten?" There would be some extra complications if they had. Mountains of paperwork. Immigration and Customs Enforcement would have to get involved. After the Reveal, ICE had caught the responsibility of keeping track of the newly turned. It was yet another impossible law to enforce, but looked good on paper, and politicians could jabber about it as if it would make a difference.

"No," the senior officer answered. "We had a squad take them over to Hialeah to get checked out."

"So they got lucky," Alex said. "The guy in there is probably a good guy. Solid." He didn't keep the admiration from his tone.

"Wait, what? He almost killed them," the rookie said.

"No, you've got it wrong. He *saved* their lives. He had enough control left to get them away from him." Alex made the decision that killing this vampire wasn't going to be an option.

"What do you have going for response?" Alex asked. "SRT on the way?"

"Just Nocturn Affairs—you guys catch all these calls now. Director's orders," the primary answered.

Alex sighed. One Nocturn Affairs cop instead of a Special Response Team. In his case, that certainly measured up, but they had no way of knowing that.

"Is he armed?"

"He's a vampire," the rookie said.

Alex let his annoyance show through. "Does. He. Have. Any. Weapons?"

"Not that we know of," the primary answered.

Alex considered the men taking cover behind the police cars. The sun was doing more for them than those cars ever would if a blood-frenzied vampire decided to have a taste.

He looked around. Press trucks with long-distance mics listening to every word. That was a problem.

"So it's my scene, right?" Alex made a show of surveying the area. "See you guys later."

Alex walked back to the SUV.

"Whoa, you're not going to deal with this?" the rookie shouted after him.

"In about eight or nine hours. Sun's up. Even in a blood-frenzied state, he's not going anywhere. That's probably the only thing his brain can even understand right now."

Let the press weigh that. Was it really worth sitting around all day to get some B roll of cops waiting out a vampire?

The younger man trotted after Alex. "Um, he might not be alone."

Alex whirled back to the senior officer. "You didn't evacuate the area?"

"The surrounding buildings, but not—"

"The store itself." Alex shook his head in disbelief. "CCTV?"

"Nothing we can tap."

Alex looked over at the press. They weren't going anywhere. Time to get a bit fascist.

Alex raised his voice so everyone on the line could hear him. "Does anyone know if there are still civilians in the building?"

The response was a bevy of shaking heads and shrugging shoulders.

Alex clapped his hands over his face and rubbed his eyes.

"Unbelievable," he muttered through his hands.

Menkaure could easily take a metaphysical look, but that took time, and there were too many eyes on him right now.

He remembered Salbatore, the man who had named him Alejandro and taken him in after he'd reawoken. Salbatore's advice sounded as clearly in Menkaure's mind now as it had one hundred seventy-odd years before.

Do what they do, talk like they do, think like they do. Or they will destroy you out of ignorance and fear. Salbatore had been right, and the locals in Cartagena had nearly gotten Menkaure because of his carelessness.

A duality flowed within him like the Asian concept of yin and yang. Alex was modern, a skilled operative who could kick ass and take names against the best wetwork teams the world had to offer. But he was also Menkaure, son of Khafre, son of Khufu. An ancient pharaoh who'd taken it upon himself to stand between humanity and the most terrible evil he'd encountered in all his long years. A king who'd made a pact with incalculable powers from far beyond the mortal realm for a chance to walk in Asar's footsteps and wield immortality as a weapon.

He was Alex, a man shaped over nearly eighteen decades— vintner, explorer, scholar, soldier, spy, enforcer, assassin, and cop. He was the oncetime pharaoh Menkaure, a has-been deity. Now intimately bound to his direst foe, reliant on his brother god Re and the Path of Asar until his ultimate task was complete.

"Shit." He pressed his hand against his forehead in frustration.

He was burning daylight. The sooner he was done with this, the faster he could get back to his own business.

"Okay, first things first. Get the press out of here. I don't care how. We can't have our TTPs showing up on the evening news. Next, get me a blanket out of one of the cruisers."

"What? TTPs?" The younger cop looked perplexed.

"Don't they teach you anything anymore? Tactics, techniques, procedures. Now, get them out of here." Alex pointed at the press trucks and the civilian spectators.

"Um, they're not going to want to go," the young cop answered.

"If they're not out of here in the next few minutes, you'd better be. Got it? Now, one of you get me a damn blanket."

Alex stalked back to his SUV and opened the rear door. A blood-frenzying vampire was going to be a hardcase. No way to reason with it. Alex needed to take him down a notch.

Nocturn physiology precluded the use of a direct sedative. However, there was a loophole. The same traits that made a vampire immune to diseases and drugs also made the creature incredibly efficient at processing blood. And extremely fast at it, too. While the loophole wasn't effective with diseases, blood collected from a human under the influence of some substances might have a similar effect on any vampire ingesting that blood. Bottom line, while a vampire couldn't dope up on its own, a vampire drinking blood from a doped-up human would feel the effects of the drug. That fact alone had given rise to all the illegal blood clubs that dotted the city. With the help of vampiric sources within UMBRA, it hadn't taken operatives long to use this trait to their advantage.

It wasn't exactly on the up-and-up within the eyes of the law, post-Reveal, but then again, Nocturn Affairs, which was full of ex-UMBRA operatives, tended to fall on the shady, gray side of Legal Street in almost everything it did.

Alex opened a refrigerated case in the back of the SUV and pulled out a small vial. Its blood product had been extracted from a human who'd nearly OD'd. Alex slid the vial into a small handheld syringe gun, the same type used to administer vaccines to cattle, and loaded it with a CO_2 cartridge.

He walked back toward the barricade and the primary.

"Do you have my blanket?"

"Sure do. Much good it will do you." The cop handed him the blanket.

Alex started walking toward the grocery store.

The older cop put a hand on his shoulder. "You're not going in there, are you?"

"Sure am."

"What exactly do you think you're going to do with a blanket? Against . . . a monster?"

"Use his survival instinct against him. If he's truly frenzying, there's no talking to him. His cognitive mind is gone. It's something they teach us over in Nocturn Affairs. It's like bullfighting." Alex nearly laughed. It was complete horseshit.

"You're crazy."

"Crazy is a requirement for Nocturn Affairs. Well, crazies and vampires. You ought to put in. Strikes me, you might be qualified."

The older cop scowled and waddled back to the cover of his squad car.

Alex stopped at the entrance. The trumpets from a Celia Cruz salsa version of "Guantanamera" blasted their way through the otherwise silent store. The savory smell of fresh *pastelitos* mixed with the coppery scent of Hemo-Synth greeted him. If it weren't for the Hemo-Synth, there'd have been no Reveal, and vampires would still be wetwork, covert ops, instead of a law-enforcement problem. If this blood frenzy was anything like the other two recent cases, it was likely this vampire had consumed some tainted blood product. If that was true, it wasn't just a theory anymore. Someone was poisoning the artificial blood. If the vampires couldn't trust the Hemo-Synth, then . . .

He stomped his way in, kicking around the broken glass and generally making his movements as loud as possible. He crossed the first aisle and knocked some cans onto the ground. There were no civilians. It looked like the store had emptied out the moment the vampire started to frenzy. Lucky.

Suddenly, streams of water burst from the ceiling, and the fire alarm began blaring.

Alex stopped and tightened his hand on the vaccine gun. Flashes of memory assaulted him. Cartagena. He really didn't need a fire right now.

Forget flames. The vampire was overhead, crawling along the ceiling.

Alex pretended he didn't know where it was. He moved halfway down the aisle, then bent over to examine the broken bottles of Sangri and Hemotopia that littered the ground. Both were popular Hemo-Synth products, and they came from different distributors. The contents formed a large pool of artificial blood. The combination of the store's fluorescent light and the sprinkler water bouncing off the pool of Hemo-Synth made it look like it was raining blood.

Alex splashed down the aisle, continuing to make as much noise as he could. The forensics team would be hard-pressed to get much of anything from the mess on the tiled floor, especially now that it was watered down.

A slight rush of wind whispered next to him, as he'd expected. He turned, in time to catch one of the vampire's arms as the creature pounced on him. The vampire reacted as Alex thought it would, lunging for his throat, piercing him with its fangs. It suddenly recoiled and gagged.

"Too bad, *amigo*. No lunch for you. I'm already dead."

The vampire hissed and pushed at him in an effort to escape. Alex slammed the vaccine gun into the vampire's neck and squeezed the trigger. There was a sharp pop-hiss as the device delivered its payload. The vampire reeled in surprise, but didn't go down. Alex dropped the vaccine gun and grunted as he held the vampire with one hand and tried to maneuver the blanket into position with the other. The cops outside had been right. This guy was strong.

Alex flapped the blanket out onto the ground and switched his grip on the vampire. He pinned it to the floor with one hand and used the other to wrap the blanket crudely around it. It wasn't pretty or neat, but it was good enough.

He grabbed the bundle of struggling vampire in a bear hug and shuffled to the front of the store. In the short time it had been on the ground, the blanket had absorbed a surprising amount of the Hemo-Synth, which was now seeping into Alex's clothes.

Day ruined, shirt ruined. That was never going to come out.

Swearing under his breath, Alex reached the front of the store and tossed his burden out into the sunlight.

Immediately, the vampire freed himself from the blanket and stood transfixed, caught in the sun's rays. It took some time for the pain to penetrate the fog of the blood frenzy and sedative. The creature screamed and darted back toward the front of the store.

Alex blocked his path and pushed him back into the sunlight. The vampire whirled, looking for any escape from the pain. Then he noticed the blanket.

"That's right, buddy, there's shade under there."

The vampire snatched the blanket and wrapped himself in it. Before the nocturn could move again, Alex knocked it back to the ground.

"Get me some ties!" he shouted at the police line. None of them moved. Slack jaws gaped at him.

"Hurry up!"

Two of the braver officers responded, tossing him the plastic zip-ties they used to restrain problem suspects.

Alex linked some together and tied the straps around the blanket while the officers kept their distance. He could feel the vampire weakening, as the sedative finally kicked in.

"I'd have never believed it if I hadn't seen it," one of the officers said.

Alex affixed another strap. "Yeah, well, don't try this at home, kiddies."

"What now?" the same officer asked.

"I'm taking this big boy to holding so he can sleep it off and we can ask him some questions."

2

7:37 P.M.

Below Alex, the city was aflame, lit by the fading rays of a rapidly setting sun. The strong wind pulled at his open shirt and carried
strange tastes with the impending nightfall.

Time for his preshift scan. He let his *ka*, his consciousness, his
soul, slip free of his flesh and into the spirit realm. His body stood
against the dying sunbeams, which graced his dark skin with a tawny
glow. His true self soared forth, leaving its fleshy confines on the rooftop. He was Menkaure, the Great Bull of Horus, once more.

The city felt off-kilter, punch-drunk, stretched apart. There was
always a melody, the song of the world, lurking in the background,
giving Menkaure the sensation that it was a familiar tune, but one
he couldn't quite make out. Tonight, it was riddled with dissonant
tones.

He received only the vaguest of impressions. For the third day in
a row, he sensed a new power in play. It hummed in the ether, a raw
live wire, rolling thunder accompanying an unseen storm—primal
and ancient.

Corrupt.

It, whatever *It* was, eluded him like a name sitting on the tip of
his tongue.

It was not *the Other*. Neithikret, Nitokris, Ayesha—whatever she was going by these days. Of that much, Menkaure was certain. He knew her particular melody.

This tasted of vice and degeneration, an ill scent on an otherworldly wind. He couldn't place the source, yet had no doubt that it lurked nearby.

Beneath him, the city mewled and whimpered in myriad voices. His altered state-of-being afforded him senses beyond the mundane five. He saw the soft orange-yellow presences of the souls of the living. Seeded among them, rare as shooting stars in the night sky—yet more common than they should be—he saw the telltale blue-white presences of lost souls who had not yet crossed. These had no remaining flesh to animate, yet haunted the periphery of the mortal world, confused, aimless, and full of raw, unchecked emotions.

Since the Reveal, they were multiplying at a steady rate.

Because of the vampires.

Menkaure saw several vampires now, still indoors, their soulless existence appearing as negative presences violating reality. Those he sensed were going about the mundane business of preparation for their night shifts at various jobs. Nearly the entire economy of the city had shifted to a twenty-four-hour schedule, and the vampires, numerous as they had become, had to contribute to society.

Some notes in the evening's song grew louder.

Someone was coming. Apparently, a few minutes alone was too much to ask for.

Menkaure let his *ka* snap back into his flesh. He stretched his arms out before him and grasped the railing to steady himself. He felt the momentary drain of the effort; then Re's dwindling beams restored his strength.

The door to the rooftop crashed open. The wind here, twenty stories up, often caught the door and slammed it into the side of the building. Tonight was no exception.

Before he even turned around, Alex knew it wasn't one of the vampires. Whoever it was, was entirely too loud. Alex turned around as a young woman struggled with the door.

Latina, athletic, just shy of six feet tall, early to mid-thirties—not much younger than Alex appeared to be. She had her hair in a ponytail and wore casual clothes. Had to be the FNG, the fucking new guy, Stephanie Garza.

Garza fought to close the door. It probably felt like a hundred pounds. Garza finally shut it and walked over to where Alex was standing.

"Detective Romer?"

"Let me guess, Narcotics, right?"

"That obvious?"

Alex laughed. "Read your file. You don't look like what I was expecting."

"I get that a lot. It's the height, right?"

"Yeah. You've got no problem with the hours, I take it?"

"Yeah. I mean, no. No problem." The gal couldn't stop smiling. That would be gone soon enough.

"You're sure you're ready to jump down the rabbit hole?"

"I've seen my share already, that's why I transferred. Well, that, and the pay is a lot better."

Alex buttoned up his shirt and tucked it in his slacks. He re-adjusted the holster and the detective's badge clipped to his belt.

Garza laughed nervously. "Captain Roberts wants to talk to you."

"Any hint as to what's up?"

"He didn't tell me."

"Well, welcome to Nocturn Affairs. Full of secrets within secrets within secrets. Everyone plays things close here. That's not bad advice, by the way."

Alex walked toward the door, and Garza followed him.

"Regular cops want nothing to do with us weirdos," Alex said.

"That's one reason we're out here in the boonies, renting office space in an empty building instead of having a proper precinct or space down with Metro." The Miami-Dade Police Department hadn't been called Metro-Dade in about two decades, but while names changed easily, habits didn't. He was going to correct himself, but Garza didn't seem to mind.

Alex opened the door, and it swung in his hand as if there were no wind at all. He let Garza walk past him, and then pulled it shut.

It slammed home with an unintended finality. That was it. Time to start rationing. No more sun for today.

They moved down the short flight of stairs toward the elevator. Alex pushed the call button, and the doors opened. They stepped into a world of synthesized remade music, droning at the edge of consciousness, banal, and stripped of all its original glory.

"Do you have any first-day advice for me?"

Alex pushed the button for their floor.

"You're paired with Zorzi Cigogna, right? Listen to him and do exactly what he says. Keep your head on straight. Don't act like a boot. He'll see and hear things you can't, and you can pick up things he won't. This won't be like Narcotics. Regular cops are growing their balls back and dealing with the youngbloods. We get the hardcases. Every one of the vampires—"

Garza's intake of breath interrupted him.

"Old habits," Alex continued. "Every one of the nocturns in this unit has several hundred years of experience behind them. Marcus, our Ancient, has disarmed some situations just by showing up."

"An Ancient? Wow! What's he like?"

Alex gave Garza a sidelong glance. She must not have dealt with any real hardcases in Narcotics. It took vampires a couple of centuries to work up to their full potential for depravity.

"He's like an Ancient. Between you and me, he's kind of a prick. I'll let you make up your own mind."

The elevator stopped and the doors opened. The familiar smells greeted Alex like old enemies. The recycled office air. Scorched coffee. That metallic tang of the Hemo-Synth that seemed to catch you in the back of the throat.

They stepped into a dark gray cubicle farm more suited to an accounting department than a police section. Alex turned toward the break room. The place was empty. The majority of the personnel, most of them vampires, would trickle in over the next hour. The only sound came from the cheap off-white blinds as they clacked softly in the stream of the air-conditioning. The blinds were only there for show; the windows behind them had been painted opaque long ago.

"You deal with thropes much over in Narcotics?" Alex entered the break room and took a large metal thermos from the refrigerator.

"I heard about a case or two, but that's as close as I got."

"You will here. Hopefully, it won't be soon. Just let one of those poor bastards go off his meds during a cycle and then we've got big problems."

Alex stepped out of the break room and headed for Captain Roberts's office, Garza still in tow.

"That happen a lot? With the therians, I mean."

"Less than you'd expect, but more often than you'd like."

"Therians." There was another PC word. Derived from "therian-thrope." It amounted to skin-changers, shape-shifters, call them what you will—cursed bastards who'd lose control about once a month. At least now there were meds to help them deal with it. Granted the word "thrope" didn't make much sense by itself if you thought about it, but then slang words often didn't.

Alex continued. "You know only one in every three thropes is actually registered? Folks don't report attacks, for obvious reasons."

Captain Roberts called out from his office, interrupting Alex. "Taking your sweet time, Romer?"

"On my way, Captain." Alex tipped his thermos at Garza. "I'll talk at you later." He bit his tongue not to add in "kid." After all, he was supposed to be only a few years older than she was.

He walked into the captain's office.

Roberts was a solid cop, who should have collected his pension a couple of years ago. A sense of duty had kept him from retiring after the Reveal. His wife, now his ex, had been losing her fight with breast cancer. When word got out about the vampires, she was one of the first high-profile cases to go over to the other side. That was before Washington passed those idiotic laws and ICE got in the business of trying to control the vampire population. Far too late of course, but then that was the rule if you counted on the government to react to a trend.

Now, instead of a few thousand, there were roughly 1.2 million vampires in the good ol' U.S. of A. And they needed their own special brand of law enforcement. So when the city was looking for good cops with a solid sense of command and familiarity with the nocturn situation, Roberts had been the logical choice to head up the section.

He sat behind his desk, tie undone, and ran a hand through the few strands of hair still on his scalp. He looked like he'd had the mother of rough days.

"Close the door, Alex. I wanted to talk to you before everyone else rolls in. Any chance you've got your report done?"

"What do you think?" Alex smiled.

Alex closed the glass door, a pretense of privacy. Vampires in the area would be able to hear whatever they said anyway.

Roberts wrinkled his nose. "You could take it a little easier on the aftershave."

"You know how it is. I wear it, humans bitch. If I don't, I get to hear how much I smell of death from all of *them*," Alex said.

"Sorry, Alex. I've had an ass-kicker of a day."

"Join the club." Alex sat and made a gesture of opening the thermos. "You mind?"

"Go ahead."

Alex opened the top, and immediately a powerful smell of chamomile, thyme, and frankincense filled the small room.

"That holistic stuff help much?" Roberts asked.

"Some." Alex took a swig from the thermos.

"I've got to hand it to you, not going for the vamp blood, you know?" Roberts said. "I'm not sure what call I'd make if I was sick. I just don't know."

Roberts and a lot of other folks thought Alex had some rare terminal disease. Alex let them go right on thinking that. It kept people from asking too many questions.

"We all have different ways of coping. You shouldn't judge too harshly," Alex said.

Roberts glanced at the blank space on the desk where his wife's picture had once been.

"Yeah, it's just . . . it's not the same. Never can be. Like these vampires out there. You can't ever really trust them, right? It's like they're always withholding something. Every one of 'em . . ." Roberts censored himself. You never knew who could be listening.

"I know what you mean. Who lives as long as they do to be 'on the job,' right?"

"Don't get me started. What'd your partner dig up?"

"Haven't talked to him yet," Alex said. "Marcus is checking in with an old source now. We should have a lead soon. I hope."

"You want some good news or more bad news?" Roberts made little finger-quotes in the air when he said the word "good."

"Let me guess. Constance got bureau commander?"

The rumor mill had been alive with tales that the Nocturn Affairs Section was going to get bumped up to a proper bureau and that they were going to get a vampire to head it.

Roberts nodded. "Word is Lelith handpicked her. What's the deal between those two anyway?"

Alex didn't like Constance Howe. He didn't trust her and couldn't be sure she wasn't one of the bad guys. But Marcus assured him that having her head the Nocturn Affairs Bureau, while Lelith thought she had her in her pocket, was a closet win.

Alex kept his face noncommittal. "They're both vampires, I guess. Does that mean you'll be out of here?"

"After a transition period. I filed my papers today." Roberts didn't look happy. He stared down at his desk.

"Well, that's the first bit of good news I've heard all day. Good for you. You've dealt with enough of this bullshit." Alex smiled for him.

"You know a guy named Trent Summers?"

Alex felt the smile vanish.

"Yeah, he's a fed with the Behavioral Analysis Unit out of Quantico. I used to work with him back in—well, I used to work with him."

"He sends his regards," Roberts said.

"So we're on to the bad news now. When did you talk to him?"

"He was on a telecon at City Hall. Says he's coming to town in the next couple of days."

"That's not good. Abraham?"

Roberts nodded.

As of that morning, Abraham had sent some kind of manifesto to the media. The talking heads had been going on about it all day.

So much for damage control using that old copycat idea.

"So the manifesto is real?" Alex asked.

"Looks that way."

Alex shifted uncomfortably in his chair. "And the murders we thought were copycats?"

"Probably the real deal. That means Abraham is sitting right in our laps."

"That's just fantastic. And it's only Wednesday. How're they sure?"

"The manifesto *The Standard Bearer* printed—"

"Yeah?"

"Someone leaned on 'em and they finally gave up the original. Postmark came from our fine city."

"Damn. Listen, Captain, if you want me and Marcus to play hosts to the feds and drive 'em around—"

Roberts held up a hand. "That's not why we're having this talk."

"If the feds want this one, they can have it. I'll even wrap it up with a bow and a gift basket."

Roberts nodded. "Frankly, they're better equipped to deal with this sort of thing."

"I sense a 'but' coming." Alex braced himself for the next piece of news.

"You'd be right. City Hall wants this to go away pronto. You know as well as I do they have friends in D.C. They made some calls and someone tossed out your name."

"Ah."

"Yep. I don't even want to know what you and Marcus did before, but someone in D.C. was impressed with your handiwork. So folks told me to tell you, regarding this Abraham deal, they're willing to turn a blind eye and let you and Marcus do what you have to do."

Alex laughed halfheartedly. There it was. The ever-present "they." The puppet masters. People the conspiracy nuts would have a field day with if the truth ever came out.

"In this political climate? They don't even know what they're asking. Tell them I want full immunity, in writing. For starters."

Alex knew they'd never agree to any such thing, but this way it wouldn't look like he was completely unwilling to play ball. He had a decent idea who was making the request, and that person would know this was bullshit right from the start. If they were really serious, they wouldn't have asked. They'd have ordered.

"I'm just the messenger."

Alex crossed his arms. "They don't want us dealing with this problem. Nobody's ready for the fallout. As soon as the bodies start piling up, it would be our asses out in the wind."

Why were they asking anyway? If Abraham had started his activities before the Reveal, they would have probably recruited him right into UMBRA. Were the Lightbearers getting so powerful they could pressure the men Alex suspected were behind the request? If that was the case, everyone was pretty much screwed. Fucking politics.

He stood up and his voice involuntarily rose. "They wanted this to become a law-enforcement issue. They don't get to pick and choose when the gloves come off."

"You don't have to convince me."

Alex nodded and let out a breath. It wasn't Roberts's fault. He sat back down and took an angry swig from the thermos.

"You heard what happened this morning?" Roberts asked.

"I was there, remember? Did the guy I bring in sober up?"

"He died. Docs say it was some kind of system shock."

Shit.

"Can't catch a break, can we?"

"Might have. While you were handling your business, another sanger . . ." Roberts corrected himself. "Another nocturn had just downed a pint of what he thought was Hemo-Synth. Just like the others. Blood-frenzied out into the street and took down three of us before the pain kicked in and he burned enough to realize it was daylight. Only this time we got the original bottle and there was enough fluid left to test. Lab tells us it was human blood. Not one hundred percent pure though. They'll tell us more when they run more tests."

"There's a new shitstorm," Alex deadpanned.

"You have no idea. The FDA has opened a formal investigation, though no one will admit to it openly. The Lightbearer Society is doing their best to keep it quiet. At Lelith's direction, Media Relations is in the dark. She's got her PR machine in full spin mode. Any hint there might be something wrong with the artificial blood supply . . . Well, I don't have to spell it out for you."

"No, you don't. But that requires you to brief me personally?"

Roberts sighed. "I know you don't give two shits about half this stuff. But like it or not, you and Marcus have more experience than almost this entire section combined. As long as I'm still in charge, we'll be eating this shit sandwich together, all right?"

Alex nodded, his lips pinched together. What the captain didn't know was that the government still had their foot on Alex's neck. And Marcus's, too, for that matter. Nearly all of the older nocturns had some Sword of Damocles hanging over their heads. Ever-present, yet increasingly unknowable, elements in the government were blackmailing them into doing this cop thing. He didn't know what the government had on the others, but in his case, they had some rather important canopic jars they suspected he couldn't do without. Alex didn't know for sure and was reluctant to find out. They'd been extorting him for as long as Alex had worked with them, back on the UMBRA special program with the NSA, and before. There was no reason to expect any change now.

"You and Marcus are dropping all your other cases. I want you on this blood thing and Abraham exclusively. Hell, for all we know the two are connected."

Alex doubted it. That wasn't Abraham's style.

"Are we okay here? Anything you want clarified?" Roberts asked. "That all?"

Roberts shook his head. "What, you want more?"

Alex considered it. Roberts was right. It wasn't even true dark yet.

3

Rhuna Gallier finished putting on her white thigh-high stockings and tried to ignore the yelling outside her room. They'd been going at it for at least two hours now and it was unraveling her last nerve.

She smoothed out the elastic tops to make sure there were no wrinkles. The stockings were an inch shy of the bottom of her black skirt, which left just a touch of alabaster thigh teasingly exposed.

The low-cut crimson blouse highlighted key parts of her anatomy and just barely met the top of the skirt. Rhuna's subtlest movement would reveal a tantalizing glimpse of her flat stomach. Perfect.

Most importantly, she could shed the entire ensemble quickly, if it came to that. And sometimes, Rhuna had to admit, it did, though not for the more pleasurable of reasons.

Voices outside the room rose again. Rhuna rolled her eyes.

The crux of the argument was that they'd risked their lives and tipped their hand by striking at a decoy. Half of the group thought it had been a wise move. If the woman had truly been Lelith, they would have dealt the Lightbearers a severe blow. They should have known it was too good to be true. Instead, they had likely played directly into the Lightbearers' plan, and that meant Abraham wasn't dictating the terms anymore.

Some of the group thought Roeland had become careless and rash. They'd seen his manifesto, an ultimatum thrown in the face of society and the vampires. It was full of innuendo and threats. Roeland's defense was that it really was not his manifesto at all, that the publisher had tampered with large portions of it and changed the overall message.

That wasn't the real problem. At issue was whether he'd shown his hand too early, and whether their foes would call or fold.

Rhuna's bet was that the vampires would raise. It thrilled her. They'd been stalking for too long. The endgame was near.

Besides, the others were probably more upset that he hadn't consulted them before sending the manifesto to the media. He'd been ranting about it long enough and reading parts of it to them; they were fools if they hadn't seen it coming.

Rhuna sat down on a rickety metal stool in front of the cheap pressboard dresser. She'd propped up a mirror and used a desk lamp to help her apply her makeup. At least this apartment had come furnished. Other places they'd stayed could barely count as a roof overhead.

If some of the others were really leaving, as the raised voices outside promised, maybe she could have her own room again. Not that the bed here was any prize, but a sleeping bag and foam liner on the floor was getting old, no matter how a girl got used to "roughing it."

Rhuna smiled.

She teased her white-blond hair into a trendy "just out of bed" look and pressed her lips into a pucker to apply her lip gloss. Next came eyeliner and a dark purple eye shadow, applied so that it flared outward from her blue-green eyes for a stylish and dramatic effect.

She had tried using more eye makeup before, and though it looked good, it hadn't worked out well. Mascara had once run into one eye and nearly blinded her. If that had happened at a critical moment, she'd have been in real trouble. No, it was better not to chance such things.

Especially since the whole point of her outfit was to invite trouble. Instead, she chose to make her eyelashes thicker and longer naturally. A moment's concentration and it was done. She stood up from the dresser and admired her handiwork. She was the ideal image of a twenty-something desperate Wannabe. For their target tonight, she was the perfect piece of bait.

She stepped into her heels and opened the door.

The argument still raged, but all the yelling came to a stop when they noticed her.

Diana, a black European woman, spoke first. "Dear Lord, he has you posing as a streetwalker now?"

Rhuna noticed she'd been tossing her sparse belongings into her large camping backpack.

Tom, Diana's mate, had been looking in the opposite direction, at Roeland Jaap, their leader, "Abraham" in the flesh. Tom turned at his wife's statement.

"Rhuna, you don't have to do this."

Rhuna saw a backpack in his hand as well. She'd known the argument was serious, but she hadn't realized just how grave.

"You're leaving?" Rhuna asked. Tears threatened to well up in her eyes, but she fought them back.

"It's too dangerous now, honey," Tom said. "Roeland has put us all at risk."

"To be fair, we were always at risk."

The new voice belonged to Arthur Holmwood. His rich English accent instantly seemed to bring a measure of civility back into the conversation. He looked more like a pudgy accountant than a vampire killer. "We aren't babes in the woods, and I thought we all had equally good reasons to be here."

Diana turned to him. "But you don't tell them we're coming, you don't broadcast it—"

Tom interrupted her. "We've said our piece. If you lot want to get yourselves killed, that's your own lookout. We're leaving."

"Come with us, Rhuna," Diana said. "You don't have to go about all tarted up anymore."

A keen whistle cut through the air.

A summons! It startled her. Subconsciously she drew her lips back from her teeth. The others hadn't heard it—couldn't hear it. She regained her composure. Too much was happening too quickly.

Rhuna's eyes flitted toward Roeland. He alone knew what she really was.

Roeland's voice was calm. "Rhuna is 'tarted up,' as you put it, because our mark likes Wannabes so desperate for sanger attention they're practically whoring themselves out. In that outfit, I think we can all agree, Rhuna is going to be hard to miss."

"But you can't keep using her as bait. What happens when something goes wrong? What if you lot aren't there to save her?" Diana asked.

"Rhuna can take care of herself," Roeland replied.

The whistle cut through the argument again. Rhuna winced and moved toward the door.

"I need some air."

Rhuna stepped out into the narrow stairwell and made her way down to the alley in the rear of the building.

"Can't you see the girl is terrified?" Diana said, as the door closed behind Rhuna.

She mentally blocked out the rest of the conversation. Even with the nearby Dumpster doing its best to obscure all other scents, she could already smell her contact. He had that wet-dog smell of the Luperci, the Wolves.

Lou (most definitely not his real name) let out an appreciative growl when he saw her.

"Wow. Are you in season?"

That was all the males ever thought about.

Lou was tall, with rakish good looks. In most circumstances, he was the kind who could have any female he wanted. All but one.

Rhuna chuckled. "If I were, it wouldn't concern you. And you can take it easy on that whistle, I heard you the first time."

"I couldn't be sure if you'd heard over all the shouting. What's that all about?"

"They're starting to unravel. I don't know how much longer they'll be effective. Now hurry up, why did you call me out here?"

"I've brought you some flesh. And something more serious."

Rhuna's mouth began to water as soon as he mentioned the meat. She crossed the short distance to him. It had been long since she'd properly fed.

"Where is it?"

"Hang on, little kitten." Lou held a package over his head, well out of Rhuna's reach.

"Give it." It barely sounded like words. The sounds tore forth from her throat in a wet snarl that told him clearly she was not in a play-ful mood.

He placed the fist-size package of plastic-wrapped meat in her hands. She tore it open and took a large bite.

Though it was still cold from refrigeration, it did not have the sterile antiseptic taste of their usual sources. She would have preferred it warm, but this tasted like the hunt. It was excellent.

"What was the other thing?" she asked, her mouth still full as she chewed.

"Have you heard from Gail at all?" Lou asked.

"Gail?" Her blood was rushing from the effects of the flesh and she was finding it hard to care about anything Lou had to say.

"She's been out of contact for two days. The Conclave has con-cerns. She's succumbed to lack of control in the past."

"Have you heard anything?" Rhuna asked. "The humans haven't reacted to any attacks, so she didn't lose it. If she does, she'll prob-ably regain it without incident. Why the worry?"

Rhuna gobbled the last of the meat and licked her fingers. She could hear her blood pounding in her ears. She wanted to run and jump, but in these heels, that would be foolish.

"It's probably nothing. The Conclave sent her to check out a new blood club. Very exclusive. In some industrial park . . ." Lou trailed off.

Rhuna's nipples pressed against the thin fabric of the blouse, and Lou's eyes drifted in that direction. The mongrel had probably planned it this way. She started getting angry.

"They sent her alone? She wasn't ready for that. She can't even change at will. The fools."

Lou inched closer to her and she could feel his warmth through their clothes. He nuzzled her neck.

"Have you thought about taking a mate?"

Rhuna laughed, full-bodied, without restraint.

"Oh, you'd like that? Why not right here against the Dumpster? We can be quick."

Lou stood back, incredulous. "Really?"

"No, you idiot." Rhuna fought to regain her wits. "Find Gail. Maybe she'll be more receptive to your advances. I have mischief to do tonight. And when I choose a mate, you can be sure it won't be one of the Luperci."

She laughed again to let him know she was joking. Lou wouldn't be a bad pick, though Rhuna could have any number of suitors if she desired it. But there was much to do before getting to that.

Rhuna headed back toward the building. "Did you really think you could play me with an offering of flesh?"

"You can't blame a guy for trying." He laughed.

She chuckled again. "No, you can't. Try and try again, little wolf."

Rhuna stepped back into the apartment. Diana had finished packing. She put a hand on Rhuna.

"Are you sure you won't come with us? I can see how upset you are. You don't have to do this."

Rhuna gave her a wan smile. Despite both of them having had their reasons for joining the group, Diana and Tom were too idealistic. It was only a matter of time before their ideals would compromise a mission, or worse, the group. Though Rhuna was sad to see them go, perhaps it was for the best.

"I have to do this. But I won't forget you."

Diana nodded, tears forming in her eyes. Without looking at the others, she opened the door and stepped out.

"Be careful, girl. Don't let those boys talk you into anything you don't want to do," Tom said.

"I won't."

He followed Diana out and the door closed behind him.

Rhuna stared at Roeland, who hadn't moved from where he'd been sitting—his head in his hands.

"We're going to miss them," she said.

Roeland looked up at her. "Don't you think I know that? As soon as John gets back, we're going." He added, "You'll have to do something about your hair if there's time."

"What?" Rhuna asked.

"Our target prefers brunettes," Roeland said.

"Does he?"

Rhuna glanced about her, ensuring no one but Roeland could see. She could hear Arthur moving around in the kitchen. Annoyed, she concentrated and ran her hands through her hair. In a matter of seconds, her hair was dark brown.

4

Jolted awake by an explosive noise, Gail found she was lying on her side in some kind of cage. Her muscles refused to obey her, making her move in fits and starts. Her head weighed tons. The bars and the straw pressing against her face came into focus.

"Wakey, wakey! Come on, you've been out damn near two days, least you could do is get a move on now."

The voice, almost pleading, came from a hulking brute wearing an undersize wife-beater shirt and darkly stained coveralls. Gail raised her bloodshot eyes, and the room briefly swam out of focus. A nagging sense of danger and urgency pulled at the back of her thoughts, just out of reach.

"Two days?" she repeated dully. She clawed herself onto all fours, designer jeans sticky and covered in straw. The straw scratched her naked belly where her blouse had ridden up. Where was she? She could remember the club, the drinks. What happened?

Something was very wrong. What was that terrible stench? Was it coming from her? It was everywhere.

There was another smell, cloying and succulent, which hung just beyond recognition. Fear scratched at the edge of her consciousness. The feeling of danger grew; also, those other feelings, the ones of urgency, to run, to rend, to scream with reckless abandon, to give in to lunacy.

Gail's eyes flitted around the room and finally began to take it in. Small pale yellow tiles covered the floor and crept halfway up the wall to meet with crumbling discolored whitewashed plaster. A large stainless-steel counter with a lip ran along one wall, ending in a deep sink. Dark stains pointed from the counter to drains set into the floor every few feet. The half-working fluorescent lights flickered with annoying irregularity.

"Get your skinny ass out here or I swear I'm gonna pull you out by your fucking hair!" The brute smashed his massive hands against the cage again. The crashing noise as the bars rattled threatened to split her skull.

Instinct sent her retreating into the farthest reaches of the tiny cage, which was no bigger than a large dog kennel. Somehow, those few extra inches offered her a sense of safety.

A loud clank startled her. A massive door screeched open, and another man, lanky and gaunt, backed into the room pulling a small tool cart. The car battery on top dangled alligator clips. The man looked over his shoulder.

"You fallin' in love there, Pete? We need her in the chair."

Pete hung his head briefly. He half mumbled, "Get off my back, Stan. She's taking longer to wake up than normal, that's all."

"Well, she is a cutey. Ain't they all? But you're droppin' the ball, man. Get her out of there. Our guy is here already."

Pete looked at Gail and shrugged his shoulders. "Can't say I didn't give you a chance." He reached in and grabbed a handful of matted hair. She kicked, clawed, and screamed as he yanked her small body out of the cage. She lashed out blindly, at the cage, at the floor, at him. She howled in pain as she tried to slip out of the agony radiating from her scalp.

He whipped her around on the floor by her hair. His other colossal hand closed about her neck, strangling her cry and cutting off her air. She tried to escape his grip but it was like trying to move the floor.

Pete brought his face close so he could look into her eyes. "I'm only going to tell you once. Shut up. You're going to be screaming your throat raw in a couple minutes, so there's no point runnin' your damn mouth now. Understand?"

Gail blinked at him, her face flushed red. Her mouth gasped, inhaling nothing. Clutches of gray crept into her spotted vision. Instinct responded again: She slashed her hand across his face and raked viciously, gouging deep marks into his cheek. Somewhere in the recesses of her mind it felt wrong; the marks were not deep enough.

"Bitch!" He let her go as he recoiled, clutching at his face.

She retched and sucked in air. That first lungful of breath was full of the scent of him, day-old cheap booze and BO. She managed to crawl back up onto her hands and knees before he kicked her.

That brief breath rushed out of her. A second kick, a third, and her insides felt like they wanted to squirm out her throat. She writhed.

The other man laughed, "Cat has claws, huh? I told you you're too nice."

"How's this for nice?"

He punctuated his question with another kick, which lifted her off the ground and rolled her over. He straddled her, and plopped his bulk down on her stomach, then smashed his fist into her face.

Stan whirled at the sound, turning away from his work on the little cart. "What the fuck did you do?"

He ran over and yanked Pete off the girl's limp body. Blood ran freely over her face.

"You broke her goddamn nose? Fantastic! You asshole."

"She tore up my face!"

"You had it coming. You're lucky you didn't get worse. Now you can explain to the client why his little angel is tenderized meat. You better hope he doesn't take the tools to you, shithead."

"Sorry." Pete hung his head like a small child.

"If he wants a discount for that, it's coming out of your cut." Stan strode back over to the cart and continued laying everything out.

"You think you can manage to get her in the chair now since she's done struggling? Or do I have to do that, too?"

Pete tugged her by an arm and began to lift. Then he remembered the last girl.

"Pants on or off?"

"Off. They were a bitch to cut off last time."

Pete grabbed the girl's hip-huggers and started to yank. They clung to her.

"Damn, she must've greased up to get into these."

He changed his grip, seized the jeans from the bottom, and yanked. Her body came with him at first, dead weight flopping against the floor, but finally slid back as the pants, wet with urine, gave up their grip on her thighs. He tossed them aside and they landed with a wet slap.

He grabbed her small limp body and carried it over to a large wooden chair with discolored leather straps. The chair looked like something off death row. All function, no form, and blemished with stains that were best left unconsidered. He dumped her into it, drawing a small low moan from her, and began to tighten the straps around her thighs and ankles.

The massive door screeched open again. An effete man, androgynous features bordering on feminine, strode in with an air of someone accustomed to owning the place. He made a disgusted face at the smell of the room and took off his business jacket. He shook his head after a quick look at the girl. He hung his jacket on one of the many savage-looking hooks on the wall, hooks that weren't for jacket hanging. He rolled up the sleeves of his peach-colored shirt. He, a specialist in his trade, considered the girl more closely, "Hmm, I thought you were supposed to be professionals. That face is going to cost you. At least a thousand I should think."

GRAVEYARD SHIFT ✦ 53

Stan exchanged a glance with Pete. Pete muttered something under his breath but went on tightening the straps on the chair. They creaked with tension.

"Her arms are a little skinny for the straps. She'll just wriggle out of 'em."

Stan opened a drawer below the top surface where he had been laying out the tools and grabbed a bag of long black plastic ties.

"Zip-tie 'em then." He tossed the bag to Pete.

Pete slid them tightly over her wrists and the chair's arms. He pulled them taut, enough to draw thin streaks of blood.

"We're sorry about that. But she was a fighter."

"Can't be helped. Her sleeping through this is a problem, however. It affects the final product and that won't do. Wake her up."

Stan dug around in another drawer on the cart. This one broke the trend of organization and brimmed with assorted junk, tape, and supplies. He pulled out smelling salts and waved them under her nose.

Her head snapped up. For an instant her eyes were wild and unafraid. Stan stepped back reflexively. Then her eyes focused as she came back to the world and recognized her situation.

He wheeled the cart next to the chair, and with the flourish of a waiter presenting the finest desserts, he revealed the tools he had been laying out. There were scalpels, pliers, needles, surgical tubing. The sight brought another moan from the girl. Her eyes were wide with terror. Good, that was a start at least.

"No. Please, no," she started to sob.

"Oh please, no tears yet, sweet child. We've not yet begun," the specialist said.

"I'm out of here," Pete said. "Don't have too much fun."

Pete left the room, the door clanging shut behind him. Stan wished he could follow him. He hated this part. But in an hour or so it would be over and he'd have some cool cash to help him forget.

The specialist picked a scalpel off the cart. The girl squirmed in the chair. The straps and ties cut deeper into her flesh but did their job of keeping her still.

"Don't worry, my dear. We always start small."

He dragged the blade of the scalpel almost tenderly against her hand, leaving a cruel line of crimson in its wake. She gasped. The gasp turned into a scream. Then the scream turned into a rasping almost choking sound as she began to buck and strain against the straps.

At first, it looked to Stan as if she was trying to pull free, but with more energy than he would expect considering the ordeal she had already been through. Quickly, he realized she was having some kind of fit.

"What did you give her?"

"We didn't give her shit. Maybe she's epileptic or something?"

"You don't screen for that sort of thing? Her blood will be useless!"

Stan didn't hear the specialist's comment. The girl was shaking so violently now that it looked as if the chair might actually come apart. He stepped in and slapped her across the face.

Her eyes snapped open, yellow, feral, almost glowing—eyes that didn't belong to a teenage girl or anything remotely human.

He yelped and jumped back, nearly tripping over his own feet as he flew for the door. He had to get the hell out!

"What? What's the matter?"

"She's a thrope!" Stan's throat had constricted in terror, choking the words meant as a warning cry into a strangled croak.

Stan reached the door. Almost against his will, he turned his head back toward the chair and the girl. The specialist apparently hadn't heard him, or didn't care. The idiot was still there!

The specialist leaned in to get a closer look at the girl. She was still screaming, and the longer she screamed the lower in pitch and more bestial-sounding the noise became. Then it became a low growl, and a tongue that he couldn't believe would even fit in her mouth strained and wriggled forth, seeking purchase.

Stan could hear cracks and pops. Things were shifting under her darkening skin. The restraints on the chair creaked and strained, then snapped, one by one, the zip-ties first, then the leather.

Her hand shot out, lightning quick, and struck the specialist in the abdomen. He gave out a sharp surprised cry and then fumbled with the slick gray-red ropey mass that spilled out of him.

Stan whirled his attention back to the door and pulled at it. It didn't budge. He groped clumsily at the lock, panicking. There were terrible sounds, slurping and crunching, coming from where the girl had been, but he didn't dare look back. Then the chair, or rather what was left of it, smashed into the wall next to him and showered him in splinters.

"Open the door, for fuck's sake!"

Outside the room, Pete sat in a chair with a shotgun across his lap, acting as gatekeeper. Opposite him, another man sat and gaped at photos in a thoroughly used bondage magazine. Pete laid his head back against the wall, closed his eyes, and tried to get some sleep. He heard muffled sounds coming from inside the room. To hear anything through that door meant that it had to be loud as hell inside.

"This one's making a racket early."

"Why don't you go in there and tell her to keep it down?" the other man muttered.

"Naw, that ain't my bag. Fuckin' 'em's one thing, that shit is something else entirely. I want no part of it."

Then something hit the door.

Hard.

The impact made both men jump.

"What the hell?"

Another loud bang and the top hinge popped out with a loud, almost comical, ping.

Pete backed away and racked the slide on the shotgun.

Something smashed the door again, and this time it swung open, off kilter, the bottom scraping a deep gouge into the floor.

Now Pete could see into the room. There was so much blood, and there were other things, parts of things.

Gore.

An explosion in a slaughterhouse.

"Are you shitting me?"

The other man pulled a pistol from his waistband. "A bomb?" His voice was a shallow whisper.

Pete shrugged.

Using baby steps, the man stepped across the threshold, crouching, pistol at the ready. He stood, started to lower the pistol, a puzzled look on his face.

Pete let out the breath he hadn't realized he'd been holding.

The man started to say something but a black shape in tattered clothes and moving way too fast hit him from the side. It slashed into his neck as he screamed and gurgled on his own blood.

"Oh shit!"

Pete fired the shotgun, indiscriminately hitting both figures, racked, and fired again.

The thing left the dead man, his head lolling to one side, nearly ripped from his body. Arterial flow pumped over the slickening tiles.

The shotgun had done no damage. It just got the thing's attention.

Pete tried to back up, to buy time to get another shot. He racked the shotgun again and then stared dumbly at it as the thing snarled and swatted it from his hands.

He started to scream, but was cut off by more pain than he'd ever known. He dimly thought that the thing was some kind of half animal. By then he was drowning in his own blood.

5

8:50 P.M.

Alex drove the dark blue Explorer out of the parking garage turned makeshift motor pool. He waved at Lopez, a human who was on desk duty after being injured, and then pulled out past the AUTHORIZED VEHICLES ONLY BEYOND THIS POINT sign and into the street.

It was the first true darkness of the evening. The "magic hour" had given way to night a little while before, and the dim light that seeped into the violet edges of the sky had just winked out.

He hoped he could make it back into the center of the city before the first night rush hour began. The economy had shifted dramatically in the last two years. It created more jobs, more money, more opportunities, and sadly, more crime. Shortly, mobs of folks would be crowding the choked streets. Most folks would be heading in to work for the night shift; others would be prowling for prey. Miami had always had a reputation for being a place that never slept, but now it was true.

Alex looked at his watch. If he was lucky, he might make it to Aguirre's church before services.

Aguirre headed a church for vampires seeking redemption from God through purification of the flesh and denial of their vampiric tendencies. Marcus had been stuck there all day, quizzing Aguirre for intel, and no doubt being served up a sanctimonious helping of religious mumbo jumbo.

Aguirre was their lifeline to the many networks that were no longer friendly to Marcus or Alex. They'd done their share of bridge burning in UMBRA for the NSA. Never mind that the government had forced their hands, or that the monsters they were hunting were truly evil, even by vampiric reckoning. Too many insiders wouldn't trust them now. They needed Aguirre.

Still, being cooped up in that place for an entire day would have left Marcus in a foul mood. If he hadn't fed, then his mood would be downright nasty. Alex couldn't be sure what Aguirre's regimen was these days. It would be best if he had some Hemo-Synth on hand to placate Marcus, just in case.

He saw a convenience store on one of the cross streets. He pulled the Explorer in, got out, and noticed a small gathering of people near the front door. Six of them, all young men. They were agitated and he couldn't make out what they were looking at. As he got closer, he could see they were huddled around a newspaper and their conversation became clear.

"Those bloodsucking bastards! When are people going to stop this shit?"

"They don't stand for this kind of stuff over in Europe. Over there they'd have already staked half these motherfuckers."

Alex got right next to them and glanced at the paper over one's shoulder. The story was about the morning's blood-frenzy attack. The second one. The one Alex hadn't stopped.

So much for keeping it out of the press.

He walked into the store. An old black man was minding the counter. He was watching Lelith give a press conference on a tiny old-style TV set imprisoned in a locked Plexiglas box. That set had probably been in there since the store had been built. Lelith looked radiant, her pale skin a sharp contrast to a mane of red hair that no doubt took some hairdresser an hour to set right. She wore a dark power suit that hugged her figure and accentuated her sexuality.

Matching boots came up to her knees. She looked like a supermodel turned movie star turned CEO who was a dominatrix on the side. Alex had to hand it to the Lightbearer Society. They'd have been hard-pressed to find a better spokeswoman to extol the benefits of being a vampire. Of course, it was all bullshit, but Joe Bag-o'-Doughnuts didn't know that.

Alex nodded to the old man and headed back past all the snacks and soft drinks. He found some Sangri and Hemotopia on one of the end caps. They'd come out so quickly after the announcement of the discovery of A-PFC4—the scientific name for the key ingredient in Hemo-Synth—and the Reveal, that there had been accusations of insider trading. Whether through bribes, intimidation, or worse, those allegations had gone away shortly thereafter. Alex happened to know that vampire shell companies owned both distributors for Sangri and Hemotopia. It just seemed that no one cared to do anything about it.

Something was off here. Everything was marked down. He picked up three bottles of different blood types of Sangri with large 75% OFF stickers on them and headed up to the counter.

"Having a sale?" Alex plopped the bottles down on the counter.

The man looked down at the bottles then looked back up at Alex. His second glance held more scrutiny.

"Aw, what's a young brother like you messing with that stuff for?"

Alex shrugged. "Why's everything marked down?"

"We're not going to carry that stuff anymore. Folks around here . . . well, they don't care much for the kind who buys it."

Two of the younger men from outside came into the store. Alex heard one comment to the other when he noticed what Alex was buying.

Alex pulled out his wallet to pay the cashier and one of the men swatted it out of his hand. It landed on the floor, open and facedown. This guy was taller than Alex by a head and, given

Alex's slim frame, must've thought he was easy pickings. He chested up to Alex.

"Hey bro, go buy your blood shit somewhere else, sanger!" the man shouted, volume apparently tied directly to his bravado.

So that's what this was about.

The men outside couldn't have helped but hear their friend.

He should make this guy eat some teeth. He looked over the man's shoulder at the four others and decided to take a different tack. He could easily handle them, but there was no telling what the night held in store. He needed to conserve his energy and it was an additional mess he just didn't need right now.

"Do I look like a vampire?" Alex looked him right in the eye.

The man stared at Alex, a dumb look flashing across his face. Alex had shaken his expectation; sometimes that was enough.

"Then, why are you buying that shit, man?"

"For a friend. Oh, and you might want to think about a thing or two."

"Oh yeah?" The man stepped closer to Alex, invading his personal space. He came just short of physically bumping into him. He could smell the beer on his breath. The man was back on high ground now; by Alex's own admission, he was guilty of dealing with a vampire, and that apparently made him fair game.

"Yeah." Alex bent down and recovered his wallet. He held his jacket as he stood so the man could get a good look at his badge.

"You might want to think before bothering a cop."

The other man, the first guy's backup, hastily backed to the entrance.

"Oh man. I'm sorry, I didn't . . ."

Alex didn't let him finish. "And you also might want to think, if you're harassing vampires buying fake juice, do you really want 'em going for the real stuff?" He paid the cashier.

The cashier took the money from Alex and handed him the bag.

"Think about it." Alex brushed past the man, nodded to his friends at the entrance, and walked back to his Explorer. If that little encounter was any indicator about how the rest of the city felt, tonight wasn't going to be pretty.

6

9:05 P.M.

For Filip, the cloak of night did not just signal the transition from day; it heralded a transfer, a change of thought and ownership, a shift of attitude. It was an almost palpable thing, oppressive, hanging just beyond the bright streetlights, waiting for the opportunity to smother the city.

Night in parts of Miami had never been what you could call safe. Now you needed eyes in the back of your head. Night was when everything, everyone, blended. During the day, you only dealt with humans for the most part. Now everyone would start to move about and mingle, and you couldn't even be sure who you'd be dealing with until they asked you for what they needed. Be it some vamp blood for whatever use, some human blood to shake off the plastic taste of the artificial stuff, or maybe some drugs to stave off the cravings for a little while. It was exciting, dangerous, and full of possibilities.

Filip's father had been a Tonton Macoute for Baby Doc Duvalier. He'd had a lot of stock in that lifestyle, and then, overnight, it was over. They'd barely gotten out of Haiti. The experience had taught Filip to always have a backup plan.

Filip's specialty was possibilities. His world boiled down to delivering potential, and the more exotic it was, the higher the price. He'd started in with coke in the late nineties, gotten busted, done enough time to earn cred. He got out and rebuilt some wealth on designer drugs, mostly X and higher-end weed, selling Rolls and Krippie to the club crowds and tourists. Then he'd diversified, got mixed up with some human trafficking, girls from Eastern Europe and the islands. That's how he'd found out about the vampires. They made for good customers. And he found he could make good bank selling their information to government types who were in the know. Post-Reveal, the government money was gone.

Now he'd branched out into other products, with a much higher profit margin. Many of the nocturns were loaded, and that's where the real money was. All of them had a blood habit that was more demanding than any coke fiend's dealer could dream of. They weren't going to shake that shit and they couldn't OD.

His many commodities put him in a unique position. He dealt with everyone without prejudice. He was an equal-opportunity exploiter. As far as his world was concerned, people boiled down to three kinds: "saps," normal humans; "sangers," vampires; and "thropes," the shape-shifting bastards who could turn into animals. You'd be a complete moron if you trusted any of them.

Filip knew he'd dealt with the first two categories, but until recently, he didn't think he'd ever met a thrope. How could you be sure? Those poor sick bastards looked and acted like everyone else, until they went off their meds. The next thing you knew, something would set them off and you'd have a rabid bear, or wolf, or big cat tearing up some bar or club or school.

He was sure his new customers had something to do with thropes. They wanted an awful lot of meat. Meat you couldn't just stroll into your local megamart and buy. They paid extremely well and asked even fewer questions than the sangers did, which was fine with Filip.

Sure, their business came with more threats, and they wanted personal delivery from him and not one of his guys. With the money he was going to make this week alone, he could give up the whole gig. Hell, by the end of the month he might just do that, what with some of the sangers attacking folks in the open. He didn't need any of that shit. He'd go somewhere that got lots of sun. Maybe Hawaii or somewhere like that. But not back to Haiti.

For now, he had to keep his head in the game. He'd already had some hiccups tonight. He was still waiting on half the expected shipment, and that asshole Stan hadn't called him. Zagesi's folks would be pissed if it was late.

He had a couple of beauty addicts to meet, too. A little bit of the old red stuff from a sanger could take years off a person for a short amount of time, if you used it right. All the Hollywood stars were using it, just to keep their careers going for a few more years.

Filip had his regulars. No one famous. Just vain men and women pushing it a little too hard for Botox to be much help, looking for some kicks for a day or so, and going through their whole if-only-I-knew-then-what-I-know-now phase. With a little bit of the sanger good stuff, you could actually exploit that knowledge, which most of the time boiled down to who you'd be sleeping with that night. Filip smiled. He knew a couple of those broads would be hard up for his product. He'd normally send Mitch to meet them, but Filip could actually use a freebie himself tonight, so maybe he'd go instead.

He might even give them a discount if they agreed to do him a favor or two, after they'd dosed up of course. There was no point getting a blowjob from an old biddy. In the end, the discount wouldn't amount to much.

He'd give them half off, or more, that first time; then afterward they'd all pay whatever he asked. If the women didn't, their husbands did. A couple grand for the special occasion, and their aging husbands would get to diddle a twenty-five-year-old again. Who wouldn't pay? Even knowing that as soon as their tired heads hit the pillow after the deed, their wives would be out and about, hunting for younger fare, if only for the night. They were frantic about it, desperate, fucking against the clock, before the blood effects wore off and they were pumpkins again. Cinderella had nothing on these bitches.

What he didn't exactly advertise was that when the stuff did wear off, well, the human body wasn't built to take that kind of stress. They would come out on the flip side feeling just a little bit older, a little more tired, a lot more used up. There was a good reason for that. As far as their bodies were concerned, they *were* older. Sanger blood could knock back time for a day or so, but those years came back in a hurry and brought a few friends back with them.

He pulled onto Fifty-third Street, where his small corner bodega—the front for his whole operation—squatted between Lemon City and Buena Vista. Lemon City sat right on the other side of the Toll-way. His clients could come and go quickly and it allowed for easy deliveries, and getaways, if the situation warranted.

He drove by for a quick look-see, more out of habit than anything else. Emil was working the counter. The kid was a little slow, but Filip needed someone to run the front so he could work the real clients. Everything looked okay. He took a turn around the block and pulled the van into the small lot in the rear. He honked the horn once, put the van in park and shut it off, then honked again.

He honked the horn two more times.

Mitch opened the back door and waved to him to kill the head-lights. He did, and then stepped out of the van.

"What's going on?" Mitch asked.

"Not much. I got two coolers in the back we need to unload. Who else is around?"

"Me and Emil."

"That's it? Where're Gus and Lonzo?"

Filip stepped to the side of the van and unlocked the side door.

"They headed off to the Pork and Beans," Mitch said. "In case Stan called. Figured they'd already be kind of in the area."

"Did he?" Filip asked.

"Did he what?"

"Call. Did Stan call?"

"No. Haven't heard a word," Mitch said.

"Shit. Think he got pinched?"

"Don't know."

Filip didn't like that at all. One set of customers would like it even less, since now he'd have to tell them he only had half their order. Filip slid the side door of the van back. Inside were two industrial stainless-steel coolers roughly the size of refrigerators.

"Holy crap, Filip, we can't move these. Not just us two."

"Well, we're going to try. I ain't having these things sit here all night and everything getting ruined. Go get the handcart, will ya? Give Lonzo a call. No point having those jokers driving around all night. Never mind, I'll call him."

Mitch moved back inside, muttering as he went. "I should get a cut of their share. They ain't ever around to do the heavy work."

"Quit your bitching. It's not like you're working for a living."

Filip tried to reposition one of the coolers on the pallet cover to make it easier to prop onto the handcart. It wouldn't budge. He stepped inside the van to get more leverage. Nothing.

Bright headlight beams shone directly into the open door of the van, partially blinding Filip. Someone pulled into the rear lot. He patted his back to reassure himself the pistol was still there. He stepped out of the van, shielding his face with his left hand from the light. The lights died, but his night vision was still shot and he could only see silhouettes as they opened the doors of their small truck.

"I hope that's our stuff."

Filip recognized the voice. And a little bit of tension eased out of him, replaced by annoyance.

"Nico? Are you out of your fucking mind coming down here?"

Nico was a petty thug who had hit the big time through his association with the vampires. A *chusma* Cuban lowlife who was likely to wind up with his throat slit for his trouble. The sangers didn't abide small-timers.

"Our boss, well he got a little impatient." Nico stepped close. He swished a bit of toothpick from one corner of his mouth to the other.

Three other men stood behind Nico. One stood a head above all of them.

"Shit, do you have any idea the risk you're taking? You could blow everything."

"Fucking that's your problem, *cabrón*, not ours."

"Prick," Filip muttered under his breath, but he couldn't deny that Nico was right.

The rear entrance of the shop opened up, sending a triangular spear of light into the small lot. Mitch backed the handcart out of the doorway.

"Well at least you brought some muscle. Let's hurry up and move this shit."

The four men stepped toward the van, and as the big man stepped into the light, Filip realized he was a vampire.

"Whoa. Is he gonna be okay? I've seen what this shit does to sangers."

"Watch your mouth, little man," the vampire shot back as he brushed past Filip.

"He'll be fine. So, these are both ours?" Nico asked.

"No. Only the one on the right, and not all of it is yours either." Filip braced himself for Nico's reaction.

"What the hell? This isn't what we agreed to," Nico said.

"Well, it's all I've got. One of my suppliers didn't come through. I can still make good on the order, I'll just need a minute."

"Again, not my problem, bro."

The men stepped into the van and muscled the cooler toward the door, sliding it back and forth.

"Hey, you can't take the whole cooler. Like I said, not all of it is yours."

"For the amount we're paying, we should be able to take whatever we want. I have a good mind to withhold payment until we get full delivery."

Nico opened the cooler and stared inside a moment. Mist from the dry ice inside spilled over the lip and briefly looked like liquid as it ran down the side. He reached in and came up with a package of frozen plastic-wrapped meat. "Oye, what the hell is this shit?"

"Camouflage. You know, in case someone asks why I have two huge coolers in the back. Look, I can hook you guys up with some other stuff at a good discount to make up for this. That other cooler's got some sap juice, all blood types and you know my stuff is always clean."

The big vampire answered, "We can get that shit right from the source. And better quality than you can offer." He moved quickly, for effect, and seemed to melt from his location near the van to be standing right next to Filip and talking into his ear. "Now, where's our order?"

"Shit!" Filip took a big step back. "Under the meat."

Nico dug around and found that the bottom of the cooler was full of large bags of blood. He held one up. The frozen contents crunched as the bag shifted.

"What do you think?" Nico asked.

The large vampire's nostrils flared, and Filip saw his fangs extend as if he was ready to feed.

"That's the good stuff right there," the vampire said.

"Okay, great. Hurry up and take it and get the hell out of here," Filip said.

Nico and one of the other men began scooping the packages of meat out of the cooler, dumping them onto the van's floor.

"Make a mess why don't you." Filip hoped the dry ice would burn them as they did.

"We shouldn't have to be doing this. Your service is slipping, Filip."

"If you'd waited for me to deliver instead of coming down here to take the shit, I'd have had it ready for you."

The large vampire and the two other men manhandled the cooler out of the van and onto the handcart. Mitch helped them load it into the back of their truck.

"Hey, and the money?"

"You get it when we get the rest of our order, bro."

"Not how it works."

Nico got right in Filip's face. "Fucking that's how it's gonna work this time. You don't do right by Mr. Zagesi and he doesn't do right by you. *Claro?* Unless you want to talk to him direct."

Filip was on unfamiliar ground. "No. No. I don't want to talk to him."

That brought chuckles from the other men. "He doesn't tolerate fuckups. I'm already going to pay for your screwup. So I'm holding on to your share until you come through." He spit the bit of toothpick at Filip and it bounced off his chest.

"You better hurry if you want to see any of that cash."

The men got into the truck and left.

As both men watched the truck's red lights disappear into the night, Mitch asked, "What are we gonna do?"

"Fuck if I know. Tell Lonzo and Gus to go in and see what the hell Stan's up to. What choice do we have?"

Filip balled his fists up and kicked absently at the ground. "Those assholes. They think they can just push me around like that, like I'm a fucking nobody? Prick thinks he can keep my money? I'll fucking show him."

7

9:35 P.M.

Alex pulled up at Aguirre's church complex and parked in the front. Aguirre had built the church, and the associated campus, out of gray stone. Years of acid rain and pollution had pockmarked the stone and turned some of it black, especially where the water had run down the little channels in the mortar between the large blocks. The church was traditional Gothic construction. In many European towns, it would not have stood out as exceptional in any way, except for the enclosed walkways connecting it to the other buildings on the campus.

The church looked far more ancient than it actually was, just as Aguirre had intended. There were even rumors that he'd had it brought over stone-by-stone from somewhere in Europe and reassembled here in Pinecrest, an old-money suburb of Miami. Alex doubted that, suspecting that it merely duplicated an existing structure.

Light streamed from above the double doors of the entrance, illuminating the short set of stairs leading up to it. A modern white sign with black replaceable letters advertised the hours for services. This being a nocturn-only church, all the services were at night. The illumination inside backlit the stained-glass windows. Alex's gaze went to two words at the bottom of one of the large windows, SANGRE SANCTI. He shook his head.

Those poor misguided fools. Well, if they found solace in it, what

harm could there be? The double doors opened and two recognizable figures stepped out onto the top steps: Father Lopé Aguirre in
his monk's robe, and Marcus in a black tailored suit. They looked so
"normal"—Aguirre the stereotypical monk and Marcus the sharply
dressed executive—yet one was a former conquistador and the other
a former Roman governor. Each of them was responsible for his own
particular brand of genocide. Both were pretty much assholes. That
was one price of immortality, along with the tendency of friends to
become enemies and enemies friends.

They spoke for a short moment, and then Marcus broke off and
came toward the car with long strides, which effortlessly ate up the
distance.

Marcus was a little over six feet tall and had the patrician features to go with his history. He wore his dark hair slicked back, and
along with his pallid skin tone, it made his vampire look unmistak-
able. Marcus couldn't pass for anything else.

"You are late." He opened the passenger-side door of the Explorer.

"Sue me. I had to get a pep talk from Roberts."

"Oh? Did I miss anything good?" He closed the door and waved
at Aguirre.

Aguirre raised a single hand. Alex couldn't tell if he meant the
gesture as a farewell, a salute, or a blessing. He decided to wave back
as he drove away.

"Some good, some bad," Alex answered.

The radio interrupted him. "Two-seven-three Delta, in progress,
residential. Nocturn support requested four-eight-two Charles, Le
Fanu Court."

It sounded like a domestic dispute gone out of hand. The request
for nocturn support meant that there was a vampire involved.

Alex ignored it.

"Constance got the promotion. She'll be heading the full-blown
Nocturn Affairs Bureau at the start of the month."

"Excellent." Marcus didn't sound like this was news to him. As connected as he was, it probably wasn't. "The way things are getting, the field's not for her."

"You afraid she'll relapse?"

"Things have been tense lately."

Marcus changed the subject. "When was the last time you were in the church?"

"Been a while."

"You really should go see it. Lopé put a small garden in the cloister. It is quite remarkable."

"Huh. You don't want to hear the bad news?"

Marcus stayed silent.

"Well, bad news is that your hunch was right. Feds confirmed Abraham's in our neck of the woods."

"All the signs have been there for some time. We are sure it is not some protégé?"

"Nothing's sure. Might be. They screwed up royally this morning and got one of Lelith's decoys. Shows the war is heating up if they're willing to take a potshot at a target of opportunity like that."

"I've heard," Marcus said.

"Figures. Here's something you might not have heard already. Roberts and I had a little chat. He was just the messenger understand, but someone in the leadership is asking for the UMBRA treatment for this special case."

Marcus sat up a little straighter. "Do they understand what they are asking?"

"No. You know how it is. It all sounds sexy on paper. Things would be a hell of lot harder to cover up now, that's for sure. It jibes with folks believing it's really Abraham. They're scared."

Marcus changed the subject again. "What is to be our first stop?"

"Roberts wanted us to shake down some CIs. I figure we'll start with Filip. His hands are always dirty."

"We'll have to stop before we go there."

"Yeah?"

"I'm famished and I do not want to face one of his special offers on an empty stomach."

"I figured. I grabbed you some Sangri."

"Always thoughtful."

"Not an entirely pleasant experience, by the way. Some folks felt they needed to share some opinions with me."

"News got out, I take it?" Marcus twisted around and reached back for the bag in the back seat of the Explorer. He grabbed two of the bottles, a Sangri type O and a Sangri type A. He looked at the two bottles, grimaced, and put the type O back in the bag.

"Yeah. I figure we're in for a rough night. Hey, if that stuff's bad, you're not going to go all blood-frenzy on me when you swig it, right?"

"It would have to be especially potent to affect me. Besides, it is not as if you have got anything to worry about." Marcus sat back down in the front seat, straightened out his suit jacket, and opened the bottle.

"Wasn't worried about me," Alex answered, "was worried about having to chase your ass down."

Marcus sniffed cautiously at the bottle, and then took a long pull.

"Ah, Sangri-A, there's nothing like it." He pronounced the word "sangria."

"That joke never gets old, does it?"

"One of life's tiny pleasures, but it really should be warmed, you know." Marcus chuckled to himself, but then his tone turned serious.

"Disturbing news from Aguirre and his sources. There's evidence that there is another Ancient in the area."

"And he didn't check in to catch up on old times? How rude."

"I am serious. There are few enough of us about, and I do not have to remind you the rest of them do not have anything but their own interests at heart."

"You say 'the rest of them' like it doesn't include you." Alex got no response for his prodding. He decided to let it go. "Aguirre say who it was?"

"There is no hard evidence, just the unusual ripples that occur when a large fish splashes into the pond. Some movement indicators and lack thereof from Our Friends in the See. They've asked me to take a professional interest."

"Our Friends in the See" was a euphemism for the Order of the Eternal Watch, the Vatican's organization that had dealt with all things vampiric throughout the ages. Marcus had been a knight commander a long time ago. If anyone checked, Marcus had severed ties with them, but Alex knew firsthand that a person could never truly leave those kinds of organizations.

"They asked us? That's new."

"Well, no. They did not ask us. Not directly. They ask without asking."

"Ah, the usual." Alex shook his head. It was always secrets and layers of secrecy whenever you dealt with vampires. The Catholics could be just as bad. Plausible deniability. Multiple levels of CYA. When you dealt with folks that lived as long as some of these vampires and who had memories just as long, you had to be doubly careful how you dealt with them.

"There's a lot of activity coming our way, I suspect." Marcus took another sip from the bottle.

"Are you wearing two hats again?"

"I have always been a Roman."

"Hmmpf. Getting to be more and more like the old days, except it feels like we're the only ones playing by the rules. I really hope that doesn't blow up in our faces."

"Lopé feels he has a solid chance to get to the bottom of the Hemo-Synth problem."

"If there is one," Alex tested.

"If there is one," Marcus echoed. His voice held no doubt.

"The Lightbearers are up to something at Haley House. He is trying to get some of his people up there to have a look. If I know Lopé, I'd wager he has something in place already. Though he isn't very likely to tell us."

"You have to love all the trust going around. With the folks he knows he should be able to get someone in there for recon."

"I doubt it is as easy as you'd think." Marcus turned his head to look out the window.

Haley House was a lavish mansion complex on the outskirts of the city. It had once belonged to a wealthy industrialist turned bootlegger and had become notorious for the outlandish parties thrown there. Prohibition ended, but the parties didn't. After the Reveal, the Lightbearer Society had purchased it for an undisclosed sum. The parties suddenly got a lot more exclusive, but they were still happening. Rumor had it that the only things that had really changed were the types of beverages served.

"Why not? Wait till Lelith and her cronies have another blood orgy up there, which no one can ever prove of course, and have Constance invite herself. Word is Lelith has a thing for her anyway. Then Constance can get Aguirre all the intel he needs, if she's still on our team that is," Alex said.

Marcus groaned. "You really should not malign Constance so."

"Yeah, well she thinks I'm an asshole and I think she's a bitch. Turns out, we're both right. For someone who's going to be running the first Nocturn Bureau, she's awful cozy with the enemy."

"Lelith is the voice and face of political vampirism in this city and Constance would never have been appointed to the post without her support."

"Exactly. You don't see a conflict of interest there?"

Marcus said nothing and went back to looking out the window.

"Besides, if you're willing to escort me up there, I could get a nice look around and no one would even be the wiser."

Marcus looked back at him, his face full of concern.

"Sometimes, Menkaure, I forget that you have only walked abroad for a brief time. There is still much you have to learn about Ancients. The foremost fact you must never forget, is that you must never under-estimate one."

Alex read something more in his expression. "Why am I getting the feeling I'm not seeing the whole picture here?"

The radio burst on again, letting Marcus off the hook.

"Two-seven-three Delta, in progress, residential. Nocturn support requested four-eight-two Charles, Le Fanu Court."

"That's the second time that call has gone out."

"So what? Not our problem. Captain's orders." Alex let his annoy-ance creep into his tone.

"How far is that?" Marcus asked.

"I don't know, ten maybe twelve miles? You're serious. You want to kick off the shift with that BS? Come on."

Marcus keyed the handset. "Fifteen Nora forty-two responding."

Alex glowered at Marcus, then jerked the wheel into a sharp turn at the next intersection.

"Damn it."

8

Two parked police cruisers bracketed the entrance to Le Fanu Court when Alex pulled into the cul-de-sac. Around its circumference were midscale townhomes, neatly piled against one another. He could see a small group of people and two Miami-Dade police officers huddled under a streetlight.

He pulled the Explorer past the first police car and parked. As he stepped out of the Explorer, one of the uniforms called out to him.

"You guys Nocturn Affairs?"

"What do you think?" Alex tilted his head to indicate Marcus, who was just emerging from the SUV. Even in the haloed glare of the streetlight, he could see the apprehensive looks on their faces.

Alex dropped the volume of his voice so it was scarcely above a whisper.

"You wanted this one, you can take the lead."

Marcus pretended not to hear him.

Alex let out a sigh and walked toward the group of people. The officer who had first engaged him filled him in.

"We just started setting up a perimeter. We were about to call for more backup when you guys pulled in."

"More backup? What's going on? I thought we were dealing with a domestic."

"That's what we thought, too. But now I think it might actually be some kind of Hemo-Synth poisoning."

Alex looked at Marcus. He wasn't ignoring that. Marcus stepped into the shadows. Okay, he was playing it cautious until they knew more of what was going on.

A woman charged forward out of the group. "You've got to do something about this. We could have been killed."

"All right, ma'am. What exactly happened?"

"My daughter's boyfriend"—she spat the word—"is one of those goddamn vampires."

She seemed to remember Marcus just as she uttered the last word. She tried to swallow it. The look on her face played between mortification and terror, like she'd just farted at her Sunday social.

"Where is he now?" Alex asked.

"He's still inside. Probably going insane or God knows what." She turned now to address a young woman in the crowd: "Do you see? See what happens when you mess around with those types? What if I hadn't been home? He'd have torn you apart." The woman covered her mouth with her hand, the thought of her daughter's potential fate enough to silence her for the moment.

Alex turned his attention to the young woman. Textbook Wannabe, the neo-goth makeup, the short skirt, the stockings, her shirt tied in a knot above her midriff to reveal her pierced belly button. Somehow, the Wannabes had got it into their heads that the sexier they dressed, the more likely a vampire would turn them—never mind that it was illegal under human law, and vampire custom frowned upon it. Those facts had done little to curb the movement, and just about every blood club was crawling with Wannabes and bleeders. It seemed to be a lot more prevalent among young women than among young men, but that might have been only because the young men didn't dress as provocatively and therefore weren't as easy to identify. Alex could have told her that only the youngbloods would still care how a bleeder dressed, because among vampires, only they would still be into vanilla sex. But he doubted it would make any difference at all.

She was only in her late teens, if that. It was hard to tell under all that makeup. Couldn't hurt to treat her as a grown-up.

"Miss, you saw what happened?"

Her mother answered. "That vampire had some of that fake blood and started going crazy! He almost killed her."

Alex turned back to the mother. "Ma'am, were you there?"

"No. I was in the kitchen, but I heard her scream and heard him getting sick."

"Okay, I'm going to need to hear it from your daughter."

He turned back to the girl. "What exactly happened?"

"Draven . . . he—"

"Draven is your boyfriend?" Alex coaxed her along. *Draven.* The name sounded false, like something somebody thought a vampire would go by.

"Yeah. He came over so we could like make out. But he said that I was overwhelming him." Her eyes flitted to her mother.

Alex understood.

"It's okay, walk with me." He led her out of earshot. Alex could feel her mother's eyes boring into his back.

"Now go on."

"He said I was overwhelming him. That he wanted me so badly. I thought about it, I really did. But I thought maybe he was just hungry."

"So you gave him some . . . ?"

"Some Hemotopia. I wanted to surprise him. I got some and went and heated it up like you're supposed to and everything."

"Let me guess, he wouldn't drink it."

"Not at first. He said he wasn't hungry and that's not what he meant when he said he wanted me. But I told him he was hurting my feelings and so he had some. And then he went crazy."

"How did he go crazy?"

"Well he made a face like he was trying to hold something in and then he threw up everywhere and after the stuff in the news I was like, Oh, my God!"

"And you got out of there. Not a bad idea under the circumstances. Before you ran, did you see what color his vomit was?"

The girl gave him a questioning look.

"What?"

"When he got sick. What color was the vomit?"

"Umm, puke-colored. What kind of question is that?"

"The most important kind." Annoyance crept back into Alex's voice. He grabbed the girl by the arm and led her back toward the group. "The kind of question these guys should have asked you before calling for us." He pointed at the uniformed cops.

Alex stomped toward the house. "He's still in here, right?"

The mother answered, "Yes. Be careful."

Alex was sure Marcus had heard everything and he was hoping he was on the same wavelength. What a colossal waste of time! He slammed the door open and stalked into the house. He could hear someone sobbing.

He followed the sound into the girl's room, where he found a thin young teen sitting on the bed, a half-empty bottle of Hemotopia at his feet. In one hand, the boy held a clump of paper towels he'd been using to mop up his puke.

"Draven?" Alex stepped into the room.

The boy looked up. His eyes were red-rimmed and filled with tears. Normal tears. No way in hell was he a vampire. Alex's suspicions were right. He and Marcus had just wasted a half hour.

"Oh, for crying out loud."

"I thought, how bad could it be, right? Just one swig and then Katy'd like me."

"Be honest, kid. You were trying for something way past 'like.' Let me guess, nobody knew you at school until you decided to be 'Draven,' kid vampire, right? Then you had to turn away girls. But Hemo-Synth doesn't go down well for humans at all."

"Am I gonna be okay?"

"What, from the Hemo-Synth? From the looks of things, you pretty much puked it all up. You'll be fine. That's if Katy's mother doesn't kill you. Tell me, how'd you get the school to approve you for night sessions?"

"Um, they never checked."

Alex shook his head at the stupidity of it all. Parents' groups were still flipping out about newly turned vampires being allowed to share schools with human children. This wouldn't help that situation a bit. The small upside was that instead of a teenage impostor, he could have been dealing with a real vampire in full blood frenzy, and that would have been unpleasant.

"You don't have to tell them, right? I mean, I fit in now. And Katy thinks I'm cool."

"No, I don't have to tell them. But my partner might have a thing or two to say about that."

"Your partner?"

Marcus sat on the bed next to the boy. His eyes were still blood-shot from the Sangri he'd drunk in the car, and he'd lowered his fangs. The kid was still looking at Alex and hadn't realized Marcus was there.

"Ask him." Alex nodded in Marcus's direction.

The kid turned and gasped just as Marcus grabbed him by the neck. Marcus leaned in close.

"Do you know what vampires, real vampires, do to impostors?"

It was scary, terrifying. Alex would have put money down that the kid had just shit himself. The truth was that vampires didn't care about impostors at all. But after another minute with Marcus in full-on prince-of-darkness mode, that kid would confess everything to Katy and her mom and the school and probably anyone who would listen. They wouldn't have any problems with him anymore, not vampire-related anyway. Alex had to leave before he started laughing.

9

Roeland Jaap stared at the club's entrance from the driver's seat of the van. Beside him, John Seward's hulking body squatted in the passenger seat. Behind them, Arthur Holmwood sifted through a novel, his battery-powered book light providing faint illumination.

"She should've been out by now," John said. "How long's it been?"

Roeland didn't move or answer.

Arthur noticed the silence and peeked at his watch. "It's only been fifteen minutes."

John fidgeted in the front seat.

"She'll be fine, John. How many times has she done this?" Arthur said.

"Not with this bloke. And you heard her talking about her friend, Gail? Rhuna said that girl went missing doing the same bloody thing. Tom and Diana—" John said.

Roeland snapped his gaze away from the club and focused it on John.

"Tom and Diana lacked the will to see this through. I only pray they regain a measure of strength before the vampires catch up with them," Roeland said.

He saw the puzzled look on John's face. Half of John's face couldn't move, paralyzed by the parting gift of a vampire that had gotten too close. The attack had left John with a missing eye, a terrible scar, and facial muscles that didn't work right.

"What? You didn't think the vampires would forgive them simply because they left our merry band, did you? Rest assured, should any of the Lightbearers catch up with them, they'll share just as unpleasant a fate as any of us." Roeland added, "We don't stop until we've driven a stake into Lelith's chest."

"That won't stop whatever the Lightbearers are up to. You know that, don't you, Roeland?" Arthur said.

"It is a step in the right direction. These creatures need to know fear."

"We've heard it all before, Roeland. You have to admit, we've been taking larger risks lately," Arthur said.

"The risks have risen with the stakes. Wouldn't you agree?"

"Well yeah," John interrupted. "But it hasn't been us taking them for the most part."

"Rhuna can handle herself."

"You keep saying that. But she's the one in there being bait. What if—"

"She knows the risks," Roeland said.

"So, if it came down to putting her on the line to get at Lelith?" John asked.

"That'd be up to Rhuna," Roeland said.

"Would it? She's no more than a girl. And she listens to you. She shouldn't be doing this." John leaned forward in his seat, his shoulders flexing as the conversation grew more agitated. He adjusted the patch over his ruined eye. A nervous tick Roeland had come to recognize.

"How else are we to find Molony's club, huh?" Roeland asked.

Arthur interjected. "You're still committed to trying to take down an active blood club then?"

"That's why we're here."

"Just making sure. I was hoping you'd changed your mind," Arthur said.

"We've been over this."

"Yes, I know, Roeland. But we—"

"What's your plan then?" Roeland asked.

"Well, if it were up to me, and I know it isn't, we wait till Rhuna brings Molony out and ambush him. Same as we've always done and a hell of a lot safer," Arthur said.

"That makes good sense, Roeland," John said.

Roeland countered, "Same as we've always done. Like you just said. And then what? Molony's club goes right on doing business though we know his isn't the kind of victimless blood joint the Lightbearers would like us to think they all are. We know he takes his victims there and they never leave."

"And we know you want to send them a message. But at what cost?" Arthur asked.

"If we can show the humans around here what the vampires really are, and that they aren't invulnerable gods to be tacitly worshiped, that they can be killed by a few dedicated individuals with the will to see it through . . ."

Arthur had gone back to reading his novel.

"Am I boring you, Arthur?" Roeland turned in his seat to glare at him.

"I'm part of the choir, lad. We've heard it all before. I'm here because I don't need convincing. We all want revenge same as the next. And I won't let you walk in there alone. You know that."

"You really think the three of us can take out a club full of vampires who've just fed?" John asked.

Arthur shrugged.

"We'll have the element of surprise," Roeland answered, "and someone on the inside. There are, after all, four of us."

"Right. Rhuna, right in the middle of it."

"John. It's nice you're sweet on the girl, but you aren't her bodyguard. You don't know her half as well as I do. I'm telling you she's up to it. If you don't like the way we're doing things—the door's unlocked, mate."

An awkward silence followed.

"We're with you, Roeland. We told you we'd see this to the end," Arthur said. He pulled himself up between the driver and passenger seats. "Now's not the time to go having second thoughts. It's too late for that anyway."

"Here we go," Arthur said. He pointed at a couple coming out of the club.

Roeland snapped his eyes back to the front. The stress was affecting them all. He'd allowed himself to get distracted. He quickly saw their quarry. Even with her darkened hair, the woman was unmistakably Rhuna. The man, the vampire with her, was their target.

Fionan Molony was Lelith's right hand, a borderline oldblood, hundred years and change. He liked virgins. Not just the literal kind, but also those new to the S&B lifestyle. He'd been dining on a smorgasbord of Wannabes since the Reveal. The poor girls didn't even know what hit them. They fell for his charm, they fell for his tour-guide act, and in the end, they just fell.

He left a string of missing girls in his wake, all in their late teens or early twenties. Their lives snuffed out by his vampire lust. Tonight, Roeland had served him up Rhuna, tailored to Molony's tastes. He would not, could not, refuse.

Now that Roeland could see him, he felt a knot of doubt growing in his chest. Oldbloods didn't live to become oldbloods through lack of caution. Maybe John was right. He watched Rhuna flirting with the monster as he shepherded her toward his Jaguar convertible. She wrapped her arm around his waist and pressed herself too close to him for Roeland's comfort.

Beside him, John dug his fingers into the dash.

"She'll be fine," Roeland said. He was trying to convince himself as much as the others.

Molony reached for a key fob and lowered the convertible's top remotely. He watched Rhuna giggle and excitedly clap her hands together in delight.

He thought back to the moments after Tom and Diana had left. Rhuna had acted strange. Even for her.

How much of this was an act?

Molony opened the passenger door and Rhuna got in. She waited until he sat in the driver's seat before stretching her arms backward over the seat and arching her back. Roeland could only imagine the view Molony was getting.

He let out the breath he hadn't realized he'd been holding.

He started the van's engine and waited for Molony's Jaguar to pull away, then slipped out in pursuit.

10

10:15 P.M.

Filip's anger hadn't diminished at all over the last hour. He was still cleaning up Nico's mess. They'd just dumped out everything that wasn't a part of their order on the floor of the van, taken the entire cooler, and left. He pressed another armload of frozen meat against his chest as he tried to keep the plastic vacuum-sealed packages from sliding against each other. He passed Mitch on his way back out to the van. Mitch paused and held the door open for him.

They had the routine down now. Filip had lost count, but this had to be at least his eighth load. He turned immediately right upon entering and passed into a small room. On the floor were several large, cheap Styrofoam coolers he and Mitch had coopted. He dumped the armload of frozen packages into one that still had room. It wasn't hard to ignore what it was, packaged like this. It looked much like the ordinary meat he'd always used to mask the blood products he dealt in.

He headed back out to the van, holding the door open for Mitch as he came in with another unwieldy armload.

"Maybe one more trip and then the other big cooler."

Filip grumbled what passed for a reply. He still couldn't figure out how he was going to move that damn cooler with just him and Mitch. He had to get Gus and Lonzo back here, and the hell with Stan and his order. They couldn't risk the whole operation over one fuckup. He reached the van and snatched at the remaining packages of meat. He piled them up in his arms and they slid frustratingly against one another, several falling back to the floor of the van as fast as he could pick them up. He wasn't going to make it in one more trip.

Then Filip had an idea. He let the packs of meat in his arms fall to the floor and opened the second cooler. He slid some of the meat around to make more room and shoveled the packs from the floor of the van into the cooler. A few more packs wouldn't hurt; he and Mitch weren't going to move it alone anyway. He slammed the cooler lid down several times, and after he'd moved some of the packs around a bit more, it finally closed.

He stood leaning against the cooler and pulled his cell phone out of his jacket. He dialed Gus. No answer. Then he dialed Lonzo. Straight to voice mail. It seemed like he'd just spoken to them earlier. Filip had a bad feeling. If those guys got pinched, too . . .

A noise caught his attention, the steps of someone walking across the gravel of the lot. The footfall didn't sound like Mitch's heavy steps and Mitch would have been coming from the other side anyway, unless he'd decided to walk around the block for some reason. Filip held his breath to listen more carefully. The footsteps stopped right outside the van.

Was it the cops?

Nico's crew?

One of his new customers? No, those assholes had been as quiet as the vampires.

He thought of the pistol holstered in the small of his back.

Mitch would have said something by now. Filip decided to put on his buddy act. He was good at it, and it would help throw whoever was out there off their guard.

"Hey friend, what can I help you with so we can both go away happy?"

"I'm glad you're feeling so accommodating tonight, because we could use your help."

Filip tried to place the voice and it came to him. It was a cop, but one he had an arrangement with.

"Alex? Jesus, you damn near made me shit myself."

Filip came out of the van and saw Alex standing there alone, one hand in the pocket of his khakis. That hand was probably holding an automatic. At least he and Alex understood each other. That he could deal with.

"I shouldn't have, I made enough noise coming up here." Alex looked into the van. "You a little shorthanded tonight? You're bringing in a little juice supply and you have nobody else around? Are you getting stupid on me?"

"Come on, man, you know my rep. Everyone's my friend, right? Who'd want to hurt me?"

"Well, me for starters. You planning on moving the cooler by yourself?" Alex asked.

"Me and Mitch. We could use a hand if you're feeling helpful."

Alex gave him a look and stepped into the van. "What's inside, I wonder?"

Filip's heart turned to ice. He didn't want Alex, of all people, looking too closely inside. What completely shitty luck to have him come down right now. "You know, speaking of getting stupid. You come down here alone and start talking shit, poking around and stuff . . ."

Alex took his hand out of his pocket. It was empty. It wasn't a gesture of peace, but a sign meant to convey to Filip that he didn't need whatever was in his pocket. "Never said I was alone."

"Your partner around?" Filip, dark-skinned as he was, still managed to lose a shade or two of complexion.

"Always."

The back door of the bodega opened up, sending a triangular spear of light into the small lot. Shadows danced and Alex shrank behind the front seats of the van. Mitch was backing the handcart out of the doorway.

"Mitch, go ahead and head back inside. I'll come get you when I'm ready."

Mitch half turned, his hands still on the handcart. "You want I should get Jean?"

Filip liked Mitch even better right then. He was smart, not like those other two idiots he had working for him. Jean wasn't a person. Jean was a shotgun Filip kept upstairs.

"Naw, it's cool. Just give me a couple minutes."

"You got it."

Filip turned back to Alex. "Now, what do you want, bro? You can see I have a busy night ahead of me."

"Okay, I got a couple things for you." Alex opened the lid of the cooler and started poking around absently at the packages of meat. "First, have you heard anything about vigilantes taking down vampires? I'm not talking about the onesy-twosy nut thinking he's going to get a quick payback. I'm talking about semipro, holy-avenger types. Organized."

Filip kept staring at Alex's hands in the cooler. Was Alex just toying with him? Then the importance of Alex's question hit him.

"What, the uh Nocturn Killer? Abraham? Holy shit, the rumors are right. That manifesto was real? He's here ain't, he? Whoa. You guys need to pull your heads out of your collective asses on that one before it blows up in your faces. Folks are talking like he's some kind of folk hero, gonna take the night back from the sangers."

"Fantastic. Are folks scared? You know, your nocturn customers?"

"Not more than normal. They're pissed. Only a matter of time until some sanger goes to take the law into his own hands as payback. You sure that's not what happened this morning?"

Alex ignored the last sentence. "What about folks out to get some vamp juice on the cheap?"

"What? Someone rolling a sanger?"

"Been known to happen."

"So's folks playing Russian roulette, but it ain't smart. Anyways, I wouldn't know anything about that."

"Right."

"I'm a legitimate businessman selling a product in demand. Hell, if the dicks in D.C. were a little more open-minded, my whole operation would be aboveboard."

Alex chuckled. "I'll believe it when it happens. Second thing, there's a new source of juice out. Human stock, heavy adrenaline, not synthetic. Hard to find and extremely expensive. A new cut, we need to know who's running it."

"I ain't heard nothing about that." How the hell could the cops know about that already? Filip had been running it less than a week, and if Nico hadn't shown up to grab his order early, there'd be a whole cooler of that shit sitting right where Alex was standing!

"So if I dig a little deeper in here, I'm not gonna find any blood products, right?"

Filip laughed nervously. "Didn't say that. Just I don't know about any new adrenalized juice. Have yourself a look."

"Just like that? Preemptive offer, so then you think I won't look? You know me better than that."

Alex shoved his hand into the cold packs of hard frozen meat. He shoved the tightly crammed packages aside, digging farther down. Under the top layer, the packages had frozen together almost as one solid mass. They wouldn't budge. Alex grunted and pushed the packages aside. Loosened packs spilled onto the floor of the van.

Filip could have sworn he saw the cooler move.

"What is this? How come you don't get your stuff through regular suppliers?"

Filip thought quickly; could it be possible Alex didn't realize what he was digging through?

"You know me, man. I only deal in the best stuff. That right there is straight from the farm, all choice, all organic, no hormones or any of that crap. I know you're into all the healthy stuff. I could throw some in for you, you know, give you a police discount."

"Sell it to someone else." Alex grunted. He continued to scoop meat off to the side, digging deeper into the cooler.

"It's all kosher, you know. Or halal, if you swing that way."

"Kosher and halal? Nice."

Filip laughed nervously. "Hey, it's whatever you want it to be if it allows me to charge more. Like the song says, 'If you've got the money, honey, we've got your disease.'"

Alex found what he was looking for: plasma bags, frozen blood packs.

"What the hell is this?" Alex held up a pack in mock surprise. "Are you telling me you're a juice dealer?"

"Uh gee, I ain't ever seen that before, uh, honest, it ain't mine," Filip joked.

Alex reached into his pocket and came up with a small tactical flashlight. He thumbed the touch switch on the back and the light shifted, going from white to dark purple. He brought one blood pack to eye level and moved the light over it. The blood inside the pack, dark crimson and blackish under the white light, now fluoresced noticeably. This was vampire blood. Very expensive and hard to come by. And Filip needed every single drop, especially if he expected to have any fun with clients later that night.

Filip lost all expression of amusement. "Hey, that ain't UV, is it? Turn that shit off! You're gonna ruin it!"

Alex tossed the pack back into the cooler. He fished around and came up with one from another batch. He did the same thing to it. The blood did not fluoresce. This was human stock.

"You had better have donor papers for this."

"Yeah, yeah. You want to see them now?"

"Yeah."

"Shit. Why are you busting my balls, bro?" Filip opened the passenger door of the van and picked up a large metal-enclosed clipboard, the kind delivery people used to carry before everything went electronic. He always kept some fakes on hand just in case. They wouldn't stand up to a full check, but he hoped Alex wouldn't go that far. If he did, he could shoot him and make a run for it.

Not that he'd make it. Alex's partner would be on him faster than he could move. That pistol wasn't going to do anything to an Ancient.

He was getting pretty tired of people ordering him around tonight. The thought brought Nico to mind and formed the seeds of an idea, a little payback for both of his pains in the ass.

"Here you go." He handed the clipboard to Alex.

Alex took it and opened the top. He leafed through the papers absently. Then he put the clipboard on the corner of the open cooler.

"You're going to have to get rid of all this meat," Alex said.

"What?" It wasn't what Filip had been expecting. He was still formulating his plan.

"Selling juice is one thing. Those customers know what they're getting into. I can't have you selling strange meat to the neighborhood housewives out of a van. That's not happening. And I'll know if you try anything."

"That cost me a shitload."

"I'm sure you'll pass on the cost to your customers. Call it the cost of doing business. Why pack it in with the juice?"

"Because it masks the scent of the blood products from them, you know, the ones with more sensitive noses."

Another voice joined the conversation, quiet and icy.

"It does not."

Filip jumped in his skin. The voice, vaguely European in accent, seemed to bring its own chill to the air.

"Wha—" he managed to stammer.

"It does not mask the scent." A phantom slid from shadows Filip would have sworn weren't dark enough to conceal anyone. He saw a tall solid man with pale skin and hair so black it looked as if there was nothing there at first, until he stepped into the edge of the light's glow.

Filip didn't move, though he had met Alex's partner before. He was beginning to wish he never had. Each time he saw the ancient vampire was as disconcerting as the first. It was one thing to meet a vampire in a well-lit room, quite another in a dimly lit parking lot. Filip had met enough killers, human and vampire, to know one when he saw one. This man, this vampire, was an old hand at killing.

"That's not what we need, Alex," Marcus said. His voice never really rose above a whisper, yet it seemed to come from everywhere at once.

Alex stepped out of the van and put one hand on Filip's shoulder. "You're lucky, Filip. It would have gone very badly for you if that was the stuff we were looking for."

Filip thought again of Nico picking up the other cooler early. Oh yeah, he wanted everyone to suffer a little. He put his plan into motion.

"Uh yeah. Hey, if your partner's up for something, you know, he can help himself. As you saw, I have some really good stock there."

Alex answered for Marcus. "No thanks, just keep an ear to the ground for us, okay?"

"Yeah sure. I've got something for you right now, if you're interested. There's a new juice joint. Very exclusive. They screen everybody. High-quality bleeders, not your normal emo Wannabe stock."

"So?"

"So, they've only been going a couple of days, but word is they're running through booze and broads like the world's about to come to an end. It's like a party to end all parties. I'm thinking maybe they might know something." Filip hoped it sounded convincing.

"Wow, just like that? What's your beef with them?"

"They're moving a lot of product out of there. Performance enhancers, vamp . . . er . . . nocturn blood. Some human stock for those that don't want to get personal with the bleeders. Competition is already stiff, man."

"So you sic us on them hoping your troubles go away?" Alex asked.

"Hey, a guy's gotta do what he can to stay ahead in this economy, right?"

"We'll check it out. If they do as much trade as you say, we might even raise an eyebrow or two. Speaking of which, you need to start cutting back, you're starting to get too big for the big boys to ignore. As long as you stay small-time we can help each other out."

Filip almost laughed. Alex thought he was a hard-ass cop, but he really was clueless.

"So a businessman can't get rich?"

"You're already past rich. You've been playing it smart, so stay smart and not smart-ass. I've been doing this longer than you think. Nails that stick up too high tend to get hammered down. If someone needs a trophy to put on the wall to please the mayor or the media, guess whose head gets whacked and mounted. The smart-asses who aren't playing smart."

"I knew deep down you liked me."

"We do not," Marcus said. He slid across the gravel in the lot and made no sound. Marcus was doing that shit on purpose just to get at him. It worked. "A word to the wise is sufficient. Now, if you would be so kind as to give us the location of the club you spoke of."

11

Rhuna was pumping out enough pheromones to make a normal male weep from lust and frustration. She was putting on quite a show, too, making sure to stretch her arms and legs in the right places, letting Molony get an eyeful. In her outfit, it wasn't very hard, especially with the convertible's top down. She almost felt violated by the wind. She let her hand brush along Fionan Molony's leg just long enough to place a suggestion of potential impropriety in his mind.

Sure, he was a monster. But he was also a good-looking rake. And there were no rules against a girl having a little fun before getting down to business.

She was still feeling heady from the meal Lou had brought her. To be truthful, she was a bit on the horny side, too. She went with it. It helped her play her role all the better.

Fionan, for his part, hadn't shut up. He was going on and on about the sangers and bleeders, the S&B lifestyle. She had to keep up the act that she hadn't heard about any of these things a dozen times before. She concentrated on observing the minutiae of his facial features. She stared at the white skin of his neck, and gave the illusion of offering her rapt attention, all the while thinking of how it would feel to sink her teeth into that flesh and rend it to shreds.

Fionan continued his lecture, speaking a bit too loudly over the wind blasting through the open top of the convertible. His voice had taken on a pedantic quality that annoyed Rhuna.

"S&B has been around for centuries in Europe. It was the pastime of kings and the stuff of the most secret societies. Everyone knows that bleeders are humans who willingly allow vampires to feed on them. But what you don't know is who some of them were: Marie Antoinette, the Marquis de Sade, Oscar Wilde, Lord Byron, Coleridge, and the Shelleys. Yes, both the poet and the novelist. Almost all the Romantics.

"On this side of the pond, let's see, you have, Benjamin Franklin, Daniel Webster, and Doc Holliday. That's just for starters. In the old days, you had to be careful. A nocturn could wind up in the whole 'villagers with pitchforks and torches' situation, the villagers would accuse the bleeders of conspiring with spirits or the Devil, and it was off to the big bonfire for them. Now, well, it's still technically illegal, but no one's going to lose a life over it."

He didn't even wait for a response from Rhuna. He just kept right on rolling. Which was fine by her; Fionan was easy on the eyes. She didn't need to talk to him to do her job.

"Show me a nocturn who says he doesn't occasionally enjoy the juice straight from the source, and I'll show you a poor liar. It's our nature, but it takes some folks longer to come around than others. It's like you could get all your nutrition from drinking soy protein. You'd still want a steak now and again. Except that's not really a good analogy, because you'd have to kill the cow to the get the steak, and we don't have to kill the bleeders to get a little juice."

Except that you do anyway. Rhuna ran a hand across her neck and pretended to rub it. She wanted to take a surreptitious look behind. Was the van there? Were they following?

"Something wrong?" Fionan asked.

"I'm freezing. Can you put the top back up?"

"I could. But we're there." Fionan smiled. The smile lit up his face and made him irresistibly gorgeous. His vampire charm tugged at her heart. How many lives had that smile ended?

He slowed the car down and pulled up to the curb. Rhuna looked around. Nothing strange. It was a simple side street with some office buildings and some small shops. Darkness swallowed everything except for an all-night drugstore on the corner.

A youngblood male nocturn in stylish clothes walked seemingly from nowhere up to the car as soon as Fionan cut the engine. The youngblood opened Rhuna's door and held a hand out for her. She took it and helped herself out of the convertible.

"Good evening, Mr. Molony."

"Evening, Reggie." Fionan tossed the keys to the youngblood, then walked around the front of the car and put out his arm so Rhuna could take it.

"There's a blood club around here?"

"One of the nicest in the city."

They stepped around the nearest building and into an alley. At the end of the alley, lit by a solitary light, was a large male sitting on a metal folding chair. He had been watching something on a small tablet computer but looked up as they entered the alley.

A long alley, a single point of entry with a guard—this wasn't good. Rhuna felt her heart start pounding faster. She let it. Fionan would be expecting it. A normal Wannabe going into an exclusive blood club for the first time would be understandably excited.

The male stood and reached into his pocket. It was a man. A human. Not a youngblood.

"Good evening, Mr. Molony. New girl tonight?" His tone indicated that Rhuna was some kind of prop. He didn't acknowledge that she was even a person.

"Just showing her the ropes."

The man pressed some kind of button in his pocket, and the door gave off a buzzing sound.

"Normally, there's a hefty cover charge to get in here. You know, to keep the riffraff out. But I'm good friends with the owner." He shot her a wink as he held the door for her.

Rhuna felt her heart skip a beat as their eyes met. Part of her wanted to come clean and tell him everything, that this was a trap, that she was bait, that Abraham would be there tonight to kill them all. She wanted to fall to her knees and beg his forgiveness. She would do all this if he would have her.

Then the bestial part of her stirred, its defenses shot to the fore, and she regained her senses. She suppressed a growl and flashed him a tight closed-mouthed smile as she crossed into the foyer.

Inside, the lights were dim. Down-tempo electronic music droned at the periphery of normal hearing. A young-looking beautiful female vampire stepped from behind a small podium. She had long straight blond hair and wore a red dress with a vaguely Oriental cut. She didn't move like a youngblood.

That was bad news, too. A couple of oldbloods in here could make the difference between victory and disaster.

The hostess smiled at Fionan and Rhuna.

"Modviv?" she asked Rhuna.

It was short for "modus vivendi"—lifestyle. It was a broad question. It covered whether or not a bleeder drank or used drugs. What kind of foods they ate, whether they were vegan health nuts or fast-food addicts. How often they worked out, sexual orientation and frequency. Normally, a vampire could sniff out most of those traits, but the close confines inside most blood clubs made it more difficult to single out an individual's scent.

Regular bleeders would know the answer to this question and would be able to answer it in a series of category words. The hostess would input it into a small handheld computer and, using something akin to ink-jet technology, spray out a little infrared stamp onto the back of the bleeder's hand. That way, only the vampires would know who the regular bleeders were.

Rhuna played stupid.

The hostess didn't seem surprised, but made a sly glance at Fionan. "Another fresher? Where do you find them?"

"It's a talent. Someday, if you're really nice to me, I might tell you. Let's skip the modviv tonight. She's with me in any case."

The hostess lowered her head in deference.

"As you wish." She stepped to the other end of the foyer, where a bead curtain hung over a doorway. She parted the beads to one side and made a show of formality.

"Of my own free will I invite you to cross this threshold."

Fionan responded, "For your freely given welcome, I will return no harm."

Rhuna had done this dozens of times, and the vampires always expected her to be thrilled. She supposed a real Wannabe would be beside herself crossing the threshold into the vampiric world. So she acted accordingly.

Fionan passed through the bead curtain, and Rhuna followed. They moved into a larger room that was halfway between a bar and nightclub. The lighting was dimmer here than in the foyer. Small cabaret-style tables spread across the floor so bleeders could mingle with their prospective vampires. Smaller, more private rooms branched off from the main room, and Fionan was leading her toward one of those.

There were perhaps half a dozen couples seated at the tables engaged in small talk, some males with males, some females with females, and some males with females. As usual, sexual orientation had little to do with it. Instead, the kind of experience the vampire or bleeder was seeking that night dictated the pairings. Conversations would stop as Rhuna and Fionan passed by and when they resumed Rhuna was always the subject.

They didn't think she could hear them, but she could. Fionan was the object of their envy. And she was what they coveted. That was good. She could use that to her advantage if she had to. If the vampires were already leaning toward hostility toward Fionan, how-ever small, and lust for her, it would take only a little bit to set off a potential blood frenzy.

She'd been secreting subtle pheromones all night, enough to keep Fionan off his guard. If she needed to, she could dial it up and have all the vampires in the place fighting each other over her. She started to formulate a plan.

Fionan led her into one of the smaller rooms. The audio design was superb. As soon as they crossed the threshold, different music, more New Age, drowned out the main room's sounds. A central pillar with a fake fireplace rose in the center. Around it was a large very plush circular couch finished in red velvet.

There was a light smell lingering under the surface of everything. It smelled like cinnamon, but not real cinnamon, like cinnamon candy. Two couples kissed and petted one another and scarcely ac-knowledged their entrance.

The circumference of the room had little booths with high walls meant to give the occupants the illusion of privacy. Fionan guided her into one of these. The confines of the booth were far more inti-mate than Rhuna had suspected from the outside. It pressed them tightly together.

Fionan leaned back, and as Rhuna went to sit next to him, he pulled her down and sat her sideways across his lap.

"It's a lot more comfortable this way, don't you think?"

He flashed those eyes and that smile at her again. Rhuna felt the room swim around her. He was much stronger than any other vam-pire she'd faced. Her heart beat faster. Fionan leaned in for a kiss and her lips parted willingly. He kissed her and she found her arms wrap-ping around his shoulders of their own accord.

The animal within her recoiled and raged. He was hitting her hard with his glamour. Human girls wouldn't have stood a chance. The thought helped her control her arousal. Instead, she concentrated on what unpleasant things she would do to Fionan later that night.

She kicked her heels off as he broke away from the kiss.

"Wow. That was very nice," Fionan said.

A waitress stepped up to the booth. "A drink for the lady?"

Fionan shot her a look of annoyance but masked it quickly when he saw that Rhuna had seen it.

"Go ahead. We'll be here awhile."

"Okay. I'll have a Red Bull and vodka."

Fionan interrupted her. "Make it a double."

The waitress nodded, then stepped away.

"Hang on now. You ordered a double for me and you're not going to drink anything?" Rhuna already knew why, besides the obvious fact, but felt it was in character to ask.

"Well, it's part of the experience. That's the whole point of the modviv question. Nocturn physiology is very robust. Everyone knows that. But our digestive tract is the chink in our armor so to speak. That's why nocturns can't eat normal food once we're turned. If we drink alcohol, our bodies will either pass it right through, or it winds up coming back up, rather violently, I'm afraid. But if, say, I bought you a couple of drinks . . ."

He winked at her.

". . . and then had a little sip from you, I would get the same effect as if I drank that alcohol. Drugs work the same way. In some of the other rooms there are nocturns buying bleeders joints, or needles, or whatever they're into, so that they can share the rush."

Rhuna nodded and feigned interest. Would it be possible to poison a vampire? Her mind moved on. A place like this was bound to have security, and she needed to know who they were and where they were.

"But if the sangers . . . oh, I'm sorry . . ."

"It's all right. We know it's the slang. They're just words." He smiled disarmingly.

"If the nocturns and bleeders are both getting high, aren't people worried things might get out of control?"

Fionan pointed past her to a camera in the corner and to two large male vampires standing in the shadows. Rhuna was surprised that she hadn't seen them before.

"That's their job. Aside from being regular bouncers and taking care of things when folks get too rowdy, they're here to keep nocturns in check as well." He returned to his original train of thought. "Sangri and Hemotopia and the other synth-blood stuff, it's just not the same coming from a bottle. The whole other rush is gone. It's the difference between watching porn and fucking."

Rhuna acted a bit shocked at his language. His hands moved to cover her stomach and her back.

"Easy now," she said, "my drink hasn't even gotten here. Aren't you getting ahead of yourself?"

He ignored her. "Like I was saying, if a nocturn starts to get too carried away, those guys step in and pull the nocturn off, hold them down until their senses come back, and make sure everything is okay. The system works. A couple of centuries back, you might get some unfortunate circumstances in the community because nocturns would lose control. They'd feed too long and then they'd be left with only two choices, turn the bleeder or let them die."

"And the bleeders wouldn't fight back?"

"That's part of why the clubs started in the first place. When we feed, we give off an enzyme that is a very powerful drug in its own right. It makes it so we don't have to worry about blood-borne diseases other than a bad taste. It's what gives bleeders a rush. There are no victims. Just consenting adults."

He slid his hand on her stomach up to her chest and pulled her in for another kiss. Before she knew it, she was kissing him back. When he pulled away, she was breathing heavily, as if she'd just run for miles.

Where were Roeland and the others? She wasn't going to be able to hold this off much longer. The effects of the flesh she'd eaten earlier combined with Fionan's glamour had weakened her rational defenses. It was hard to think.

She felt a sharp pinch on the soft skin of her arm. To her surprise, she realized Fionan had bitten her and was feeding. She let out a soft gasp and felt a low moan building within her as her muscles went slack. One of his hands had her arm pinned to the booth's side wall; his other hand worked its way under her blouse and sought each nipple in turn. Suddenly there was a river between her thighs. She wanted to shout, to scream, to pull away. All she managed was a weak groan and a gasping whisper.

The beast inside her struggled to assert itself.

"Don't fight it. Go with it," Fionan cooed. He returned to feeding.

She had to fight it. Her body surged as if attached to an electric current. She felt impaled on a high-tension line.

The hand on her breast moved lower. Much lower. A piece of her wanted it there; her legs parted, and he moved her panties out of the way.

She couldn't breathe. Her body fought itself. She was a live wire and bucked against his hand in paroxysms of ecstasy.

He pulled his mouth away from her arm and the euphoria died away.

Rhuna sucked in a breath and looked at him. She saw the look of surprise and horror on his face. He had tasted it in her. He knew!

How could she have been so stupid? She'd have only seconds to act.

"Oh don't stop!" she murmured. Her senses were crawling back to her through the aftermath of the orgasm. Her hand moved down to rub the bulge in his pants. She simultaneously hit him with a burst of pheromones that would drive vampires insane with lust and hunger the instant they caught a whiff.

She saw his eyes begin to glaze with the start of a blood frenzy.

She knew he wouldn't be lucid for long. In moments, every vampire nearby would be fighting for a chance to get at her.

She leaned in close to him and smiled.

"Did you think you could glamour me?"

She moved her hands behind his head, the fingers already shaping themselves into flesh-tearing talons. She relished the look of horror on his face. How many young girls had felt the same at his hands?

Her eyes turned yellow as she started the change. "My turn."

12

10:45 P.M.

The unmarked Ford Explorer glided from lane to lane, shifting elegantly as it slid around the obstructing cars. Alex couldn't help but smile. He loved driving, particularly this large SUV. He adored the sense of power. He was easily topping ninety and didn't need to check the speedometer. He could feel it. But then he'd always loved physical speed. His thoughts flew to heady days skimming along the cataracts of the Nile, where the waters grew swift, heedless of the rocks and a dozen different dangers.

He snarled and buried the brake pedal into the floorboard. The taillights in front of him nearly disappeared beneath the hood as his tires screamed in protest. The SUV stopped just shy of kissing the other car's bumper.

Alex smacked the wheel. There used to be a time when traffic grew thinner after dark. Everything was twenty-five/eight now, three-sixty-five. There were vampires about now and they were customers like everyone else. So as much as they might drain their victims of blood, the economy could drain them of money. So everything was work, work, work—go, go, go.

Marcus was unfazed as usual. He reached back and pulled out the other bottle of Sangri. The cap made a popping sound as he twisted it open. After a cursory sniff, Marcus drained the contents in one long pull.

"Thirsty?" Alex asked.

"It helps to curb the baser instincts. If one is to be infiltrating this 'juice joint' it doesn't do to have one's head muddled by the younger patrons."

"I wonder what Aguirre would have to say about that." Alex had dropped all pretense of his cover accent, and his words now carried the cadence of his normal speech, tinged with the inflections of foreign times and ancient lands.

"Some such thing about temptation blocking the path to redemption. Every time I go into one of those places it gets a little harder not to let loose and allow nature to take its course. The temptation to just give myself over to the lusts and passions of my kind is very great sometimes."

"For some nubile young girl of twenty summers to legally open up her neck to you, at your age, you're going to have to pay for it."

In truth, Marcus didn't look over forty, but it was his disposition that made him act his full age of over two millennia.

Alex's attempt at a joke was poor, but he needed to do something. He could feel Marcus's humors falling out of balance, spiraling into dangerous territory. That was the last thing either of them needed.

"Of course," Alex said, "the bleeders get something out of it, too. They say the bite exceeds anything in the human experience."

"That is not how I remember it. I struggled for my life with an emaciated creature ripping at me, his fetid stench blending with that of the mud-and-shit-covered street, one dark night, in a forgotten province of the Imperium."

As feared, Marcus was already sour. The constant badgering of Aguirre and his penitents was enough to put anyone off his game. Alex had heard that the Romans had been known for their mercurial moods. That probably went quadruple for Roman vampires. Marcus was providing a stellar example of it, and it wasn't even midnight yet. He needed to get him thinking about something else.

"Did you not find it odd that Filip is suddenly choosing to sell meat?"

"*Certes*. He had a good excuse for it, though he was wrong," Marcus said.

"That it didn't camouflage the scent of the blood?"

"It did not. As I told him. I also doubt that he should rid himself of it gratis."

"He wouldn't dare sell it. I warned him." Alex unconsciously put iron into his words.

"Your words no longer carry the weight they once did, old friend."

Alex drove on in silence. His words scarcely had, even when he'd ruled. It was his secret shame.

The traffic was beginning to open up again. His mind began following threads he might have missed earlier. The color of the meat was off, or was it just the lighting? If it didn't conceal the scent of the blood products, then Filip would have known that. Filip should have known that. One didn't stay in the blood trade long by making an error like that. Alex pursed his lips; he should have paid closer attention.

"Put another way, have you ever known Filip to waste anything?" Marcus continued.

Alex grudgingly shook his head.

"I wonder how much profit he is able to garner from it?" Marcus didn't direct the question toward Alex, but posed it rhetorically, pensively.

"That would go well with your pedigree." Alex laughed. "Marcus Scaevola, patrician noble, governor of Lower . . ."

"Pannonia," Marcus finished for him.

"Lower Pannonia. Knight commander in the Order of Malta. Purveyor of meats of dubious origin."

He managed to get a crease of a smile from Marcus.

"I could use the additional coin. The gods know Juno Moneta has not lent her grace to me of late. If I had half, no, one-third of the relics this fool government is keeping from me . . ."

The Roman goddess of money wasn't going to be much help to Marcus these days. Her time had passed. Marcus had frittered his substantial wealth into a long string of poor investments. First, the dot-com bubble burst; then he'd tried to double down with real estate before the bottom dropped out of that, too. By human standards, he could be considered wealthy, but by vampire reckoning, particularly Ancient standards, he was a pauper.

"Try having your entire civilization plundered and scattered to the points of the compass by barbarians and thieves. Then having to buy back your original possessions in the world's shadiest back alleys and black markets at triple the cost," Alex said.

"*Concio ad clerum,*" Marcus said. Preaching to the converted.

"If you need some extra coin, you could probably part with a pint or two of your own rare vintage. Given your esteemed bloodline, and coming from an Ancient, you should be able to fetch, what . . ." Alex put on his best Laurence Olivier. ". . . one thousand golden sesterces, or some such, per pint."

"First, the plural is 'sestertii.' Second, they were silver. Third, I would hope to get much better than that. Finally, Romans are not British."

"Forgive me. I was misled." Alex made his tone drip with mock contrition.

"What of you? Do you not routinely summon armies of scarabs to undo your foes or guide sandstorms to follow your every whim?"

"Ah. Poor maligned Imhotep. The subject of so many tales. In my day, he was revered as a god. Now, he's but a petty villain in a children's tale. There is a difference," Alex answered.

"How?"

"I've never tried to summon sandstorms or armies of scarabs. For all I know, the tales might be right. In any case, Imhotep was a powerful sorcerer and I am but a simple deposed king, trying to account for the error of his ways."

"In a sort of exile to be sure."

"Don't try to change the subject. We were speaking about you turning meat merchant for a few coppers. That's what bothers me about this age. The people are lazy. They've so completely forgotten what a day's honest sweat can bring, no less what it took to make brick for Pharaoh, or build a temple with their bare hands."

"Ah. Because you have a wealth of experience in such matters."

Traffic was opening up now and Alex let the SUV charge forward. "Hardly the point. My favorite of the work gangs," Alex continued, "once moved three blocks up from the harbor and into position in a single day. These were granite blocks mind you, not limestone. I rewarded them with the finest of Hathor's *yrp* wine and from that day forth they called themselves Menkaure's Drunkards."

"Carried that moniker with pride, did they?"

"They certainly did." Alex smiled with the memory. The smile died with the bitterness of other memories, which rode through his mind on the coattails of the first. The death of his son and daughter. Knephren-Ka and the Battle of Inebu-Hedju. Neithikret, who lurked out there somewhere, doing Isfethotep's mischief.

Marcus interrupted his thoughts, "You should tell the people how it was done."

"What?"

"You should tell them of your honest day's work and how you built the pyramids."

"Eh. Why bother?" There wasn't much of a trick to it. Water applied in the right places and the copious application of a massive workforce. Modern people overthought everything.

Alex checked a street sign and turned the SUV in to the entrance of an industrial park. He drove past long rows of buildings with multiple loading docks. They all looked abandoned except for the security lights.

"Besides," he continued, "if they want to believe ancient aliens did it, why ruin their fun?"

Alex killed the Explorer's lights. Even though he could only see to the next streetlight, it would enable Marcus to see farther.

"Keep going. Up ahead," Marcus said.

They passed what started as a spattering of parked cars along the side of the road. The spattering grew into an unbroken line parked bumper-to-bumper and overflowing into the lots of some of the industrial buildings.

"Well, well, looks like someone is throwing a rave," Marcus said.

Alex killed the engine and Marcus rolled down his window. The two sat in silence for a moment.

Alex spoke up. "I hear nothing. If Filip's lying, I'll let you do whatever you want to him."

"Shh. You do not hear that?"

Marcus had his head cocked to one side and almost entirely out the window of the SUV. The Sangri was doing its work. His eyes had taken on the reddish bloodshot quality of a vampire just after feeding. His skin looked flushed, almost human.

Alex strained his ears, trying to hear something, anything, that didn't fit. For a long while, all he could hear were the muted sounds of I-95 behind them. Finally, he heard it, one sound that didn't belong. A musical bass line pulsing beneath the noise of the city.

"I've got it now. How do you want to play this?"

Marcus thought for a moment.

"You take a look about?"

"I can do that."

Alex sat back in the seat, relaxed, and let his *ka* pull free of his body. There were no pretenses in the ether. The club ahead was swarming with golden souls and negative-image vampires. There were also the blue-white spirits, lost and confused, dozens. Then he saw more. More than he could count. How many were they murdering in there?

Then he felt *It*. That presence of malevolent primeval corruption he had sensed earlier. *It* was here! *It* was in that club.

Then, he felt something else.

An otherworldly probe sliced across the ether from inside the club. It scanned the astral plane like a searchlight, and instinctively Menkaure knew it sought him.

Simultaneously, the spirits swarmed in his direction. Their activity drew the attention of whatever was inside. He felt its malign gaze focus on him and he knew its power.

Alex retreated into his body.

"Shit, I think I just got made." He was thinking not as a pharaoh anymore, but as a cop again, and subconsciously slipped back into his modern voice and accent.

"What?" Marcus asked.

"There's something in there. Something old and unholy. It saw me."

"Aguirre's Ancient?" Marcus's voice took on a hint of concern.

"I don't know. I've never felt anything like it. The body count is in the hundreds. The spirits were attracted to my *ka*. Still want to go in there?"

Alex knew the answer just by looking at Marcus. All signs of melancholy had vanished. Next to blood, there was nothing a vampire liked more than the prospect of a territorial fight.

"More than I did before. I shall play the gate crasher, you be the cavalry."

"Cavalry implies rescue. Let's keep it to recon for now, okay? No heroics."

Marcus gave him a look. "Don't get your bandages in a bunch. I promise just to look around."

"Remember, we don't know what we're dealing with and we're not prepared."

"I will try not to forget. Maybe it is just a truly excellent party. If so, I might be a few hours. You know what they say about good vampire parties?"

"What's that?"

"They haven't really started till several dozen people have died. Judging from what you've seen, there hasn't been a party like this in centuries. Do not wait up." Marcus smiled.

"You know I don't sleep. Don't make a vacation out of it. Filip isn't the only guy we need to talk to tonight." Alex tried to be casual, but he didn't like it. He couldn't tell if Marcus was trying to lighten the mood or not. Vampire humor often eluded him.

"Well, I shall endeavor to try, but the nubile young women make better company than you, even if I do have to pay for it."

Alex smiled. "Can't argue with that. We're burning moonlight. Get going."

Marcus stepped out of the Explorer and wove his way through the line of parked cars. He strode confidently in the direction of the bass line. Alex saw him as he entered the light pools thrown by the street-lights, but soon he was lost from view.

Marcus saw something—two somethings, actually: two vampires, young, large, and inexperienced, posted as guards. They were trying to hide in the shadows but were doing a poor job of it. Both of them were dressed in black slacks, black shirts, and black sports jackets. He pretended he didn't see them.

He kept walking toward the loud throbbing of the bass line. One of the guards said something into a radio, probably announcing his approach. The man's jacket moved awkwardly. The concealed weapon was too large to be a mere pistol. In all probability, it was some sort of personal-defense light machine gun. That kind of hardware would be overkill to keep the unwanted from entering a rave.

Marcus kept moving up the sidewalk. The building the sound came from loomed ahead, an industrial warehouse, nondescript. On one side of the building there appeared to be an opening sunk into the ground. As he got nearer, it resolved into the entrance to an underground parking garage.

He started down the ramp, trying to keep his gaze casual. He was certain they were watching him, but he didn't see any security cameras. Temporary velvet ropes had been set up on the parking level just as they would be outside a normal club. Only here they were arranged to form a switchbacked line, as at an amusement park. There was no one waiting there now. A garish neon signed spelled out the name ABZU. Marcus reached the parking level and began to wend his way through the velvet ropes.

Along the edges of the walls, he could see lines of dust and dirt at regular intervals. The marks left him puzzled. A bit farther, in an area of the garage the lights didn't reach, he saw their cause. Large pallets had been stacked in blocks and set against the wall. The dirt and dust marks were the traces of other pallets.

As he got closer, he saw that the pallets were of bottles, but from this distance, he couldn't see what kind. They were probably blood products of some kind. It would fit with the description Filip had given them, and if they had this much supply on hand, then they surely were a threat to Filip's little enterprise. Marcus wanted to get a closer look. But to do so, he would have to break free of the velvet rope maze. He wouldn't be able to get a better look at the pallets without arousing suspicion. He would have to go with his best guess.

He walked the maze of velvet ropes until he came to a concrete wall that jutted from the main wall at a hard right angle. He stepped around it and followed a smaller wall that turned back in on itself. It formed a short hallway, a natural choke point that kept anyone from directly attacking the door. Marcus looked at the formidable door. It had a tiny shuttered window set in it. It looked like it slid sideways when opened, like something out of a 1920s speakeasy—

but not a real one, only the kind you saw in films. Next to the door was a small button.

As Marcus pushed the button, he reflected on what he'd seen. None of the other buildings had parking garages, or even subterranean storage. This building was different. The door certainly seemed more like a prop than something functional. He thought of how many people it would take to construct a place like this. How many bribes it would take to keep them quiet. No, not bribes. Something else. Fear.

A gruff voice spoke as the shuttered window slid to the side in the door.

"What do you want?"

Marcus was so taken aback, he laughed. This couldn't be for real; it had to be some kind of themed establishment.

"Joe sent me," he chuckled, using an old password from his days as a vagabond in the "wet" districts of New York.

"Get lost. You know the rules. One time in and one time out. You missed the opening, you're out."

Marcus protested, "But I didn't know the rules. When can I get in?"

Even as he spoke, the peephole slid closed with a snap of finality. At the same time, Marcus heard movement behind him. Someone trying to be quiet, but in actuality crude and clumsy. It wasn't quite loud enough to be a human, so it was most likely a vampire. Judging from the amount of noise, there were probably two of them, doubtless the pair of guards he'd spotted. He stood there for a moment trying to decide how to play it. He decided to stay in character as someone just trying to get into a party. That wasn't entirely false in any case.

He turned over what he knew while he waited for the guards to get closer. He wanted them to think they were in control. So, this club was some kind of lock-in facility—an excellent security measure. This way they could easily control the flow of the patrons, keep any unwanted out, and minimize the personnel needed to monitor the entrances. Well, *entrance*, singular, Marcus corrected himself. Places like this only ever had one way in. There might be a bolt-hole or sally port or two, but these things wouldn't see regular use and were there just to let the proprietors escape. They wouldn't be there for the benefit of the patrons.

Marcus heard the guards moving through the velvet rope maze now. He decided to meet them there. He turned and moved out from between the door and the tight cinderblock entrance. Playing stupid was one thing—being stupid, quite another.

Just as he rounded the corner, he nearly bumped into the lead guard, exactly as he had planned it. He gave a startled little gasp and decided to play this as the vampire playboy out for a good time and just a little ashamed of his habit.

The lead guard oozed false authority. "Sir, you're going to have to leave now."

"Ah yes, well, it's just that I, erm . . . I do not know when to come back. Your doorman mentioned there was a specific time . . ."

"You'd know if we wanted you to know. This club is by invitation only."

The other guard was trying to move out of Marcus's peripheral vision and get slightly behind him as the lead guard lifted the velvet ropes out of the way and gestured for Marcus to walk beneath them.

Marcus decided to try another tack. "I've brought lots of money. Come on, can you not make a small exception?"

"No."

Then Marcus caught a new scent. Fear. They were afraid of something. Him? He needed to test this theory.

As he stepped underneath the velvet rope he suddenly stutter-stepped. To the unsuspicious, it would look as if he had tripped over his own feet and caught his balance. If they were frightened of him, it might look as if he were going to try something. He turned his head as he did this to get a better look at the guard who had been trying to get out of his field of vision. He saw the youngblood jerk his hand toward whatever weapon he had under his jacket.

Marcus caught his balance and let forth a little chuckle, as if ashamed of his own clumsiness. The two guards were definitely afraid of him. If they suspected he was associated with the police, it might make them nervous, but it would not make them afraid.

No, they would only be afraid if they suspected who he really was. And that meant that between the time they'd seen him approach the building and the time he reached the door, someone inside had recognized him. If they hadn't wanted him to go in, why let him come all the way down here? Both guards had seen him and allowed him to make his path to the door.

Marcus chided himself, *Menkaure might be right.*

Then again, the way Menkaure had been behaving lately, maybe he had just wanted to go home. As much as Marcus liked him, Menkaure hadn't been a model detective recently. To be honest, he did not share the same connection to the world Marcus did. As Menkaure had once put it, there might be vampires killing humans, and vice versa, until the stars burned out; he wasn't going to make a dent, and he wasn't going to waste his time worrying about it anymore. Menkaure, rightly or wrongly, believed he had a higher purpose.

Marcus was jumping to conclusions about the situation. He could try a quick test to be sure. If he was wrong, there'd be no harm done except they'd have to send someone else to check out the club. If he was right, then that was a dire development, and Menkaure was correct. He secretly hoped Menkaure was just being lazy.

He reached the bottom of the ramp. Unexpectedly, he whirled on both of the guards, deliberately making his movement sudden and hostile. He dropped all pretense and manifested the presence that came with over two thousand years of experience.

The nearest guard stumbled backward so quickly that he lost his balance and fell to the ground. The other guard backed up and drew his weapon, a small MP5K-PDW–model submachine gun. He stammered out a warning.

"Don't try anything." He was trying to sound brave, but it came out panicked and unsure.

Marcus let his presence ooze from him like a miasma; he filled it with scorn and contempt, knowing these two would be able to pick up on the emotions. He let them know they were facing an Ancient.

He laughed with derision. "You think that *thing* could stop me?"

The vampire on the ground received a message in his earpiece. Marcus barely made it out, but wanted confirmation.

"What was that? Speak up!"

"This is not your demesne, you have no authority here. You . . ." The man stammered, as if he expected his words to provoke a terrible consequence. ". . . must go."

Marcus keyed on the man's choice of the word "demesne." It was far too archaic. No one spoke like that these days. Who was pulling his strings? There was no point pressing the issue now; Marcus was at the disadvantage.

"Another time then." He let the phrase hang in the night air, letting the unseen watcher know that he was not cowed. Then, after a carefully calculated moment of stillness, he turned briskly and walked back up the ramp and into the darkness.

Alex started the SUV and drove it toward Marcus as soon as he came back in sight.

Marcus opened the door and got in. Alex could tell that Marcus had his dander up.

"So?"

"So, you were right."

"Well, that's bad."

"I believe that might be the understatement of the evening, my friend."

"By the way, it gets better. Right about the time you were trying to make it to the door, those cars pulled up. No one got out. They're just sitting there."

"A security force?"

"Looks like."

There were two Lincoln Town Cars parked about fifty meters behind them, engines idling, ready to cut them off.

"I see. It seems my two idiot friends down there overstepped their bounds. No doubt, they were supposed to wait for those gentlemen in the cars—a more proportional response. Now I'm sure Aguirre's information was correct. There is another Ancient in the city and we've stumbled onto him."

"Are you sure it's an Ancient? I mean, I've never felt anything like that, not even around you."

"I'm one of the good guys."

"Right." Alex let the word stretch out in sarcasm.

"There are more profane things than I in this world and they've walked its surface for eons longer than I can fathom. I haven't survived this long by not trusting my instincts. And those say it is one of my kind. An Ancient. More powerful than we had first surmised. We have a major problem."

"I think *that's* probably the understatement of the evening. What do you want to do about those jokers in the cars?"

"Let them make the first move."

In the old days, the UMBRA days, they'd be calling in a team to level that club just on Alex's word. But now, nothing Alex and Marcus just *knew* amounted to a hill of beans. If it couldn't hold up in court, it didn't mean anything, and astral projections and vampiric instincts weren't legally binding. Now the world of warrants, due process, and probable cause allowed the real monsters all the advantage they needed.

"We're going to need to find out more of what Filip knows about this place. Try to drum up something for the DA."

Of course, any talk with the DA meant that Lelith would hear about it and this place would be deserted by the time anyone who could do anything about it showed up.

"Agreed, and this time, I shall not skulk in shadows."

Abruptly, Marcus jerked his head toward the police-band radio. "What was that?"

"What?"

Alex had left the volume turned down after that first bullshit call. He wasn't going to spend the rest of his shift chasing crap calls.

Marcus's fingers whirled the volume dial, and the dispatcher's voice crashed in.

". . . again. Ten-ninety-one Victor in progress, code eleven and code twelve. Vicinity of Liberty Square."

"A thrope on the rampage? Are you kidding me? There's not even a full moon for another week. It's probably a stray dog or something. What is it with folks nowadays?"

Marcus pursed his lips together so that they formed a thin line. Alex knew that look, and he knew what Marcus was thinking.

"Damn it."

He snatched the microphone from its clip on the side of the radio. "Fifteen Nora forty-two responding."

Then he hit the concealed lights and, with the siren blaring, sped past the Town Cars and toward Liberty Square, the Pork and Beans projects, one of the worst areas of Miami.

13

Roeland and Arthur sat in the van, waiting for John's signal. It had been a little over ten minutes since Rhuna had gone into the new club, and all of them were nervous.

After driving around the block to get the lay of the land, Roeland had John get out of the van so he could ambush the youngblood valet. The guard at the end of the alley was going to be a little tougher to get, but Roeland had a good idea on how to execute that.

"Blast, what is taking him so long." Arthur peered through the windshield for John's signal.

Roeland looked at his watch. From where they'd dropped him off it should have taken John two, maybe three minutes to move stealthily up to the youngblood. Then just seconds to dispatch him, unless something went wrong. John wasn't overdue just yet. He was still well within the window.

The two of them sat in silence for a few more seconds. Then Arthur started squirming.

"Calm down."

"He's overdue, Roeland."

Arthur reached down into the bag at his feet and pulled out a .44 Magnum Desert Eagle. He had heavily modified it, chopping down and threading the barrel so he could fit it with a long suppressor. To compensate for the loss of the front sight, he had attached a holographic sight to the top of the pistol. The arrangement looked absurd. However, it did have the advantage of being able to knock a vampire down and cause considerable injury, leaving it incapacitated long enough to finish the job. Arthur had even killed a youngblood with a head shot from it, once upon a time.

"I'm going to go help him." Arthur unlocked the van's door.

"Hold on a moment. Look." Roeland was pointing to the bushes out in front of the curb where they'd first seen the valet. A flashlight was flashing intermittently at the van. John's signal.

"Good lad. Rhuna's been in there long enough. Let's get in there."

"Agreed."

Both men exited the van. Arthur carried a long black duffel bag in his left hand and shoved the Desert Eagle under his left armpit in an effort to conceal it, yet still have it ready.

They crossed the street and moved directly into the alley. The guard at the end of the alley looked up from whatever he'd been doing when he heard them. Roeland quickened his pace and stepped a little in front of Arthur to keep Arthur's actions partially concealed.

By the time they reached the halfway point to the door at the end of the alley, the guard had left his seat.

"Hey. You guys don't want to come down here. Turn around."

Roeland kept walking. Just a little farther.

He bought time. "Hi. We were wondering if you could give us directions."

The guard's hand went to his side. Roeland couldn't tell if he had a holstered weapon there, but it made sense that he would.

"Get lost. Go on, get the fuck outta here."

Fifteen meters away from the guard, Roeland stepped to the side suddenly. Arthur had been expecting it and fired a shot directly into the guard's chest. Despite the suppressor, the shot was excessively loud in the close confines of the alley. Roeland broke into a full sprint, closing the distance to the fallen guard within seconds in order to finish the job.

It wasn't necessary. The guard was dead.

"What? It's a human."

Arthur caught up to him. "What the hell? Why post a human as a guard?"

"No time to wonder now. Come on, come on."

Arthur dropped the duffel bag and opened it. Roeland reached in, brought out a wrapped package, and laid it down on the alley floor. As he did so, a figure appeared at the end of the alley. It was John.

Arthur flashed him a thumbs-up sign, and John disappeared. He reappeared a moment later dragging the body of the youngblood valet.

Roeland spread out the contents of the package gingerly. It was made of six small rectangles of Semtex, a powerful explosive, strung together with detcord. Together they formed a breaching charge that would take down just about any reinforced door, with the added bonus that it turned anyone on the other side into paste. Anybody who managed to survive the blast would be in no condition to put up a fight. Roeland removed the bits of paper covering the adhesive on the breaching charge and applied it to the door.

Arthur dug through the duffel bag and laid the remaining contents out on the ground behind Roeland: shotguns, machetes, grenades.

John dropped the valet's body and picked up a machete in each hand. He was big, athletic, a former rugby player; he'd been a prop, one the largest individuals in the scrum. His job was to dispatch any vampires that Roeland and Arthur dropped. Decapitation was his method of choice.

Roeland finished applying the shaped charge. He picked up one of the shotguns attached to a three-point sling. The sling would allow him to "drop" the shotgun, freeing his hands, yet still have the gun hang at the ready. Arthur did the same. Both shotguns were loaded with slugs, for maximum knockdown power against vampires. They might even kill youngbloods, and though an oldblood might conceivably shrug it off, it hadn't happened yet.

Roeland picked up the last shotgun from the ground, a modified double-barreled Benelli that he'd cut down and fitted with a duck-bill adapter. The attachment would funnel all the shot into a lethal horizontal fan of destruction that made clearing rooms decidedly easier.

Finally, Arthur handed each of them shooting glasses and a set of headphones. The headphones looked like the standard electronic hearing protection people wore at pistol ranges. But these were different. Known by the nickname Wolf Ears, they were an active hearing-protection system that cut down loud sounds like explosions and gunshots while amplifying soft sounds, like speech and footfalls.

They donned the glasses and hearing protection. Less than thirty seconds had gone by since Arthur had shot the guard.

Roeland took a deep breath and let it out. The moment of truth; this was the most vampires they'd ever attacked. Rhuna had better be as good as she boasted. They had to send these bloodsuckers a message that they weren't safe anywhere.

"Paint?" he asked Arthur. He'd almost forgotten.

Arthur handed him a spray can of black paint. Roeland stepped in front of the door and painted out a symbol—Abraham's symbol. It looked like a winged diamond bracketed by two vertical lines and bisected in the middle by a horizontal line. This whole exercise would lose much of its meaning if the vampires didn't know who was responsible. He tossed the can aside.

"Remember. Check your targets. Rhuna is in there somewhere."

They took up their positions, stacked next to the door, Roeland on point, Arthur behind him, and John taking up the rear position. Arthur put his left arm through the straps of the duffel bag and slung it like a backpack.

"Everyone ready?"

Arthur patted him on the shoulder and John grunted a noise of assent.

Roeland turned his face away from the door and pressed the detonator. The door disappeared in cloud of deadly fragments. He waited for a two count and then moved in, sweeping the Benelli in front of him.

Inside the small foyer at the entrance, he saw a bloodied woman getting to her feet. Half of her dress had been burned or blown away. She was covered in burns and grisly wounds. By all rights, she shouldn't have been moving at all. That could mean only one thing.

"Oldblood!" Roeland called out.

She rounded on him at the sound of his voice, fangs extended, eyes crimson.

He squeezed one trigger and the shotgun jerked in his hand. The fan of shot nearly cut her in half. He couldn't count her as down; oldbloods had been known to survive worse. Roeland moved past her to let John do his work.

He moved to the remnants of a bead curtain at the entrance to the next room. He could hear sounds of carnage coming from the other side. He was dimly aware of the butchering sounds behind him as John finished the female vampire. Holding the shotgun at waist level, he swept into the next room.

And walked into a battle.

Vampire attacked vampire in a violent rampage of ichor and carnage. The room was in shambles, the coppery tang of blood thick in the air. He noted two bleeders huddled behind an overturned table as the vampires near them attacked each other.

Rhuna had started early! And she had outdone herself this time.

Roeland barely had time to register the bedlam. His training took over. He checked his corner and moved into the room, his eyes sweeping for Rhuna. He didn't see her.

"Hot!" He yelled their signal to indicate that his fire zone was free of allies and they could fire indiscriminately.

He heard Arthur and John call out in turn, almost simultaneously, "Hot!"

He fired the Benelli and cut down several vampires. He tossed the duckbill shotgun aside and brought the slug shotgun on the sling up to his shoulder.

One of the bleeders broke cover and came toward him.

"Don't shoot! We're humans!" the woman yelled, holding her hands in the air.

No, not humans anymore. They were part of the problem. They were bleeders. He fired a slug into her and racked the shotgun, loading the next round into the chamber.

He moved through the room firing slugs into the vampires and bleeders alike. They were so intent on fighting one another in the throes of the blood frenzy that they hadn't realized the new threat among them.

He fired blast after blast. He heard Arthur's shotgun firing nearly as an echo of his own.

In a moment, it was over.

He took a knee, reaching into his vest for more ammunition, and called out, "Reloading!"

He shoved slug after slug into the shotgun. This was when he was most vulnerable. He racked it and brought the shotgun back to ready, his eyes sweeping the room for movement.

Nothing. He turned his head quickly to assess the others. Arthur's shotgun hung loose in front of him from the sling. He had transitioned to the Desert Eagle. John made short work of prone vampires, his machetes thudding home, sending heads rolling free.

Roeland heard sounds of combat coming from a side room and moved to it, weapon at the ready. The sounds stopped as he crossed the threshold and he saw the source.

Rhuna was putting the finishing touches on a fallen vampire. There were at least six others, or parts of six others, who looked like she'd torn them limb from limb. He'd never seen her do this much damage.

She rose from all fours as she saw him. The feline characteristics she'd taken on melted away as she stood. She stood before him naked. The stockings were the only part of her outfit that had survived her rampage in any shape to be recognizable. They were drenched in blood, as was her hair, now a blood-splattered white.

She snarled an acknowledgment as she saw him, and his stomach clenched in terror. He was sure she could make it across the room to him before he'd be able to yell, much less get off a shot. Despite himself, he felt real panic at seeing her in midtransformation.

"Be right back." He retreated from the room. She looked more dreadful than he had ever seen her. What terrible force had he allowed to become his ally? Had he made a deal with the Devil to deliver vengeance on the vampires?

He moved toward Arthur.

"Change of clothes. And blood."

"Is Rhuna okay?" John asked.

Arthur met Roeland's eyes. Arthur understood. Arthur dropped the bag and dug around inside.

"She's fine, John. Start prepping the room. We're gone in five."

Arthur tossed him some coveralls and slid a plastic pint of blood across the floor. Roeland retrieved both and went back to Rhuna's room.

She was scraping bits of gore off her body with her hands. He threw her the coveralls.

"Where's Molony?"

She indicated the direction with a tilt of her head. Roeland noticed she was bleeding from puncture marks in her upper arm.

"What happened?"

She looked down and her face flushed. Then she turned away hurriedly, blocking the sight of her arm with her body.

"It's nothing."

It was the first time he could remember Rhuna showing any hint of modesty. There'd be time for questions later.

He found Molony in a booth, eviscerated and missing an arm. He had lost too much blood, but for the moment, he was still alive.

Roeland held up the pack of blood. Molony's eyes tracked it.

"The blood is the life, isn't it, Molony?"

"You're fucking dead. That little fucking bitch thrope—the lot of you." His voice was a ragged gasp, a wisp of its former self. The end was near. Roeland kept on guard. Vampires could be at their most dangerous when their end was certain.

"That's no way to speak to your potential benefactor, Fionan. Besides, I think you've got things a bit turned around. I'll chalk it up to blood loss. This pint here could save your sorry hide."

That was a lie. That pint might keep him talking long enough for them to get what they needed. It was looking like that might be a long shot.

Roeland pulled out a knife and poked a tiny hole in the bag. He let the blood drip over Molony's face and into his mouth.

Despite his defiance, Molony struggled to get at the blood.

"Now, boyo, we're going to have ourselves a little chat. And if you're very good, I might just drop this bag for you and leave you to the fates, instead of ending you for certain."

"Fuck off."

"Fair enough. I could kill you now. But from the looks of things, you've got some unfinished business with my fucking bitch thrope friend, as you put it."

He saw the light of fear ignite in Molony's eyes. Rhuna had really done a number on him. It must truly be a terrible thing to be an oldblood killer and have all your century of power stripped away by a hundred-and-twenty-pound girl.

"What do you want?" Molony was clinging to the only hope there was. He had little choice, really. No honor among vampires. Roeland had made a career of exploiting that particular flaw.

"You're going to tell me everything I want to know about Lelith and what she has going on at Haley House."

Arthur and John came into the room. For a brief moment, John wore a look of bewilderment on his face as he saw the aftermath of Rhuna's handiwork. Then John moved toward Rhuna. The poor lad had no idea what he had a crush on.

"Room's ready," Arthur said.

Roeland held the bag of blood over Molony's head. The blood dripped out in a steady stream.

"Talk fast, laddie."

14

11:32 P.M.

Alex saw two SRT vans and a hunter truck. There were at least twenty cruisers, probably more, forming one side of a perimeter; their spinning lights pulsed against the tenement buildings, first blue and then red. Technical crews were setting up the large tactical lights. In another ten minutes, the whole area would be lit up like a ballpark.

This was standard policy. The city responded to any thrope reports with an overwhelming show of force. The illusion of control hadn't been a problem until a year ago when Joe Bag-o'-Doughnuts found out about what had been there all along. Someone had always been able to cover it up. Most times what Joe Public didn't know made solutions a helluva lot easier.

The press trucks erected their sat-feed antennae, set up their cameras, and dolled up the field reporters. If the threat was real, there'd be no chance of covering it up this time. But it was likely all this hoopla was for a false alarm. A thrope's cycle might not coincide with the lunar cycle, but that was rare.

In the first days when therianthropes surfaced publicly, people reacted with more fear than when nocturns revealed themselves. There was something even more primal about the idea of a person actually transforming into an animal and losing control. Things shut down at the first hint of darkness, as if whether it was day or night affected thropes—it didn't. Society developed a sudden and acute case of agoraphobia. It couldn't last. Everyone knew that. However, it stirred local and federal governments into action. They had to show they were doing *something*.

It wasn't the transformation so much as the lack of control that most people feared. TV shows, films, books, role-playing games popularized the transformation part. The public should have known. Where there were vampires, there were thropes. But the truth was a lot darker.

The public couldn't deal with the feral lack of control, with confessions from victims of the disease that in some cases they had been aware of what they were doing but unable to stop the beast within. In the end, there was just something about thropes that people feared and abhorred because they had no way to relate.

Alex parked the Explorer near the patrol cars, killed the lights, and pressed a switch to unlock the rear door. He and Marcus got out and met at the rear of the vehicle. Alex opened the rear door and unlocked the large metal case that was standard issue for all nocturn units. He lifted the heavy metal lid on its hinges, uncovering a hoard of weapons and equipment: silver-plated spikes, four SPAS-12 assault shotguns, a pair of razor-sharp machetes, two high-powered tactical flashlights, night-vision goggles.

"Looks like they're starting without us."

"I've always hated these 'hunts.' The best outcome is unpalatable."

"Heard that. Badge." Alex tossed an extra police badge on a chain to Marcus. He threw his own around his neck, where it hung like a gaudy necklace.

Alex grabbed a pair of the night-vision goggles. Both he and Marcus picked up SPAS shotguns from the small armory and loaded them with silver-shot rounds. First, several slugs, rounded out with double-ought buck.

Thropes normally closed with anything that attacked them, so the theory went. You could supposedly hit one at about forty yards with the buckshot. That was the official range, but in practice, you really didn't do much damage until about twenty-five yards and closer. Past that, all you were going to do was piss it off. As it got closer, the plan would be to try to finish it with the slugs. If you missed with the slugs, you wouldn't have to worry about it. It would be the next guy's problem.

Alex secured the Explorer; then he and Marcus proceeded to the center of activity. As he entered the perimeter, Alex called out to some uniformed officers, "Hey guys, anything go down yet?"

"Nothing yet. Who're you guys?"

"Nocturn Affairs. Where's the primary?"

"Over by the hunter truck."

Alex waved his thanks and they made their way in the direction the officer had indicated. As they walked away from the squad car, he heard the officer mutter to his partner, "Nocturn Affairs. Sangers and thropes, like letting the fox guard the henhouse."

The hunter truck loomed before them, a large bread-truck-looking monstrosity slightly smaller than a fire engine. The official name for it was the NTFRV, the Nocturn/Therianthrope Fugitive Recovery Vehicle, but even as an abbreviation that was a mouthful, so everyone just called it a hunter truck. It came equipped with everything a team would need to hunt down a fugitive nocturn or rabid therianthrope: machetes, a dome-shielded infrared camera on top, night vision, and enough firepower to give just about anybody a run for their money.

It had a small containment compartment in the rear, little more than a cage, in case they managed to take a thrope alive. Never mind that only a fool would try. Official policy was to resolve such incidents without loss of life, but Alex couldn't recall anyone even making the attempt.

There had been a case of a thrope beginning to transform back into a human when the hunters cornered it. The pursuers hadn't hesitated in opening fire, even though the creature was in midtransformation and at its most vulnerable. Had they waited a few moments they could have apprehended it easily and taken the human into custody.

There were several cases where police had arrested thropes wandering naked and confused near the remains of their latest victims. The trials were hard for everyone involved, but prosecutors had so far made criminal negligence stick, on the grounds that the thropes refused to remain medicated. In those cases, the courts had been careful to avoid associating their rulings with the death penalty. Officially, those thropes had been "euthanized."

In any case involving thropes, there were only victims.

There was a small group huddled near the passenger-side door of the hunter truck. Alex could pick out several SRT members. Their M4 carbines and other tactical equipment gave them away. He could see Zorzi and the new kid, Garza. Zorzi also saw them.

"Marcus! *Buona sera*, you old long-tooth. You hear about Const . . . the lieutenant?"

"I have, and we're well into *buona notte*, my friend."

"So we are, so we are. And what's new with you?"

"You know, the same old thing. Had a lovely chat with our friend Aguirre, I must tell you of it."

Alex could see the incredulous look on Garza's face. Many of the SRT members' faces shared the same look. Here they were at the inception of a major operation and these two vampires were jovially greeting each other and gossiping. Alex could tell them the truth, that when you got right down to it, the vampires just didn't care. At least, these two didn't, and he could throw himself in and make it a threesome of apathy. They'd seen it all and worse. Garza took it upon herself to get the situation back on track and cleared her throat theatrically.

Zorzi and Marcus seemed to notice everyone again.

Alex spoke up. "Who was first on scene?"

Zorzi rolled his eyes in their direction. "They're over by the EMS truck, say they responded to an unknown-trouble call and discovered the two pretties by that van." He indicated a van parked near one of the buildings. Even from where he was standing, Alex could see the blood spatter.

"Unknown trouble, huh? That's an understatement." Despite the situation, Zorzi's mood remained jovial.

"So what have we got?"

"Just like old times, eh, Alex? Always to business with you. Very well. We've got a wolf again, friends. This time a young, damned fast one."

"Are we sure? I would have guessed we'd have another week. Couldn't it be someone trying to make it look like a thrope—"

"Alex, I'm hurt. Do you think all this is due to a stray dog? We have tracks showing size and speed and we have the aftermath over there. At least four down in total."

Alex looked back at the van. He could make out officers covering the bodies while SRT members stood guard.

Zorzi continued, "We're safe to say it is not over there. Eyewitnesses spotted the last kill and saw it dart down that way."

"How big is the perimeter?"

"Roughly two square blocks. We're as sure as we can be that it is still within the boundaries. We're still evacuating the last of the buildings. That's where the bulk of the men are. When they're finished, which should be any moment now, we'll try to drive it this way."

The first of the several bright light stands turned on. Even Alex winced at the change in lighting. Zorzi and Marcus shielded their eyes.

Marcus swore under his breath. "Blast, there goes any advantage we had."

With loud cracks, two more banks of lights turned on. Alex saw more lights warming up on the far side of the perimeter. He was sympathetic to Marcus, but could relate to the officers. Somehow, making things brighter made humans feel braver, more in control. An air horn's loud blast violated the night air. It was followed by another and then, farther away, two more.

The evacuation was complete. Now the hunt could begin in earnest. The horns also served a secondary purpose. The blasts could work in either of two ways: to drive the thrope off or attract it. You never could be sure. It varied by the animal.

A powerful howl, haunting and eerie, full of anguish, answered the horns. Alex felt his stomach drop to the ground and something press at the back of his throat, making it hard to swallow. No matter how many times he heard it, his reaction was the same. If there had been any doubt they were dealing with a werewolf, it was certainly gone now.

Marcus hefted the shotgun in his hands and looked at his watch. "We best get to it."

He headed toward the building with the truck and the latest victims in front of it.

Zorzi called after him, "Marcus, do you want this one?"

For the first time that night, Zorzi's tone was not buoyant, but deadly serious, almost pleading, hoping Marcus could rescue him from running this operation. Zorzi hadn't been at policework very long. Before the Reveal, he had done government work as a technical advisor on the NSA's UMBRA special program. He was ill suited to fieldwork.

"No, old friend. You have this well in hand. Besides, would you rather be going after it?"

"*Va bene.* I had to ask. You are far more qualified at these things than I am."

"You know I'm better at getting my hands dirty than at coordinating and commanding."

Alex was a bit surprised at the pretext. Marcus was giving Zorzi an out so he wouldn't look sheepish in front of the other men. To anyone who knew Marcus, it was an obvious lie. Marcus had been governor of Lower Pannonia, once upon a time, not to mention the countless other offices he'd held throughout the millennia.

"When we call for the cavalry, just make sure to haul ass," Alex said.

They reached the van with the recent victims, the side of it grotesquely coated in arterial spray. Two SRT members stood with the building and the truck at their back, their eyes scanning ahead of them for any movement. Alex knelt next to one of the bodies and lifted the sheet covering it. He immediately wished he hadn't. The corpse had a wide slash from the shoulder to the hip. The thing had ripped a chunk from the neck so large Alex could easily see the man's exposed trachea. He dropped the sheet back into place.

As Marcus moved ahead, his eyes dropped, scanning the ground for signs of the thrope. The harsh lighting from the banks of tactical lights made the dark streaks of blood stand in sharp contrast to the rest of the pavement.

Marcus stopped in front of the stoop that led into the building.

"I have a good print here. It's most likely a female, wounded, but not seriously. Part of this trail is thrope blood."

Alex hung back so as not to spoil Marcus's sense of smell. Marcus raised his head, sniffing the air deliberately.

"There is a lot of blood. And something else. Chemicals. Ammonia or bleach? There are more dead inside, and something strange. I can't tell from here."

"Drug lab? Easy guess for this part of town."

Marcus didn't answer. He was looking at the ground again. Alex tried to see what he was looking at. The tracks bounded across the sidewalk and continued through a small basketball court. Marcus followed them.

Alex started after him. The stark tactical lighting was throwing harsh shadows everywhere. He remembered the night-vision goggles hanging from their straps. He switched them on and looked through them. The night became much too bright green and everything looked overexposed. There was too much light now; these were useless. He hoped the lights weren't affecting Marcus's eyesight the same way.

Marcus moved in on the basketball court. He stood still for a moment, then started spinning in a seemingly random circle. It would look strange to anyone who didn't know what was happening, but Alex had already figured it out. Marcus had lost the scent and he was trying to find it again. Then Marcus stopped and looked up at the twelve-foot chain-link fence that surrounded it. In one fluid motion, he crouched down and then hopped over the fence as if he were taking a flight of stairs two at a time.

Some of the SRT members near him gasped involuntarily. Marcus turned and motioned for him from the other side of the fence. Alex and the SRT members near him were falling too far behind.

One of them said, "Copy that."

"What's going on?"

Alex led the team around the fence.

"Squad Three says they have movement. They're going to investigate."

Marcus reversed and bounded back toward the main group.

"Tell those men up there not to move. I can hear it. They are close." Marcus projected his voice to them. It wasn't loud, but every single one of them heard it.

The SRT officer started to relay the message but it was already too late. Another howl shattered the night—then growls, screams, and gunfire. Everyone moved at once. Marcus melted away. Alex broke into a dead run, shotgun stock at his shoulder, the barrel swept back and forth ahead of him; the rest of the team performed the quick-step "Groucho walk" favored by tactical shooters as they cleared the basketball-court fence as quickly as they could.

As soon as they cleared the corner of the next building, Alex could see the men easily. In addition to their silhouette in the banks of lights, the men had activated the tactical lights on their weapons. Alex could see they were surrounding another man, who was down; their backs were to the inside of the small circle they had formed.

Alex heard a man shout, his words unintelligible with fear. The beams of light swung as one, and then muzzle flashes dazzled Alex's eyes.

Then he saw it—a quick streaking shape, silhouetted by tactical lights, bounding across his field of view. Damn it! It was between them!

Two sharp cracks split the air nearby and Alex instinctively hit the ground.

"Check fire! Check fire!" he shouted at the top of his lungs, hoping they heard him. Those men were so worked up they were going to shoot at anything that moved. He looked behind him. The other SRT members were all prone. One of them was shouting into his headset. Another shouted something at Alex. Alex looked at him, puzzled, and then realized the man was asking if he'd been hit.

"No. I'm okay."

Alex looked back. Marcus hadn't stopped. He had just changed the course of his run. Alex stood up, hoped the other men had regained a measure of discipline, and ran after him.

Marcus slowed without looking, letting Alex catch up to him.

"Look there," his voice hissed out, full of tension. He held his arm outstretched.

Alex looked, his mind scanning for a wolf or something wolf-shaped. He saw nothing.

"What?"

"There."

Then Alex saw what Marcus had seen, a storm drain leading down away from the street. "Aw hell."

Chasing a wolf into sewer tunnels was a nightmare he didn't want to relive.

"It's like Paris again. Damn."

The face Marcus made told Alex he was thinking along the same lines. "Try to distract it. I'm going to make sure it does not go down there."

"Try to distract it?" Alex laughed. "How the hell am I supposed—" Another thought interrupted him. If Marcus wanted him to distract it, then Marcus knew where it was.

"Where is it?"

Marcus shrugged his shoulders and made a "damned if I know" face. He moved his arm in a wide arc to denote the general direction he thought the wolf had gone.

Then Marcus was gliding toward the storm drain, in a way only a vampire could move, nearly melting from one place to another. And then, there was one shadow too many.

Alex fired. A yelp rewarded him. He'd winged it at least. Then he could see its eyes. Despite his years of experience and even given what he was, his breath caught in his chest and it was as if his entire body were suddenly heavier. Ambient light reflected back at him through the thing's eyes, and gave the impression that they were glowing.

Alex racked the shotgun and fired again. This time he missed. He couldn't figure out how and then realized he'd overshot it. It was damned fast. The blast turned it from its charge.

Now the vague shape moved into a light pool under one of the streetlamps. It was a black blur. Maybe only twenty yards from him. Time slowed to a crawl. Alex could see gore and spittle spilling from its jaws. Even as his hands racked the shotgun again, he knew he would not be able to get off another shot. He was moving too slowly.

Another blast hit the wolf in its hindquarters, half spinning it around. It yelped, lost its footing, and went down hard. Automatic and semiautomatic fire erupted from behind Alex, sending a hail of bullets in the direction of the wolf. Alex had a chance to fire. More silver shot flew at the wolf. The pattern of the shotgun made half the pellets go wide, sending them to strike sparks off the pavement surrounding the injured animal. Alex racked the shotgun twice more, getting rid of the shot rounds and loading a slug.

Another blast struck the wolf midbody just as it was getting to its feet. It made a tormented gurgling sound. Its eyes stared at Alex, into his soul. Imploring. Pleading. He took careful aim.

The wolf snarled and opened its jaws wide, its feral nature once again asserting itself. Alex fired. Just as the slug smashed into its skull, automatic weapons fire from multiple weapons raked across its body.

He could hear the men behind him shouting exultantly, "We got it! It's down! It's down!"

Alex felt sick to his stomach. This wasn't so much a hunt as an execution.

He heard one of the men from the other group call for medical attention. The man on the ground, his voice high-pitched with fear, was saying over and over again, "No, it just scratched me. It's not a bite. It's not a bite. It just scratched me."

Alex didn't know if he was trying to convince himself or the others; probably both.

He looked at the wolf. It had that misshapen quality to it where it looked like something in between animal and human. There was no question it was dead. The body had suffered an incredible amount of damage but it was still all too recognizable. Already it was shedding much of the hair and starting to look more and more like the thin naked body of a young woman. The SRT members reached it and started to huddle around it.

He stood over it—her. For a brief moment, he was looking down on his daughter's face and the high priest was telling him that there was nothing they could do—that the accursed, vile, and vengeful Neithikret must have her payment. That was long ago, in his black land of Kemet, and there were matters that pressed in the present.

Alex wrenched himself away. As he turned, his gaze met Marcus's dead eyes and he knew that Marcus was lost with his own ghosts, and feeling similar, if not the same, emotions.

Marcus went to the body and crouched down next to it.

"Are you seeing this? No, of course not."

"What?" Alex didn't want to turn around.

"She's got a stamp on her arm here. A blood-club stamp."

Alex forced himself to turn around. That didn't make any sense. The vampires would never feed on a thrope if they knew what she was.

"She was a bleeder?"

Marcus gingerly moved the body. He checked the inside of the upper arms, the inside of her thighs, her neck, looking for telltale signs. Alex thought it was an impossible task. The body had innumerable wounds on it.

"I do not think so."

"Could she have masked her scent in some way? I mean, why would they even let her in the club?"

Marcus said nothing but Alex could see he was lost in thought.

"What have you got?"

"Nothing. Nothing. It reminded me of an old . . ." Marcus paused, searching for the right word. ". . . story. Very queer."

Marcus stood and walked away from the body. Alex left him to his thoughts as they headed back toward the hunter truck in silence.

Several SRT members ran past them. One of them asked as he ran by, "Hey, is that it?"

Neither Marcus nor Alex answered.

They heard the man shout, "Fuckin' A! They got it!" Then they heard him emit a surprised "Oh" as he saw the body. His exuberance turned to shock, horror, and disgust, and he lost his dinner in loud splashes.

That seemed to break the seal, and Alex heard other members of the team stepping away from the body and retching.

Yeah, they got it all right.

15

Thursday, August 12, 12:34 A.M.

Alex walked past the hunter truck without saying a word. Marcus and he both nodded to Zorzi and Garza as a sort of signal that it was their problem to deal with the cleanup. Although it remained unspoken, both Alex and Marcus wanted to get away from this place before Constance arrived. She was always a by-the-book person, but with her promotion and pending command of the Nocturn Affairs Bureau, she'd be even more of a stickler for detail.

There would be questions and a post-op out-brief. That would probably happen anyway, but if they could make it back to the Explorer and secure the weapons, there might be a chance they could slip away.

Alex's mind was already drifting back to the club and the Ancient within. The recent thoughts of his first life had brought back the memory of the feelings he'd had at the club, the sense of that primeval malevolence seeking him out in the ether. He hoped that Marcus was wrong, though his long centuries of experience meant he rarely was. If there actually was an Ancient in that club and he hadn't made contact with Marcus, that pretty much meant one of two things. Either he didn't know that Marcus was in the city, or he didn't want to have anything to do with him. The first wasn't that big a deal, but Marcus's treatment at the club told him it was more likely the latter. That pretty much signaled that among the handful of Ancients left in the world, this one was not one of the good guys.

They passed the squad cars, which were already breaking up the perimeter. The city couldn't afford to have this many resources in one place for too long. If word got out . . . Alex didn't want to think about it. They reached the Explorer, and Marcus began unloading the shells from his shotgun. They were momentarily plunged into darkness as the large banks of tactical lights switched off.

Alex fumbled with the keys, his night vision useless for the moment. He managed to open the back of the Explorer and they put the weapons and equipment away.

Marcus spoke quietly: "Someone's in a hurry."

Alex stopped moving and could hear rapid footfalls coming their way.

"Damn, I thought we'd manage to sneak out of here. I can deal with the report tomorrow."

"No such luck, apparently."

A uniformed officer came running out of the night. "You Detective Scaevola?"

Marcus answered.

Alex looked at Marcus. "Don't tell me Zorzi's gonna have the balls to make us write this up now?"

"You guys are Nocturn Affairs, right?"

Marcus gave him a look.

"Oh yeah, sorry. Anyway, you're gonna have to come with me. We may have found where she came from."

"You know, the dirty work's done. No nocturns involved. Get Homicide to look at it."

"The lieutenant back there asked for you guys specifically. I guess it's bad. She's holding the crime scene unit back until you two can get in there."

"Constance got here fast."

Marcus glanced at his watch. "It's later than you think, Alex."

Alex closed and locked up the rear of the Explorer. "After you."

They quickly reached the hunter truck's location. Already, the scene looked different. The medical examiner's people were present and there was a hive of activity on the sidewalk. They were putting the two bodies next to the van into body bags.

The folks from the crime scene unit were scouring the front of the building and the area around the van with large flashlights and taking photographs of the evidence. Not much of a mystery here. This one looked open and shut. Alex wondered why Constance needed them there.

One of the crime scene techs saw them. "Zorzi's already inside." He pointed to the building.

Alex nodded and he and Marcus walked toward the building. They walked up the front stairs and into the small lobby, being careful not to disturb any evidence. It was fairly standard government-built low-income housing dating from around the late 1930s or so. From the looks of things, not much had been done since then.

There were streaks of blood and one nearly perfect bloody paw print on the gray and white linoleum. It looked very small in the yellow-tinted light.

Alex stepped back and let Marcus proceed first. Marcus sniffed the air.

"It smells like there has not been anyone upstairs for months. Everything is coming from over there."

They moved through the door Marcus had indicated. They looked to the right and left. Long hallways stretched to either end, lit every few feet by bare bulbs that were less than effective. The walls had been painted and repainted, the layers cracked and peeling to reveal the colors of the years beneath. Combined with the gray cloud-patterned linoleum on the floor, it completed the image of putrefaction and decay.

Alex had been inside the tenements and other low-cost housing projects before. Those buildings had vibrancy about them, stories they could tell about the tenants who lived there. Alex didn't need Marcus to tell him this building was dead. Its soul had long gone.

They saw Stephanie Garza crouched against one wall with her head between her knees. Behind her a cracked backlit sign marked STAIRS with a little stair icon flickered with the telltale indications of a fluorescent light about to give up the ghost.

"They down there?" Alex asked, reaching into his jacket pocket for some latex gloves. He handed a set to Marcus.

Stephanie looked up at them and they could see how pale she was. Her eyes took a moment to focus on Alex. She nodded. Alex could see she was barely holding back her gorge.

"First time on one of these?"

"I've seen my share of homicides but . . . but nothing like this."

"Yeah, a thrope attack is a whole other ball game."

"Are they always like this?"

"Welcome to the jungle, kid."

Marcus grabbed the steel handle on the door and yanked it open. A variety of smells assaulted them; blood and decay, stale urine and feces, ammonia and other chemical smells. It was almost enough to make Alex's eyes water. Even Marcus blanched. Stephanie Garza ran for the front door. She didn't make it. They heard her heaving in the lobby.

Alex held his hand over his nose and mouth and started down the stairs. As his eyes adjusted to the even dimmer lighting in the stairwell, he could make out a dark wet lump on the landing. A severed arm still clutched a submachine gun. It was so badly clawed and chewed that it took his mind a moment to know exactly what he was looking at.

"We think this guy was a guard," Zorzi shouted from the bottom of the stairs.

Alex and Marcus walked gingerly past the body, careful not to disturb anything. Zorzi was at the bottom holding open the door to the lower level.

"I must tell you, Marcus, I've never seen anything like this. Not even before . . ."

Every muscle Alex had tensed. He and Marcus had seen, and done, some unspeakable things in UMBRA. He inwardly prayed that Zorzi had been more sheltered than they had been. Besides, the aftermath of a thrope attack was always bad. Alex braced himself.

They stepped into the lower hallway. Alex could see several bodies. There was a shotgun, the barrel just slightly curved, lying like a broken, discarded toy roughly twenty feet down the hall. A savaged body lay near the stairwell door. Its rib cage was cracked open and its chest cavity nearly empty, the contents strewn about on the floor nearby. A bloody streak and a trail of internal organs on the nearby wall told of the horrendous claw swipe that had gutted the man.

Marcus gave the body a cursory glance and moved on. His shoes splashed lightly in the thin pool of congealing blood.

"Oh shit. Zorzi, I owe the new kid an apology."

Two metal chairs with plastic seats lay overturned in the hall; spent shotgun shell casings and a crude porn magazine covered in sticky blood added to the picture.

"He actually got a shot off," Zorzi said in a bemused tone.

"Probably just pissed her off."

A third body lay in the entrance to a larger room. It might have been a utility room or a gymnasium in the past, but someone had converted it to something else, judging from the massive door that lay on the ground. Without moving into the room, they could see the nearly decapitated third body.

"Would you get a load of this door?"

"Constance is inside. You should go in first." Zorzi motioned to Marcus.

This was the standard procedure. Zorzi would tell them very little so that they could form their own ideas of what had occurred without tainting their outlook. He would follow Marcus so as not to contaminate or mask any scent Marcus might pick up. Honestly, with the reek of this place, he doubted that Marcus would be able to smell anything helpful.

Marcus walked into the room. Alex paused for a moment and stared at the door lying dented and bent on the floor. The door was about three inches thick, painted a dull gray, and looked to be made of steel. Alex could see where claws had gouged deep marks into the metal.

"Where the hell would someone even get a door like this?" he said aloud. Zorzi shrugged.

He stopped briefly to look at the twisted hinges and did a mental calculation of how much force it would have taken to twist the hinges in their moorings and pull them wholesale from their anchors in the concrete. Anyone who still debated the preternatural power of a thrope would have lost this argument categorically. Exhibit A, Your Honor, if it pleases the court . . .

Marcus called him from inside. "Alex, get in here."

He stepped past the nearly decapitated corpse and took in the room at a glance—the splintered remains of a large wooden chair, discolored leather fastenings instantly betraying its purpose, the yellow-tiled floor that sloped down to inset drains, the wide stainless-steel counter with the sink at the end. He saw the overturned tool cart, a punctured car battery seeping fluid, a bone saw, and knives. There were two other corpses, one so badly mutilated it was simply a red and grizzled mass of flesh; only the shoes, elegant and expensive, hinted that it had once been a man.

His eyes stopped on the three wire-mesh cages lined up in the corner of the room. If it hadn't been for the chair, he could almost fool himself into thinking that this entire setup was for animals. He stared at the straw-covered floors of those cages, empty water bottles strewn along the bottom of two of them. He saw a stained set of blue jeans tossed to one side.

"Must you bathe in that cologne?" Constance's cultured New England tone bounced across the room at him. Alex was astounded that she could pick out that smell among all these others, and more so that it was the smell of his cologne that was causing offense. Then he saw her, her nose slightly wrinkled at his scent, her tongue subconsciously running across her fangs. Her eyes were glazed and bloodshot. Not as if she had just fed. But as if she was about to blood-frenzy. She had her fists balled up at her sides.

Lieutenant Constance Howe was a stunning nocturn, or rather, she could have been. Her stereotypical pale skin contrasted beautifully with her black hair, giving her an effortlessly classy Gothic look. She had a figure most women would kill for but covered it with long sleeves and high collars. She had the look of a nun. Not the kind that take up the cloth to love God; the kind that hide behind the habit because they can't bear the guilt of the myriad sins they are trying to atone for. In her dark past, her appeal had encouraged men and women to throw away caution and, with it, their lives.

Right now, she looked terrible.

Alex's eyes flickered over to Marcus. Marcus looked back at him and he knew they were on the same page. Marcus kept making a show as if he were just investigating the scene, but he was positioning himself behind Constance in case she decided to make a move.

Constance shivered as if she had a chill running up her spine.

"Are you feeling all right? You look a little peaked." That was a massive understatement. She looked terrifying, like she was about to cut loose.

"I'm fine," came her answer, the words pronounced a little too slowly for Alex's taste.

"Yeah? If I were someone else, I'd be crapping my pants about now. You look like you're about to blood-frenzy."

"I'm not." Again the slow speech, the last consonant enunciated so loudly it sent a little echo bouncing around the room. She spoke again, this time to Marcus. "Don't think I don't know what you two are trying to do. I'm in control."

She said it again, trying to convince herself. "I'm in control."

Zorzi came in and looked around. "So, what do you gentlemen think?" Then he saw Constance. "Oh."

She snapped her head at him and shouted, "I'm in control!"

"Okay, no one is saying otherwise. Take whatever time you need," Alex said.

Now Alex could see blood tears coming from her eyes. She really was trying to fight it off. All the blood and gore in the room, it could set off a hunger response in a vampire. It would be the same thing as asking a hungry man to keep his mouth from watering when walking him into the kitchen of a restaurant. Alex had seen it happen before, though not like this, and only to younger vampires. This was different. It was as if Constance had been starving, not merely hungry. Now he looked at Marcus again for reassurance but his eyes were taking on the same blood-crazed look, and his fangs were descending.

"Oh shit. Guys, what the hell is going on?"

Marcus shouted, "Zorzi, get her out of here. We need to make sure we stay in control. There's fear blood in here. Pure. A lot of it." That last bit was a warning.

Zorzi spoke up. "There's a door back there, Marcus. Some kind of freezer. I pulled it closed before she got down here. I didn't think she could handle it." His voice was contrite, but also taking on the slurring affectation that indicated that his fangs were extending as well.

He stepped toward Constance, but she was already moving toward him, her legs stiff. She seemed to be relaxing a bit.

"You can smell it, too?"

Alex could hear the relief in her voice. She was terrified she was going to lose control, and now she knew her body hadn't been reacting to the scene.

Zorzi pulled her out of the door and called back, "Are you going to be all right, Marcus?"

"I will be fine. Besides, Alex is here to keep me in line."

Zorzi launched a quick glance at Alex, the skepticism in his expression speaking for him.

Alex reassured him. "We've been through this drill once or twice. I'll be okay."

Zorzi and Constance moved out of view. Alex could hear them going back up the stairs.

"Okay, what gives? This is bad, but we've seen worse. What's getting to you guys?"

"It's intoxicating. It is why some of us choose to stalk and dally with prey, rather than seduce, or take part with willing partners. There is a lot of it here. A lot of the fear blood. It is not affecting me as much as Constance, because, well . . ." He was beginning to slur a little as his fangs fully extended themselves.

"When you feed, you're a seducer, Constance . . . Oh. Oh, damn. So our Constance wasn't always so nice, huh? Go figure. I guess there's more to Constance than I know."

Marcus chuckled. "My friend, if you truly understood the extent of that understatement, you could fill volumes."

"Yeah? Someday, you're going to have to let me in on what exactly the deal is between you two."

"Of course, I shall do that when you finally enlighten me as to your *full* history. About this so-called sorceress you're bound to. Perhaps all the inner workings of live mummification and the spells which reside in the Scroll of Thoth? Perhaps over respective drinks?"

"Touché."

Alex examined the long stainless-steel counter with the sink. The counter was clean, but there were thin scratches in the steel. It had the feel of the familiar, but he couldn't quite place it.

"As I was saying, the adrenal content of this blood is abnormally high. You can see it is eliciting a response from me as well. To some, the fear blood is too much to resist. No matter what we tell ourselves, we might go wild and gorge. Depending on various factors, like when one last fed, for instance, it can make one lose self-control."

"So what would happen if a vampire drank a bunch of this stuff when they thought they were guzzling Hemo-Synth?"

Marcus moved over to one of the drains in the floor. He removed the cover and looked down at some sort of catch basin there. He didn't answer.

"Yeah, that's what I thought. The blood frenzy. Are you doing all right?"

"Really, Alex. This is rather curious, these drains . . . it reminds me of something."

Alex examined the sink. It was deep and could easily hold gallons. It looked like something you'd see in a large restaurant or cafeteria. He didn't need a vampire's sense of smell to notice the chemical stink coming from it.

"This is like a butcher shop or slaughterhouse." Then he remembered the door Zorzi had mentioned. He looked toward the back wall, where it loomed imposingly—a large freezer door.

"I don't even want to look."

Alex took hold of the big latched steel handle and yanked. A cloud of frigid air greeted him as he peered into a monstrous walk-in freezer. Immediately, he could see bodies hanging in the back, gutted, and awaiting the butchering process.

"Oh fuck. Yeah. This is . . . wow."

Alex stepped into the freezer. As cold as it was, he wouldn't be able to stay here long. His body didn't handle the cold very well.

There were pull-out shelves along one side. They were on rollers so a person could slide them in and out for easier access. There were jars, boxes, and empty bags. He grabbed the end of the shelf, the cold steel stinging his hand through the latex, and pulled.

The shelf bucked forward in a fit of jerks and starts on sticky wheels. Now he could better see the contents in the flickering fluorescent lights. There were jars filled with some sort of yellow fluid. Floating in them were eyes, hearts, and other organs he couldn't easily identify.

Alex pulled one of the boxes off the shelf. It was constructed out of a foamy-feeling plastic, something like Styrofoam but harder. He reached for the lid. His hand hovered over the handle.

Marcus squatted down beside him. "How much worse can it get?"

Alex opened the lid. Inside, tightly packed against one another were roughly three dozen frozen blood bags. He reached inside the box and grabbed at one of the bags. The latex glove on his hand wanted to stick to the frozen plastic. He wrenched one of the bags out.

"Well, here's your fear blood. Zorzi was right. I've never seen anything like this."

Marcus wasn't listening. It looked to Alex like he was miles away, in his own little world.

"Marcus? Stay with me, buddy."

Alex hurriedly threw the bag back in the box and closed the lid. "Are you all right? You want to take a step outside?"

Marcus's eyes finally focused. "I'm sorry, you were saying."

Alex considered his options. "I was saying you might want to step outside and get some air. Maybe see how Constance is doing."

Marcus waved him off.

Alex knew he wasn't going to win this argument. He looked at the remaining boxes on the shelves.

"Assuming all these are full . . . Mass production just reached the blood trade, didn't it?"

Marcus was shaking his head in disbelief. "They've been abducting people off the street, bringing them down here, and keeping them for some time."

"Why keep them? Why not just kill them outright and harvest what they need?"

"They need the fear. More probably, they need an expert. You noted what was left of the chair?" A long string of bloody drool dripped from Marcus's lower jaw.

"Yeah." Alex made a "you've got something on your face" gesture to Marcus. "It looks like something out of the Middle Ages."

"You are not far from the truth there, my friend." Marcus wiped the bloody drool away with annoyance. The glazed look was finally starting to leave his eyes. Alex could tell his fangs were receding simply because he wasn't slurring his words as much. The mystery had him in its grips now, and the urge to solve the puzzle was greater than that of the blood lust.

"To maximize the fear and the adrenaline, they would want to torture the subject as long as possible. Possibly even attempt to harvest a few organs while the victim was still alive. It takes a measure of skill to do something like that and keep the victim responsive."

"I don't want to know how you know that. What bothers me is that we know that humans did this."

"Oh? And how exactly do we know that?"

"You're slipping, Marcus. A nocturn, even a youngblood, can smell a thrope. Or at least smell that their blood isn't like the others."

"And yet this lot was caught unawares. Very good. I nearly missed that. They were totally unprepared. And the stress of the situation must have forced the change upon her. It's been known to happen. Or . . . No."

"What?"

"I'm just considering possibilities."

"That or they were damned unlucky to pick her up and have her be offset from the lunar cycle." And then they, the police, had killed her. The unspoken words hung between them. He looked into the freezer again, at the hanging corpses, the shelves, the boxes, the jars.

"Wow." That was all he could bring himself to say.

"You have a penchant for understatement tonight."

Alex couldn't stand to be in the freezer any longer; his body was growing stiff. He walked back into the other room.

"I've seen something like this before." Marcus followed him.

"Seriously?"

"Perhaps thirteen hundred years ago? In Neustria. I was with Charles, son of Pepin, helping him to consolidate his rule. We came upon a charnel house not terribly unlike this one. We did not know what to make of it then either. You understand those were somewhat rougher times. Gods, I thought they'd have died out by now."

"Apparently not. We never heard about anything like this." Despite himself, Alex lowered his voice. "Not even in UMBRA."

"They have been at this for some time. A well-funded operation. They cleared out the entire building above us simply to hide this."

"I'm willing to bet they started with the tenants, or at least some of them. Then used the usual tricks to drive the rest out. Even in this part of town, folks would notice a whole building going missing."

"Would they?"

Alex considered that. The mind's capacity to come to terms with the unthinkable and ignore it never ceased to astound him.

"One thing really bothers me. I mean, thinking this out. The blood makes sense. After seeing the effects it has on you guys, it's a valuable product. Some vampires will pay top dollar for it. But why save the organs, or store the corpses?"

"I have no idea."

Alex knew Marcus was holding something back. He also knew that there was little point in calling Marcus out on it. He'd tell Alex what he suspected when he was ready. At this point, prodding him would only tighten his lips.

Zorzi walked back into the room and looked at the freezer door, which still hung open.

"See what I mean? This is new," Zorzi said.

"Not to Marcus. How is Constance?"

"She is herself again. She is trying to placate the crime scene unit and the press. Something else is going on out there, something big."

"Bigger than this? I don't want to know."

"That is what I thought, my friend. She wants all of this destroyed."

"Ah. She may have a point. We should keep all this in the

strictest confidence. If word got out somehow, with the city the way it has been these last weeks . . ." Marcus let the sentence hang.

Zorzi finished the thought: "None of us would be safe."

"No, you're right about that. It'd be open season on nocturns. Shit. There's no way . . . Damn it! What a mess. You know, I'm inclined to agree with her."

"I'm surprised to hear that coming from you, Alex." Zorzi's eyes were taking on that blood-glazed look again.

"You shouldn't be. Constance wants it destroyed which means Lelith wants it destroyed. I'm just going with the flow."

Marcus huffed and walked back into the freezer.

"You're not suggesting we close our eyes and let this go on?"

"Part of me is. We can't fight back against an operation like this. Maybe in the old days, but not with our hands tied. This is bigger than we are. Vampires have been preying on humans for all of history."

Marcus called out. "This was humans preying on humans, Alex, as you so recently pointed out."

"Humans on behalf of vampires. They weren't saving this blood to use themselves. They're selling it. It implies major blood trade, the likes of which we have never seen. Think of the experience between us, and this is something new. Shit, I'm feeling like Garza up there. How much are you willing to bet this isn't the only place they have?"

"This is a major operation, so far all human. The clout to clean out a whole building, to convert this into this slaughterhouse, we're talking organized crime. Right?" Alex asked.

"That follows. That would not be new. The mob started working in the blood trade as soon as they discovered there was a market for it," Zorzi said.

"And this product is so good that it's got you and Marcus drooling, and nearly reduced our most pious and proper lieutenant to a state of animal lust. I mean, I don't even know what the street value is for this stuff. We have no idea what they used half of this stuff for. We're in over our heads."

"I won't disagree with you there. It was very sad to see Constance like that. She will be hitting the blood clubs hard in the coming days. And that isn't good for her." Zorzi stole a glance at where Marcus was pulling out shelf after shelf and examining the contents. "Or anyone," he added for Marcus's benefit.

Marcus ignored him.

"So it's safe to say, if a youngblood got a swig of this, say in a tainted bottle of Sangri . . ."

"Yes. They would go wild. It would drive them immediately into a blood frenzy."

"But no one would want that, right? I mean, who would want a bunch of vampires to go on a killing spree. Let's say that was an accident. They're moving this stuff disguised as legitimate Hemo-Synth. But something went wrong, and some of their bottles made it onto a store shelf somehow."

Zorzi stood by quietly, listening to Alex sort it out.

Marcus called from the freezer, "I saw pallets of blood products at that club. I assumed they were legitimate. I certainly didn't smell anything out of the ordinary."

"Could it be masked somehow?"

"I do not know."

Zorzi stepped to the door of the freezer. "What are you doing?"

"Me? I am looking for a clue," Marcus answered. "I have the scent of something familiar. If my suspicions are correct, then it is more bad news."

"You know, I liked this job. It was easy. Kick in the doors of a few blood clubs, get some kickbacks to let them keep operating, give Filip some grief over some illicit blood. It was cushy. You said it yourself, Zorzi, this is like nothing we saw at NSA. This is far worse."

Zorzi interrupted, "Except Lagos."

"Or São Paolo," Marcus added.

Alex shook his head, "São Paolo . . . shit." Internally he conceded the point.

"I wonder . . ." Marcus stepped behind the shelves and dragged something large and heavy to the front of the freezer.

"Found something?" Zorzi asked, stepping into the freezer.

That got the better of Alex's curiosity and he went to see what Marcus had found.

Alex threw up his arms in vain when he saw the object Zorzi and Marcus dragged from the room. It was a large industrial cooler, exactly the same make and model he had inspected in the back of Filip's van.

Marcus opened it and peered inside. After a moment, he reached in and tossed a vacuum-sealed bag of meat at Alex, who snatched it from the air.

"I think we now know where Filip was getting his meat."

"Fucker. I think Filip . . ." Alex turned the plastic package over in his hand, reflecting on what kind of meat it was. "I think Filip isn't gonna like our next visit."

16

Alex raced the Explorer in and out of traffic, dodging from one lane to the other trying to make the best speed. The damn traffic was killing their time. The blaring siren and the flashing lights behind the front grille sent cars leaping out of the way.

Alex bashed the horn with his hand. "Damn it! Get out of the way!"

"Lighten up on the rage, Menkaure. We need to arrive in one piece if we are to give Filip a piece of our minds."

"That slippery son of a bitch. You realize if we don't get to him tonight, he's gone. He's got to be right in the middle of it. Once he knows that we know . . . that's it."

"He may not even know what he is dealing with. Consider his behavior on our prior visit. He behaved as he always does."

"Yeah, I never would have figured him to be that good an actor."

"I detected no untoward nervousness."

"You didn't detect human meat either."

Marcus was silent.

"What about that?"

"I thought I smelled the human blood. I have no explanation."

"So Filip was right when he said the meat masked the scent. It was just a bit vice versa. He's set to turn his customers into unwitting cannibals. It's like some kind of weird Sweeney Todd thing."

"I am not quite so sure."

"Huh?"

"There is a level of organization, a level of sophistication shown here. Human and vampiric organized crime working together, and if not for a miscalculation on their part, we would not know any of it. I doubt it was all for Filip's benefit. The quantities of the meat . . . Surely, a bit more than needed to bake into a few pies, if you catch my meaning."

"Except that Filip knows something. He sent us to that club, you know? Supposedly, he doesn't know anything about it. Just that they might be selling some rare blood products and we're supposed to take it at face value that he just wants to cause his competition some heat."

"Yes. And we investigate and find something we weren't expecting, a highly sophisticated operation."

"And we're not welcome. We can't make it in the door."

"Because . . . watch that fellow . . ."

Alex swerved and narrowly missed the car Marcus had indicated. "You were recognized."

"By another Ancient." Marcus grew quiet. He began again tentatively, "What if our friend Filip sent us there not to help us in any way, but to hinder them in some way."

"Which them? The people behind the club? Or the people behind the torture chamber?"

"Are they different?"

"That's a pretty big damn leap to say they're the same bunch."

Tires screeched. Alex cut off a car trying to make a left turn. The driver flipped them off.

The balls on that guy, flipping off a cop car. People nowadays.

"True. I will grant you that. All right, the people behind the club," Marcus conceded.

"Yeah, so they are creating trouble for the smaller less-organized juice dealers so Filip sends a couple vice cops their way. We've covered that."

"Only he didn't," Marcus said.

"Didn't what?"

"Send a couple of vice cops their way. He sent a former UMBRA team their way. A team which, without bragging, has accumulated quite the legendary and notorious list of exterminations. A team he counted on being recognized."

"Yeah, but Filip knows that UMBRA's gone. He knew that when all our extra kickback money dried up. He's not on a payroll anymore; his information is his only payday now, and only while it's good and worthwhile, which is just barely enough not to get him hauled in. One thing is really bothering me."

"Only one?"

"Figure of speech. What the hell is the meat all about?"

Marcus didn't respond. Alex was sure he knew, or at least suspected something, but it was always about secrets with vampires, even in a work situation like this one. When any secret might come back to haunt someone, decades or even centuries later, they tended to keep things prudently close. He pursed his lips and jerked the steering wheel a little more forcefully.

Marcus changed the subject. "If instincts serve us well, there is an Ancient behind that club. Which, based on Aguirre's intelligence is my current theory of preference."

"Or, someone who knew us from UMBRA made you," Alex said.

"Far less likely."

"There's a third possibility," Alex said.

"Yes. An Ancient, who also knows of our activities in UMBRA, recognized me."

"There's no upside to this, is there?"

"No. Certainly not for Filip. He's underestimated whom he's dealing with."

"Yeah on both sides. Those guys will kill him outright just for sending us down there and alerting us to their operation. They can't be that stupid. They'll find out it was Filip who sent us."

"And us?"

"Well, after he tells us what he's going to do with the meat, I'm inclined to kill him myself. Depends really. I'm kind of on the fence about that one. Cross that bridge when we get to it."

They were approaching Filip's bodega. Alex killed the police lights and the siren. He slowed the Explorer down and blended in with traffic.

"Okay, how do you want to play this? Go in all Machiavelli like we already know everything? Or go in buddy-buddy like we're there just to check up?"

"You know, Machiavelli wasn't such a bad sort. Zorzi was good friends with him."

Alex made an exasperated face at Marcus.

Marcus conceded, "Oh all right. I think it's high time we scare the shit out of that little man. Your other idea, how did you put it? The 'Prince of Darkness' treatment. I've grown rather keen on that idea."

"I'm getting the itch to start cracking heads."

Marcus pointed out two Lincoln Town Cars parked near the bodega. "Damn them all."

The bad guys had one car parked in front of the entrance, the other around the corner along the high wall that blocked visibility into the rear lot.

"Your head-cracking antics may have to wait."

"I hate it when you're right."

Marcus lowered his passenger window and craned his head to try to hear anything. Alex knew the drill. This maneuver was old hat for them. As he drove past the front of the bodega, he put the Explorer in neutral and killed the engine, coasting by as quietly as he could without letting the vehicle lose much speed.

When they reached the end of the block, he turned the engine back on and popped back into drive. He pulled around the corner, and then turned off the Explorer.

"What have you got?"

"It is as we feared. There are at least six individuals inside, mostly on the upper story. There is blood and the smell of death, although that may just be Filip's trade. I cannot tell. There was some screaming and crying and other sounds—blows being struck?"

"Well, hopefully Filip's still alive." Alex paused. "Never thought I'd say that and actually mean it."

Alex picked up the radio's handset.

"Dispatch, this is fifteen Nora forty-two, requesting immediate backup to the corner of Fifty-third Street and Sixth Court. The grocery on the corner. Two-eleven in progress, possible two-oh-seven. Nocturns involved. Two officers on scene."

"Roger, forty-two. Stand by, one."

Marcus opened the car door. "I don't think there's going to be enough time. It sounds like some people are leaving. I heard one of them say, 'Stay behind and take care of it.'"

"Shit." Alex considered his options. "How badly do you think we need Filip?"

"That's cold, even for you. But I would say, badly."

"Yeah, unfortunately I agree. Can you hear him? Can you tell if he's still alive?"

"Sorry. There's too much yelling going on."

The police radios squawked through their conversation. "Fifteen Nora forty-two, stand by for backup. ETA is about eight minutes. Non-nocturn units. Other nocturn units occupied. Copy?"

Alex wondered why other nocturn units were occupied. He'd have to get his answers later. He acknowledged the radio, "Copy. We're going in. Officers in plainclothes."

Marcus was already at the rear of the Explorer. "Pop the back."

Alex did. Marcus opened the metal case and grabbed one of the shotguns.

"Those youngbloods in there could use a few hits of shot, I would warrant. In fact, I think they deserve it."

Alex picked up two Taser pistols; fifty thousand volts would drop a vampire just as easily as a human, and more easily than gunfire. He took off his jacket, threw on an ultraviolet-flash vest, and checked the power pack. The vest looked similar to the reflective kind that crossing guards wore, except that along the sides and the back, where the reflective strips would normally go, were strategically placed banks of superbright ultraviolet LEDs. A rip cord extended from either side like on the life vests flight attendants demonstrated on every flight. The idea was that if a vampire grabbed you, you could pull one of the two rip cords and it would set off a bright ultraviolet flash, which would hopefully cause the vampire enough pain that you could break free. The concept was dubious at best, but it was simply another tool. Like many things when dealing with vampires, it was probably better than nothing.

The power pack's indicator showed he had enough power for two bursts. He hoped he wouldn't need any. He made sure his sidearm was secure, more out of force of habit than anything. He threw his jacket over the top of everything to hide the vest for the initial approach and used the buttons on the outside to hold it closed rather than zipping it up.

"Let me guess. I'll be the scapegoat."

Marcus smiled his tight-lipped smile at him.

"Yeah, what was I thinking? I'm always the damn goat."

"A singular benefit of having your unique talents."

"Yeah, just because I'm not as easy to kill as everyone else doesn't mean it doesn't still hurt."

Marcus's eyes flickered as he heard something. "One of the cars is pulling away. They're starting to go to work up there. It's now or never."

"Okay," Alex said, "I'm going in John Wayne style. See you inside."

With a light run of several steps, Marcus vaulted straight at the building wall opposite the Explorer. His right foot hit the wall about four feet off the ground and he pushed off in the other direction, planting a foot on the Explorer's roof and leaping onto the corner streetlamp. One arm outstretched, he caught the streetlamp and planted a foot roughly halfway up and swung around the pole, using his momentum to slingshot himself back around. With practiced ease, he let go at the right time and vaulted onto the second-story rooftop of the building, leaving the streetlight vibrating like a tuning fork. He looked down, gave Alex a thumbs-up, and then he was just another shadow.

17

2:42 A.M.

Alex moved into his part of the plan. He stepped around the corner and walked briskly down the block to the bodega. He had one of the Taser guns up the sleeve of his coat, palming the front so no one could see what he had in his hand. The car that had been in front of the store was missing. That meant that the one around the block might be gone as well. Safer to assume it was still there.

He did some quick math, given what Marcus had heard and how many people could fit comfortably into two Town Cars. He was guessing there'd be about eight maximum. That could get very ugly. One car gone, left about four of them if luck was on Alex's side. Hell, Marcus could handle that by himself. If they were all youngbloods . . .

Alex caught himself smiling.

He approached the storefront. He didn't need Marcus's hearing to hear the racket coming from upstairs. He took a deep breath and hoped Marcus was in position. Then he threw himself into his role.

He sauntered up to the storefront glass door and gave it a tug. Locked. He saw movement inside.

They had left a lookout, one of the club vampires from the look of him. He pretended to be working the register. The man was wearing a thick gold chain; it was so big and gaudy that it looked like something you'd lock up a bicycle with. It glittered and called too much attention to the wearer.

Alex tapped lightly on the glass door.

The vampire looked up, curious, but trying to look like he was not even interested. Then he looked back down to whatever he was doing behind the register.

All right, if that was the game he was playing, Alex would play along. "Hey man. Door's locked."

The vampire called back, "We're closed. Come back after daylight."

"Listen, all I need is some milk. Just off the graveyard shift. Open up, will you?"

"Are you deaf? We're closed. Beat it."

Alex heard a car engine slowly approaching. He didn't like this. He had nowhere to go.

In his peripheral vision, Alex saw the car pull around the corner. He turned his head and confirmed the make and model: Lincoln Town Car. He noticed the driver, pale face, probably a youngblood vampire. Worst-case scenario, the first car hadn't left. It had moved. They were doing some kind of patrol and he'd missed it because he was concentrating on the inside of the store. Now who was the amateur?

He instinctively understood how exposed he was in the front of the store. His eyes flickered back to the man behind the counter. Only he was no longer behind the counter, he was moving toward the front door, and was about halfway there.

Just then, there was a shout from the upstairs. Someone screamed, "It was nothing like that! I didn't know!" That last word stretched out, changing its meaning from "know" to "No!" Then there were two quick gunshots.

The vampire walking toward the door looked right at Alex and they both knew what he'd heard. No chance for more talking now. Talking hadn't really been a part of Alex's plan anyway. As the man's black T-shirt passed in front of the door, it made the glass act like a mirror and Alex could see the Town Car behind him, the two side windows lowering.

Alex dropped and let the Taser gun slip out of his sleeve into his hand. He used the butt and smashed it into the door. Glass shattered. He heard the telltale "pfup" sound of a suppressed weapon and the snap of the bullet passing right over him, where his head had been just an instant before. He heard the vampire inside grunt in pain.

Alex dove through what was left of the glass door. He hit the vampire inside right in the shins. The man, already off balance, fell forward, his heavy body falling on top of Alex, who was already scrambling through the shards of broken glass and farther into the store.

Another couple of "pfup" sounds and the glass cabinets holding the cold beer and energy drinks had spiderweb cracks spreading from new holes.

Alex struggled on all fours to the end of one of the aisles. He'd lost one of the Taser guns. He switched the one in his palm to his off hand and drew his sidearm. It wasn't loaded with the right ammunition to end a vampire—that wasn't allowed on the police force yet—but they'd know he'd hit them.

The vampire inside the store crunched broken glass as he got back to his feet. Alex needed to make it to the back. If he could make it upstairs and regroup with Marcus, they could hold a slew of them off, at least long enough for backup to arrive.

It reminded him he had to play it straight. This wasn't the old days. There were rules now.

He identified himself: "Police officer! Drop your weapons and place . . ."

He never finished. A flurry of bullets peppered the back of the store, shattering more of the refrigerated compartments and this time breaking through a case of Hemotopia bottles directly above Alex's head and drenching him in sticky synthetic blood.

The vampire in the store screamed, "Hey assholes, you know you're hitting me, right?"

Laughter came from the ones in the car, and then Alex could hear the car doors opening and closing.

A voice outside the store: "Quit being such a pussy. It's not like you're going to die."

Glass crunched underfoot as the store vampire moved down the aisle. Then the "bing-bong" chime as the ones outside walked through the shattered door and stepped inside. These were all youngbloods, newly turned; they were still moving and still thinking like human thugs. He put the Taser down for a second, unbuttoned his jacket, and pulled his left arm out of the sleeve. He needed to get this jacket off. His hand reached back down for the Taser. Just as he grasped it, a large hand grabbed him by the throat and yanked him out into the aisle.

Alex choked as the store vampire lifted him clear off his feet like a small child. The vampire's other hand knocked Alex's pistol from him. Synthetic blood splashed everywhere. Alex was drenched in the stuff. It dripped onto the floor.

"Hey, look, guys, he's gone and marinated himself for us!"

Laughter from all of them. Now Alex could see there were four. His throat ached. His lungs started to burn. Three more upstairs?

He heard a crashing noise from upstairs and a surprised exclamation. He hoped that was Marcus's doing.

Alex smiled through the pain. If there was one thing he was certain of, it was that you never let a vampire know when you were afraid. He thought about the Taser; hitting the vampire while it was holding him wasn't part of the plan, but then neither was getting grabbed. Any way you cut it, this was going to hurt. The Taser would have less effect on him than on the youngblood.

The vampire gave him a puzzled look.

Alex's hands clawed at the hand holding him up. "You were faster than I thought," Alex managed to squeeze out. Then he tried to shoot the Taser into the vampire's neck. Again, the vampire was too fast. He intercepted Alex's arm with his elbow, all without releasing

Alex. It was enough to send the two wires and their leads shooting harmlessly into the air.

"You little shit!" The enraged vampire cocked his other arm back in preparation to deal Alex a horrific blow.

Alex squeezed his eyes shut and turned his head away, as if he didn't want to see the blow coming. Then he pulled the rip cord on the UV vest.

He could see the bright flash even through his closed eyelids. The vampires, who were all looking in his direction, and with eyes designed to see in low light, never had a chance.

They all howled in pain. The vampire holding Alex reflexively dropped him to cover his eyes. Alex would only have a second, maybe two. He opened his eyes, punched the larger vampire in the throat, and then spun him around to use the larger man's bulk as a shield. He reached up around the taller man's collar and grabbed hold of that large gaudy chain. He gave it a quick half twist as he yanked on it and simultaneously punched the vampire in the small of the back. With his hands clutching at the chains, the man bent over backward.

Then the shots started, just as Alex had suspected. They were firing blind. Alex didn't want them to. He had a shield, so he might as well use it.

"To your right, you cocksuckers!"

He shuffled backward, toward the stairs, towing the larger vampire back in front of him. More shots came at him and he felt the vampire shudder with several impacts.

He heard Marcus actually laugh from upstairs. Well, at least *someone* was having a good time. He stole a glance behind him: a few more feet and he'd be able to make a run for it. He passed the counter with the cash register. He risked a quick look. What had the vampire been playing with earlier? Despite himself, a wicked smile crossed his face.

Lying on the counter next to the register was a snub MP5K-PDW submachine gun. The kind high-end bodyguards defending ridicu-lously important clients dream about. Alex started to consider the problem of how to release the vampire he was holding to make a grab for the weapon.

A blur of motion fell screaming outside the front of the store. There was a tremendous crash as a body smashed down onto the Town Car, shattering the rear and side windows and pancaking the roof. Marcus had hurled someone from upstairs, and it looked like it hurt. He felt a brief glimmer of satisfaction.

The vampires in the store whirled toward the noise. They saw one of their companions feebly trying to climb out of the crater his body had made. Alex saw his chance and made his move.

He changed his grip on the vampire, reached over the counter, and snatched the submachine gun. Once it was in his hand, he raised his right knee almost straight to his chest, let go of the chain he was using to choke the vampire, and kicked out his leg. It sent the choking vampire sprawling into the nearest shelf. It toppled over with the vampire on top of it, strewing all manner of snacks, chips, and onion dip across the floor in another loud crash.

The other four vampires turned again. Alex snapped the bolt back on the machine gun. He absently noticed that an unspent round ejected from the chamber, but better safe than sorry. He let fly three short bursts.

Three of the vampires fell clutching their faces, and the fourth dove for cover. Vampiric constitutions notwithstanding, bullets to the head hurt. A lot. They were out of the fight for now. The fourth vampire peeked from his cover behind a shelf. Alex shot at him through the shelf, but couldn't be sure if he'd hit. All the gunfire had ruined his hearing. Everything sounded muted and dim. He hopped backward to the stairs, shook the remaining jacket sleeve off his arm, and made a run for it.

He'd have a couple of seconds before someone would be after him. Then he corrected himself. He'd been underestimating these idiots the whole time. He gave them the benefit of the doubt and fired another burst blindly toward the bottom of the stairs. The vampire with the chain ran right smack into the hail of bullets. The bullets hit his upper chest and neck before the vampire went down coughing and sputtering.

Alex took the remainder of the stairs two by two, hopped across the narrow hallway, and bounced into the first room upstairs.

There was no one there, just the body of Filip's assistant, two gunshot wounds in his head, and another vampire, clearly dead, his body broken in unnatural ways. The window was smashed out, undoubtedly where Marcus had thrown the other vampire out onto the car. That still left . . . how many?

They must be down the hall in another room.

He moved to exit the room. He stopped near the doorjamb and peeked his head out, snapping it out and back.

A bullet snapped through the drywall, millimeters from his face. He dove away from the door, his mind still resolving what he had seen on the landing in that split second. Two more vampires came cautiously up the stairs, the fates of their comrades still fresh in their minds.

Sure he had joked with Marcus and Zorzi about missing the "good old days," but right now, he wasn't missing them much.

His mind worked quickly. He moved over and grabbed the corpse.

"Hey, buddy, looks like you'll be able to do some good after all," he whispered into its ear as he picked up the body around the chest and half hefted, half dragged it to the window. He pressed the body high over his head and heaved it outside. Then he backed up away from the window. He barely heard the body hit the car. He hugged the wall with his body and clutched the MP5 like a lifeline.

Almost immediately, one of the vampires was at the door.

"He went out the damn window!"

The vampire peeking into the room forgot caution and ran right through the room to stare out the window. Alex hoped the other was rushing down the stairs.

Alex stepped out from his position flush against the wall and fired a burst into the back of the vampire's head. The loud roar ended in a muted clack. At such close range, the vampire's skull blossomed in a flower of carnage and gore. Alex knew he'd killed him. There was only so much damage a body, any body, vampiric or not, could repair. For a youngblood, that kind of wound was fatal. The vampire's body kept walking; it jerked in awkward steps, eerily looking as if it were trying to maintain its balance. Then it, too, toppled out the window.

Alex took a quick glance at the submachine gun in his hands. Its bolt was locked open, and wisps of smoke rose dreamily from the hot metal.

He pulled the magazine out just to be sure. Hoping against hope for a jam of some kind. Nope. Empty.

He had to get down the hall.

He heard shouting coming from downstairs.

"Leave 'em! Come on! Let's go!"

"Take the other car!"

He heard the muted tinkle of broken glass. Where the hell was Marcus?

He moved quickly to the room at the end of the hall, brandishing the empty machine gun in front of him in false bravado. If he ran into anyone else, a bluff was all he had to defend himself.

He passed the broken body of another vampire, hands still clutching the ruined throat that Marcus had ripped open. The guy was twitching feebly. He didn't have much time left. Alex reached the closed door at the end of the hall and tried to hear what was going on inside the room. He heard Marcus's voice.

". . . stop being stupid. Don't you hear the fight is still going on? We need to get out of here."

Now Alex heard sirens. He had the answer to why the other

vampires were leaving. Backup. Took them long enough. In any case, he'd better get through that door; if any of them stayed around, he'd be better able to wait them out in there. He hoped Marcus was still armed.

He opened the door cautiously and took in the scene. Filip was in the corner, beaten and bloody, with a shotgun pointed at Marcus.

"Friendly coming in," Alex announced.

Filip shouted at him, "Stay the fuck back!"

Alex stole a glance behind him. "What the hell, Filip? I'm not staying out here with those other assholes running around."

He eased the door open and stepped slowly inside. He closed it behind him, making a show of being more worried about what might be outside. It was hard to do, turning his back to Filip with a shotgun, but he hoped the ruse would work. If not, he was counting on Marcus to be damned fast.

Marcus spoke up: "I think it might be over. I can hear our backup arriving. You're safe, Filip."

"Bullshit. What about you? Huh? What about him?"

"What? Marcus? You can't be serious."

"They could have sent him to kill me."

"And what, they sent in the B team downstairs to rough you up, so we can come in to rescue you from them but then kill you? Filip, think straight, does that make sense?"

"Nothing they do makes fucking sense, man."

Alex tried to lighten the mood. He needed to get that shotgun out of Filip's hands. He turned to Marcus. "He's got you there. You don't make a lot of sense."

Marcus nodded; his eyes never left Filip.

"There's something real big going on. Shit, I don't know what I've got myself into."

"First you've got to make this right, Filip. You know how? You have to tell us who you're in bed with."

"Shit, just trying to make a buck, man." Filip wasn't listening.

Alex decided to try another tack.

"Filip, you tell us who you're dealing with and Marcus and I will make sure you never get screwed with again."

Filip looked at him. He was getting through with the revenge angle.

"The meat in the cooler, it's human, isn't it?"

"Yeah, man. Shit. I wasn't going to sell it out of the store. I just said that to get you out of here."

"I know that, Filip. You're not a bad guy." Alex noticed Marcus standing statue-still. He was doing his thing where he could almost make someone forget his presence. He hoped it would work. He needed to keep Filip's attention on him.

"Who was that meat for?"

"It's a special order."

"For vampires?" Alex doubted it. That didn't make sense.

"No. I don't know."

"Come on, Filip. You have to help us out here. If we're going to bring payback to the guys who did this, we need something."

"The Pact," he whispered, as if just saying the words would bring dire consequences. He seemed even more scared, if that was somehow possible.

"What?"

"I don't know, man. That's all. They weren't the guys who did this anyway."

"Yeah, that's right, these guys were vampires. Who are they, Filip?"

"They're fuckers from that club I told you about."

"Yeah, that club, we went to check it out."

Filip lifted the shotgun away from him. "Damn it, Alex, I really fucked up. I really fucked up this time. I just sent you down there to give them some shit, you know. They were coming around making all kinds of threats and talking shit. So I wanted to let them know they're not the only big dicks in town. You know, send a message that I got friends, too."

Filip was calming down. Alex decided to let him keep talking.

"You guys hadn't been gone three hours when these assholes came back. Roughed up the customers and killed one of the girls back in the storeroom after doing God knows what to her. I could hear her screaming. Then they went to work on me and Mitch, telling me that they'd given me a special privilege in dealing with them. And that I'd violated a trust by sending you two down there."

"Who are they?"

"I got nothing, man. This guy Nico runs with them. He's another juice dealer. He'd been trying to move on my shit for months, then all of a sudden everything is cool and he wants to deal with me. They said they were going to kill all of us slow, except me. They said . . ."

"Do you have a name, Filip? Think. Anything."

"Yeah, they kept saying Mr. Ziggy or something. A fucked-up name, Lugosi or something. I don't remember. They said . . ." Filip broke up. He lowered the shotgun to his side. Alex took a hesitant step toward him.

They could hear people shouting instructions over a PA downstairs.

"Cavalry is here, man. Put the shotgun down."

Filip snapped it back up and pointed back at Alex.

"No! They said, if I didn't off myself, they'd hunt down, torture, and kill my whole family!"

Alex quickly glanced at Marcus. A thought flickered across his mind: If those people were behind that torture chamber they'd found, then Filip's family was already dead. The look on his face must have given it away.

"Aw no . . ." Filip moaned. The shotgun moved up.

"Marcus!" Alex screamed, trying to rush forward.

The ancient vampire was nearly across the room when the shot fired and blew the top off Filip's head.

Marcus stopped, standing over the slumping corpse, a fine mist of blood and brains raining down on him. He stuck his ring finger in his ear and jiggled it around while pumping his jaw up and down.

Alex looked at him. "What happened to that Ancient speed? You could have cleared the room and grabbed the gun easy. Did you trip or something?"

Marcus stared at him. "What?"

Alex couldn't even hear himself talk, just the ringing in his ears. Besides, for now, there was nothing more to say.

18

3:40 A.M.

Alex was tired. They had three hours and change until sunup, and
he doubted that he was going to do anything else tonight. He was
looking forward to the daylight. He needed to recharge. His body
was stiffening and the skin was beginning to look taut and drawn
over his limbs.

He sat on the rear bumper of the crime scene unit's van, and drank
from his thermos. Someone had brought him a wet towel and he was
able to clean up his head and his hands, but his clothes were a complete mess. As the synth blood coagulated, his clothes had become
heavy and gummy. Changing out of them was rapidly approaching
"Number 1" on his to-do list.

There'd been a delay in how long it had taken for the lieutenant,
the crime scene techs, and other responders to arrive. Alex and
Marcus had been left in the dark as to why their crime scene was
suddenly playing second fiddle. Then they'd found out why. Someone had hit a blood club across town and left no survivors. From the
rumors he'd heard, it might have been Abraham, and he might have
left behind a crime scene worse than the one in the torture chamber, though Alex found that hard to believe. Zorzi and Garza were
taking lead on that case. The new kid was having a whopper of a
first day.

Now Alex was waiting for the guy from Internal Affairs Section to call him back in after he'd had his look around. Constance was with the medical examiner investigating the bodies, both human and vampire, that littered the inside. She was having a hell of a night, too, trying to micromanage every little thing. It was one of the many things Alex didn't like about her.

Marcus paced near the front of the store. They'd been told to stay apart. IA didn't want them to get their stories "straight." Just one more thing Alex preferred about the black ops world.

In the UMBRA days, this would have been a win. Not a big win, admittedly, since they were still in the dark and had lost an asset that produced a lot of intel. But when bad guys were down and the good guys were still standing, black ops folks didn't ask too many questions. There'd be time enough later for finger pointing. Nowadays they treated cops like perps just for doing their jobs.

One of the forensic technicians walked over to the van, holding some equipment.

"Detective?"

"Yeah? They ready for me?"

"Don't know. I think they found your weapon."

"Well, that's good. I had no idea where the hell it went." Alex stood up and started walking toward the bodega.

"They're going to need some time with that weapon before they can clear it."

"They don't need to. Bastard knocked it right out of my hand. Didn't even get a shot off, like some damned noob."

"Well, I think you did a hell of a job in there. You two against . . . ?"

"Eight or nine? I don't know." Alex's thoughts drifted back to the action when the vampire had grabbed him. He'd gotten sloppy. If it hadn't been a youngblood . . . He vowed it wouldn't happen again.

An awkward silence passed between him and the technician.

"You know," the technician said, "some of the other guys, they're not really cool with the whole Nocturn Affairs thing."

Alex nodded. Constance was talking to Marcus while the Internal Affairs guy loitered nearby.

"I just wanted to say, you guys are okay in my book. I mean you did a hell of job in there. They should give you a medal."

"I don't think they give out medals for goat ropes like this."

The technician looked a little crushed.

"Didn't mean to come off so hard. I appreciate the thought. Just have a lot on my mind."

Alex walked away as the technician opened the side door of the van to put away his equipment, and came within earshot of Constance and Marcus. They spoke in those damn hissing vampiric whispers no one else could make out. His footsteps on the broken glass gave away his approach. They cut off their conversation and watched him. It was probably nothing, but he couldn't shake the feeling that they didn't want him to hear what they were saying.

"So, who's got my piece?" Alex asked.

Constance gestured at one of the crime scene techs, who brought the pistol to him. "This is quite the mess, Alex."

"Tough night. As if the earlier ten-ninety-one wasn't enough."

"I may have to pull you two off this, until some of this blows over."

"What?" This surprised even Marcus.

"Blows over? What the hell?"

"Constance," Marcus said, "this was a front run by our longtime CI. He provided us with a tip earlier this evening and was—"

"I've heard it. And you mean to tell me that you had no idea that this CI of yours was connected to the chamber of horrors we discovered earlier?"

"I swear to you we did not know," Marcus said.

"And no idea he was moving this kind of product, both human and vampire?"

Marcus was quiet this time. Alex felt he needed to speak up. "Look, he had documentation for all of it. Besides, he's got to move some product if he's going to maintain any cred, right? Come on, Constance . . ."

"Lieutenant," she corrected.

Alex glared at her. "Are you shitting me? Listen, you deal with Boy Scouts if you want to cross the street, not if you're trying to catch the bad guys."

The guy from Internal Affairs decided to interrupt them. Alex hadn't bothered enough to remember his name.

"And that's why I'm looking into it. Didn't I ask you to wait outside?"

"I asked him to come," Constance covered for him.

"This isn't the Wild West, Romer. I don't know why you and your partner think you can flout procedure. There was significant loss of life here tonight. And I'm not sure you two didn't do everything you could to instigate a confrontation."

"Are you for real? You've got our statements," Alex said.

"And they're full of holes. Why didn't you wait for backup? Your CI committed suicide? Maybe you were cleaning up a problem you were afraid was about to turn on you?"

Alex balled up his fists. He'd had just about enough of everyone.

"You have about two seconds to walk away," Alex said.

"And now you're threatening me?"

Marcus stepped between Alex and the investigator. He faced Alex.

"Let it go," Marcus said, making eye contact with Alex. "We've had enough excitement for one night."

Alex wanted to smash the man's face. The insolence! The thought of that man speaking to him like that. To *him*! He should leave and let the vampires and thropes deal with the lot of them.

Constance talked to the Internal Affairs officer. "Let's call it a night? I assure you, you'll have their report by this afternoon. And we can continue the investigation when we've all settled down."

IA sneered at her. "Have it your way. Your little bureau is getting off to a hell of a start. Your unit is full of cowboys, and you may not care, but you're going to get good people killed. Who the hell decided to give you assholes your own bureau? God help us all." Without waiting for a response, the man stormed out the front.

"That didn't help things, Alex," Constance said.

"We're not the bad guys here. What, we're going to wait for every dotted 'i' and crossed 't' before doing something? We should be kicking in the doors to the club right now."

"Hold on." Marcus stopped him. He turned to Constance. "There is no time to do things tonight. This coming evening, we need to hit that blood club. Hard. We must force our way inside."

"Nothing tactical," Constance said.

Alex shook his head. "There's probably an Ancient inside!"

"And you have no evidence of that except Marcus's instincts."

"That's good enough for me. Or do you want to clear it with Lelith first?"

Constance glared at him. "It's not good enough for a warrant."

Marcus conceded the point. "All right, nothing tactical. I don't like it, but we will have nothing to rely on but bravado." He paused, coming up with a different plan. "We'll use a lot of cruisers with sirens and lights just to affect their clientele. We shall count that their greed outweighs any secrets they wish to keep. Patrons will be disinclined to attend the establishment with a significant police presence. That will give Alex and I our leverage to get them to invite us in."

"I don't know." Constance shook her head. "I'll think about it. What makes you think any persons of interest would still be there after tonight's fracas?"

"If there is an Ancient there . . . Well, we are nothing if not arrogant."

"Plus, there isn't enough time. Daylight is coming," Alex added. "And if it's politics you're worried about, at the very least, if Marcus is wrong, we shut down a big illegal blood club. That should be good for a feather or two in your cap. And make the new bureau look good with City Hall."

"You have to change your attitude, Alex, if you're to succeed in the new world," Constance counseled.

"Look who's talking."

Now it was Marcus's turn to glare at Alex.

Constance's pale countenance actually flushed and Alex saw her eyes flash red with vampiric ire.

"I've got a good mind to put you on a desk just for that. You've had a tough night, so I'm going to attribute your lack of respect to that."

"Lack of respect? Have you forgotten who *you're* speaking to?"

"Not at all. A king who was a failure in his old life and is a failure in his new one."

Marcus interceded. "We've all had a tough night and we could all use a spot of rest. Alex, why don't you take the Explorer, head in, and start working on the report. Constance and I will meet you this evening."

Alex caught the clue. Nothing good was going to come from him hanging around.

He turned away and walked over to one of the shelves. After looking at the contents for a moment, he picked up a box of trash bags.

Constance glared at him.

"What? This? Filip can bill me. Anyway, I'm not getting this gunk all over the seats in the Explorer. I'm going to head home first to change."

"And then you may want to see Aguirre," Marcus added.

"Yeah?" Alex said.

"What about?" Constance asked.

"About something Filip said. A group called the Pact?" Marcus said.

Constance gave Marcus a blank stare. Alex saw through it. She had a pretty decent idea what Marcus was talking about. "Some vampire secret, I take it?" Alex asked.

"I have my suspicions. This is something new. But old Lopé may be able to tell us a thing or two," Marcus said.

"Fine. But then you're back at the station," Constance said.

"Constance . . ." Alex started to retort, but then thought better of it.

Constance nodded. She'd won this round.

One of the forensic technicians stepped out of the back room. The man was pale and looked as if he was about to vomit. He noticed them looking at him.

"That stuff in the cooler. I think it's human flesh. Oh my God."

Alex spoke up. "Good news for someone, anyway."

"How is that?" Constance asked.

"That son of a bitch Filip got off easy."

19

4:51 A.M.

Alex's gut was not letting things go this time.

He could hit home, grab some essentials, and be gone. He'd have at least a twelve-hour lead and could be out of the country. One quick stop in the Caymans to tap his stash, and then he could shed this identity and disappear. Why not let Marcus, Constance, even Aguirre deal with this? They wanted to keep their damned secrets, let them.

Even as he thought it, he knew that it was just a fantasy and that he'd never go through with it.

It wasn't as if the government would let someone like him wander too far from the reservation in any case. He thought of his friend Grigori, a Ukrainian expat who'd been Zorzi's human partner in UMBRA. They'd found him in an upscale brothel in Rio after someone had given him a dose of something that hadn't agreed with his health. This happened only one week after he'd announced that he wasn't going to play ball anymore and that he was going to retire and be "nose-deep in Brazilian butt floss" for the rest of his days. Well, Alex had to admit, that part had been true. He couldn't help but think that the end of his days had come a hell of a lot sooner than Grigori would have liked.

Alex arrived at his condominium complex and pulled up to the gate. He lowered the window and reached out to the small keypad on the drive-up stand. He punched the key code but nothing happened. Annoyed at having "fat-fingered" the code, Alex started to punch it in again. He felt sticky and tired and wanted nothing more than to have a nice pull at his water pipe and then maybe go down to the beach and soak in the daylight.

That paperwork could wait. They couldn't really do anything to him anyway.

He froze as he continued punching in the code. He was getting a bad feeling. Maybe it was wired. No. It would have just gone off after he punched it in the first time. If someone had really recognized Marcus for who he was, anything was possible.

He was compromised. Maybe he was just being paranoid. On the other hand, he'd been sloppy lately. He decided to err on the conservative side.

He briefly slipped his *ka* from his body and headed skyward for a bird's-eye view. Everything looked normal. Except . . .

There was a white sedan on the corner with two humans inside. They were just sitting there. It didn't make sense, unless, of course, they were a surveillance team. Whose surveillance team? That was the real question. And why? If they were there to remote-trigger a bomb, they'd had plenty of time to set it off already. If they were there to verify that a bomb had gone off, well, they didn't have to be sitting on the corner for that.

He was overreacting. They wouldn't use a bomb, not in this political climate. It would be too big, impossible for the media to ignore. No, they'd be coming at him sideways. The damn gate was just broken. He decided to let things play out for a bit and see where the situation would go.

He snapped back into his body, but the effort left him more drained than he'd expected. The sun needed to come up soon.

He heard tires squeal. He checked the mirrors and could see that the white sedan was moving to bracket him in. He threw the Explorer into reverse and waited to see what they would do.

Just as Alex had expected, the sedan stopped directly behind the Explorer. To use such an obvious tactic meant these guys thought that they were tough, that they had the upper hand and had nothing to fear. They'd be common thugs thinking they were dealing with a common cop.

Doom on you, assholes.

Alex floored the accelerator, and the Explorer lurched backward and T-boned the white sedan, knocking it back into the street with a crash and a spray of broken glass. He slid from the driver's seat into the passenger side, opened the door, and climbed out of the SUV. He ran down behind the white sedan and saw that the driver already had his door open and was getting out.

The man was dazed, woozy, but already reaching for something at his side.

Alex reacted instinctively, right hand clearing his jacket and drawing his pistol in one fluid motion, finger on the trigger. He had to consciously keep himself from pulling it.

"Hands! Now! Let me see 'em!"

The driver put his hands up and then turned around to face Alex. Alex's eyes flickered back to the inside of the car. There was a guy still in the passenger seat. He backed up so the Explorer would give him some cover, but he lost sight of the passenger.

The driver shouted at him, "Ease up. We're just bringing a message."

"Shut up!" Alex needed time to think. He was exposed. Did they have a backup team? He hadn't seen one, but he hadn't had time to look. He stole a glance down the street.

"Relax and listen up. Your sanger partner can afford the bravado. You're just a sap and we can end you anytime we want, so lose the attitude." The man paused, letting his words sink in. "It's weird how you can own this whole building on a cop's salary. I mean, you don't even try to keep it a secret. Pretty dumb for a dirty cop."

Okay, so he'd been at least partially compromised. They'd checked

188 ✦ MICHAEL F. HASPIL

his finances; so, minimum, he had to assume they knew everything about this identity. It was exactly for situations like this that you always used an alias. First-day tradecraft.

Good news was that this might not be a hit. Most times, you didn't do a background check on someone you were going to rub out.

Alex didn't relax his guard, but decided to see where this might go.

"Who says I'm dirty? Maybe my partner was good to me. Maybe I just invested well."

The man chuckled. "In this economy? Be serious. Look. Like I said, I'm just a messenger. The guy we work for and you, well, we have mutual friends. We might be able to come to some arrangement."

"I'm listening."

"Our friend would like you to know that he rewards his friends well. And that he regrets the recent unfortunate events. That was the fault of some overzealous recruits, you understand. They'll be dealt with. We don't want more incidents like earlier tonight. You know and we know it's bad for business. No one wins."

"You mean Filip?"

The man didn't answer directly. "Just know that there's something in it for you to drag your feet."

"You're going to need to be a bit more specific. My caseload is full right now."

The man continued as if Alex hadn't spoken. "If you don't, we know who you are, and we know where you are."

Now Alex understood the game they were playing. He was familiar with this dance. He had to show them he was interested. It would mean exposing himself but it might be worth it. Of course, if they shot him, then he'd have to kill them both. Karmically, it kind of worked out.

He lowered the pistol, still pointing it at the driver, but more casually, as if he'd forgotten it was in his hand.

"Okay. Let's talk numbers. And I still need the details. Can't throw all my cases in a cold drawer, can I?"

"You're not so stupid you'd expect us to discuss the specifics in the middle of the street, are you?"

"I don't know. I can be pretty stupid."

"We'll be in touch."

Damn. It was worth a try anyway.

"Well, next time be a little more discreet. I might not be so slow on the trigger."

"If you'd harmed either one of us, you'd be dead in seconds."

"That a fact?" Alex looked around. He still couldn't see any evidence of surveillance. Maybe the driver was just bluffing.

"It is. I'm going to get back into the car now and we're going to leave. We'll be in touch." The driver brazenly lowered his arms and turned his back to Alex in an obvious demonstration that he didn't regard him as a threat.

The sedan pulled away, scraping against the rear of the Explorer and leaving mementos of white paint along the dark blue and constellations of broken glass on the pavement. Alex could see that he'd crushed the passenger door so badly it wouldn't open without a trip to a body shop. He smiled.

"Sorry about your car!" he called after them, but received no acknowledgment.

Okay, so from now on, he had to assume someone was watching him. Shit. He got back into the Explorer, dug out his phone, and placed a quick call to Marcus. He doubted Marcus would answer. Judging from the past night's activities and the conspiratorial way Marcus and Constance had been talking to each other, he was sure they'd be up to something they knew Alex wouldn't approve of.

Sure enough, the call went straight to voice mail.

"Marcus, I just had an interesting visit at my condo. Assume you're being watched, if they haven't tried to contact you."

They'd know better than to try to bracket an Ancient. There were reasons they lived so long and being tolerant of threats wasn't one of them. Part of Alex wished they would try to corner Marcus—even better if he had Constance with him. His only regret would be if that actually went down and he wasn't there to see how quickly Marcus and Constance dealt with them.

The next order of business was the gate. Alex got out and opened the gate with his key. He pulled the Explorer through and parked. He took a multitool out of the glove compartment and walked back to the keypad.

Despite owning the whole complex and residing on the top floors, he wasn't the only one who lived here. If they had done something malicious to the keypad beyond just rendering it inoperable, Alex needed to know. It wouldn't do to have a resident blown sky-high on his account.

He carefully removed the screws on the faceplate and pulled it away. They had just disconnected the front plate from the internal electronics. Pretty simple. Alex pushed the connector back into place and tried the code. The gate reacted. Alex made a show of putting the plate back on. But his eyes were scanning the other buildings. He could see nothing.

He finished and walked back through the gate, letting the time delay shut it behind him. He climbed back into the Explorer and drove to the parking garage.

He still had another bolt-hole in this city. Some office space leased through a dummy corporation that interested parties would have trouble tying to him. If he had to, he could still get away.

He could have easily sent a code word, the one that would erase Alejandro Romer from the world and establish someone new. That would imply he was running. Which might also imply a chase, depending on who was paying attention.

He had one more stop before he could go up and shower this gunk off him.

He pulled the Explorer into the parking garage and backed it up to the entrance of a storage unit. He got out and got his first good look at the damage to the rear of the SUV. It had survived the crash in much better condition than the sedan and had taken the brunt of the damage on the bumper. Still, the metal was dented and warped around the door. He hoped it would still open. He tried it. It stuck.

He pulled at it long and slow, using the last measure of his reserves. The metal groaned in protest, but after a moment, it gave way and swung open. Okay, now he just hoped it would close. The lock mechanism looked shot. His joints were beginning to stiffen up and his skin was turning ashy. If he didn't get some sunlight soon, he was going to look like a mummy again, and that wouldn't be helpful to anyone.

He unlocked the door to the storage unit and flicked the light on. Everything was as he'd left it. Shelves bracketed the walls covered in items Alex had hoped he'd never need again. This was UMBRA stuff. Stuff no one had asked for when UMBRA ceased to exist. Alex had helped himself—but, again, better safe than sorry.

He reached under one of the shelves and pulled out what he was looking for, a large black Pelican case. It looked like those pricey cases that people used to carry around very expensive electronic equipment, and in a way, that was appropriate. He knelt down, his knees groaning and popping with the effort, unlocked it, and opened it up. It was just as he'd left it.

There was a black LCD panel with an entry keypad and a keyhole. The associated keys were still taped to the faceplate after all this time, just as he expected them to be. Alex knew that beneath the matte black faceplate was enough octanitro to blow this building—any building—sky-high. Octanitrocubane was currently the most powerful nonnuclear explosive known to man. Civilians had only recently been able to manufacture small quantities. But UMBRA had had it for years. It was very stable, it was shock-insensitive, and it put out a very very big bang. This was a doomsday device. If you ever had to use this, it meant you were officially having a really bad day. Marcus had dubbed the device Rubicon, after the river in northern Italy.

The story went that Julius Caesar was marching his army back from Gaul. Roman law prohibited any Roman general to march an army south of the Rubicon. Caesar deliberately violated the law and marched his army toward Rome. His actions signaled his intentions against his rival Pompey and the Senate, and helped make a Roman civil war inevitable. As far as the case was concerned, it was Marcus's way of saying that if you used it, there was no going back.

Alex took the battery out of the device and fetched a fresh one from the charger. He carefully inserted it. Took one of the keys, placed it into the keyhole, and turned it to the first position.

The LCD screen lit up. Alex checked the settings and made sure to link it to his phone for remote detonation. He thought briefly of turning the key to the second position, arming the device, then thought better of it. He removed the key, put it on his key ring, and closed the case.

He put the case into the back of the Explorer. Then he went back into the storage unit and brought out other tools he hoped he wouldn't need—pistol crossbows with silver bolts, industrial-strength garlic spray foam. The police did have some garlic Mace. But they'd designed that stuff to subdue. The Mace Alex had just loaded would throw your average vampire into anaphylactic shock. This was a product designed to kill, stuff the police couldn't have because it just wasn't PC to carry a substance expressly designed to terminate members of the new population.

He threw a box of silver-plated stakes and some silver-plated machetes into the back. The whole deal with the silver might be over-kill. Sometimes it worked, sometimes it didn't. People had gotten the idea about silver affecting vampires and thropes from early movies. The idea had caught on for a reason: Sometimes it was true. He wasn't sure where Hollywood had gotten their information for those early films. However, he had to admit: Sometimes even cheesy movies were right on the money.

One more trip brought out a case of electronic flash-bangs. These emitted a higher frequency than humans could hear and gave off a lot of UV radiation. It was nonlethal, but caused vampires extreme discomfort. He took one of the cylinders, about the size of a road flare, out of the case and slipped it into his jacket pocket, just in case. He made a mental note to pick up a fresh UV vest when he made it into work.

He hoped he'd be putting all this stuff back soon. His gut told him he was being an optimist. He locked the storage unit and slammed the door on the Explorer. He pushed the door hard against the frame. The entire vehicle rocked forward under the force of the impact. The metal made a crunching noise he didn't like the sound of, and he thought of the additional paperwork he was going to have to do to explain the damage to the department vehicle. But now the door was more secure than any lock. No one other than him was going to be able to open it without hydraulics.

He could deal with the paperwork and explanations later. For now, he would park the Explorer in a monitored slot, and then he could finally take a shower and recharge. He only had a few minutes left. He could feel himself shutting down.

Alex stepped out of his private elevator and checked the alarm system. No alarms. Nothing had tripped the motion detectors. Motion detectors could be defeated, but that usually took time, and his were set so that anything larger than his cat would set them off. He'd take the risk and assume that no one had made it up here.

He unlocked his door and took in the scene, looking for anything out of place. Nothing. The first rosy fingers of dawn were creeping into the large-pane windows. The warm dry air greeted him.

He stepped inside, closed the door, and set the security system to "stay" mode. He took off his shoes and checked the carpet carefully. It was clean. He hadn't tracked any gunk in with him.

He stripped off his synth-blood-covered clothes. Most of it had dried and clotted, but it still felt tacky to the touch, and boy, could this stuff stain. A black cat poked its head inquisitively around the corner and gave him a dubious look, as if to say, "What kind of mischief have you been up to? And where is my food?"

"Hello, Bastet, are you hungry?"

Balling his clothes up into a bundle, he made his way toward the kitchen. He quickly navigated a small maze of pedestals with various ancient artifacts displayed on them, and lighted cases filled with treasures that would make any antiquities museum outside of Cairo pale in comparison. If knowledgeable investigators ever set eyes on his collection, Alex would have a lot of explaining to do. After all, how could he convince anyone that he was the original owner?

Once in the kitchen, he opened a drawer and after some quick, blind fumbling retrieved an old plastic shopping bag. He thrust the soiled clothes into it. He wouldn't be wearing these ever again. He tossed the bag in the trash. The jacket would be a different story. That would have to go to the cleaner's. He set his phone, his keys, and the flash-bang on the counter, and then took a cat-food tin out of the pantry.

He opened the refrigerator and took out a premixed bottle of his tonic. He gulped down more than half of it before coming up for air. The cat leapt nimbly onto the counter and meowed at him insistently.

"Patience, okay, I'm getting to it." He grabbed a fork out of a drawer and scooped the food out in to a small glass dish. The cat didn't even wait for him to finish, digging into the food as he was putting it in. He left the fork on the counter for Bastet to lick.

Carrying the bottle, he walked into the bathroom and turned on the shower. He let the water get good and hot as he polished off the bottle's contents. He stepped in and let the six showerheads scourge the night's activities from his body. Somehow, the water just never seemed to be hot enough, though he knew it was nearly scalding. He stood there just enjoying the luxury of the shower and appreciating that for a small amount of time, he didn't have to do or think about anything.

After what seemed like a mere instant, he stepped out and dried himself off very briefly. Just enough so he wasn't dripping wet. He would let the air dry the rest of him. He wrapped a towel, shendyt-like, about his waist and stepped back out.

He couldn't wait to greet the day. He opened the door to the solarium, dropped the towel from his waist onto a lounge chair, stepped naked into the light of the rising sun, and let it wash over his dark skin. The solarium was his favorite room, by necessity if nothing else.

Massive windows rose from the floor to connect to the glass ceiling. Artwork from the Egyptian Old Kingdom decorated the mostly open space, which was broken up by large pillars meant to recall those of the temple of Het-ka-Ptah, at Men-nefer, which the Greeks had called Memphis. A waist-deep pool dominated the middle of the room. Soon the sunlight would contribute to the room's greenhouse effect, making it much warmer than most people would like. Alex didn't mind; it served to remind him of home. His first home. His real home. Kemet. The Black Land. Egypt. Even now, after all these years, that last name sounded very foreign to him.

Already he could feel his vigor returning. He bathed in the sunlight's golden glow. A sun worshiper shouldn't have to work the graveyard shift. Throwing his hands over his head, he stretched his tired body and paid his respects. And Re did restore him, as only a god could.

The weariness of the night passed from his sinews, and new reserves of strength poured into him. He decided that Aguirre and the paperwork could wait a few more hours. He would have a lie-down in the solarium, among the framed papyrus artworks that adorned the walls, and just relax. He was starting to feel a lot better already.

Then the phone rang.

20

Marcus let the heady rush from the wine wash over him and tried to forget the night's troubling events. Filip had revealed disturbing developments, thropes and vampires working together with humans in the middle. It didn't make sense, but the evidence at Filip's, and at the fear-blood-laden crime scene earlier, suggested that they were at least receiving goods from the same supplier.

Next to him, a shapely young blonde stirred in her sleep. Marcus had requested she consume at least half of a bottle of a rare Sassicaia wine before feeding on her. He ran a hand through her silk-fine hair and felt the warmth of her.

A groan of ecstasy caught his attention. He diverted his eyes to the other divan. Constance was now feeding on her third. Their bodies entwined in a lovers' embrace. She fed while he thrust into her. Nearby, two other young men with underwear-model bodies slept naked.

A moment passed and Constance continued to feed. She was feeding too long. Marcus readied himself to intervene. He propped himself on one arm and prepared to move across the room to wrench the young bleeder from Constance if she did not break the embrace on her own. This wasn't that kind of place. Having a bleeder die here would cause unnecessary complications for everyone.

From the outside, this was just another upscale house in the suburbs with high privacy walls. Inside, it was one of the most elite blood clubs in the world. It was a closely guarded secret for the aristocracy of vampires. No one even suspected its existence. Certainly not Lelith and her cronies at the Lightbearers, not even the other boys from UMBRA, when they'd still been interested in such things. It was Marcus's gift to himself and his closest friends. But if Menkaure ever found out, Marcus would never hear the end of it. Alex just did not understand.

He carefully screened his stable of bleeders. What other vampires chose to control through fear or withholding of favors, Marcus chose to secure through luxury. In exchange for their voluntary service as bleeders exclusive to Marcus and his friends, he granted them access to a lifestyle of extreme affluence they stood little chance of enjoying otherwise. They could leave whenever they wanted, but why would they want to? And when Marcus grew tired of their blood, he rewarded them with a healthy stipend to retire on in exchange for their continued silence.

He cleared his throat loudly and Constance got the hint. She broke off contact with the young man, pushing him from her.

The man glared at her for a moment; then he regained his senses, nodded as he moved off the divan, and joined the other bleeders on the floor.

"*Leave us,*" Constance said in Latin.

The man nodded. He roused his companions and the woman near Marcus. There was some brief activity as they gathered their varied articles of clothing and left the room.

Constance's lips moved into a coy smile. "*You're of a mood.*"

"*I have had a long night.*"

"*So have we all. But you still dwell on the events. Let them pass for now. Night will return soon enough.*"

"*And carry with it new mysteries. There is something strange at play I cannot quite grasp.*"

"I don't want to talk shop." She slipped back into English.

He followed her lead. "What do you want to talk about?"

She shrugged. That particular movement did delightful things to her anatomy. He never tired of looking at her.

"Have you seen the renovations at Aguirre's church? I would not have thought it possible."

She let out an exasperated sigh. "I'm not in the mood to speak of Aguirre, and especially not of churches. *Come here and let me slip your mind of such things.*"

He shook his head. "No, you come here. Aguirre might be on to something."

Constance moved off the divan with her face in a playful pout. "I'm not interested in Aguirre's progress or his lifestyle of denial and guilt. To answer your question, yes I have seen the renovations. I'm not as easily impressed as you are."

She pushed him onto his back and straddled him.

"When did you see them?"

"Last night. I just missed you, as a matter of fact."

She pushed Marcus's hands over his head and held them pinned at the wrist with one of her hands. He let her do it.

"Is that so?"

"It is."

She grabbed the girth of him and slipped him inside of her.

"Now, can we stop all this talk of priests and churches? *My thoughts reside on much baser things.*"

Marcus laughed. "You are insatiable."

"Prove it."

21

The phone's insistent ringing brought Alex from his reverie. The automated voice of the caller ID announced, "Secure Caller." That meant work, probably Roberts, most likely calling to nag him about stupid paperwork.

He answered the phone.

"Romer."

"Good! At least you're home! Why aren't you answering your cell?" Captain Roberts sounded put out.

"It's in the other room. Didn't hear it." Something about the captain's tone bothered him. "What's going on?"

"How . . . You don't know? It's all over the TV."

"I don't have one."

"Well, it's about to get a lot more interesting. There's a general recall. Maximum deployment. We've got fucking vampires killing a family, a whole family, in retaliation for Abraham's handiwork last night. Fucker started a war."

"We know he did it?"

"Not like it matters, but yeah, his calling card was there. What matters is that the sangers hit back. Mayor's panicking. Word is the governor is calling up the National Guard. Lelith's calling for heads, literally. Everyone has to come in. The city's gonna blow up."

"Fill me in."

"Sangers hit a random family as far as we can tell. They filmed the whole thing. Made sure they didn't catch themselves on camera, at least not clearly. We've got people going over every frame. Anyway, they posted it on the Internet and sent it to the media. Some of those fuckers are airing it! They killed the whole family, mom, dad, the kids. They say there's gonna be another tonight unless Abraham turns himself in or we catch him first."

Alex let out a sigh. It really had only been a matter of time. He was a bit surprised it had taken this long.

"You wouldn't happen to know where your partner is?"

"No. He's with the lieutenant. You know how they are with their secrets. I doubt you'll be able to get a hold of any nocturn right now."

"Figured as much. That's the trouble with this Nocturn Affairs Section. Half you fuckers are vampires! I need you here ASAP."

"I'll be there," Alex said, but then he had an idea. "Actually, give me a couple hours. I have a source that has an ear to the ground. He might be able to help."

"Old friend or new."

"Very old."

"Don't take too long, I need all my good heads in on this."

22

By the time Alex battled through the horrible traffic, it was almost midmorning. It looked to him like the entire human population of the city was ignoring the suggestion to remain indoors and was using it as excuse to skip work and skip town. The last time he'd seen congestion like this, people thought a category-four hurricane was on a collision course with Miami. It made the commute miserable. But more people clearing out of the city now would mean less chaos tonight. Hopefully.

He spent the time surfing from radio station to radio station, listening to the news and reactions to it. The talk-radio people were loving it and entertaining the ideas of all kinds of wackos today. Everyone with an opinion needed to voice it on the air. Most were calling for the Nocturn Killer to do the right thing and turn himself in. How likely was that? Alex wouldn't put odds on it.

Then there were folks calling in who were genuinely terrified. They were the ones that really made Alex nervous. They said that they'd kill any vampire that came near them, guilty or not. They weren't going to take any chances. Alex knew that the majority of those people would be unable to carry out their threats, but they could dish out a lot of collateral damage trying.

All the while, Alex kept calling Aguirre, Marcus, and Constance, with no success. He hoped that Aguirre was keeping to his faith and would be up during the daylight. More than that, he hoped Aguirre would have something for him. The identity of the new Ancient in the city would be fantastic, or Abraham's identity; or, failing that, any lead on these new killers who murdered the family would be a welcome treat. It was a long shot that he would get any of those things.

Alex pulled into the lot at Aguirre's church complex. It looked deserted, as usual. The dark gray buildings stood out against the bright blue sky and held their ground against the strong sun. The campus sprawled, each building connected through covered and enclosed walkways. Though it should have been emitting an aura of sanctity, it generated an ominous impression instead, like a black hole.

He walked up the stairs to the nondescript entrance and rang the bell as a small sign requested. He waited, consciously forcing himself to enjoy the fresh air and the nice day. After a moment, he pressed the button again and then banged on the doors literally loud enough to raise the dead.

A buzzing sound came from the door, and Alex pushed it in. There was a sign on an inner set of doors: PLEASE ENSURE THE OUTER DOORS CLOSE BEHIND YOU.

Alex did. Marcus was correct when he said that Aguirre had changed the interior of the church. Already this was different. This "airlock" version of the two sets of doors was ostensibly for keeping the sunlight out, but Alex knew better. This was more in tune with Aguirre's sense of security.

He pushed against the inner set of doors. They didn't budge. Alex looked around the small vestibule, waiting for the inner set of doors to open. He was sure someone was watching him.

The inner set of doors opened tentatively and Alex could see a smallish figure in a dark gray robe. After a moment, it threw back the large cowl of its hood, revealing a stunning auburn-haired female vampire.

He was taken aback. The idea that a woman was greeting him shocked him more than the fact that she was a vampire.

"Welcome," she said, "how may we be of assistance?" Her accent was hard to place. Bavarian?

She wrinkled her nose as she took in Alex's scent. She could smell him through his cologne. He mentally reproached himself. He should have taken that into consideration; it might be trouble.

Then he saw compassion come across her features. Before he could say anything, she continued. "You are ill? A terminal disease?"

Alex decided to go with that. That story was as good as any and easier than the truth. He nodded.

"I'm sorry. I hate to turn you away, but we are a sect that deals exclusively with nocturns. If you wish, I can put you in touch with a human organization that would be better able to help you."

"I'm beyond their kind of help," Alex replied, then realized it came off as a defeatist statement when he was just trying to state a fact. He smiled. "I'm here to see Lopé. Father Aguirre. I'm an old friend and I need some advice."

"Oh, of my own free will I invite you to cross the threshold."

Alex made a show of crossing the threshold. He paused and considered how much he should give away. Then again, he'd just told her he needed to see Aguirre.

"For your freely given welcome, I will return no harm."

She didn't bat an eye. This woman was old-school. Good manners always got you farther, even with vampires. An old wives' tale tied a building's threshold to one's ability to deal with a vampire. It was a variation on the old "having to invite a vampire in" myth. The vampires had turned it on its ear; entering "of your own free will" simply meant that you did not intend any harm. Kind of a "live and let live" promise. Alex hadn't thought anyone even bothered with that kind of show anymore. Apparently, he'd been wrong.

She turned away from him and led him into the church. The changes to the interior surprised him. He'd been expecting the dungeon-like atmosphere he'd seen the last time. Very dark, with all the windows covered in heavy drapes; a cavern lit with candles. Generally, it had been the perfect atmosphere for those given to self-flagellation and self-loathing.

Now, large banks of lights lit it brightly. Sunlight streamed in through the numerous stained-glass windows. The drapes were still there but they were now white where they had been dark crimson before. It looked to Alex like a proper church, a place of worship. He wouldn't have given it a second thought, except that the vampire with him was walking down the center aisle apparently without a care. She walked in and out of the brilliant stained-glass sunbeams. Vibrant greens, yellows, and reds illuminated the long rows of hardwood pews.

"You've perked up the place quite a bit since I was last here."

"Oh yes." She paused to stay with Alex, who had stopped to better take in the refurbished room.

"We've had a change in philosophy and we've changed our decor to reflect our optimism."

In the light, she didn't appear as beautiful as he'd first thought. She was still very pretty, but her skin was almost transparent and he could see every vein. She was also too thin and had a look about her of someone who hadn't had a good night's sleep in years. Aguirre encouraged members of his flock to abandon their nocturnal lifestyle, eschew all blood except for synth blood, and try to incorporate actual human foods into their diet. They were putting themselves through hell, and it showed on this woman.

She caught him staring at her. "My apologies. I am Adeline." She held out her hand to greet him.

Alex took it. It felt warm. Not like a vampire's at all. But not human either. Stranger and stranger.

"I'm Alejandro Romer. But everyone calls me Alex."

"And which do you prefer?"

"Whichever. It doesn't matter much to me."

"Alejandro then. It sounds truer to you. Though not entirely true. You seem older than you look."

Alex smiled but said nothing.

She continued walking down the aisle, but now Alex's curiosity was aroused. He was sure she was a vampire. They approached another wide sunbeam and he saw her make a little halting stutter step before crossing it. He would have missed such a slight gesture had he not been looking for it.

He stopped and let his *ka* slip out of his body. He had to know.

Adeline had the negative-space projection of a vampire, but a golden glow suffused it, almost like an electrical discharge. Aguirre's methods were actually getting results.

He slipped back into his body and almost fell. He stifled a gasp and put a hand on one of the pews to steady himself.

"How is it possible that you're crossing . . . ?"

"Into the sunlight?" She gave a little laugh. "Well, we've known for years that it is the ultraviolet component in sunlight that damages us. Not much different than humans really, except that the damage done to vampire physiology happens much more rapidly. Humans tan. We burn. We've discovered a nice film, clear to the eye, that filters out the ultraviolet wavelengths. Father Aguirre had all the church windows covered with it."

Alex wondered why other vampires hadn't thought of this. The technology wasn't new. UV protection had been in sunglasses for how long?

As they reached the crossing, she turned right, toward the south transept.

She led Alex to a cloistered garden. Previously there had been a large storeroom with benches for studying. Aguirre had changed his plans to turn it into a library. Now, Alex could see sunlight streaming in through open archways. Each archway had two gauzelike drapes fastened in the middle by Velcro strips. Alex could see gray-clad figures tending the garden.

They were covered head-to-toe in a gray clinging fabric that looked like spandex, making them look like superheroes or faceless assassins out of a Hollywood film. Some wore gray cloaks over the outfits. All of them wore goggles.

"Father Aguirre," Adeline called out. "You have a visitor."

One of the figures stood up from where it had been squatting near some flowers. It waved, and then moved with urgency when it saw Alex. The figure stepped toward the archway and peeled apart the gauzy drapes. Alex noticed that Adeline stepped well out of the way. Aguirre turned and pressed the Velcro strips together again. He turned to Alex and pulled off his balaclava and goggles. He moved his hand through his dirty brown hair in a useless attempt to straighten it and gave Alex a reserved smile, which quickly turned sour.

"Marcus sent you, did he not?"

"Yeah. I've been trying to reach him all morning. Have you heard from him?"

"No. We must talk." He turned to Adeline. "Thank you, my dear. You may return to your work."

She gave a slight bow and smiled, then stepped back into the main church.

"She's helping restore the pipe organ. She is quite the accomplished musician. Played with Bach I'm told." Aguirre's tone never changed, never lost that "hey, how's it going" kind of feeling. But Alex could tell that something was wrong.

"I don't have much time. There are things going on this morning . . ."

Aguirre smiled again. "Not here, Alex. We'll speak in my chambers. It's worse than you think."

"Shit."

Aguirre spun and glared at him, and pointed upward at the church's ceiling. "Language, Alex." Then he continued onward.

Alex followed him through an opening and into one of the

covered walkways. Here it was darker, with only minimal lighting. Alex's eyes had trouble adjusting to the sudden change.

"I must apologize for these conditions. We have not renovated this section yet. Can you see?"

"I'll manage." Alex put one hand on the wall to help guide himself. "That renovation project is really something."

"Yes. We're making great strides."

Aguirre's voice was strained. He was trying to hide it, but wasn't doing a very good job. Alex could tell him what great strides he was really making. What he'd seen when he'd taken an astral peek at Adeline hinted that Aguirre's people might be growing their souls back. He decided it would be a subject better broached later. He didn't need Aguirre going off on a metaphysics tangent right now. He wasn't here to speak to Aguirre the priest, but Aguirre the operative.

Aguirre broke the silence by continuing the discussion of the renovation. "That film that covers the windows, the same company produces a fabric that does the same. It still tingles a bit, but it makes things tolerable. It isn't cheap, but I have no shortage of resources. The old decor with all the candles and somber plainchant atmosphere, it drove the newer nocturns away. I was fond of it, of course. But the youngbloods thought it seemed rather too medieval for the current age and to be honest it did grow rather depressing at times. So we undertook the renovations. Ironically, we did most of them at night. Once they were completed we returned to normal."

"Normal? You've got women in here now." Alex smiled, bemused.

"Ah. Well. They need guidance as much as the men do. And we've never claimed to be celibate, Alex. We surrender much when we take up the battle against our burden. We don't have to surrender it all. Besides, it's become quite plain Our Friends in the See will never give our order the nod, despite their claims of tolerance and cooperation. So, what does it hurt? It makes the other inconveniences a bit easier to tolerate. We don't have to be miserable while we seek salvation, even if our discipline takes its toll."

Given the vampiric tendency of gravitating toward excess, Alex thought Aguirre's sect might have just started down a slippery slope. He kept his own counsel. It wasn't his problem.

They entered the residential building. Alex was thankful there was more light here, and they quickly reached Aguirre's small room.

"Cell" was the word that came immediately to Alex's mind. Faith was a wondrous and terrible thing. Here was a vampire who had once been a conquistador, who had taken part in violence on a grand scale, and then stood against the might of mother Spain. Yet now he was more than content to dwell in this tiny spartan room, with nothing more than a single bed, a small desk, a wall locker, and a crucifix for decoration. A Bible, a rosary, and a laptop lay on the desk. Aguirre closed the door, crossed the room, and sat on the bed. He motioned to Alex to sit in the chair.

Once Alex sat and made himself comfortable, they paused in a brief silence, as neither could decide where to start.

Aguirre finally spoke. "You're the guest, Alex, you first."

23

9:42 A.M.

Alex briefed Aguirre on the Abzu club and their encounters of the previous night. He told him Marcus suspected that someone in the club had recognized him, and that the Ancient believed to be in the city was somehow associated with it. He also told him of this morning's murders, the vampiric response to Abraham's attack.

"Yes," Aguirre answered, "We've heard of this last news. It is deeply troubling. What I find more troubling, Alex, is that we've heard no advance word of this. None. I had not heard anything even hinting at nocturns striking back at humans. The consensus in the nocturn community was that Abraham was a lone psycho, a serial killer that the authorities were doing everything within their ability to apprehend. This retaliation, from our point of view, comes unexpectedly. It could undo much of the good that has come about. It seeks to increase the divide between the human and the nocturn communities."

"Yeah, kind of dovetails nicely with Abraham's manifesto calling for a race war, don't you think?"

Aguirre was distant. It was clear to Alex that he was thinking of something else.

"Lopé?"

"Yes. Well, the whole thing is beginning to sound very orchestrated. From what we know of Abraham, there has always been a possibility that he was not a lone killer, but actually a group of individuals. Could we be talking about the same group?"

"I don't know if I buy that. You mean nocturns pretending to be serial killers and then taking reprisals against themselves?"

"No, I mean it could be humans playing both parts."

"That's even less likely."

"Don't be too sure. It would not be the first time such an event was engineered to bring about a larger conflagration. However, I understand your hesitation. Our survey data shows that nocturns and humans are finally beginning to accept each other for whom and what they are and are working with one another to the mutual benefit of both."

"Maybe on the surface. You're not out there. It's getting worse in my opinion. *The Standard Bearer* didn't print Abraham's manifesto out of the kindness of its heart. The publishers know that kind of message resonates with a lot of people. It has an audience, and judging by its increase in circulation since it ran, a damned big one."

"You have a point." Aguirre's thoughts were elsewhere again.

"What are you thinking?"

"Oh, a number of things. First, consider your theory that Abraham is a nocturn, or group of nocturns."

"Not my theory."

"Beside the point. It does explain a great many things."

"Do tell?"

"Just to start. It explains how one lone serial killer could overpower and kill a vampire."

"Most of his victims were youngbloods. But yeah, you're right, there were a couple of older ones. Last night, he took down a whole blood club, sangers, bleeders, everyone. Hard to believe that's the work of one dedicated individual."

"Marcus could do it. Or you."

"That's giving us a lot of credit, and do you really see an Ancient taking the time out of his busy schedule to hit a rival blood club?

I don't. He'd be much more likely to frequent the establishment and try to buy it out."

"True. Yet we know Abraham is powerful. Many consider him responsible for the death of Lelith's predecessor at the Lightbearers."

"There's no evidence to support that. I don't know all the specifics, but I'm pretty sure that aside from Abraham's own empty boastings, there's nothing to tie him to that."

"Yes, well, something to consider."

"Something else is bothering you. Why didn't you want to talk until we were out of earshot of everyone else?"

"That subject is something else entirely. I will tell you in a moment. But there is something else I find troubling with your information."

"Go."

"Your informant, you said he was trafficking in human meat."

"Yeah, freezers full. You have any idea what it's for?"

"Unfortunately, I might. Your informant said it was for 'the Pact'?"

"Yeah. Does that mean anything to you?"

"Could he have said 'the Pack'?"

"Sure, the guy was blubbering and about to blow his own head off. Why? Does that mean something?"

Aguirre shrugged. "There have always been rumors of a secret organization of therianthropes. It was doubly hidden, both because of the stigma attached to therianthropy and because of its practices. We never discovered their identities, nor could we confirm they actually ever existed, but there were some among us who never doubted their presence."

"You're talking something more substantial than a support group for folks suffering from the Curse, I take it."

"Most certainly. Members of this group were rumored to take part in certain rituals. During these rituals, they would be encouraged to embrace their beastly natures, to commune with the monsters within, and try to mend their fractured natures into one. The culminating act of these rituals was that of consuming human flesh."

"The same could be said for your—"

Aguirre's eyes flared. "Watch your blasphemy, Menkaure!"

Alex laughed. "I'm sorry, but when you've been the Morning and Evening star, it's a little hard to take these things seriously. I used to be a god once, you know."

"But now you know better, right?"

"Now? I'm not so sure I'm not. Given what I've done, what I've endured. Perhaps it is the priests, such as yourself, who are to blame by overselling what a god can do."

Aguirre threw up his hands. "You are the proof, Menkaure."

"Hardly. I've conversed with the foulest denizens of this plane and worse—"

"You were deceived."

"And that absolves me?" Menkaure asked.

"Though I wear the vestments of a priest, if it is absolution you seek, you've come to the wrong place."

Menkaure sat quietly for a moment, then continued. "I'm so very tired. It weighs upon me, this existence. This life without living."

"You wish you could find her and be done with it?"

"Neithikret? Aye. Some days, when I see what has become of the world, I'm not entirely sure she was wrong. Maybe I was simply unlucky to have gotten in her way."

The two unlikely beings, the immortal pharaoh and the conquistador-cum-priest vampire sat for a few minutes in silence.

Aguirre broke it. "Are you through feeling sorry for yourself?"

"Yeah. I guess. What were we talking about?"

"The Pack eating human flesh. In any case, I am not speaking metaphorically. They did it literally. The point of such rituals was to allow them to control their dual natures, to allow them to control the change. Their human aspect would become more animalistic and the animal would become more human. You may have stumbled onto them."

"You just said you weren't even sure they existed. That it was all rumors and speculation."

"Yes, but you act as if you've never heard this before."

"I haven't. I thought all the thropes were loners by default. The only time they get together is in support groups. The only secret groups I knew about were before the Reveal, and UMBRA used to keep tabs on them. To make sure they were medicated or put them down if they got out of hand."

Aguirre's laugh was sharp and incredulous.

Alex continued in surprise, "So you're saying they're something else."

"Most assuredly."

"But you don't know anything about it."

"I've told you what I can. Have you never heard of the Luperci?"

"No. I mean, I can figure out it has something to do with wolves, but I can't say it's ringing any bells."

"And the festival of the Lupercalia?"

"Look, I haven't been up and about forever and a day like you. Just spill it, okay?"

Aguirre looked uncomfortable.

"Lopé. Seriously. Does Marcus know about this?"

Aguirre chuckled. It was the kind of "I know something you don't" chuckle that pissed Alex off.

"Marcus was a knight commander in the Order of Malta. That's all I'll say. And honestly, it is such a better story coming from a Roman."

"So what I'm hearing is there's no way he wouldn't know about this, but he didn't say anything last night. You damned vampires and your secrets." Alex got to his feet.

"Alex, wait."

"Why?"

"I've heard your side of things. You have yet to hear mine. Sit back down, Alex. It's worse than you think."

24

❈

Alex sat down.

"We've had numerous incidents with nocturns entering a blood-frenzied state after consuming what they thought were artificial blood products. We all believed that it was some new effort to smuggle bootleg blood supplies disguised as legitimate Hemo-Synth blood products. It happens with alcohol, cigarettes, almost everything there is a demand for. The quality of the counterfeits is always lacking and the producers are somewhat more compromising in their selection of ingredients.

"With any other product, there would be public notices, product recalls. The FDA would be out there reassuring the public that there was nothing to worry about. Why not this time?"

"The answer is pretty obvious, Lopé. Folks would panic, both humans and vampires."

"Have you given much thought, Alex, as to exactly what would happen if someone were to deliberately tamper with the supply of synthetic-blood products in this city? In this country?"

Alex sucked in a breath.

Aguirre continued, "It is something I consider every single day. I've carved myself a nice little niche here. I'd like to believe I'm somewhat self-sufficient. I can even pray to the good Lord under the sun and I can light the church the way it should be. I'm self-sufficient but for one thing, the truckloads of synthetic blood that arrive here on a weekly basis and allow us to survive.

"Those followers out there, you understand we must sequester them from all human contact. Temptation is the first tool of the Adversary after all. But no matter how strong our faith, our true nature always intervenes."

"The blood is the life," Alex added.

"Yes, the blood is the life. Do you know this is not the first time I've tried this scheme? I'm not even the first to try it. Others tried to make similar religious orders of like-minded nocturns—during the Reformation, the Great Schism, after the Inquisition, and here, in the New World. We swore oaths, gave offerings, and prayed. We all forswore the taking of human life and consumed only animal blood. It was so hard, Alex. I cannot even convey. Our nature drives us back to making humans our prey. Some think that is proof of our damnation, that God has forsaken us. Myself, I see it as a test of faith. Animal blood allows us to survive, but not to live. After a time, years, decades of torture, it wasn't enough—it isn't enough. Every single one of us relapsed and reneged on our promises, broke our vows, and fell again."

Aguirre opened the wall locker and took out a small bottle of Sangri. He tossed it to Alex.

"Untainted, that is literally a Godsend to us, Alex. There's something in the key ingredient, in the A-PFC4, that helps us to suppress the urges, allows us to get by on Hemo-Synth. The craving for human blood is still there; but we can manage it through discipline and faith. I can tell you that on the good days, I hardly notice it at all."

"So where are you going with this?"

"Just reminding you how the entire balance of the new world, the world as it is now, relies on the product within these little bottles. My sect actively tries to avoid taking human life. Other nocturns, the real *vampires*, won't be so discriminating should anything happen to this supply."

"Yeah, and the FDA knows this. They keep a pretty tight control on the production of all synthetic-blood products."

"Bear with me." Aguirre put his hands out, imploring Alex's patience. "As you can guess, the FDA is not the only organization closely monitoring the status and supply of synthetic-blood consumables. Blood clubs are no secret. While they are enough for nocturns, there are always our darker kin, the true vampires, who want no part in the consensual process. They loved the chase and the hunt, the rape, and the kill. It is they who love the thrill and taste of fear. What you uncovered last night was a form of fear-blood factory. I can be sure of that much from your description. But I've never heard of one that large or run by humans."

"It's some powerful stuff. I saw the effect it had on Constance, Marcus, and Zorzi."

"Yet Constance had the harder time of it. Marcus and Zorzi are seducers. They don't take pleasure in the thrill of the chase, in the kill. Constance, well, without disclosing too much, once, she was a true vampire. It wouldn't be hard for her to slip back to her old ways."

And now she's the one we're supposed to trust as a buffer to Lelith?

"That stuff, the fear blood, it's some kind of gourmet stuff to you guys. I figure, some elitist clients are paying top dollar for it. The blood trade isn't that different from the drug trade, Lopé."

"But what if it is?"

"What do you mean? We knew about the new blood stock, that's why we were leaning on Filip. We figured he knew something. Turns out he was right in the middle of it."

"Assume for a moment, Alex, that Filip wasn't selling his stock to many customers, as you would expect in your 'drug dealer' model. What if he was selling it to just one?"

"What do you know? Come on and cut the crap. Make your point." Damn him, Aguirre loved his riddles and mysteries.

"We're still putting pieces of the puzzle together. What we know is that there is a very small clientele for this fear blood. Perhaps even just a single client. Even more curious, we think that those random bottles that showed up on store shelves and resulted in blood-frenzy incidents were not random at all."

"So they were a screen to lower suspicion on something else? That makes sense if you're trying to hide a deliberate murder—"

Aguirre interrupted, "Or test a product. Your department tested the blood, yes?"

"Yeah, but I haven't heard the results beyond that it wasn't pure human stock and it had a high adrenal content."

"They need to test it for a form of methamphetamine. It's in small amounts, but you must remember nocturn physiology is significantly different from human."

"Meth? You're kidding."

"I wish I were, Alex. We suspect the high adrenal content of the fear blood masks the different taste or simply makes the nocturn victim ignore it. The methamphetamine boosts the euphoric effect of feeding on the fear blood, ten-, maybe a hundredfold."

"So this is a hell of a recreational drug. It's going to put the blood clubs out of business."

"No, Alex. Any nocturn who drinks this would experience euphoria initially, but then they would lose all control. The need to glut themselves on blood would overcome any rational thought."

"And bam! You've got blood frenzy." Alex sighed, as if they needed more shit right now. "Do you have any proof?"

"You are holding it, Alex."

Alex stared in shock at the bottle of Sangri in his hand. He was momentarily at a loss for words.

"What? How?"

"We have operatives throughout the city. This particular bottle was retrieved for us at great risk from the Lightbearer Society's new headquarters."

"Haley House?"

"It is secluded, and is known for secret passages, caches, and bolt-holes. It even has a distillery and winemaking equipment left over from the Prohibition days and the Haleys' aborted foray as vintners. We suspect the Lightbearers are using that equipment for making these illicit and very dangerous blood products. We suspect Lelith is serving a new master. We know he's there, but he is keeping his identity closely guarded."

"Any idea why they're doing any of this? Why didn't you tell Marcus about this before?"

"Well, primarily because we did not know about it when I last spoke to Marcus. That might have been for the best. We suspect that the other Ancient in the city is more than likely behind this. Everything is circumstantial. You know how territorial our kind can get and that increases with time. Marcus might have tried something on his own and played our hand too soon."

"Like we did last night. We might have screwed up your entire op."

"I do not think so. Our source brought this to us last night. Not long after Marcus departed as a matter of fact."

"And you were just tending your garden, without a care in the world. You've got ice in your veins, you know that?"

"I have a responsibility to my flock. I cannot give them any impression that something may be wrong. You have no idea how close some of them are to relapse. If they lost confidence in the Hemo-Synth, they would lose all hope. Besides, there is very little a humble priest can do against such forces."

"Secrets and more secrets. Okay. Who's your source? I need to talk to him."

"I'm afraid that's quite out of the question. That individual has already taken a tremendous risk."

"Damn it, Lopé, no one's going to go for this. I just turn up with a bottle of tainted Sangri and we're supposed to go kick in doors at Haley House and take down the Lightbearer Society? Do you know how many power players Lelith is in bed with? Figuratively, if not literally. That's not going to happen. Even if she didn't have her talons sunk into every major politician, it's not going to happen. I need to worry about due process, warrants. There are rules now."

"Are there? All that is necessary for evil to triumph is that good men do nothing."

Alex shook his head at the situation. "Don't lecture me. You can't play me like some damned asset and throw a guilt trip my way. You can't just wash your hands of this. This isn't my problem. What about when one of your people guzzles down a pint of this shit?"

"We're screening all the product that comes in here. Now that we know what we're looking for. The real danger lies out there. There is some hope we may have discovered the plot before its completion. There haven't been widespread incidents. Perhaps they don't have enough to do what they want. They might be stockpiling it until they can put enough out there that it would overwhelm any human capability to counter its effects. It is literally in your hands now, Alex."

"Thanks for that." Alex reflected on potential options; all of them were dreadful. He'd wasted enough time here. He needed to get back.

"Do you have any idea what they're trying to pull off here?"

Aguirre shook his head. "We've been trying to figure out the angles on this. I've got nothing concrete. They don't trust our asset enough to let them in on whatever the big picture is. I don't need to lecture you on vampires and their secrets. There are some pet theories floating around out there. My personal favorite is that we're witnessing a power player trying to make a bid to corner the artificial-blood market. Causing incidents that would sow distrust about competing products? And then when the time is right, they can release their own 'guaranteed' safe product. There's millions of dollars at stake there. That makes the most sense to me. But there are some who think it might be some kind of pseudoterrorist false flag, engineered so the Lightbearers can gather more power. We just don't know."

"Well, that's comforting."

"You will figure something out, Alex."

"And what if I don't?"

"I have faith in you." Aguirre opened a drawer in the desk and took out a small silver crucifix about the size of his palm. He handed it to Alex.

Alex looked at it incredulously, "You're joking, right?"

"God has faith in you to do the right thing. Do not spurn His aid."

Alex sighed and put the crucifix in his pocket. This was no time to get into a debate on theology. Aguirre wasn't one of his favorite people right now.

"Faith will always prove useful."

"I'll walk myself out."

25

✤

Ma'at. It meant a myriad of things in Old Kemeti. Truth, Balance, Justice, Morality, Law, Harmony, Order. It was the latter that Menkaure now craved the most. He drove as quickly as he could back to the Nocturn Affairs Section. The tainted bottle of Sangri rattled gently in the center console as he wove through traffic. As Aguirre's information sank in, he allowed his thoughts to stray, the better to let his subconscious digest the new data. Once again, things were changing too quickly.

Since he'd awoken in the mid-1800s, it seemed *Ma'at* was constantly in short supply. The world had given itself over to *Ma'at's* ideological counterpart, *Isfet.* Chaos. Certainly, the last century had been proof of that much. Destruction on a scale previously unimagined formed a new order of its own. This century didn't seem to be headed on a much better course. Volatility, uncertainty . . . change was now the new status quo. How anyone expected to bring stability to a nation when the government changed more often than Menkaure's own had conducted cattle counts was beyond him. It was something he'd never grown to accept about the new order of things. Power to the people. But when had the people known anything about power?

He thirsted for stability; but he wasn't likely to get any. Constant change appeared to be the one thing he could count on not to vary.

And now he couldn't easily shrug off what he'd seen in Aguirre's church. Vampires with souls. It bothered him and drove his thoughts to consider the state of his own spirit.

The dispatch radio squawked something he knew he should be concerned with. He ignored it.

How would his heart fare now, balanced on the scale against the feather of truth? How many of the Forty-two Declarations could he honestly cite without betraying himself?

Well, he hadn't stolen any cultivated land yet. So that was at least one out of forty-two.

The radio squawked again, this time calling him by name. "Detective Romer, Nocturn Affairs assistance required at the Ponces."

Roberts must've told someone he was the only NA guy out and about. "The Ponces" was the name of a luxury rental apartment complex in Coral Gables. Alex was just a few minutes away.

He needed to get the Sangri to the lab. He needed to brief Roberts on what Aguirre had told him. He didn't need to be chasing what was likely to be another crap call.

In spite of his better judgment, he reached for the radio handset. "Romer. Passing U. of M. now. I'll be there in about five. Out."

He pulled up to a group of beige apartment buildings laid out like a campus. Two large towers that looked like they'd been designed by a Frank Lloyd Wright protégé dominated the property. Fountains blasted clear water high into the air amid immaculate tropical landscaping.

Alex stepped out of the SUV and into a cool mist that spread from the fountains. He had to admit it felt magnificent and helped take the edge off the heat. The whole place felt more like a resort than an apartment building.

A uniformed officer, who'd been waiting, jogged up to him. "Detective Romer?"

Something was off. The man was entirely too calm given the call for Nocturn Affairs support.

"Yeah."

"You're Nocturn Affairs, right?"

"Yeah."

"Good. She's through here." The officer hardly waited to see if Alex was following him and stepped off toward the lobby of the nearer tower.

Alex quickened his pace to catch up.

"What exactly are we dealing with?"

"Homicide. But we don't know if she's one of yours or not. We've got a bus on the way, but figured we could use you to take a look-see. I mean, if she's one of yours she might not be dead, right?" The man gave off a nervous laugh.

"Yeah." That explained the lack of tension. A dead vampire, or even one mostly dead, didn't engender the circus-sideshow atmosphere of a vampire on a blood frenzy. Still, someone had managed to take down a vampire?

They crossed into the lobby, and the lavish decor momentarily pulled Alex's thoughts away from the scene. A homicide in these surroundings felt utterly incongruous, and the decor made Alex's own condos appear squalid by comparison.

"Hey, how much do you figure the rent is in this place?" Alex asked.

"I heard it's like three grand or so."

"Seriously? A month? Damn."

Alex needed to step up his game if he was going to stay in the real-estate market. Then again, he only rented out the rest of his building because he didn't have a use for all the extra space.

They stepped from the lobby into an inner courtyard with a large swimming pool. Patio furniture and lounge chairs peppered the pool's surroundings, and there was a large community bar, which was currently closed. Another uniformed officer faced a small crowd.

The first officer continued, "I swear, I've vacationed in worse places."

"Heard that," Alex said.

"Enrique," the officer called out to his partner, "Nocturn Affairs is here. You get anything?"

The other officer, Enrique, stepped away from the crowd and toward them. "Nah. You know how it is. Nobody saw nothing."

"Who called it in?" Alex asked.

"Anonymous."

"She's over here." The first officer led Alex to the covered body.

Alex pulled on some gloves from his pocket and knelt next to the body. He pulled back the sheet.

"Ah. She's just a kid."

A young woman lay beneath the sheet. She had black hair, and wore goth-style makeup and a stereotypical Wannabe outfit, probably from Hot Topic. Her skin was pale enough that he knew she hadn't been out here sunbathing. If she was a day over twenty, Alex was going to lose a bet. A wooden stake jutted up from her chest.

She was no vampire. But he went through the motions for the other officers' sakes. Checking the length of her canine teeth, looking at her eyes. Rigor hadn't even begun to set in yet. That couldn't be right.

"She's a sap all right. Not one of ours. When did this happen?" Alex asked.

"We caught it about an hour back," Enrique said.

"Wait, so you're telling me that residents of this fine establishment brought her out here in broad daylight and yet were still so convinced that she was a vampire they staked her down and killed her?"

"Looks like. Maybe a reprisal for the family thing this morning? Maybe tied in to Abraham?"

Alex scarcely heard what the young man said. "Then this city is fucked."

"You said it."

Alex felt the anger rising within him. "And nobody heard or saw anything? That's horseshit." He stood and raised his voice so he could be sure that everyone in the crowd, and anyone else who might be watching, heard him.

"We're gonna want heads on this one. We're gonna have people up in here tomorrow. And the day after that. And the day after that. We're gonna be in everyone's shit twenty-four/seven until someone says something. Someone saw. Someone knows. And if I have to come back and personally burn this shithole to the ground myself, we're going to get answers."

He had to get the Sangri in and brief Roberts now more than ever. If citizens were beginning to rationalize behavior like this, there was no telling what would happen when the sun went down. He snapped the gloves off his hands and headed for the lobby.

"Hey, where are you going?"

"To try and get ahead of things for a change. And hopefully to keep incidents like this from becoming the norm."

26

Alex barreled into the squad room expecting a hive of activity; instead, a tomb-like atmosphere greeted him. Even though this was the Nocturn Affairs Section and they did most of their work by night, there was usually something happening during the day, someone typing up a report, following up on a lead, something. He knew Roberts was here.

"Captain Roberts?"

No answer. Alex went over to the office and saw Vince Roberts on the telephone, jotting down notes. Roberts looked up, saw Alex, and waved him into the office. Alex walked in and sat down.

"Yeah, I understand. I don't know what to tell you, most of my unit is out. Listen, one of my best guys just walked in. I'll send him down ASAP. Okay. Good luck to you to." Roberts hung up the phone and took a deep breath, then looked up at Alex.

"Okay, so what the hell's so important you can't talk about it over the phone?"

Alex thumped the tainted bottle of Sangri on the captain's desk. "Someone's cutting Hemo-Synth with meth. That's what's making the sangers go all bugshit."

"A new drug?"

"That's what I thought. My source says that it wouldn't work like a drug. At least not the kind anyone would consciously take. Any vampire that has a sip of that stuff will go loco and blood-frenzy inside ten minutes."

"So the stuff on the shelves, not accidental I take it."

"Naw, figure it for a test run of something bigger."

"Shit." Roberts ran a hand through his thinning hair. He looked like he'd aged years since yesterday. "Today of all days. Damn."

"Yeah, it gets better. Last night Marcus and I found a new upscale blood club called Abzu in an industrial park."

"Before or after the chamber of horrors."

"Before. We didn't get a chance to follow up on it thanks to the rest of the fun last night."

Roberts nodded and gave Alex a "get on with it" face.

"Marcus went. I didn't. He got made. When he came out he said he saw pallets full of Hemo-Synth products down there. Now, we don't know if it's this bad stuff here. But I'm thinking probable cause, right?"

"So what do you want?"

"We need to get in there. With this new intel, we shouldn't wait till nightfall. We should go now, catch 'em with their pants down. Get me a warrant and cut loose whoever you can spare."

"First off, we can't spare anyone. The city's tearing itself apart. That's why no one is here. There's rioting outside gun stores and anti-vampire lynch mobs running around."

"Yeah, I just came from a scene over at the Ponces. Not an hour ago, some poor goth girl got pulled out of her apartment and staked by her neighbors, because they thought she was a vampire. She wasn't. Just give me—"

"I'm not done. You've been out this whole damn morning so you're in the dark. You haven't got a clue what's going on. So at least let me fill you in."

Alex made a face but leaned back in the chair.

"Secondly, we're not sending a bunch of humans to raid a known nocturn establishment without nocturn aid. It is bad politically and it's damn near suicide."

Alex opened his mouth to protest, but the captain was ahead of him.

"I know you think you can handle yourself. But you wouldn't be the only one there. Besides, the DA's office is in bed with the Light-bearer Society. We know this because this squad wouldn't exist without a lot of deal making and substantial campaign contributions to various politicians. Hell, that woman Lelith is down there at least once a week and they're thinking about giving her a chair on the city council. The second we even ask for a warrant they'd be tipped off."

"So what? We hit 'em during the day, they still can't move the stuff."

The captain's phone rang. He put the line on hold without looking.

"You're assuming they don't have humans working in their organization. If they're cutting that stuff with meth, they could be involved with anybody. Or do you think they're cooking it themselves?"

Alex started to answer, then thought about the torture room with the fear blood and the men who had threatened him at his building that morning. "Yeah. Okay."

"This whole conversation is moot anyway."

"Why is that?"

"You know that attack this morning? The family thing?"

"Tell me you caught the guys."

"Already? That would be a good day. Does it look like we're having a good day?"

Alex made a face again.

"Abraham turned himself in. That would be a good day, too, right? Except at last count, we have more than a dozen Abrahams who turned themselves in. More who we've gotten tips on. City Hall wants us to follow up on each one. Every whackjob who's ever read an article on him is showing up with a claim. It's like the Zodiac

Killer times ten. They're routing everyone to the Doral facility, yeah, even normal saps, where we get to interview these kooks. Trouble is, somewhere in there, we might actually have the real article."

The Doral facility was a segregated holding facility on the west side of the greater Miami area. It had been constructed shortly after the Reveal, so that any apprehended thropes or vampires wouldn't have to go through the system with humans. Since vampires seldom got caught and thropes were even more rarely taken alive, the facility didn't see much use.

"Come on, you really think he'd turn himself in? That doesn't fit the profile."

"Doesn't matter what we think, the politicians are doing the policework today. In any case, we need someone down there. The only guy we have there is Garza."

"Shit. We have bigger things to do than this."

"No you don't. Not right now. Get down there."

Alex stood up. He could see that all the lines on the captain's phone were blinking. He picked up the bottle of Sangri.

"What are you going to do with that?"

"Taking it to the lab."

"I'll take it. You need to get down to Doral. It's already a fucking zoo."

Alex hesitated with the bottle. Then again, if you couldn't trust a guy who hated vampires so much he'd left his terminal wife when she decided to turn instead of die, whom could you trust?

"Have them test it for meth against the other samples we've got."

"What am I, a boot? And I need your source, Alex."

"My source got it from his source. And he won't tell me who that is. Don't bother, I've already barked up that tree. Not happening. You know how vampires are."

The captain nodded. "You're burning daylight and I've got phones to answer."

27

12:55 P.M.

The booking hall at the Doral facility wasn't generally what one would call a hive of activity, since it normally accommodated only vampiric and therianthropic suspects. Today, with the admission of large numbers of human suspects into the small space, it was insane. Even though Roberts had painted a picture of what it was like, Alex was taken aback. Outside the building, a substantial mob had gathered. Word was out that Abraham had turned himself in. Hordes of people had turned out, either to cheer him on, or to curse him. The two camps were close to coming to blows and it was impossible for the handful of officers to control the situation.

Alex couldn't even park near the building. He had to leave the Explorer almost four blocks away and fight his way forward through the crowd. When he reached the frail wooden sawhorse barricade hastily erected around the building's entrance, it was like a tiny sanctuary from the rabble of shouting and slogan-chanting fanatics.

He felt a bit guilty when he showed his badge and looked into the pleading eyes of the much-too-young policeman trying to maintain order. Alex walked past him and told himself everyone had his role to play.

He called the officer over to him and deliberately turned his back to the crowd in a show of bravado. It was risky and dangerous, but he felt he needed to at least to maintain an illusion of confident authority.

"Listen, kid, most of these guys are just talking big, okay? They're not interested in taking on a cop. They aren't ready for that kind of trouble. Don't let them forget that. Don't act in charge, *be* in charge."

The young man nodded, fear still in his eyes.

"Don't forget there's a building full of cops behind you who've all got your back. This crowd turns ugly, it will be uglier for them."

Alex stole one last glance at the chanting and screaming crowd and walked forward into the building, trying to forget about the young patrolman.

Inside the building, there was only one officer at the security desk. Alex showed him his badge. The man didn't speak, but his eyes said everything. Welcome to bedlam.

As Alex walked farther into the building, a cacophony of chaos greeted him: telephones ringing constantly, people shrieking, shouted orders, pandemonium. He crossed into the main room. There were way more civilians here than he expected. The officers inside were almost as badly outnumbered as the ones outside.

He looked around and saw Stephanie Garza vainly trying to fingerprint one of the suspects. The man was resisting fiercely. Stephanie battled with the man's cuffed hands but made no progress. The man had about as much a chance of being the real Abraham as Alex did. Alex pushed his way over to them.

He put his hand on the back of the suspect's shoulder, in an "I'm your pal" kind of way.

"Is this Abraham?" Alex asked Stephanie. The detective looked like a wreck.

The man interrupted, "I'm the only real one! These other people are liars!"

"It's been like this all morning," Stephanie said.

"Okay, Abraham, why'd you turn yourself in?"

"Someone has to save those families from those bastards."

"Yeah, we've got a real martyr here."

"Okay, Abraham, we've got to fingerprint and process you or those bastards aren't going to believe you turned yourself in. Understand?"

Some measure of comprehension seemed to show in the man's crazed eyes.

"Yeah. I get it."

"Right, so the faster Detective Garza can get you processed, the faster we can get the word out, and the killing can stop. So please cooperate."

The man turned to Stephanie, and his entire demeanor changed. He was docile and helpful. Stephanie continued printing him.

"What's the deal? I thought there were about a dozen?"

"About two hours ago. I lost count somewhere around twenty." Stephanie had bags under her eyes. She looked like she could use about a week's worth of sleep.

"Bet you wish you'd stayed in Narcotics, huh?" Alex tried to lighten the mood.

"What's the secret? You look like you've just come off vacation."

"That's easy. I never sleep."

Stephanie laughed. "Convenient."

Another voice interrupted, "Holy shit! Alex!"

Alex whirled at the sound of his name and instantly recognized his old friend. "Trent? They've got you in this mess?"

"Yeah, I got roped in." The man, a six-footer built like a lineman, thumbed the ID badge clipped to his suit's lapel. The letters across the top spelled out FBI.

"You're with the feds now?" Alex was quite surprised. Trent had been let go when the administration dissolved UMBRA, and he had been bitter. Alex had been sure he would never see him back doing government work. Then again, Alex had thought the same thing about himself.

"Yeah, they've got me consulting on nocturn behavior and psychology."

"Nice."

"There's only two of us on the ground so far. We got in this morning, right in the middle of this shitstorm. The rest of the team is flying in piecemeal. Figured I'd lend a hand."

"Mighty fine of you." Turning to Stephanie, Alex asked, "Where can I make myself useful?"

Stephanie answered, "Just grab a desk, the crazies just seem to find you."

"I'm not crazy!" the man he was still fingerprinting hollered.

"She meant the other crazies," Alex answered.

"I'm going to be heading out to follow up on tips. You wanna come with?"

"Sorry, Trent, I've already been running all over the city this morning. I don't feel like chasing my tail."

"You're missing out. We might get lucky."

"I'll pass. If I catch anything, you feds will steal all the glory anyway."

"Well, that's what we do." Trent walked away laughing.

28

4:35 P.M.

Rhuna bounded back up the steps into the apartment. Three more trips, maybe two, and she'd be finished with her part. She stood to one side as Arthur moved down past her, his arms holding a suit-case and a plastic bag of groceries.

"We can buy more food."

"No sense in letting it go to waste."

She shook her head. The haul of cash they'd taken from the blood club would see them well provisioned for months, if not longer. There was no need to be frugal. The blood-club op had been a gratifying success. As Molony's life had leached away from him and he'd grown progressively more desperate, he'd spilled his guts and given them a wealth of actionable intelligence. Whether or not it was all accurate was still in question. But not whether Molony thought it was. Rhuna was sure that Molony had died believing he was telling the truth.

She walked into the apartment and ran into John. He gave her playful pinch on her waist. She jumped away.

"Ow!"

"Stop horsing around," Roeland interrupted, his tone serious. He was still angry with Rhuna for Molony dying earlier than he should have. Like it was her fault.

"What do you have left?"

"Nothing," John said. He held up a small gym bag. "This is it."

"Just a couple of things in the room," Rhuna said.

Fifteen minutes earlier, Diana had called Roeland. She was frantic and said that Tom had gone missing. She'd already been looking for him for hours. Vampires could not have gotten to him in broad daylight, but they did have human thralls. They'd been getting ready to go help her when Roeland received a code-word text from Diana's phone. It was a preestablished code to warn him that she was being coerced. Almost immediately afterward, Roeland's phone rang again, but that time, he didn't bother answering it and left it on the kitchen table.

That had been five minutes ago.

"Good. We leave in five. John, go help Arthur." Roeland waited until John had left and closed the door.

"Rhuna, a word."

"Look, if it's about me and John, we don't have time for this—"

"It's not. You and I both know that with Molony's information we could take down the Lightbearers' operation at Haley House. But we four aren't going to be able to do that alone. What help can we—"

"—expect from my people? None. I told you that when we started. I'm it. I'm all the help you're going to get. Just me being with you makes them uneasy. The Pack's Conclave doesn't . . ."

There was something outside. Arthur was having some kind of coughing fit. Rhuna knew a fake cough when she heard it.

Roeland reacted. "What is it?"

"Someone's outside."

"Shit!"

Rhuna peered around him.

John was on his knees, his hands over his head. There was no sign of Arthur.

"Someone's coming up the stairs. A lot of someones," Rhuna said.

Roeland drew his pistol from his holster.

Rhuna smiled and let the beast awaken within her. Immediately she felt stronger, her senses sharpened, fingers extending into talons.

Roeland peeked out the window again. He gasped.

"The FBI?" He backed away from the window and tossed the pistol onto the kitchen table.

"Okay, we stick to the plan. They don't know who you are, I'm the only one they're after."

"It could be a trick." It was harder to talk now; her teeth were getting in the way. The power of the beast was coming to the fore, ravenous and raging, hungry for carnage.

Roeland stared at her.

"No, Rhuna."

Then he did the dumbest bravest thing she'd ever seen. He charged her and wrapped her in a tight hug.

"They'll kill you. They. Will. Kill. You." He wrestled with her.

She forced the beast back with a terrible effort, just as the door-jamb exploded in a storm of splinters and the entry team burst into the room.

29

Alex did a double take at his watch. The last five hours had flown by. They'd had a steady stream of "Abraham" pretenders and a good amount of normal riffraff to be processed. As the day wound on and Central Booking became overwhelmed, some genius up the chain had decided to use Doral as the hot backup. Numerous rioters, looters, and ersatz vampire vigilantes were brought in. The arresting officers barely had time to drop off the offenders and record their offenses before the city needed them back on the streets to continue trying to control the mayhem.

He'd gone outside two hours earlier to catch some sun and recharge. In contrast to what he heard coming in from the rest of the city, he'd been glad to see that the crowd outside had thinned. It had calmed down as well. When he'd first arrived, it looked as if it could go full-blown riot. It seemed as if the really fervent polarizing elements of both camps had either left or tired themselves out. The remaining bunch were the looky-loos just wanting to catch a glimpse of the infamous Abraham, or just wanting to be part of the moment.

Alex rubbed his eyes and looked up at the new arrival an officer had just placed in the chair opposite him. This was number what? He'd lost count. They had to be setting a record for crazies today. Alex had processed at least eighteen Abrahams by himself. This was a colossal waste of time. The department had real threats to deal with.

Alex wished the latest man could be a joke. The man looked like he'd just popped out of a Cecil B. DeMille biblical production. Alex sighed and almost dreaded asking the question.

"Name?"

"Abraham, son of Terah."

"Okay, so no surname I take it. Any aliases."

"Avram, I am also called Abram. I am the chosen father of all the Israelites, Edomites, Midianites—"

"Uh-huh. Sorry to be rude, Abraham, but as you can see we're really very busy today . . ." Alex trailed off.

Across the room, he could see that Trent had returned. Trent had a concerned look on his face and was moving with a sense of urgency. He had a large sheaf of papers in his hand and moved one of the officers off his computer so he could input data. Whatever was going on over there was a hell of a lot more important, or at least more interesting, than what was going on here.

". . . from the land of which was mine . . ." The man was still going. Alex realized he had been ignoring him, but the man continued, ". . . to the land of Canaan."

Alex stood up. He saw Stephanie Garza just getting back to the desk where she'd set up camp. She had a cup of coffee in her hand, but looked like she was going to fall asleep on her feet.

"Garza. Can you handle this guy for me?"

Stephanie gave him a terrible look.

"Something's come up."

"Abraham" began getting agitated. "You do not wish to speak to me?"

"Sure, sure. Detective Garza wants to hear all about it."

Alex walked away and left Stephanie to deal with the man. He crossed the room quickly and reached Trent just as he finished entering whatever information he had into the computer.

"I know that look, Trent, what've you got?"

"Alex. Good. Good. I didn't have to come find you. I'm going to want you in there with me when we talk to these guys. Can you believe it? We might actually have him."

"The real Abraham? No shit? That's awful lucky."

"No luck about it. We were following up on a tip. The tipster has been calling all day repeatedly, but because of all this noise, we hadn't gotten to him yet. He had real detailed knowledge. Might be one of Abraham's own crew getting a guilty conscience. Anyway, we roll up on these guys just as they're finishing loading up a van. Looks like they were about to do the bug-out boogie, right? Hadn't even ID'd ourselves and two of them surrender."

"Just like that?"

"Just like that. I think they knew what was up. Also, I think three of them are just accomplices. Not hard-core enough to be the real deal. But the last guy. Wow. Anyway, what a find. Their van, loaded with countervampire shit. Nothing pro, homemade improvised crap for the most part. But I'll be really surprised if all the evidence we need isn't in there."

"Dropped right in our lap?" Alex's instincts told him something was wrong.

"Hey, don't look a gift horse in the mouth, right?"

"Right."

"Anyway. They fit the profile. They're all European. We got two Brits, a German—he's the real deal, I think—and a woman. Can't pin down her accent though, something Scandinavian, I'd guess. She doesn't talk much. She had this look in her eye like she'd just as soon tear out my throat as talk to me. Strong for her size, too, and not a little bit crazy. Took three agents to subdue her. If I didn't know better, I'd have bet money she was a thrope. But she popped negative. Hoping Interpol or ICE will have their prints on file."

The computer kept churning through the search.

"We're moving them to the interview rooms right now. We need something more concrete as fast as we can get it. That's why I want you in there. I remember how you'd get us stuff from the old days. Figure we should be able to make an announcement to the media before nightfall with any luck. Maybe save some lives. You still got it in you?"

"Sure. But you don't think people will actually believe it? There'll be pundits out there saying that we'll say anything to prevent another family-slaughter video from hitting the Internet. And they'd be right."

"Christ, Alex. Do you ever look at the upside? Who cares if these guys are the real Abraham? We have credible suspects dropped in our laps. We'll put them on parade if we have to. Anything to calm people down. The city's already going nuts. There's no telling what will happen after dark. We've got to get on the same page here."

Just then, the computer beeped with the indication that they had received a hit on one of the suspects.

"Well, look at that, our German friend Roeland Jaap is in the system."

"Lucky us." Alex looked over Trent's shoulder.

Trent was skipping down the profile. "Sealed jacket? What's the deal with that? Oh, this guy used to be law enforcement."

Alex had seen something else. It couldn't be a coincidence, could it?

"He's not German, he's Dutch. *Now* we're on the same page. I think you might be right."

"What? What did you see?" Trent asked.

"Don't you feds read your own profiles?"

30

Roeland Jaap. Alex stared at him through the one-way mirror. Handcuffed and hunched over, he didn't look like a serial killer. Then again, outside of the movies, serial killers didn't really look like serial killers. This guy looked like an accountant. Except his arms gave him away as someone who worked out, a lot. He had a defeated air about him, as if he had known this moment was inevitable and was simply a matter of time.

"How do you want to play this?"

"Well, if he's former law enforcement he's gonna know the tricks. I think we just have to go in straight. If he is our guy he won't get intimidated easily."

Alex nodded. "Any luck with his sealed jacket?"

"Nothing yet. But this has to be our guy, right?"

"There're some signs, but it's still long odds." Alex sighed. "Okay then, might as well get started. The second my partner shows up, I'm bailing. We have cases of our own we're working, you know. Much as I'd like to sit here and help you feds babysit."

"Hey, are far as we're concerned this is still Miami-Dade's. We're here to assist, not to run things."

"Look around. If you're not going to run it, no one will."

Trent didn't say anything.

"We're just wasting time now, right? Let's get in there."

"Your DA wants us to wait. Wants to be here, afraid he'll lawyer up."

Alex gave Trent a knowing look, "I bet the DA wants us to wait. Who's pulling the DA's strings? The Lightbearers want first crack at him. Look at him. He knows he's screwed. He's smart enough to know this will never see the inside of a courtroom. Best case, he cuts a deal, worst case, the vampires get to him before he can. Either way, I'm betting he never lawyers up."

"Okay. If we're betting on the profile, our guy's just begging for someone to listen to his story."

"Let's give him the chance to tell it. I'm not going to sit on my hands waiting for the DA. Sooner we're done with this, the better."

Alex opened the door and put on his most affable demeanor. Trent followed him into the cramped white-walled room. They both sat down. Roeland didn't even look up.

"Hello, Mr. Jaap. Am I saying that right? Do you mind if I call you Roeland? I'm Detective Alex Romer, with Nocturn Affairs, and this is Special Agent Trent Summers with the FBI." Alex engaged him and managed to get him to look up.

"Is there anything I can get you? Something to drink? Eat?"

"No." The man's voice was scarcely a whisper.

"Look, we're all cops here, right? Between us, we're not entirely unsympathetic to your cause." No reaction. Trent looked at Alex.

"Off the record, you caused a mess with your choice of name. I don't even know how many guys we had walking in here claiming to be you. A lot of 'em played up the Old Testament angle. You know, out of the sixty or so crazies turning themselves in, and all the tips that came in, not one picked up on the right angle. How weird is that, huh?"

"I guess people don't read much anymore," Trent added.

Alex picked up a sheet of paper and drew Abraham's symbol. As he drew it, he spoke out the initials that, overlaid on one another, formed the symbol "A. V. H."

He pushed the paper at Roeland.

"Abraham Van Helsing. The greatest fictional vampire hunter ever. Tell me, did you pick that because of your nationality?"

Finally, Roeland looked up. "Fitting, don't you think?" His accent was not as pronounced as Alex expected.

"Yeah. I mean, it's a cinch. Hindsight is twenty-twenty, you know?"

Trent put the folder with the information they had on the table. "What's the deal with the sealed jacket?"

Roeland stared at him blankly.

"Come on, we've got the queries in to Interpol, it's just a matter of time."

"You know, Roeland, you had to know this was coming. I mean, there are only two ways your little crusade was going to end, right? Either we catch you, or the sangers do. I'm thinking you're better off in our hands at the end of the day."

Roeland laughed. "It amounts to the same thing. How long do you think the vampires will let me stay here before they come to dig their claws into me?"

"We're not going to let that happen. They want a piece of you, sure. I mean you killed, what, fifty-six at last count?"

"More."

"Well, the number really doesn't matter at this point, right? In for a dime, in for a dollar."

Roeland laughed again. "You have no idea what you're up against."

"You might be surprised. But why don't you enlighten us?" Alex got no reaction.

Trent decided to try a different tactic. "Okay, if you don't want to talk to us, there are folks talking to your compadres. You might be a hard-ass but I bet this . . ." He made a show of looking at the file. "Rhuna Gallier. She's what, all of twenty-three? She'll crack in no time. I wonder what stories she'll tell."

"Knock yourselves out. They don't know anything. They've got nothing to do with this."

Trent looked at Alex. This wasn't going the way they'd hoped.

Alex decided he'd try one more nice-guy tactic. "Roeland. Say you're right. Say the sangers are going to get to you no matter what we do. There's no point in stonewalling us, right? You're telling us they have nothing to do with any of this. We both know that's bullshit. But if that's the story you want to tell, we have to get in front of this. There's no reason your people have to go down with you. As far as people outside this room need to know, you worked alone."

Trent followed along. "That's right. Those other folks were just helping you load the van or whatever. They're not in the system. The sangers don't need to know about them. We can make up something."

Alex nodded. "We're not trying to bullshit you here. You know just as we do what we need right now is a trophy. Unfortunately for you, you fit that bill gift-wrapped with a bow on your head and we all know it. We bring in the *real* Abraham and no one's going to look too closely at the backstory. And if you're right, and the sangers are going to get to you no matter what, you and I both know it's not going to be pretty. Do you want those other folks, those people that have helped you and been loyal to you, going through that?"

Roeland's eyes flickered very slightly; for a brief instant they lost the defeated look. Alex noticed it.

Trent saw it, too. "You wrote in your manifesto that your family had been killed by vampires. You couldn't save them. You can save Rhuna, John, and Arthur. But you've got to give us something concrete. We've got to be able to convince people beyond a shadow of a doubt that you're the real article. And that you were working alone."

"My manifesto? You people haven't read anything."

"Give us something high-profile. Something you can be easily tied to."

"Do you think you're prepared for the truth? Would you even believe it if you heard it?" Roeland shook his head.

"Try us."

"Do you know that the Lightbearers' leader, Stanislaw Chakalarov, had a change of heart, right before the end?"

"A change of heart from what, Roeland?"

"This whole thing. This charade. They've been planning it for years, decades—if not longer."

"Look, Roeland. We're on a clock here. The longer we're dicking around playing games, the more folks are going to get interested. The more eyes we have on this, the harder it is going to be to tell the story *we* want to tell. Trust me, we want to be able to tell *our* version. Let's stop with the guessing games and riddles and just talk to us."

"Fine." Roeland's voice still sounded skeptical. "As you have said, you are pressed for time. Knowing what I know, I shan't be allowed to speak for long. We'll see how ready you are to hear the truth. Shall I start with Stanislaw Chakalarov?"

"Sure. Start wherever you'd like."

"I didn't kill him."

"Come on. You shouted it with pride in your manifesto."

"Are you ready to hear the truth? Or are you more interested in arguing?"

For the first time, Roeland showed signs that he might lose his cool. Underneath that defeated and depressed façade was still a lot of repressed rage.

"I'm sorry, go on," Trent apologized.

"My background used to be in law enforcement. Two years before the Reveal, vampires killed my family before my eyes. There was nothing I could do. When I tried to warn people, to tell them what had happened, I would see them regard me with that compassionate and knowing look reserved for the delusional. They explained it as a defense mechanism, a weak mind's way of dealing with the stress and the grief. I knew it was not so. I wasted away in an asylum for months.

"I put up a front of sanity, of agreeing with their version of the world, to secure my release. Once out, I started a crusade of my own, but before I could get far, members of the Unit Interventie of the DSI contacted me. They claimed to have an organization within the DSI that tracked and dealt with vampiric groups, like those who had slain my family. It was secret, for obvious reasons."

Trent and Alex locked eyes briefly. So, the Dutch had a special program, too.

"They recruited me and entered me in their training. They taught me the methods I've used. Before I could actually do anything in the field, the vampires staged their great 'Reveal.' Without fanfare, the organization I had been recruited into was dissolved as if it had never existed.

"There were those of us who did not let our guard down. We made contact with one another and formed covert networks throughout Europe. Some of the members convinced themselves they were simply acting as watchdogs. Others of us knew differently. Yet, you must understand, this was before we were completely dedicated to violence. Many of the other members believed that they could deal politically with the vampire situation. In the end, I think we were simply playing into their hands.

"I started a very vocal countervampire group in Amsterdam. In those early days, we received much support. People were still trying to make up their minds. The vampires hardly seemed a threat, as they had not yet made themselves known in large numbers. All that was before Budapest."

"Oh yeah, those riots. I remember that. That was right around the Supreme Court ruling on this side of the pond," Trent said.

"Everything seemed staged to me. Antivampire racists attacking sympathetic vampires in the street. Cameras were placed 'just so' and managed to capture the perfect angles on pivotal moments. They allowed only those holding the extremist positions to speak. Everything seemed geared to enhance discord and polarization. I made my opinion known on several forums for antivampire groups. A few days later, a vampire who confirmed my suspicions contacted me. He wanted to meet in person.

"I feared a trap, but couldn't pass it up. With associates watching my back I went to the meeting anyway. Imagine my surprise when I discovered that my contact was none other than the head of the Lightbearer Society, Mr. Stanislaw Chakalarov. I could scarcely believe what he would tell me."

"Well do tell." Alex's skepticism colored his tone. Roeland glared at him, directed his attention to Trent, and continued.

"He told me that the entire Reveal, the Lightbearer Society, the demonstrations, all of it, had been planned. According to him, the plans had been in place for more than fifty years, but science had not advanced enough to put the key portions in place. Everything depended on the Hemo-Synth products. Until a suitable blood substitute was discovered, the vampires could not make themselves known. They'd had front companies working on a synthetic-blood solution for decades in the name of medical research, but nothing ever worked until a little over two years ago."

"But why did they need to make themselves known? We know that vampires had covert organizations before the Reveal."

"They needed to make themselves known to swell their numbers. Chakalarov told me that for each member of a vampiric group, there were dozens who kept to themselves. You know how secretive they are. By making it unfashionable and impractical to remain secluded, the vampires could greatly increase their organized numbers. That was the purpose of the demonstrations. To force the various camps into organized blocs and to centralize control. You see, once you can get people to commit to an opinion and act on it, even with the minutest act, they become deaf to other points of view. They are too busy shouting their own slogans to hear anything different. Same thing with vampires.

"The most dramatic incident occurred in Budapest. That was

for the vampires' benefit. The footage, which the Lightbearer Society didn't try hard enough to suppress, clearly showed vampires lashing out in self-defense, but only after they had been provoked. If you'll remember, the media outlets followed it with only the most biased and bigoted opinions, directed toward a new generation which had been raised on a steady stream of pro-vampire propaganda. Think of it. Vampires are everywhere, in books, television, film, children's programming, breakfast cereals. The effect was predictable. Soon it became fashionable to blame the human victims of the incident for having provoked a confrontation in the first place."

"You're talking about predictive programming," Trent said.

Roeland nodded. "Countervampiric activity became extremely unpopular. Many of the antivampire groups were driven underground. Indeed, only a week after my initial meeting with Chakalarov, the Dutch government classified my own organization as one engaged in hatemongering and ordered us to disband. We did. Secretly we remained active."

Alex felt he had to interrupt. "Yeah, but that whole countervampire movement being unpopular didn't last too long on the Continent. That's why things are the way they are now."

"You are correct. Their plans did not work to their expected longterm effect in most of mainland Europe. I don't know why. Perhaps many Europeans had too much history with vampires to replace it with the glamour of a few Hollywood films and TV shows. A generation ago, maybe two, vampires were still monsters in Europe. Yet you cannot deny that their tactics worked exceedingly well in this country."

"And Chakalarov felt he needed to spill this all to you—a selfproclaimed vampire hater—out of the kindness of his heart? I'm not buying it."

"I was not the only one he was in contact with. There were others; he called us the seeds of a human resistance. For understandable reasons he kept our identities secret from one another. The true purpose for all this was much darker than anyone supposed. That's what he said. He'd had a change of heart."

Roeland reacted to the look on Alex's and Trent's faces. They were incredulous.

His speech grew more frantic. "These things were not staged to garner support for increased vampire rights or to help their integration into society! Those were certainly side effects beneficial to their cause. But the Reveal was a precursor to a greater conflict. Some kind of race war the vampires are planning. They will use it to upset the established order of things in a bid for global power!"

It was Trent's turn to interrupt. "So every single vampire is in on this?"

"Don't be stupid! Chakalarov said he had been a member of an organization thousands of years old. He called it something . . ." He paused, brows furrowed as he tried to remember.

". . . a confraternity! They had been planning and waiting for just such a moment. When the Hemo-Synth products became a reality, they seized the opportunity and set their plans into motion. Chakalarov himself had been in charge of mustering their propaganda efforts. He had once been one of the advocates of a race war. Once it started, they would turn as many humans as they could. Their numbers would swell exponentially. They would tip the balance of numbers and subdue humanity beneath a vampiric yoke. But he changed his mind when he saw how vampires could in fact adapt and become members of everyday society. When he actually saw humans and vampires living side by side, he reconsidered. He was going to try to stop it. He wasn't alone. There were others. Together they were trying to avert the conflict his own hand had helped set into motion."

"Hold on," Trent said. "You're talking about them mustering some kind of global vampiric takeover, right? If not all the vampires are in on this, they don't have the numbers. In this country, the government reports what, just over a million documented vampires?

A lot of those are youngbloods." Trent looked to Alex for confirmation.

Alex nodded; that jibed with what he knew. Even if estimates were off, the numbers were close.

Trent continued. "I mean how can they start a war? They'd be royally outnumbered. How are they going to get normal vampires who want to live as part of society to take part in this scheme? To start preying on humans? To get all the nocturns to join them, they'd have to somehow reestablish a state of affairs where humans and vampires were again at each other's proverbial throats. And we're not talking a couple of riots inspired by your shenanigans, right? I mean, you've said it yourself. For most folks, vampires are cool now. People know them now, a few threats aren't going to get people, you know, the average Joe, to run out and start staking sangers."

Alex thought about the goth girl this morning and wasn't too sure about Trent's assumptions.

Roeland shook his head. "I don't know."

For the first time since he'd started speaking, Roeland was lying. Alex was sure of it. All the air in the room turned to cement. He started getting a lumpy "oh shit" feeling in his stomach. The tainted Hemo-Synth, the blood frenzies—Alex knew.

In these terms, it was obvious. He glanced at his watch, hoping Marcus would arrive soon. He hoped he'd had the good sense to check the messages Alex had left on his phone.

Trent continued. "That's convenient. I'm telling you, from over here, it doesn't sound good."

"It's the truth!"

"Sounds good to me. Go on," Alex said.

Trent turned to Alex. His face bore a "you're not buying this shit, are you?" look. Alex hoped Trent would think it was part of an interrogation technique and just go with it. Alex was starting to think not only that Roeland Jaap was the real "Abraham," but that he was telling the whole truth and nothing but. This did not bode well.

"Chakalarov was going to get us—me and the other members of what he called the resistance—he was going to get us proof. Something happened. I don't know what. He went months without speaking to us. He was traveling all over the world under the auspices of the Lightbearer Society, so we explained away his lack of contact.

"Then he reached out to me. He actually called me on an open line, breaching our established protocols. He was panicked. Something had happened in their covert organization—in the vampire conspiracy. Chakalarov's faction was losing. He needed to meet with me. I was the nearest one to him at the time. He was going to give me definitive proof of the vampire conspiracy, so that I could pass it on to the appropriate authorities. He told me he would be in touch with the location and that I had to be on the next train to Bosnia. I did as he ordered.

"When I arrived, I received instructions from someone I believed to be Chakalarov to meet him in a churchyard in the dead of night. I felt this was unusual. After our initial contact, we had always met in public places, just after nightfall, so that humans and vampires could mingle without attracting attention. I brought members of my team with me.

"Chakalarov was already dead when we arrived. We saw them staging the scene. They must have heard us. They attacked. I lost two good friends that day. We killed one, maybe more, as we made our escape. The next morning locals discovered Chakalarov's body. There was no evidence of the other bodies or of any proof he was to pass on to me. I wanted to probe into the investigation, to discover what the local police knew. But if there really was a vampiric conspiracy, I could not afford for them to know who I was.

"I wrote an anonymous letter to the local police to tell them what had really occurred. I provided details only an eyewitness would know. I included a code word for anyone wishing to make future contact."

"Let me guess, 'Abraham.'"

"Yes. That is how it began. Except that I read in the press that there had been multiple letters, some claiming responsibility for the murder. I had been lumped in with these. That was not the last time this has happened."

"So this is just a big mix-up?" Trent asked in amazement. "You're innocent. You're not the Nocturn Killer." He was almost laughing.

"I am innocent of Stanislaw Chakalarov's death."

Alex sat in silence, contemplating what he'd just heard. It reminded him of the way they used to run ops during UMBRA. Trent might not have known. Trent was an analyst, not a field man.

"All right. Let's say I believe you. About Chakalarov's murder anyway. We'll see about the rest of it. About the other vampires you've killed, were they just random, or fit to some pattern, or what? 'Cause you know, you've kind of got us stumped there."

"Roughly a month after the murders in Sarajevo, I was contacted by another vampire. Not in person. He called me only once. From then on, we've communicated through a series of dead drops. He was an associate of Chakalarov, a protégé, and that is all he would tell me. He was discontented with how the succession had progressed in the Lightbearer Society. Within the vampiric conspiracy, the faction that wanted a race war, Lelith's faction, had won. They'd purged most of Chakalarov's people. Those lucky enough to still lurk about believed that Chakalarov's mistake had been that he had made himself too visible. This vampire was entirely more cautious. It was his plan to invent the so-called Nocturn Killer, a serial killer that the media would unwittingly bolster. That kind of sensationalism sells papers and ratings. He would feed me the identities of key members of the vampire conspiracy and I would assassinate them. We built up the identity of 'Abraham' so the press would highlight the story and we could capture the public's short attention spans."

"But you did some freelancing, too, right? Like the job last night?" Alex asked.

"Yes."

Trent stayed on the original line of questioning. "You say you were working against the race-war guys. But your manifesto, it seemed to say just the opposite."

"That's what I was trying to tell you earlier. That was not my manifesto. Parts of it were. Parts of it were not."

"Explain."

"I felt the world needed to know what was happening, what the stakes were, everything I'm telling you now. Humans needed to know about the threat they lived with. And I wanted to let the vampires know that they should be afraid. I wrote it all. I sent it to multiple media outlets, I used the identity of Abraham, since by then it was famous. No one would listen to Roeland Jaap. People would listen to Abraham. I had misunderstood the media. No one published it. No one even mentioned it."

"Well, it was published eventually. *The Standard Bearer* picked it up."

"Yes and no. When Arthur brought me the edition, I was furious. Whoever had written this new manifesto had absolutely read mine. Some passages were the same, word for word. But entire new portions had been written. Those were calling for humans to prepare themselves for a race war! The exact opposite of what we wanted."

"You'd been compromised. You had to see that."

"I see it now. How else would you have found us?"

"I agree," Alex said.

There was a loud and insistent rap against the one-way mirror. Both Trent and Alex stood.

"Give us a second, Roeland. We'll be right back."

They walked out and closed the door behind them. Trent was furious. "This guy is spilling his guts, and they interrupt us. Most of it is conspiracy-nut bullshit, but he's talking! This better not be the damned DA."

Marcus walked out of the back room to greet them. Alex looked at his watch. He was stunned to see it was nearly eight o'clock.

"Alex, I received your messages. I agree with you, Aguirre's news is not good."

"Trent, you go back in there. You feds have point on this anyway."

Trent stood puzzled. "Wait, you and Marcus are still partners?"

"Don't read anything into it. It just worked out that way."

Trent laughed. "You really expect me to buy that? Right. Go do whatever you have to do, Alex. I don't need to know. Shit, I don't want to know. Those bastards told me UMBRA was over."

"It is."

"Sure it is." Trent smiled and winked. "Go do what you have to do." He opened the door and went back into the interview room.

"Let me grab my piece and then we can go." Alex headed off down the hall. Marcus matched his pace.

"Wait till I tell you what a shitty day I had. I was cooped up dealing with crazies the whole time and just when it gets interesting you show up."

"I'm sorry to ruin your fun. As you said in the dozen or so messages you left, the situation, at least according to Aguirre, is dire."

Marcus's complexion was flushed. His eyes showed that telltale blood-filled look of having fed. It was a good bet he hadn't been binge-drinking synth blood.

"Yeah, and wait until I tell you what old Abraham back there just told me. By the way, where the hell have you been?"

"With Constance."

"Hitting blood clubs? Do I want to know where?"

"No."

Alex had the good judgment to leave it at that.

31

Alex drove the Explorer toward the industrial park in Wynwood. They planned to meet a few other patrol officers with police cruisers a few blocks from the blood club. On the way, he summed up his discussion with Aguirre.

"I think it's more than strange you didn't mention anything when Filip was going on about the Pack. Might have been a little important?" Alex asked.

"I did not think it was relevant. Besides, Aguirre has his theories and I have mine," Marcus said. "The order has known about the existence of a therianthropic secret society for hundreds of years. Save for only one other organization, it is the one we have the least information on."

"You're saying 'we' again, like you're still in the order."

Signs of unrest and detritus littered the streets. A couch burning on a street corner. A crowd of youths hanging a vampire in effigy from a streetlight. If they were lucky, things wouldn't boil over tonight, but there was no chance that would last until the end of the week.

"A slip of the tongue," Marcus continued as if everything were normal.

"How about you slip it a little more and actually cough up some info? In case you haven't noticed, clock seems to be ticking," Alex said.

"Despite what Aguirre thinks, I don't know very much about them. I always devoted my expertise and knowledge toward other pursuits, for obvious reasons. What I know is that they go by different names, 'the Pack,' 'the Pride,' or other names along those lines, as appropriate. They cannot be infiltrated, again for reasons that are rather obvious. And they are extremely secretive. Occasionally we catch a whiff of their activities, but it's no use diverting our attention and limited resources to try to intercept them. They are elusive. In any case, historically, our paths rarely intersect. I would share more if I knew it, Menkaure, but I believe they are a distraction and are not relevant."

"Have they ever worked in league with vampires before?"

"Not that I know of. You know how vampires react to thropes and vice versa. That would be highly unusual."

Marcus seemed detached. He gazed absently out the window. Alex could tell he had other thoughts on his mind.

"So it's just coincidence that Filip was supplying human meat to some of his customers and fear blood to others?"

"It has to be coincidence," Marcus said. "Perhaps Filip's people were simply being efficient and not letting resources go to waste. If the Pack had discovered the source of their meat, I suspect it would have gone even worse for Filip. Besides, I'm not entirely sure about the use of human meat to stave off the effects of the Curse. Despite what Aguirre believes about such rituals allowing thropes to control their animal selves, there is no evidence to support that. You've seen the UMBRA data and know it as well as I do."

"Yeah, but it's been a while since I looked at that stuff. I had my own problems back then. I still do. I do remember running across reports that the Nazis were trying to get thropes to control themselves or seeing what stressors they could introduce to force the change. I don't think it went into many details."

"Well, regarding the Pack, there are other theories," Marcus said.

Alex stopped the Explorer. The street ahead had turned into a parking lot. He hit the lights and siren for an instant and dodged down a cross street. As he did, he saw the source of the obstruction: A large mob of people had gathered and was blocking off the end of the street. He guessed it was at least several hundred people, but then they were out of sight.

"Are you seeing this?" Alex asked.

Marcus remained silent.

Alex took the hint. Somebody else's problem right now.

"Okay, so what are the other theories?"

"There are some in the order who believe that the members of the Pack represent a different breed of therianthrope. Creatures who are not simply shape-shifters who change on a given cycle, but who can change at will. Some believe they may be an entirely different species, somewhere between animal and man."

"The Luperci," Alex said.

Marcus looked surprised and impressed.

"Where did you learn of this?"

"Aguirre," said Alex, "but he didn't say much more. Said I really needed to hear the details from a Roman, whatever that means."

Marcus laughed. "Aguirre is not without a flair for the dramatic."

"So what's the deal? Who are the Luperci?"

"Historically, as far as the mundane world is concerned, the Luperci were Roman priests that officiated during the festival of the Lupercalia. The name means 'the brothers of the wolf' and the Lupercalia was a festival to celebrate the story of the Lupercal, the cave on which Rome itself was founded."

"Okay, yeah, I'm with you. I remember the story that Romulus and Remus were abandoned and then suckled in a cave by a she-wolf . . . holy shit." Alex let the information sink in. "But that's just a myth, right?"

"As mythical as you and I."

Alex simply sat in silence for a moment.

He still had a feeling Marcus wasn't telling him the whole truth, but for now, this was enough.

"Anything else you need to tell me? I'd like to not run into this club in a few minutes half-cocked and not knowing what the hell is going on."

"I, for one, need to let this other Ancient know he cannot enter my city uninvited and unannounced without repercussions. I may not have my old resources but I still have my pride and reputation."

There it was. Marcus looked out for number one, as all vampires did. So until he settled this business with this Ancient, the Pack and everything else peripheral to it—the case, Roeland Jaap—would take a backseat. Miami could burn and Marcus wouldn't care. Alex shook his head. There were few things as convoluted and frustrating as vampiric politics.

"So anything we can do to disrupt their plans is just a bonus at this point?" Alex asked.

"Not at all," Marcus said. "A race war will not benefit anyone. I have a hard time believing that is the actual goal. Roeland Jaap, for the few minutes I observed him, did not make a positive impression."

"Yeah, he's a nutjob. But, what if he is telling the truth? His story is so nuts it's likely to be true. You have to admit, we've heard stranger."

Marcus considered the point.

Alex refocused the conversation on the current situation. "I'm guessing going in there won't be a pleasant experience, so I brought some stuff from the old days. Insurance."

"Oh? I wasn't aware you'd kept any of it."

"I've got some flash-bangs, some Mace—the good stuff you don't like, not the crap we're using now—and I brought along a Rubicon case."

Marcus almost choked. "Rubicon! That's a bit excessive. We're going in there to intimidate and gather information, not to start a war."

Alex shrugged. "Well, you know as well as I do, if a war breaks out, the Rubicon will finish it. If I'm right, wouldn't you rather have that case on our side?"

Marcus shook his head. "Alex. Whatever happens here tonight, I seriously doubt it will be our last night in this world."

"Let's hope you're right and I'm wrong. Too late to change our minds about it."

"Just leave it in the car."

"Sure. I'll set it for remote."

They parked about a half a mile from the club's industrial park. Alex crawled into the back of the Explorer. He opened the Rubicon case and inserted the control key. He turned it to the appropriate choice, and the LCD screen rewarded him by broadcasting REMOTE ACTIVATION in bright letters. He closed the case, then crawled back into the middle seats. He got out and closed the door behind him.

"We've got about forty-five minutes."

"Now that we are prepared for your worst-case scenario, what if things only go half bad? You have had a long day, Alex. Are you up for this?"

"I could be better. I was cooped up most of the day, but I still managed to catch a few rays. If you're right, I won't need to be, you know, ready. And if you're wrong . . ."

A moment of silence passed between them.

"By the way, you know Aguirre's crazy philosophies about vampires' ascetic living and the nature of the soul?" Alex asked.

"Of course," Marcus answered.

"I think it's working. I saw some interesting developments at the church today."

"Did you tell Lopé?"

"No. I'm not letting that son of a bitch off that easily. I should assuage his guilt? What is faith if I hand him proof?"

Marcus shook his head.

The first of many police cruisers pulled in silently behind the Explorer. The patrol officers got out and approached the rear of the SUV for a quick huddle. After they all arrived, Alex and Marcus gave the officers an overview of what they were going to attempt.

They needed to hurry. If tonight proved half as problematic as the day had been, there was going to be more trouble than the department could easily handle. The city would need every available officer on the streets.

The night was pregnant with possibilities, most of them hideous.

32

Six squad cars, lights and sirens blaring, screamed into the industrial park with screeching tires and made an impressive show. They turned the spotlights on the guards standing outside in the shadows. The Explorer was right on their heels. The other cars stopped; the Explorer barreled down the ramp to the entrance of the club.

Alex nearly hit one of the bouncers at the bottom. There was a crowd waiting to get in. More than half of them were cringing and holding their ears. The siren would be playing hell with their hearing in the enclosed echo-prone space of the parking garage. Alex killed the siren, but left the lights on.

"A bit more crowded than I saw it last time," Marcus said.

Alex's swiveled his eyes, taking in the location and marrying it to the way he'd imagined it from Marcus's description. The ABZU sign was not as bright as he'd imagined it. And the name called out to him over the eons. It was old. Sumerian or Akkadian. The pallets of blood products were still there, though he couldn't tell if any were missing.

"Notice anything else different?"

"Not at first glance."

The guards regained some composure. He didn't want them thinking that this was an attack they'd have to shoot their way out of. He wanted them very much to know they could probably bargain or buy their way out.

"Let's do this." Alex stepped out and held his badge high for all to see. "Nocturn Affairs. This is a raid. Everyone place your hands on top of your heads. If we don't see hands, folks are going to get hurt."

Speed was critical at this stage. Speed and chutzpah. You didn't want to give anyone the chance to come up with a different solution than the one you were going to present. You wanted them to think about Option A until you proposed Option B. There was always the chance that some idiot would think there was an Option C. Not for the first time, Alex hoped Marcus was at the top of his game.

Alex could see people jerking in line, hands moving hesitantly to their heads. Sangers and bleeders were both wearing indecision on their faces. Should they try to run for it or weather it out? As some of the cops came down the ramp, it helped them make up their minds.

Marcus called over his shoulder to the officers, "No one leaves until you get their information." Of course, they had no such intention at all, but the crowd didn't know that. The officers nodded, looking a little less than prepared as they fumbled for notepads to jot down names and data.

One of the bouncers stepped away from his post in the line. He was a massive vampire with at least a hundred pounds on Alex. Alex hardly had to look at him to tell he was a youngblood, eager to prove himself to his new master, but still moving and thinking like a human.

"Take a hike, fellas. There are no victims here. No one's looking for trouble. Besides, didn't you already get your cut this week?"

Some people in the crowd chuckled. Alex needed to end that and instill fear in everyone there immediately. The second they weren't fearful of him and Marcus, that's when things would get ugly.

Alex closed the distance with the bouncer while seeming to voice his reaction to Marcus: "Do you believe this? Who the hell do these guys think they are?"

As he closed with the larger vampire he could see that he had undercut the youngblood's confidence.

The vampire retorted, "I'm trying to do you a favor. You don't want this kind of trouble."

"Maybe we do." Marcus positioned himself between Alex and a second bouncer. His movement made it clear to everyone that whatever happened between the first bouncer and Alex, it was going to stay between just those two.

Alex could feel Marcus begin to assert his presence. It was something the Ancients did well. It oozed from him, a miasma of experience and antiquity that forced a measure of awe in all those that felt it.

The first bouncer was now less than two yards from Alex. Alex shouted at him, "Get on the ground now! Hands on your head!"

The vampire reached for Alex. No one ever got a chance to see what he was going to do. Alex struck out with both arms at once. His left fist struck at the vampire's solar plexus while his right hand delivered a brisk open-hand palm strike at the vampire's windpipe.

The bouncer was quick. He parried Alex's left hand to the inside, but he wasn't fast enough to stop the blow to his neck, which was the one that really mattered. He stopped in his tracks, sputtering and choking. Alex used the momentum from the bouncer's parry to pivot to the right and drop to his knee. He whipped around and delivered a bone-crunching roundhouse punch to the bouncer's right knee. Before the knee started to buckle, Alex stood up rapidly, catching the vampire's head with his right elbow as the bouncer crashed to the floor.

After the miserable day he'd had, Alex had to admit it felt good to drop the youngblood.

He glanced at the crowd, defiant, the look in his eyes daring someone else to try something, anything. They'd gotten the message. The rules were different now. He could feel a measure of respect, or at least fear, coming from them.

A commotion started near the folks at the front of the line, farthest away from Alex. After a moment, Alex could see that a man was forcing his way through the crowd and stepping underneath the velvet rope barriers. The man was well dressed and reminded Alex of a maître d'. Alex shot a quick glance at Marcus. They were in business.

As the man got closer, Alex could see that he was a smartly dressed vampire. He looked like a middle-aged human and Alex couldn't tell how old he actually was. Judging from Marcus's attitude this was not the Ancient they suspected of being in the club, but he certainly wasn't giving off the youngblood vibe.

The vampire beckoned Alex and Marcus over to him. As he did so he stepped off to the side away from the crowd, inviting them to a semiprivate conference.

"Might I have a word with you gentlemen?"

Marcus stepped from where he'd been standing and Alex put on an act of annoyance. They moved toward the vampire. The other bouncer moved to help his hacking colleague off the ground.

The maître d' waited for Marcus and Alex to get close to him and spoke in a very quiet, cultured, and reserved tone.

"I am the manager of this establishment. The owner is . . . uncomfortable with the presence of this much of the city's finest. It doesn't convey the proper image, you understand."

He addressed himself to Marcus. "As well, allow me to convey our most personal of apologies for the greeting you yourself have received. Had we known we would have the pleasure of a person of such esteemed repute as yourself gracing our establishment, we would have made more adequate preparations."

Alex chuckled. He didn't doubt that one bit.

Marcus made a gracious gesture to indicate that he was not offended, and he stuck to the game. Since Alex had established himself in the role of the hothead, it was up to Marcus to play the reasonable one.

"We understand. This line down here is violating a number of codes however, you must understand."

"Of course, Master Scaevola. If you wish, we shall disband the line immediately."

Alex picked up a completely new vibe now and he didn't like it. The manager had just confirmed Marcus's hunch that someone inside had recognized him. That meant it was likely that this man knew exactly who they were. Not just who they were now, detectives in Nocturn Affairs, but maybe who they'd been more than two years ago. He winced inwardly but kept his outward pretense of authority.

The manager was at least playing along. If everyone stayed on the same sheet of music and played their assigned parts, this might not turn to dogshit. Yet Alex's inner voice was tending to his more realistic—or as Marcus called it, pessimistic—proclivity.

"If we turned away these fine patrons for the evening, until we can come up with a better way to greet their numbers, would that be sufficient?"

That was Alex's cue. "We'd have to get inside, just to look around, and satisfy our curiosity that no other codes are being violated."

"I'm sorry, but unless you gentlemen have a warrant—"

Alex decided to ramp up the loose-cannon act. He hoped he didn't cramp Marcus's style, but to tell the truth he was enjoying his role a little too much. He hoped that bravado was going to make up for a lot on this one. Alex stared right at the manager's eyes, mentally letting him know that he knew he'd made them and didn't care. He dropped his voice so it was barely audible.

"Listen, fuck your warrant, okay? You know who we are, and we know who you are. We don't give two shits about procedure right now. But we're—"

As expected, Marcus cut him off. "Please excuse my colleague. He doesn't fully understand how things are done."

Alex stared at Marcus and, putting on a show of annoyance, threw his hands in the air, and stepped away.

"Earlier, you expressed regret that you were not properly able to greet me because you didn't know I was coming. Now, imagine my embarrassment when a fellow Ancient arrives in my city unannounced and begins operations under my very nose, without allowing me the courtesy of knowing who they are. If I were another person and less polite, then I would not have come here under a professional pretense."

Marcus let his volume rise and manifested his full presence as an Ancient. Even Alex could feel the intimidation now. Marcus seemed as if he were two heads higher than the manager was, even though they were probably about the same height. The manager appeared to have shrunk where he stood.

The manager took an unwilling step back from Marcus. Alex didn't have to be a vampire to be able to read that kind of body language. They'd won this battle.

"One moment please."

The manager stepped away from them and toward the people waiting in line. "Ladies and gentlemen, I regret to inform you that our club has reached maximum capacity for this evening. We look forward to your patronage on another occasion."

There weren't any of the expected groans or complaints. People were jumping at the chance to get out of there without any penalties. Marcus made of show of nodding to the two officers near the ramp, and they left their positions and went back to the street level.

The crowd filed out in an orderly, if hurried, fashion. The manager gestured for Marcus and Alex to follow him. Tit for tat. Alex suppressed a smile—with Marcus around, "quid pro quo" was more appropriate.

He passed the two bouncers who had been overseeing the line. They glowered at him. He made a point of ignoring them and letting them know they weren't worthy of his regard. They glowered harder, but theirs was the rage of the impotent who still believed that their day would come. Alex had felt that emotion many times before and recognized it for what it was. They were youngbloods and they had bought into the notion that now as vampires they would be nearly invulnerable. To have that belief debunked publicly would irk anyone.

They followed the manager through the velvet rope line and up to the concrete security walls and finally to the entrance of the club. The door was propped open and a metal detector was set up right at the entrance. The dull thump of a low bass line pounded Alex in his chest.

Two large vampire bouncers stood inside a trapezoid-shaped hallway, which was narrow near the entrance but quickly opened up wide and then split off into the rooms beyond. On the left side was a cashier's cage. Two young female vampires sat and stared at them as they came in. When they noticed the manager, they went back to their conversation.

Several cameras covered the entrance. There were probably cameras all over the place. Whoever ran this place was either serious about security or was a voyeur of sorts, probably a little of both. If this was the kind of blood club they thought it was, what better way of scoping out premium stock right when it came through the door. Undoubtedly, there'd be a hotline nearby that the watcher could use to invite a lucky patron to a private party, where they would further screen and sample them.

As if to confirm Alex's thoughts, the manager stepped past the bouncers and picked up a phone. He addressed Marcus: "Master Scaevola, if you would wait here for just a moment."

Marcus nodded. Alex leaned in toward him, keeping his voice very low so that only Marcus could hear him. "This whole place is swank, but I'd bet it was just slapped together. I thought you people planned long-term."

Marcus shrugged.

The manager spoke quietly into the phone. Alex couldn't make out a word. He'd have to ask Marcus later what was said. The manager seemed to get a decisive answer, which, from the look on his face, he didn't agree with.

"Please, gentlemen. The owner wishes to speak to you. Of my own free will, I invite you to cross this threshold."

Marcus stopped.

"Your master observed no such courtesies when he entered my city unannounced. I shall pay him the same measure of respect he showed me."

That set the tone. In vampiric terms that was as rude as spitting in someone's face.

The manager grimaced at the show of incivility. "As you wish, Master Scaevola. Please follow me."

They moved farther into the club. The metal detector sounded as Alex and Marcus crossed the threshold. One of the bouncers stepped forward with a detector wand and gestured for them to step to the side. Alex got the impression the vampire was doing this more out of habit than anything else. Alex refused to comply and just stared at him, daring him to try something. After a moment of awkwardness, they moved on.

As they moved farther into the ground floor, the techno music in the club got louder. It wasn't as loud as Alex had expected. He could see patrons speaking in normal conversational tones. Then he reminded himself that more than half the patrons here were vampires. Music any louder than this would have been painful to them. The light was very dim and Alex's eyes hadn't adjusted yet. He was having a hard time seeing. Black light and neon ruled the space, with the occasional flashing strobe or swirling spotlight sweeping across the makeshift dance floor. A mass of silhouetted figures gyrated within. Alex couldn't tell if he was looking at a rave or an orgy. He guessed it was probably a bit of both.

They moved through what seemed to be textured walls, but as

Alex grew nearer, he saw that they were actually pallets of blood products, Sangri and Hemotopia, which had been arranged in a maze-like configuration. He saw patrons sitting and petting each other on long benches made out of blood-product crates. There was no way to tell if the contents were tainted or even if the crates were full or empty.

They followed the manager to the far side of room, where he paused at a metal stairway. He turned to make sure they were following him and then began to ascend to the second story.

Even as they climbed the stairs, Alex couldn't shake the feeling that he was walking into the underworld. Every cell in his body told him this was wrong. They should turn back. Just as quickly, he chided himself. They'd been in worse places and walked out before. Then again, they'd been better prepared in those days. He casually stuck his hands in his pockets and gripped the smart phone in one hand and the UV flash-bang in the other. His fingers brushed up against the edges of Aguirre's silver cross.

The second floor—which, Alex reminded himself, was actually at street level or just slightly above it—only extended halfway over the ground floor. A metal railing allowed patrons to look down on whatever was going on. More pallets had been arranged along the wall to form alcoves. Alex could see sangers and bleeders in various states of undress engaged in a variety of sexual and vampiric activities.

They continued following the manager, who was now crossing the length of the club again to reach a metal stairway on the far side of the room. Alex didn't like this at all. To get out, they would have to zigzag their way down through the entire club. Marcus could probably jump it, but he wasn't sure he could without getting hurt. If they needed to get out in a hurry, it wasn't going to be pretty.

They crossed an area where several pallets and crates formed a stage. A vampire herded several young women on the far end, while an MC strutted up and down making announcements with a microphone in hand. Vampires sat on either side, and it reminded Alex of some bizarre cross between a fashion show, a strip club, and an auction. He stopped to look.

The man with the microphone called out, "Belarus. Type B, with a fourteen lifestyle. Very choice and not even nineteen."

Around the improvised stage, several vampires, male and female, held up fluorescent bidding paddles. The girl was pushed farther onto the stage by her handler, and even from this distance, Alex could see she was heavily drugged. He was amazed she was even standing on her feet.

"Keep moving," a gruff voice ordered behind him. He looked and saw one of the massive vampire bouncers from the ground level. A part of Alex wanted to lash out right then and there and make a run for it. He restrained himself. If this was going to get ugly, he was more ready than they were. He had Marcus on his side, and that was one hell of an ally. He was sure no one in here knew exactly who or what they were dealing with.

At the far end of the floor, Alex caught sight of several men and women who were strapped into raw steel bondage rigs. Several vampires were thrusting heartily into the captive women, while other vampires fed on them and the captive men simultaneously. Alex found it hard to look away.

"Remind you of Rome?" he whispered to Marcus.

"Rome was never like this." Marcus looked disgusted.

"That bother you?" the bouncer asked.

"What's to bother? Consenting adults and all that, right?" Alex answered.

The bouncer laughed. "If they were consenting, it wouldn't be as much fun."

Alex glared at the bouncer and burned his face into memory. He promised himself that when he killed this one, he was going to enjoy it.

The manager and Marcus had already reached the next stairwell and were waiting for Alex and his new escort to catch up. Alex looked to Marcus for any sign of distress or any intention to change their plans, but Marcus's face was unreadable. He wore the stern countenance of a centurion prepared for battle.

They climbed the stairs and reached the third level. Unlike the first two levels, this entire floor was enclosed office space sitting over the converted warehouse space of the two lower floors. The manager opened the door, showed them inside, and closed the door behind them.

They stood in a small foyer. Some piped-in classical music served to dampen the techno music outside, but the bass continued thumping its way in. Another large vampire bouncer guarded the one doorway on the opposite side of the room. Alex didn't pick up the youngblood vibe from him. This was an oldblood.

The manager addressed him. "Yevgeny, please see Master Scaevola inside. He and his assistant are welcome guests."

He turned to speak to Marcus. "Please excuse me, but I have other matters to attend to."

Marcus waved him off as if he were an annoying insect. The manager made a diminutive bow and backed out of the room, closing the door behind him. Alex's bouncer escort positioned himself directly in front of the exit door behind them.

The old vampire opened the door in front of them and revealed a well-lit hallway with a series of doors on either side. He spoke in a thick Russian accent.

"Please, sirs, if you will follow me."

33

As they stepped into the hallway, the door swung closed behind them. Alex wondered if it was locked. The soundproofing in this area was very good. Alex could barely make out the bass line thumping away beneath them, and the piped-in classical music obscured all the sounds from outside. Ahead, Alex could hear screaming and panting. There was no way to tell if they were sounds of bliss or terror.

The bouncer led them to one of the side rooms and opened the door. Though the lighting was more subdued than the hallway, Alex had no trouble making out the interior. There were two large and lavish couches on either side of the room. A small table with drink coasters sat between the couches. On the walls were large flat-screens with some kind of porn playing on them.

The vampire showed them inside and motioned for them to sit on the couch. They both remained standing. He said something, garbled by his thick Russian accent. Alex couldn't understand him. It didn't help that he hardly opened his mouth when he spoke. He walked out of the room and closed the door behind him. After a moment, Alex deciphered the man's speech, guessing he'd said something along the lines of, "Wait here, someone will come see you."

Alex's eyes swept the room. In two opposing corners, he saw the expected and ubiquitous observation cameras. This was more in line with the voyeur that Alex had expected. A closer observation of the couches revealed the telltale stains he knew would be there. He walked over to the door and tentatively tried the knob. To his surprise, it turned freely. They hadn't locked it. He turned back to Marcus, his brow furrowed.

Marcus looked engrossed in the porn film, but Alex saw his right hand clench into a fist twice. Then he made a "got your nose" fist with his thumb placed between his index and middle finger, then quickly made a fist with his thumb on the inside. It was an old signal, but Alex wasn't so out of practice he didn't catch it. He tilted his head to either side as if stretching or cracking his neck by way of a response. Marcus was calling an audible and changing the play at the line of scrimmage. That was fine with Alex. He hadn't been exactly in love with the way things were going so far.

"Door's not locked, boss."

"Why should it be? We are guests."

"They're arrogant. They didn't even search us."

"They are confident. There is a difference. Besides, they know they are in the wrong here. The lack of respect that they have shown me and the fact that I had to reveal myself to them in person has humbled them. They shall be falling over themselves to please us. You will learn these things the more you learn about our kind. Since you are soon to join our ranks, you must learn that there are rules and etiquette that are not violated lightly. Having an Ancient as an ally and patron is a wonderful thing, but having one as an adversary is an equally terrible thing."

An ecstatic cry from the woman on the screen interrupted Marcus and drew both of their gazes to the television screens. Now Alex could see that what he had quickly dismissed as a porn film was slightly different. The man was a vampire and he was sinking his fangs into the neck of a human woman. Her hands, clawlike, dug into his back and she had her head thrown back, mouth open in a gasping O. Biceps and thigh muscles strained taut, her toes curled, and her flat belly fluttered. She looked to be in the throes of rapture. Alex had seen this before. The vampire was killing her. This was some kind of vampire snuff film.

He broke from character briefly. "I should have expected this, vampire porn. I mean you don't think about these things until you actually see them, but I should've seen it coming."

Marcus cleared his throat and Alex tore his attention away from the screen. The door opened and the Russian vampire bouncer, Yevgeny, entered. Alex was shocked to see Lelith, the figurehead spokesperson of the Lightbearer Society herself, follow him into the room.

Vampire women did nothing for Alex, but even he had to admit that vampirism had been more than kind to Lelith. Though he had seen numerous images of her on magazine covers and on television, seeing her in person was another thing entirely. She wore a tight black evening gown with a deep-cut V that went all the way to her navel. Her red hair wasn't nearly as vibrant as in the photographs, but it was still stunning, and fell long and straight on either side of the V. It heightened the contrast between the dress and her pale skin. She looked young, in her late twenties or early thirties, but Alex knew better. She had the perfect face and figure for anyone wanting to sell the glamour of all things vampiric.

She had the bloodshot eyes of a vampire who had recently fed. She glanced at Alex, made a grimace, and brought a slender hand to her nose. Their eyes met briefly and Alex gave her the lustful look he knew she was expecting to see.

She addressed Marcus. "Master Scaevola. My apologies for making you wait so long. If you're enjoying the film, I can make arrangements. That's a live feed, by the way."

Marcus began asserting his Ancient presence once more. In the enclosed room, it felt oppressive even to Alex. He raised his voice. "You have all but exhausted my patience. I have grown tired of these delays."

He whirled to the camera in the corner. "The time has come to cease playing games. Address me in person or I shall depart. When I return, it will not be to your liking."

Lelith interrupted him. "Master Scaevola, please, we only—"

Marcus whirled on her. He slid across the room so quickly it looked to Alex as if he hadn't moved but simply stretched from one place to the other. His fangs were out and he snarled. Lelith gave a little yelp, stumbled in her high heels, and fell to her knees cowering and shielding her face from an expected blow. Alex wondered how much of this was still an act. Even Yevgeny looked like he wanted to melt through the door and get out.

"You have mere moments to fetch your master. My wrath is only barely checked."

Lelith nodded and scrambled to her feet. She headed quickly toward the door, but before she could make it, a sharp knock echoed through the room. Yevgeny jumped out of the door's way so quickly that Alex wondered if he'd actually experienced pain from it.

Lelith stopped just in front of the door. She threw her hands behind her and thrust one shapely leg slightly forward. She bowed her head and affected an awkward-looking curtsy. Her voice took on the aspect of a medieval herald, and she announced to the room as Yevgeny opened the door, "The Lich King of Admah, the Dread Sovereign Lugal Zagesi!"

As she spoke, the name Admah rang in Alex's memory like a gong, but he didn't have time to place it. As she continued to speak, he heard Marcus take a sharp breath and looked toward him.

What he saw made his heart sink like a lead weight. He saw an emotion on Marcus's face that he had never seen in all their long years of working together.

Fear.

34

Early morning, forty-third day of the Siege of
the City of Acre, Kingdom of Jerusalem,
eighteenth of May, the Year of Our Lord 1291

The drums started up again. Marcus looked toward the heavens and
saw the first rays of dawn stretching their way across the cloud-rippled
ocean of the sky.

"Will those infernal drums never cease?" The complaint came
from the Master of the Hospital.

The sound of myriad trumpets answered him.

"And now they add trumpets?"

"They do this to unnerve us," Sir Buchard said. The Teutonic
Knight's accent was harsh and thick.

"Even as we are betrayed by this one." Buchard kicked a beaten
and broken man lying on the ground. Two other men tied ropes to
the shackles around his wrists.

The others knew the man on the ground as Guillaume de
Rochefort, a Templar of some ill repute. Marcus knew him by his
true name, Lugal Zagesi, an Ancient and evil vampire the Order
of the Eternal Watch had hunted since its inception almost a thousand years before.

"Bones of the martyr, why do we wait?"

The Master of the Hospital spoke again. "We wait for William of
Beaujeu. It must be his decision."

"Do you not hear their trumpets braying? Al-Ashraf comes and we talk."

"What would you have us do?"

"Be done with the man, one has but to look at him to know he's infused with Saracen blood."

Zagesi tried to say something, but Buchard kicked him for his trouble.

"Be silent, thou false knight. Is it not enough we are undone by your hands?" Buchard drew his sword.

"No!" Marcus shouted, his voice sounding hollow from beneath his helm.

Sir Buchard stayed his hand and appeared to notice him as if for the first time.

"Oh. The Leper speaks. What would you have us do? More talk?"

The Master of the Hospital turned to Marcus. "What counsel, Scaevola? Speak your mind."

A booming crash interrupted the discussion. The first of the Muslims' stones were striking the outer wall.

"It would appear our time is limited. What say you?" Buchard said.

"He must be put to inquisition," Marcus answered. Zagesi knew too much for them to simply kill him. Marcus had to know what the Confraternity of Admah had to do with the Knights Templar. Were the Templars innocent, or was Zagesi's masquerade as one of them indicative of a deeper corruption within the order?

"More talk? I knew it." Buchard glared at Marcus. "It turns my blood to see that none of you has the stomach—"

"We strip him," Marcus interrupted, "leave him with only a cloth to cover his shame, and we hang him from the Accursed Tower."

"The man is still a Christian and a Knight until William speaks otherwise. I would not see a brother put to such a fate," the Master of the Hospital said, "even one such as he."

"I do not mean to kill him, my lord. But to stretch him, hang him by his arms, and when you see the first rays of the sun grace his flesh, you will bear witness that he is the vile creature I have told you of, and a servant of the Enemy."

Zagesi raged against his captors on the ground, but he was in no condition to fight and the two men holding him rapidly cuffed and beat him into submission.

More stones smashed into the outer wall.

"It appears that Al-Ashraf is eager this morn. Scaevola, see it done. Buchard, with me. Let us see what offerings the Saracen bring us this day."

The Master of the Hospital left, his entourage and Sir Buchard in tow, leaving Marcus with Zagesi. The two men stripped him, attached the rope bound to his shackles to a pulley, and hoisted him up the wall.

"I know you for what you are, Marcus Scaevola. You are no relation to the Doge. Do not think our affairs are concluded. I shall see each and every Hospitaller put to the sword for your offenses."

"Rest assured that if I discover any of your false schemes amongst the Templars, I shall have them excommunicated and dispersed, with the full penalties of what that entails."

"You will learn nothing." Zagesi raged against his bonds.

The two men hoisted him high up the wall of the tower and secured the rope at the base.

Zagesi growled.

"Perhaps not. But it pleases me to try."

"Pray that I do not survive."

Marcus signaled the men to follow him.

"I shall return after the noonday sun has passed and see if its grace has loosened your tongue."

He made a show of craning his neck at the rapidly brightening sky. "I pray there are not too many clouds to darken your view."

He intended to keep his appointment, but the city of Acre fell that very day.

35

Marcus looked completely cowed. All expression of rage, of confidence, had vanished; even his Ancient presence was gone. It looked to Alex as if he might actually bow or kneel to the man who had stridden into the room. Lelith bent down further in her awkward curtsy, and Yevgeny stood off to the side, his head deeply bowed.

Alex had a feeling that he was the only one in the room not terrified of the man, but it was probably because he didn't have any idea what was going on. Then he felt it. The air in the room turned to stone and he knew that the man stepping into the room was the source of the malevolence he'd sensed in the past few days. This was the source of the pervasive evil in the astral ether. Part of him was glad he was finally seeing the man face-to-face.

The man who walked into the room, Lugal Zagesi, wore an elegant tailored designer suit. He looked to be Middle Eastern and was dark-skinned, but not as dark as Alex. His eyes were darkly rimmed and Alex had the feeling he wore guyliner or some kind of other makeup. He held a large metal goblet in one ring-encrusted hand, and wore a smug, arrogant smile that made Alex instantly want to wipe it from his face.

He placed his other hand, also festooned with rings, on top of Lelith's head.

"Rise."

Only then did Lelith and Yevgeny take on a normal aspect.

Lugal Zagesi gave Alex a cursory and derisive glance, then turned his attention to Marcus. He spoke as if they were old friends at some kind of reunion.

"*Salve* Marcus Tarquinius Scaevola . . . Aeternius? Or have you dropped that affectation? It did not suit you. Gave away too much. You know, I had been meaning to catch up with you. There are so few of us Ancients left and we never talk. You know how it is, things always coming up."

He turned to Lelith. "Did you know that Marcus was one of the richest men in Aquincum? Oh, but that was long ago. Now look at you, just another common dick. Is that the expression?"

Zagesi took a swig from the goblet, the contents leaving his lips dark crimson. "Oh, there I am being rude again. Would you like some? It is from our own cultivated garden. All young girls from the old country, they still remember why saps should fear vampires. Yevgeny, fetch a goblet for my old rival, will you?"

Yevgeny sped out the door. Marcus still said nothing.

"Last time we met . . . my . . . oh I remember! You were with the Hospitallers, disguised as a leper so you could go out in the day swaddled in bandages to fight the Saracen. The Leper Knight they called him! He was a sight to see, Lelith."

His mirth took on a darker tone. "Do not think that I have forgotten the fall of Acre, I still owe you for that little inconvenience, but that happened so long ago, and it could be easily forgiven. It was a different era after all and we all make mistakes."

Marcus finally said something. "We have friends outside. People know we are here. If anything happens to us, the doors of your little club will come crashing down and then you'll really have a fight on your hands."

Zagesi ran his tongue over one long fang as if contemplating the situation and pursed his lips. "No. I do not think so."

He made a gesture and Lelith stepped forward, picked up a remote control from the table, and changed the channel on one of the screens from the snuff film to something else.

Now they looked at a security feed from one of the external cameras. Alex could just make out the last of the police cruisers pulling away.

"You see the police are going to be far too busy suppressing the violence springing from random vampire attacks and the inevitable reprisals. A rather large riot should be well under way by now. I think the authorities shall be spread too thin to care about two missing officers for quite some time. That is all going off rather well, I think."

Marcus ground his teeth. "You are not so powerful that I cannot overcome this stripling girl and be at your throat in moments."

"Yes, perhaps. Lelith may be stronger than you give her credit for. Perhaps your partner might actually be able to do something with his popgun. Again, I do not think so. You were never one to behave rashly. You are going to have to play things my way this time, Marcus. We are long past the stage for posturing and threats. Your little investigation is quite impotent. No matter what it is you think you know.

"Is that why you have come? Because you thought you could actually prevent something from happening? Marcus, you are slipping. Do you not recognize a wrap party when you see one?"

Alex's mind was working again. You could never believe anything a vampire said. They'd tell the truth so that it sounded like a lie and lie so that it sounded like the truth. While the makeshift club scene might indeed be some kind of celebration, there was no way the plan was as complete as Zagesi was making it out to be. All those pallets of blood product throughout the club told a different story. At least, he hoped so.

"I am afraid I have given you the wrong idea. I did not let you stroll in here with your bluster and daring simply for the entertainment, though I assure you, you two have provided a notable, if short, diversion. No, Marcus. As I have said, there are few enough of us

Ancients left. We are only mere days away from, well, I do not want to give away too much. Come. I have an offer to make, and one which I doubt you should wish to refuse."

Zagesi stepped toward the door and opened it. He made a gesture that Marcus should head out first. "Let us leave these children to their conversation and we can speak on more adult matters."

As Marcus crossed in front of Alex on his way out, their eyes briefly met. Marcus's expression was unreadable. He walked out and Zagesi followed, closing the door behind him and leaving Alex alone with Lelith.

Alex finally sat on one of the couches. After being without sunlight since early morning, he wasn't going to get the drop on an oldblood, let alone on Lelith. Zagesi was right. He still had his sidearm, but this was no youngblood he'd be shooting at. He might be able to clear the holster before she'd be on him. Better to play things cool, for a few more minutes in any case.

Lelith walked over to the intercom set near the couch and hit the key. "Can we get a special party favor sent to Suite D, please?"

"Immediately, Mistress," the voice on the intercom answered.

Lelith turned her attention to Alex and smiled. "Did Master Scae-vola offer to turn you if you accompanied him on this fool's errand? How sick are you?"

"Sick enough to follow him into this joint, lady." Alex affected a small chuckle.

"I thought so. You smell of death. Your disease is probably farther along than you think. It's the only explanation for your stupidity. Master Scaevola still has an excellent chance of walking away from this, and even making a profit. You had to know you would not be coming back out."

Alex smiled. "Actually, I thought this was going to be a pretty standard raid. You know, we'd come in, look around, ruffle some feathers . . . pad our pocketbooks a little and be on our way."

"You must know that isn't going to happen now."

"Eh. Probably not."

"I have to hand it to you. You have made excellent progress coming to terms with your death. I can sense no fear coming from you. You're very calm for someone in your situation."

"Well, I've met a lot of dangerous vampires in my day. And let me tell you, Lelith, you aren't the worst by far. No offense."

"None taken."

"Also, I might know a thing or two you don't. Ever considered that?"

Lelith laughed. "You must be very confident in Master Scaevola's ability to protect you. Would you like to see what is happening? Would you like to see your *master* sell you down the river?"

She'd charged that last comment with racial overtones for his benefit.

She changed the channel on the televisions. They showed a top-down view of a similar-looking room. He could see Zagesi and Marcus sitting on opposite couches across from one another. Lelith turned up the volume.

Zagesi was speaking. "—everything will change. It is perhaps only a month away and I will restore the natural order of things. Think of it, Marcus, we Ancients with legions of youngbloods to serve and lead, swelling our numbers with each and every attack! The saps will not take it lying down. We can use experienced military commanders such as yourself."

"I would need to know more. Forgive me if I do not take you at your word," Marcus answered.

"In due time, in due time. *After* you accept my offer."

The door to the other room opened and Yevgeny entered holding a goblet similar to the one Zagesi had.

"Thank you, Yevgeny. Now, Marcus, shall we drink a toast to a new member of the Confraternity of Admah?"

Alex still felt he should know that name. But the memory did not come.

On the screens, Yevgeny held the goblet out, waiting for Marcus to reach for it.

"I am sorry, but no. I will not abandon centuries of my affiliations and beliefs on your empty promises. You must know this. We Ancients are anything but fickle."

"True. Still, you cannot say I did not ask." Zagesi made a gesture. Some kind of prearranged signal. Yevgeny tossed the contents of the goblet into Marcus's face.

On the monitor screens, it looked like blood to Alex. Marcus reacted as if it was acid. He fell to the ground clutching his face and writhed on the floor, his legs kicking out spasmodically in agony. That goblet had probably had some silver in it or something. Yevgeny and Zagesi made a quick exit.

"What the fuck?" Alex shot to his feet.

"He should have taken the deal. Now his chances are quickly matching up to yours." Lelith smiled. Alex could see her fangs extending. It must have been from the thrill of a well-executed plan, because he knew there was no way he was appetizing enough for her to feed on him.

"Here comes the best part!" She redirected his attention to the screens.

The door to the room reopened briefly. A thin, pale girl in her teens was thrust inside, the door locked behind her. She had long dark hair and wore gauzy bits of netting and garters. There were calculated applications of body paint that accentuated her beauty but still left all the interesting parts exposed. She struggled vainly with the door and then noticed Marcus and tried to hide in the far corner of the room.

Alex could see that Marcus was recovering from whatever had happened to him. He noticed the girl. She screamed. In less than a second, he was across the room. He ripped her throat out, gorging himself on her blood. He was deep in the throes of a blood frenzy.

"What the hell did you do to him?"

Lelith laughed. The door to the room opened. She stopped and bowed deeply as Zagesi and Yevgeny entered the room. Zagesi took one look at the screens and seemed disappointed.

"Oh, I missed it! It works faster than I had expected on someone with Marcus's constitution. You see, Yevgeny, I told you it would work on Ancients. With this footage in our possession, well, we should not need to worry about Master Scaevola for some time. His own guilt and his own people will deal with him. Now, what to do with you?"

Alex felt Zagesi's gaze upon him. He was asserting his Ancient presence, trying to get Alex to feel fear. That way he could get some measure of pleasure when he had Yevgeny or Lelith rip him apart. Alex was betting Lelith wouldn't want to get any gore on that dress. That left Yevgeny.

Alex answered, "Um, you could let me go?" He laughed.

Zagesi laughed with him.

Alex leaned back on the couch and looked at his watch.

Any second now.

"You'll forgive me if I don't get up. I've had a rough day thanks to you yahoos."

"Oh, you must mean my little diversion with 'Abraham.' Yes, well, credit where credit is due, that was actually Lelith's idea. Yevgeny here thought Abraham had outlived his usefulness, but Lelith managed to squeeze just a little bit more out of him. You see, it isn't very hard to affect the unbalanced minds of those predisposed to suggestion. With normal minds, it just takes a little longer. I just sent out a few whispers into the ether, no need to bend them to my will just yet, and let nature take its course."

So that was what Alex had been feeling all week. Somehow, using a process he didn't understand, Zagesi was ramping up the tensions throughout the entire city.

On the monitor screens, the sounds of Marcus's kill were becoming distracting. "Lelith, turn that down, will you." Lelith came out of her bow and turned the volume down.

Zagesi admired the screens. "'The brain may devise laws for the blood, but a hot temper leaps o'er a cold decree.'"

"*The Merchant of Venice*." Alex identified Zagesi's quote.

Zagesi was taken aback. "My my. You are full of surprises. Perhaps that is why Marcus would subject himself to such a terrible scent. Always nice to meet a fellow fan of the Bard. Do you know this one? 'O what schemes what schemes do the vampyrs dream?'"

Alex stalled. "You've got me there."

"I am not surprised. It is from a lost play."

"Oh? *Love's Labour's Won?*" Alex asked.

"Alas, no. I fear that play is truly lost. It is from a play called *The London Visitor*. I commissioned it from him and I maintain the only copy to be had. If we had more time, or had met under different circumstances, I might even be inclined to let you read it. Alas."

"Story of my life, pal. So you actually knew Shakespeare?"

"As a matter of fact, I did. Yes. I take it from your demonstrated knowledge that you are not simply a casual fan," Zagesi said.

"I'm a big fan of *Henry the Fourth*, both parts. And *Henry the Fifth*, of course."

"Of course."

"The whole being outnumbered five to one at Agincourt. Underdogs winning and all that. I'm sure you can see the appeal." Alex continued to stall, hoping Marcus could recover. On her side of the room, Lelith grew impatient. *Good.*

"I certainly can, particularly in your present situation," Zagesi said, clearly amused.

"Oh this? I've been in worse pickles. I'll have something to tell you about that in a moment. But, first you have to answer a question for me."

"Have to?" Zagesi seemed genuinely taken aback.

"Well, consider it a favor from one fan of the Bard to another. And I promise it is not about my situation, but it is about Shakespeare."

Zagesi looked intrigued and gestured for Alex to go on.

"You know that turn of phrase about the 'school of night' in *Love's Labour's Lost?*"

Zagesi nodded.

Alex continued, "Is that really a hint that Shakespeare didn't write his plays, that it was Marlowe or Bacon and a bunch of others!"

Zagesi genuinely laughed. "No, my boy. Utter nonsense. Each and every play was penned by William himself. That I promise you. As a point of fact, that phrase is an allusion to more obvious actors particularly of concern to you in your current predicament."

"Ah. Good to know. Thanks."

"I believe you said you had something else to say?"

"What?" Alex made a show of trying to search his thoughts. "Oh yes. Now I remember. You only get away with this kind of nonsense, with all your schemes, because you expect the rest of the players, all of society in fact, to play by the rules, while you don't. But I'm curious as to what you're going to do when you run into someone with absolutely zero shits left to give? I'm about to present you, and Lelith here, with a singular opportunity of finding out firsthand."

Zagesi still looked amused.

Until a whistling sound broke the silence.

Zagesi looked perplexed.

It was Alex's phone. The jaunty whistling ring tone repeated. That was what he'd been waiting for. The Rubicon was ready. It wasn't a great plan—in fact, it was a terrible plan—but Alex hoped it would be enough.

"What do you have there?" Zagesi asked.

"Me? Oh, no need for alarm." Alex pulled the phone out of his pocket. "Just a phone. And you're really going to want me to take this call."

Zagesi and Lelith laughed.

"I'm glad you find it funny. Lelith, can you pull up the security feed from the entrance garage? There's a good girl."

Alex enjoyed pushing her buttons.

All signs of mirth drained from her face, replaced by hatred and rage. She looked to Zagesi and he nodded. She changed the channel on the screen they were watching. They all could see the Explorer parked at the base of the entrance ramp.

The phone rang again. Alex whistled along this time. *Walk like an Egyptian.*

He stopped to speak. "Now, that really isn't optimum placement, but I assure you there's enough explosive in that vehicle to have us finishing this conversation on the far side of the underworld, if you catch my meaning. Anyone touches the vehicle and it'll trip the mercury switches and we're talking to the boatman."

The phone rang again.

"So, I'm going to answer this. And I'm going to input a code. And if I don't enter that code every fifteen seconds, kablooey. I have half a mind just to let it go off. So no fucking around."

He exaggerated the part about the code. Instead of every fifteen seconds, as he'd said, it was really more like every fifteen minutes. The part about the mercury switches was complete bullshit, but Alex hoped they wouldn't notice.

"You're bluffing," Lelith snarled through clenched teeth.

"Am I? You're the one who can smell fear. What do you smell?"

The phone rang again.

"One more and it goes to a voice mailbox that I'll never get to check. I'm terminal. How about you?"

Zagesi growled. "Answer it."

Alex flicked the phone on and punched in the six-digit code. He couldn't disarm the device remotely. This just put it in snooze mode. He held his breath and hoped he'd entered the code correctly.

Ten seconds later, they were all still there.

Zagesi snapped his head in the direction of the Russian bouncer. "Yevgeny." The large vampire bounded out of the room.

Alex playacted at entering another code into the phone. On the screen, they could see the club security detail surrounding the Explorer. One man looked in the rear and spoke into a radio.

Alex continued, "So now, here's what's going to happen. I'm going to walk out of here. Fetch my master and then we're going to disarm the bomb and drive away. Everybody lives to fight another day."

"You must be joking." Lelith was incredulous.

"Tell you what, Zags. Lelith seems to think I'm not telling the truth. Do you also think I'm bluffing?"

Zagesi seethed. "There's something about you. Something I've never felt before. You have nerves of steel. I will grant you that."

Alex kept playacting at entering codes into the phone. "You know what? We'll make it more sporting. Since you answered my question about Shakespeare . . ." Menkaure searched his mind for the correct words and then spoke haltingly in Akkadian. "*We were never ones to know fear from your ilk, savage. Forgive me if we have difficulty shaping words in your barbarian tongue.*"

Zagesi was stunned. He responded in Akkadian, "*Who are you? Name yourself.*"

Lelith interrupted. "What is happening?"

Alex turned his attention to her. "Quiet. Grown-ups are talking."

She fumed and made a move toward him. Zagesi moved with lightning speed and snatched her back.

"Good reflexes. You just saved her life. May she not be as lucky next time." Menkaure switched back to Akkadian. "*We need not identify ourselves. It is you who are the usurper. Lich King indeed. There is one who is worthy of that title . . .*"

Alex backed up to the door and used his free hand to touch his heart and then his lips in the Assyrian gesture of farewell.

"But he's not from Assyria. It's been real. Oh and remember, one false move and . . ." He waved the phone at them.

He snapped the door open and let himself out. He expected to feel the vampire's grip on him at any moment. Lelith's eyes tried to bore holes into him as he slammed the door shut.

36

9:38 P.M.

Now he just had to figure out how to get Marcus out of a blood frenzy. Nothing came to mind. Also, more security would be coming any second. Zagesi's only motivation was to get some answers to the enigma Menkaure posed. Hopefully, he'd be arrogant enough to watch every step on the security monitor. The longer he stayed watching the less he'd be doing. If Alex had been in Zagesi's shoes, he'd be trying to get out.

Alex reached into his pocket for the flash-bang that might buy him a couple of seconds at least. He wasn't so far out of the game that he didn't still have few tricks up his sleeve. Instead, he felt something else. It gave him an idea. It was a long shot, but given Marcus's long affiliation, it might work.

He saw a telltale pool of blood seeping from beneath a nearby door into the hallway. It was this or nothing. He didn't have time to go opening all the doors. He kicked in the door.

Marcus looked up from where he hovered over the girl's corpse. Gore covered his face and upper chest. Marcus snarled at him, fangs fully extended, and eyes bloodshot red.

Alex hoped his ploy would work. He needed to engage Marcus's intellect and hoped that his Ancient constitution could give him enough control again. He'd fought Marcus before and that had been extremely unpleasant. Back then, neither of them had been trying to kill the other. He wasn't clear how it would go down this time, but with his reserves already running low, he knew he'd lose to Marcus.

Alex pulled out the object he'd been grasping in his pocket. It was Aguirre's silver cross. Now he was grateful Lopé had given it to him. He held it in front of him like some vampire hunter from a Hollywood film.

"Marcus! *Gnothi seauton!* Know Thyself!"

Marcus's eyes shifted and focused on the cross. Then he shook his head as if to clear it, looked down, and saw the girl's corpse. He recoiled from it in horror. Alex could see he was struggling to become himself again. Score one for Catholic guilt.

"Hey buddy, you can repent with Lopé later. The die is cast. Time to boogie."

Marcus scrambled to his feet and rushed out of the door past Alex. He was moving with vampiric speed and it was all but impossible for Alex to keep up. He heard a sharp cry and bang come from up ahead.

By the time he reached the entrance to the foyer, the door was gone, knocked clear from its hinges. When Alex reached the stairs, he could see why. Yevgeny lay crumpled on the remains of the door, his body moving in jerking spasms and blood dripping from a ripped-out throat.

Alex jumped over him and moved onto the landing of the stairwell just in time to see Marcus leap over the railing of the second floor down onto the first. Alex had doubts as to whether he could make the jump himself. He was about find out. By the time he reached the second floor, the screams started. Marcus was probably using the remains of the blood frenzy to mow a vengeful path through the patrons.

He reached the second-floor railing, promised himself not to look down, and jumped.

He hit the floor hard, tucked and rolled instinctively, and got up on all fours. He almost dropped the phone. Luckily, everyone was looking away from him in the direction Marcus had gone. There were several bodies on the ground, blood flowing freely from numerous wounds. He couldn't tell if they were saps or sangers and, honestly, he really didn't care.

He scrambled to his feet and charged through the crowd, barreling people out of his way. He reached into his pocket and pulled out the UV flash-bang. The last thing he'd need right now was to be grabbed from behind by some overzealous youngblood. He'd drop them a parting shot.

He tossed the flash-bang over his shoulder and was almost at the entrance before he heard the sharp explosion and the accompanying shouts and screams.

Then he was out! He charged into the parking garage and saw Marcus already rushing up the ramp, chasing some of the security.

He tried to shout after him, his breath coming in ragged gasps.

Marcus either ignored him or didn't hear him.

There was still one security youngblood near the Explorer. Alex drew his pistol and emptied the magazine into the vampire. Only about half of the rounds struck home. The rest peppered the side of the car. They wouldn't kill the vampire, but they'd put him out of the fight for long enough. He hoped.

Alex moved to the rear of the Explorer and sank his fingers into the door. He pulled hard. The whole vehicle threatened to move rather than let the door give. Finally, with a scream of tortured metal he managed to wrench open the back of the Explorer. He retrieved one of the shotguns. Vampires were beginning to stream out of the club's entrance. Alex reached into the rear of the Explorer for shells. He slammed three into the shotgun but spilled the rest onto the floor. Alex fired off a shotgun blast in the general direction of the pursuing vampires. Then he raced up the ramp after Marcus and out into the night.

About a hundred yards ahead, judging from Marcus's silhouette against the headlights of some cars, Marcus had stopped running. He still appeared ready to pounce. His head moved from side to side as if he awaited a decision. As Alex ran closer, he could see about ten vampires standing in front of the Town Cars that were the signature of their organization. They formed a cordon full of automatic weapons and laughed at Marcus. It looked like he and Alex weren't going anywhere.

Alex's chest heaved and he gasped to take in air. He finished out the run to come up even with Marcus.

"Ah . . . damn . . . it," he managed to sputter out between breaths as he caught up.

"Alex, you're doing it again," Marcus said. He spoke slowly, as if it took some effort.

"Doing . . . what . . . ?" Alex gasped.

"Breathing."

Oh yeah.

It was a hard habit to break, and though for appearance's sake and to smell things, Menkaure hadn't *tried* to break it, strictly speaking, he didn't need to do it. Alex mentally chided himself.

One of the youngblood security vampires taunted, "You almost made it. But the master had you figured."

"Yeah, you are in for it now," another laughed.

Marcus made a hand signal to Alex. This was going to go down badly for the youngbloods. They were about to find out what an angry Ancient could do. Alex still needed a second or two to form his strategy. He bent over and made a show of catching his breath. He stole a glance backward and could see dozens of shapes behind him in the night.

He quickly made up his mind. One thing was for sure. He would give himself the best possible chance of walking out of here. He knew Marcus wouldn't be happy with his decision, but as far as he was concerned, life had just gotten very cheap.

He kept breathing hard, for show. He looked down, dialed the

number of the Rubicon case into the phone with one hand, and secured his grip on the shotgun with the other. He hoped they were
far enough away.

"You . . . guys . . . knew . . . I . . . was . . . bluffing?" He continued
panting.

They all laughed. "Of course, man! You can't actually believe you
were going to get away?"

Alex looked up.

"Actually . . ." He pushed a number on the phone and lit up the
night sky. Marcus bounded into the air and landed on two of the
youngbloods before they could react. Alex hit the dirt and surprised
himself by managing to get a shot off with the shotgun before the
blast hit.

Then everything turned to chaos. The blast wave and roar knocked
the other vampires off their feet and sent chunks of flaming debris
everywhere.

The tremendous heat convinced Alex that he would burst into
flames at any second. That was how it would end. He would fall to
his ancient enemy, fire.

Then Marcus grabbed him and pulled him away.

Moments later, they were inside one of the Town Cars and speed-
ing into the nighttime traffic.

Underfunded, undermanned, outgunned, and most certainly out-
matched, but like it or not, they'd just reinstated a two-man version
of an UMBRA special program.

37

9:50 P.M.

Alex's neck felt hot and stung when he touched it. He couldn't shake the last image he'd seen when he looked back. Dozens of vampires thrashing about, on fire and silhouetted against a roiling black column of glowing smoke, dust, and flaming debris. They had to be vampires; bleeders would not have survived the blast.

"Do you think we got him?"

Marcus didn't answer him. He looked away from the road for a moment and his eyes burned with vampiric fury.

"Hey. Are you back with us? Come on, talk to me."

"Do you know what you've done? What we've done?" He'd never heard that tone of anguish in Marcus's voice.

"I know. I also know if we didn't get out of there to try and stop this asshole's plans, every night to come would be worse than this one."

"Stop it? How exactly are we supposed to do that?"

"We get everyone in on this. Cops, Aguirre's people, the Order, everybody. We can't sit on the sidelines anymore."

Marcus didn't answer.

"I get it, this guy is an Ancient. He scared you in there. We were cocky and in over our heads. Now we get all *your* old friends. We gather up Zorzi and Constance and we hit these bastards . . ."

"You do not understand. We cannot contact anyone. They will

kill anyone we contact. They will all have to disappear if they can. After tonight, everything will be different. At this point I am just hoping that our own people do not come after us as well."

"These assholes will never see it coming. Hell, Zagesi has no clue who I am. And he's worried, trust me. We have a window of opportunity here. We can hit them so hard they can't recover. Stop that shit from getting on the street, and we stop this thing cold."

"You do not understand, Menkaure. That was Lugal Zagesi, the mastermind behind the Confraternity of Admah. They have plans within plans within plans. We can trust no one. Anyone could be their pawn. When the Illuminati met their end, it was at the hands of the Confraternity."

The word "Admah" sounded in Alex's consciousness again.

"So how screwed are we?"

"Very."

"Where do I know that name Admah from? It's right on the tip of my tongue."

"There were five. The Pentapolis: Zoar, Zeboiim, Admah, Gomorrah, Sodom."

"The Cities of the Plain. Oh, fuck. How old is this guy?"

"The oldest."

"Shit." Alex's gut was doing backflips. "Do you think he made it out?"

"I do not know."

"What are the odds?"

"I, for one, would not have pondered your mystery for long. We can only hope he was so arrogant. But I think we must proceed on the assumption that Zagesi, at least, is still alive."

"Yeah."

"And if he is, he'll have made contingency plans. He will want revenge. How much do you have set aside?"

"Enough," Alex answered. "If I can get to the Caymans, I have quite a bit. From there, easy enough to disappear. That's not going to happen though. Zagesi strikes me as the kind that holds a grudge. I'm not going to spend the remainder of my days looking over my shoulder for his lot and second-guessing whether or not I could have stopped a war."

"It is too late for that, my friend."

Alex didn't respond. That didn't sit well with him. If this Confraternity was so bad that it had Marcus running scared, maybe running was a good idea. But that would mean that the bad guys would win. And Alex didn't like to lose, especially not to the likes of Zagesi and Lelith. He wanted blood and he wanted it possibly more than the vampire sitting next to him did.

"I say we don't run. See, Zagesi miscalculated in there. He got to me. He pissed me off. And for the first time in years. I have someone else I want to take down other than Neithikret. I'm going to do this. We can call it a dry run for when I face her down."

That brought Marcus out of whatever he'd been thinking. "This is probably a one-way trip."

"How many times have I heard that before? We're a long way from chasing crap calls, wouldn't you say?"

Marcus smiled.

Alex explained, "You said they'll be expecting us to make a run for it. So we don't. We go up to Haley House. We roll up there like the old days, all or nothing. Sword and fire."

"And what?"

"And we burn that fucking place to the ground with everyone in it. Aguirre pretty much told me they're running out of there. He knows that's where the tainted Hemo-Synth is coming from. We know Lelith's in on it. Now if they got out of the club, where are they going to go to lick their wounds?"

"Make some sense. There are only two of us. Yes, between the two of us, we have done our share. But this is too much."

Alex chuckled ironically. "Just like a Roman to want overwhelming odds before committing to action."

Marcus snarled at him. "This is no time for joking. You will not goad me into a battle we cannot win. If we had help, and the element of surprise, maybe . . . but then it is still doubtful any of us would walk out again."

"I feel like sending a very strong message that I shouldn't be fucked with. I'd like to make it so expensive for them that they'd rather walk away."

"It cannot be done."

"We get help and get it done then!"

"I for one will not drag Constance, Aguirre, Zorzi, and the rest of our friends down with us. It will be all we can do to warn them and hope they get the messages and manage an escape."

"An attack on Haley House could buy them the time they need then. I'm going to go up there, maybe not tonight, but I need to make sure they know they've made a grave mistake. I'd like to not go up there alone."

"It is a death sentence, Menkaure. It might not mean much to you, but it matters to others."

Alex had an idea so insane he nearly brushed it off immediately. It came back to nag at him. It might get them the help they needed. Or at the very least, some cannon fodder.

"You want to hear something crazy?"

"What else?"

"I can think of four people facing a death sentence right now who might want a chance to go down swinging, if you catch my meaning."

Marcus gaped at him so long, Alex thought he was going to crash the car.

38

10:40 P.M.

Chaos ruled the night. There was widespread rioting everywhere. Several times Marcus had to take wide detours to avoid areas of confrontation. Several large fires raged out of control. Glare from the flames reflected off the low clouds hanging over the city, casting a hellish glow.

After a seeming eternity, they made it back to the Nocturn Affairs offices in South Miami Heights. Marcus hadn't wanted to. He was sure the Confraternity would be watching. Alex wasn't giving their enemies as much credit.

Alex ran into the motor pool at full tilt. There was only one officer on duty. Lopez. Good guy, he'd hurt his back and was on light duty. Alex hoped he wouldn't ask too many questions.

"Hey Lopez, I'm gonna need a hunter truck."

"We got thropes out there, too?"

"Uh, not that I know of, but that truck can be set up as a mobile HQ. We're gonna need it."

"Is it as bad as I'm hearing?"

"Worse." Alex needed intel. He and Marcus were in the dark. "What have you heard?"

"Some terrorist blew up a blood club in Wynwood. There are hundreds of sangers and humans dead. Folks are saying it's Abraham striking back for the attack this morning. They're saying the real

Abraham isn't in custody. They're lashing out at cops now, too. That's what set off all this crap. The rest of the city took it as a signal to go bugnuts. EMS is spread too thin to respond to everything."

Lopez tossed him the keys, and then looked over his shoulder. "What happened to him?"

Alex whirled. Marcus was walking into the bay. He was on his phone. *Who is he calling at a time like this?* Gore still covered the lower half of his face and his chest. *What the hell is he thinking?*

"He caught a freaking brick to the face or something. Assholes are throwing shit at anyone around, especially cops."

Marcus caught the clue and put one hand over his face as if trying to control a nosebleed. Vampires didn't get nosebleeds, but Alex hoped Lopez didn't know that.

Marcus got into the truck and Alex passed the keys to him. He walked around to the other side.

He heard Lopez call out, "Hey, you guys take care of yourselves out there."

Alex yelled back, "You bet your ass!"

Marcus started the truck and pulled out.

Alex waved at Lopez and then they were back out on the streets.

"Well, now our own people will be after us. I hope you are satisfied."

"They'll be after us anyway once they figure out where that bomb came from. Next stop, the Doral facility. There's no going back now."

"That is why I called it a 'Rubicon,' Menkaure."

Lost in his own thoughts, Alex was surprised to realize they'd arrived at the Doral facility already. Marcus changed out of his blood-soaked clothes into a set of utility coveralls in the back of the truck.

Alex took a deep breath. "You ready for this?"

"No. There is a good chance we will not even get out of the building."

"Yeah, I was thinking about that. We'll use Trent. He thinks

UMBRA might be back on because you and I are still working together. Why tell him different? We could hint this is an op, let him
jump to his own conclusions."

"Except no real op was this poorly planned or haphazardly exe-
cuted."

"São Paolo was this bad. We didn't think we were walking out of
there either, remember?"

"I remember," Marcus said. "It gives me an idea. We protect the
principals." The phrase was from the UMBRA playbook.

"That wouldn't have worked in São Paolo. But . . . we almost
pulled it off in Singapore. There we didn't have people that trusted
us. You lead. Let's hope they're buying."

They stepped out of the hunter truck and walked inside. The
building looked deserted.

"We're getting lucky," Alex mumbled. Holding wasn't going to be
empty. He knew that.

They arrived in front of the desk sergeant. There was just him—a
gray-haired old-timer—and an officer with his arm in a sling.

The old-timer spoke up before Alex or Marcus could say anything.
"What the hell brings you two down here?"

Alex answered the question with a question. "Where the hell is
everyone?"

The other officer answered, "Maximum deployment. It's open season out there. Section head called, wanted all able-bodied on the
streets and cleared the prisoners over to National Guard custody."

Constance helped clear the building? How did she even know?

Marcus talked to the old-timer, all business. "We need Roeland
Jaap and his associates brought out of holding. We're moving them
into protective custody."

"Feds are still talking to them. They're bringing in backup of their
own. I don't have to tell you they ain't happy with the manning situation here. They'd been talking about moving them. Guess they
made up their minds."

"Guess so," Alex said. He moved around the desk.

"Not so fast. Like I'm gonna let a *vampire* go back there and take them out of here?"

"You think we're here to what? Take them out?"

"Crossed my mind."

Alex paused for a moment. How were they going to play this?

Marcus made the call for him. "Good thinking, Sergeant. That is exactly why we need to move this group as quickly and as quietly as possible."

The sergeant smiled. "Still not letting you take 'em."

"Okay, tell you what. You call back there and ask for Special Agent Summers. Tell him Alex Romer is out front and needs to talk to him. We don't have time to waste, every second those guys stay here puts everyone at risk."

Alex could see that the sergeant was still skeptical. He picked up the phone and called the interview section. His eyes never left Marcus and Alex.

Alex had to fight to keep himself from pacing back and forth. He couldn't look nervous or impatient. That wasn't the way to sell this. Marcus was as cool as ever. Apparently, it helped to have blood that stayed at room temperature.

After a moment, the sergeant spoke quietly to someone on the other end of the line. He seemed to get an answer that satisfied him, because as he hung up he said, "All right, you can head back there. Seems like he might have been expecting you."

"Thanks."

Alex and Marcus walked to the door, and the sergeant buzzed them in. They turned the corner into the hallway with the interview rooms and saw Trent Summers walking out of an interview room to meet them. He looked exhausted.

"Okay, what the hell is going on?"

"We've got to get their whole crew. We're moving them to protective custody."

"Bullshit you are. Jaap's been spilling his guts since you were here."

"Trent"—as Marcus spoke, Alex could feel some of that Ancient presence going to work—"we have a very solid tip that people are going to hit them tonight. Here."

"You're kidding me. How good is this tip?"

"The best kind. You can't keep them safe here. We have to move them *now*."

"No way."

"Trent, listen to reason. You've got me and Marcus, two desk guys, and your task force."

"Yeah, that task force consists of just me and Morris right now."

Alex's heart leapt, but he acted surprised and annoyed. "What the hell? I thought you had a whole team on the ground."

"Had. Then that fucking bomb goes off and Homeland wants a federal presence on scene immediately."

Marcus glared at Alex.

"And no one else could handle it?" Alex said.

"No one else has as much experience with nocturns as we do. Besides, there's already media speculation that this is some kind of Abraham attack in retaliation for the attacks this morning."

"Yeah, Lopez said something about that."

Marcus took control of the conversation again. "So what I am hearing is we have six police officers at most. We cannot secure them here. They have to be moved."

"Look, I know that. I've got a detail on the way. They should be here within the hour." Trent was defensive.

"We just came from out there. With the riots and everything, it might be a couple of hours before they can make it here. It's like the whole city has taken to the streets. Besides, we can get them to a protective-custody team."

"Wait, you guys don't have the manpower to properly guard them here. But you can move them? And secure them elsewhere?" Trent wasn't going for it. "What's your tip? I need to see it."

Marcus looked at Alex. Time to roll the bones.

"You're not cleared, Trent. Sorry."

"Not cleared? What the fuck?" Then Trent picked up the clue Alex had dropped. Trent had wanted to believe something covert was going on, so it wasn't that hard a sell.

"Oh shit. This is some UMBRA BS isn't it?"

Alex made it look as if he were trying to keep a straight face. "Don't know what you're talking about. But you understand. Jaap and company. They can't stay here."

"Damn it. I knew that shit hadn't been disbanded. What are they calling it now?"

"Look, can't talk about it. You know how it is. It's all politics and plausible deniability. We're running out of time."

"If it makes you feel any better, your team can escort."

Alex wanted to choke Marcus for saying that. Then he could see the look on Trent's face. Trent wanted back in, in a bad way. What Marcus said seemed to have done the trick. He could see that Trent had made up his mind.

"Okay. I'll secure them for transport. What have you got to move them?"

"A hunter truck out front. I'll move it to the rear," Alex said.

"Better let Marcus move it. We don't want these guys getting spun up. No offense, Marcus, but if they see a nocturn right now and we're moving them, they might get the wrong idea."

Marcus nodded.

"Okay. Let me go brief Morris and get Jaap." Trent walked back into the interrogation room.

"I'll wait here," Alex called after him as Marcus went back out the way they'd come.

A moment later, the gray-haired desk sergeant walked in. "Your partner said you're getting ready to move them?"

"Yeah."

"You're going to need someone to let you out. There's no one back there."

"Thanks."

The sergeant walked past him down the hall and out of sight.

Alex couldn't shake the feeling that something else was going on. Even with manpower extremely low, they wouldn't just empty out the whole facility like this. Even under Constance's orders. He tried to shrug it off. Luck was on their side.

Soon Trent came back out of the room with Roeland Jaap, his hands cuffed behind him. Another agent stepped out and crossed the hallway to one of the other rooms. The agent gave Alex a quick once-over.

Trent handed Jaap over to Alex—who put a hand firmly onto him—and made introductions. "Agent Morris. Detective Romer."

They nodded at one another, and then Morris walked into the other room.

Trent went into a different room, leaving Alex and Roeland alone.

Alex knew he'd only have a brief moment to get his point across. He looked Roeland dead in the eye.

"Roeland. One vampire killer to another. You're a smart cookie. If you want any chance of getting out of this, you'll keep your mouth shut and play along, okay?"

"This is some sort of trick?"

"Yes it is. And it is very dirty. But it's not the kind you're expecting. If you want a chance for payback at the real bastards behind everything, you'll keep quiet."

Agent Morris came out of the other room. He led over a hulk of a man, a guy Alex figured Brit gangsters would employ as muscle. The man had a patch over one eye, and a nasty scar ran down his face, telling the tale of how he'd lost it.

"Who is this beauty?"

"Meet John Seward. Nocturn Killer number two."

Seward glared at Alex. This guy might be trouble. If anyone was going to try to make a run for it, it would be him. Before Alex could say anything, Trent returned, leading a man in his fifties with a sizable paunch. He looked as if he'd be more at home at a pub than in his professed line of work.

"Let me guess. Arthur Holmwood."

"Yeah. I'm getting Gallier." Trent left again.

Agent Morris and Alex lined up the three men against one wall of the hallway.

"All right, fellas. No funny business and we can get you safely out of here."

In a moment, Trent reappeared, leading a small, shapely woman. She glared at Alex from under a peroxide-white mop of hair. Alex didn't like what he saw there at all. He'd seen killers before. He was standing next to three of the most notorious in recent memory. Yet there was something—something just *wrong* about her. It wasn't the crazy gaze psychopaths got, the look that highlighted their insanity, and signaled that they experienced a different reality. This look simply said, "I could kill you all right now if I want to." And meant it.

Alex shook the moment off.

"Okay, listen up. You all know that the vampires aren't crazy about you. We've gotten a reliable tip that an attempt is going to be made on you here very shortly. The government has graciously decided to move you into protective custody. We will be the most vulnerable during transit. So obviously, the faster we move the better. And just in case any of you are thinking of trying anything funny"—he looked deliberately at John Seward and Rhuna Gallier—"we *will* use deadly force."

Alex turned toward Trent, but caught sight of Rhuna out of the corner of his eye. Was she smiling?

"All right. Let's go."

The group headed to the rear entrance, where they normally

transported criminals via special buses to more permanent incarceration facilities. The desk sergeant was waiting to buzz them out.

"You ready?"

"Ready as ever."

He buzzed the door open and Alex stepped out into the gated garage first. The hunter truck idled a dozen feet away with its rear door open. Marcus stood near the back, and the rear door opened. When Marcus saw Alex, he stepped behind the truck out of sight.

Alex looked right and saw the other desk officer—the one with his arm in a sling—standing off to the side of the door. The officer nodded at him. Alex nodded back.

"Okay, it's clear. Let's move."

The group headed out the door, Alex on point. He was making a good show of it. Of course, he wasn't really expecting anything, but just going through the motions put him on edge. Halfway to the truck he knew something wasn't right, but couldn't place it.

He kept moving. It was all he could do. Keep moving and try to see what was setting his instincts on fire. The officer was moving toward him. That was wrong.

Now Morris was helping Seward into the back of the truck and Trent was lining up Holmwood to go in after him.

The desk officer suddenly spoke up. "You're actually gonna transport them? Lelith said to do them right here."

Everyone froze.

Goddamn you, Constance.

So she'd just emptied the building so her Lightbearer friends could do the dirty work, and Alex and Marcus had just beaten them to it. Marcus was going to get an earful about whom he trusted.

"Right here?" Alex's eyes met Marcus's as the Roman stepped out from behind the truck.

Roeland saw Marcus, recognized him as a vampire, and spat at Alex, "You bastard! You were working for those sangers all along!"

Agent Morris jumped down from the truck. He had his weapon in his hand, pointed at Trent.

"You're a fucking idiot, Winston," he said to the officer with the sling, who pulled out his own sidearm. He had it pointed at Trent, too.

Rhuna Gallier made a sound. It was part growl, part hiss. It wasn't the kind of sound that should come from a human throat, let alone a woman's.

Trent had a betrayed look on his face. His eyes met with Alex's. It looked like he was thinking about going for his gun. Alex couldn't let that happen.

"Listen, Trent," Morris was pleading, "we'll cut you in. We didn't have a chance to talk. But Zagesi's got the cash, he—"

Even as he was speaking, Alex's hand shot out and deflected Morris's sidearm away from Trent. He lashed out with a knife-hand strike at the agent's throat and heard a sharp crack come from the man's windpipe. The agent fell, gasping. It was child's play to wrench the pistol from his hand.

Alex tried to bring the pistol to bear on Winston, but Marcus had blocked his shot. He could see the man's sidearm pinwheeling through the air as Marcus got him in a death grip, draining him of blood. Alex didn't like that. Marcus had always been a seducer; he didn't kill to feed. Something in that club had changed his partner for the worse.

Alex whipped around to cover Roeland and the others. It was just in time. The pistol actually struck Rhuna in the forehead as she was making a move toward him. Even handcuffed she was fast. She fell backward hard and fixed him with that feral stare. Alex tried to play it as if he had planned the move. He hoped she couldn't read the surprise in his face.

"Nobody do anything stupid!" He needed to reassert control.

"What the fuck is going on, Alex?" Trent screamed.

"Trent. The less you know the better. It looks like the vampires really had arranged an attack on these guys. They have enough pull they were able to empty the building and draw most of your team away. My guess is, we just beat their hit team and these two idiots gave themselves away thinking that's who *we* were. No telling when their real friends will get here. If I were you, I would get the fuck out of here most ricky-tick."

He threw a light kick into the side of Morris, who was choking and turning blue, hands clutched around his throat.

He turned his attention to Roeland. "And yes, I am working for bastards. Just not the ones you think. I'll fill you in on the way. Get in the truck. Now!"

"Alex, what the hell will I tell people?" Trent asked.

"Tell them anything you want."

"No. I want in. You know I can run with you guys."

"Not a chance. Trust me, Trent. This one's going to Hell and back. And we're not so sure about the back part."

He pointed the pistol at Trent. "Now get out of here. You done there, Marcus?"

Marcus dropped the officer's now-lifeless body to the ground, turned, and wiped the bloody drool from his mouth. Trent took one look at him and backed away. Alex knew he didn't need to be told again.

Trent turned and ran.

Trent's career would be over after this. It was shitty, but that was the way things went. At least he'd still be alive.

Marcus threw Alex a bloodshot glare as he walked by him to get into the driver's side of the truck. Alex satisfied himself that their charges were secured in the back. He sighed and looked out into the night at the glare from the fires reflecting off the clouds.

What a fucking mess. A choking sound caught his attention.

Almost as an afterthought, he shot Agent Morris.

39

The information exchange in the truck went a lot faster than Alex expected. The incident at the Doral facility had inadvertently created a bond between the members of Abraham and the two former UMBRA operatives.

Alex gave the Nocturn Killers the short version. He told them about the methamphetamine-augmented blood products designed to poison unwitting vampires into a blood frenzy to kill innocents. He told them about Aguirre's leads.

Roeland reciprocated and together they were able to put together a theory that tied Haley House to the Lightbearer Society and to the Confraternity of Admah.

Then Alex had to give them the hard news. He told them how he suspected that Zagesi had influence over Abraham's contact in the Lightbearer Society. While Roeland and his cohorts thought they had been striking at the vampiric conspiracy, they'd probably been eliminating its adversaries.

Marcus pulled the hunter truck onto a deserted side road in the country. They were still about a half hour from Haley House. The members of Abraham sat in silence, coming to terms with the terrible news. Alex could read their thoughts on their faces. How many potential allies had they killed while doing Zagesi's dirty work for him?

"So there it is." Alex let it sink in.

"I think I'm going to be sick," Arthur said.

"There's still a chance to make it right. Believe me, I know all about atonement. We're going up there and we're going to finish what we started. What we need to know now is, are you in or out?" Alex asked.

"Bollocks." John spoke first. "Like we have a choice, eh? We say we're out, and we wind up on the side of the road with our throats ripped out by your pale friend here."

"Not so." Marcus turned to look to the back of the truck from his position in the driver's seat. "You can walk free and always take your chances with the Confraternity. I assure you, they will hit you when you least expect it. And you will never see them coming. But this way, maybe we can do unto others *before* they do unto us."

"And there's the small issue of trust," Arthur added, acting as if he hadn't heard Marcus. "You didn't leave us to the sangers back there, sure. But that's only because you need us to charge in there like the bloody Light Brigade."

Alex looked at Roeland for his input. Two out. He was hoping Roeland would be feeling vengeful enough to be on board.

Roeland didn't disappoint.

"I'm in. I want to deal a deathblow to these bastards."

"Even if it means your life?" Rhuna asked. Her accent was light and tripped off her tongue easily. It made her voice sound prettier than it was. Alex couldn't place it.

"What life?" Roeland replied. "What life do you think any of us will have if a race war between vampires and humans breaks out in America? All they'd have to do is keep turning people. They could probably create youngbloods faster than we could kill them. Then what? Once people have their sides chosen for them . . . it's over before it even begins. No. We can strike a decisive blow, here, tonight. Send them a message that we will not suffer their manipulations lightly."

"A chance to go down swinging at least," Alex said. "Look, I'm not going to BS you about our chances of walking out of there. It's not about that anymore. It's about stopping them."

"What is to stop them from trying it somewhere else?" Roeland asked.

"Nothing," Alex said. "But we've left messages for friends of ours who watch. With any luck, they'll be more vigilant than we've been. Now that we know what we're looking for."

"The random blood-frenzy attacks have only happened in this city," Marcus said. "This is probably a trial run. It explains a great deal. It definitely accounts for Lugal Zagesi exposing himself prematurely. At this early stage, he needed to oversee the details of the plan personally. We caught him at his wrap party, remember?"

Rhuna laughed, surprising everyone. "I'm in."

"What?" John yelled.

"Bloody hell!" Arthur threw up his hands.

"Why, Rhuna?" John asked.

"You smell that coming off them?" Rhuna said. "It's explosive residue. They're not lying. They set off the bomb at that club tonight. Any cause that makes an Ancient like Marcus abandon his lifestyle and turn terrorist is good enough for me."

Alex was shocked. "You can smell that?"

"Of course."

"She's a thrope, Alex," Marcus said matter-of-factly, as if Alex should have known from the start. That did explain a lot, except that most therianthropes didn't keep any of their animalistic abilities when in human form.

"She hides it well. I was not able to pick up her scent until very recently," Marcus said. "Tell me, how are you able to do that?"

Alex backed away from her.

"Oh, you wouldn't want all the unpleasant details. I assure you, changing one's scent is a simple matter to one who knows how."

"How close are you to the change? Are you under control?" Alex asked. He was glad she was still in cuffs. If she changed, it might buy him a few seconds.

"I am under full control. You don't have to worry about that."

"Rhuna is unique, she's our ace." John spoke proudly, as if she was his, somehow. "That scent trick of hers, that's a fantastic distraction."

Alex guessed what she was. She was one of the Pack. Well, the enemy of my enemy . . .

"You're Luperci?" Alex asked.

Rhuna looked almost insulted. "Please." She shivered in mock disgust at the thought; then she smiled. "You have bigger problems to worry about than me. Like maybe your partner controlling his blood lust."

Marcus's eyes had taken on that bloodshot stare, and he looked as if he were going to blood-frenzy again. His fangs were extended and he slurred a little when he spoke. "Whatever you're doing. Stop it."

It looked as if that took him tremendous effort. He pried his gaze away from her and got out of the truck. Rhuna laughed and smiled a little too widely.

She was still handcuffed and deliberately baiting Marcus? She had to be on the wrong side of sane. That, or confident she could take on an Ancient with her hands literally tied behind her back. Alex favored the former.

"It would be a lot easier to plan if we were free," Roeland added.

Alex shrugged. At this point, it hardly mattered. If he and Marcus couldn't handle these four, they'd have no business trying to storm Haley House anyway.

Alex fetched a set of cuff keys and released everyone. He did Rhuna last. She smiled that weird smile at him the whole time. The one that said he was probably on borrowed time if she had her way. He had a feeling she was enjoying making him uncomfortable.

"You two can be off anytime you want," he told John and Arthur. "We've got plans to make."

John shrugged. "Rhuna's not going anywhere without me. I guess I'm in."

"Damn it all." Arthur was in a fix.

"We could use your help, Arthur, but there are no hard feelings," Roeland said.

For a moment, Alex thought he was going to leave.

"I was never one to stand up to peer pressure," he said at last.

"Great. You know, your Light Brigade comment isn't too far off. Except hopefully we do more 'doing' than 'dying,'" Alex said.

"Agreed."

"Here are our assets. We have this lovely truck and all its amazing toys, an Ancient who has had better days, a therianthrope with exceptional control over her body, and three of the most notorious vampire killers in recent reckoning, and just maybe, the element of surprise. Not the best, but certainly not the worst possible scenario."

"Four," Arthur said.

"Hmmm?"

"Four of the most notorious vampire killers in recent reckoning. You've gone and left yourself out."

Alex smiled. The irony was not lost on him. Even though they didn't know who he really was, he'd killed more vampires than the "Nocturn Killer" the second he set off the Rubicon device. And that didn't even take into account his UMBRA days.

"So I did."

40

The hunter truck was parked about two hundred yards from the Haley estate. As far as placement went, it was far from optimal. Inside, Alex, John, Arthur, and Roeland sat waiting for the signal.

To complicate matters, they'd had to forgo the use of radios. With this many vampires in the Haley compound, Alex didn't want to chance one of them hearing a squawk. He'd had a bad experience with that before. A burst of static at an inopportune time was such an artificial sound that even an inattentive vampire would be able to pick it out, and home in on it.

Menkaure had wanted to let his *ka* slip free, but he was simply too weak. The lack of direct sunlight through the day, followed by what was shaping up to be one of the longest nights of his life, was beginning to tell. He was running on fumes.

He stared at the screen showing the feed from the infrared camera on the truck's roof. Given their angle, the IR was better than night vision. They could only see one corner of the main house, the entrance gate, and the gatehouse. He hoped it would be enough. Occasionally they could see one of the guards, and as far as he could tell, none of them were human. They only showed up on the infrared because of the negative space they made when they crossed in front of the walls or windows.

Marcus was out there somewhere. He was circling around so that he could hit the house from the rear. It would take him ten to fifteen minutes to get into position. He wouldn't be able to move fast and maintain stealth. But Marcus was an Ancient, and Alex knew from ops in UMBRA that he would get there, true to his word. He would wait to strike until the frontal assault was well under way.

The rest of them would have to go in through the front door. Which sucked as far as a plan went, but the hunter truck would be providing ultraviolet spotlights and spewing canisters of garlic-laced gas, and Alex hoped that would create enough surprise and chaos for them to make it to the house.

Their main target was a side building where the winery and distillery had been. That was undoubtedly where any contaminated blood product would be. Once they were inside, it would take more than a few UV flash-bangs to subdue any defenders.

They had a handful of incendiary flares normally used to set up perimeters or create fire barriers. As a general rule, thropes didn't care too much for fire. Alex didn't either, for that matter, but he didn't let on about that. The idea was that you could somehow corral a thrope by starting and controlling fires with these flares. Alex had never heard of it actually working against thropes. That didn't matter now. Those flares started fires. That's exactly what they needed them to do.

As far as the entrance went, there was no telling what kind of security they had. Alex doubted it was just a gate. There were probably tire traps at the very least. He knew there would be if he had set up the security. He wanted someone in the gatehouse before they came through with the truck. Rhuna volunteered.

She assured him she could make it to the front gate and get it opened. The others testified to her skills. She boasted that only she or Marcus could have made it anyway. She was probably right.

The upside was that she did show up on the infrared camera and they could monitor her progress or come to her aid if needed.

"They'll smell you coming," Alex had warned.

She laughed lightly and retorted, "I'm counting on it."

When he handed her a gun, she handed it back with a look of disgust on her face. After Alex pressed her, she chose to take only a machete.

The plan, in a nutshell, was simple. Get in, sow as much death and destruction as they could, fire the building, get back to the damn truck, and hopefully ride off into infamy having accomplished the impossible.

Easy-peasy.

It had been set into motion ten minutes ago when Marcus headed out. Five minutes later, Rhuna departed. Now the four of them crowded around the screen waiting to see her form enter the frame.

In the meantime, Alex showed the group how to use the ultraviolet-flash vests, in case they were caught. They armed themselves with shotguns, all loaded with slugs.

Roeland laid out several MP5s and some magazines just in case. Alex felt that the shotgun was the weapon of choice. The shotgun's slugs were plated with silver, but not enough to be more than a nuisance to these vampires. Each of them carried a machete. There weren't enough stake guns or stakes to go around.

The stake guns were really just modified paintball markers that fired the stakes with compressed air. They were simple. Shove a stake down the barrel like an old-school muzzle-loader, aim, and pull the trigger. If everything worked, you'd get a silver-plated stake flying downrange at more than six hundred feet per second. They were quiet, effective, easy to use, and faster to reload than a crossbow. Trouble was, with the air tanks they were using, they'd get maybe four shots. was if the tanks were at optimum. With these gaugeless tanks, Alex couldn't say when someone had last charged them.

Arthur selected one of the stake guns, and John had the other. Roeland took some extra stakes to deliver by hand. Alex doubted he'd get to use those, but he *was* the real "Abraham," after all.

Alex chose to stick to the simple machete. They had their way of killing vampires and he had his. Unfortunately for him, experience had taught him that tangling with vampires and killing them reliably meant getting closer to them than you'd ever want to.

"There she is." Roeland pointed at the bottom corner of the screen.

They could all see Rhuna's silhouette, glowing fluorescent white on the IR as she approached the front wall leading to the gatehouse.

"She's just going to walk up there? What the hell? I could have done that." John chuckled in disbelief.

They saw a form jump down from the wall, a black silhouette in front of the slightly brighter background. A vampire. There was nothing they could do for her.

The vampire pounced, and for a moment it looked as if Rhuna were grappling with an invisible lover. Black splashes mottled her fluorescent silhouette, and she crouched for a moment, then ran up the wall. In an eyeblink, she was up and over.

"Better get ready to move," Roeland warned.

Alex nodded silently. He still wasn't sure exactly what he'd seen. Now wasn't the time for questions. He slid into the driver's seat and wedged the shotgun between the passenger seat and the center console where he could easily get at it. He put on a pair of night-vision goggles. He turned on the engine and put the truck into drive.

"Go. Go," Roeland said.

Alex pulled the truck onto the road and started driving. Seconds later, he could see the front gate opening.

"Okay. Here we go. Holler if you see anything."

Arthur quoted Tennyson from the back. "'Boldly they rode and well, Into the jaws of Death, Into the mouth of Hell . . .'"

Marcus crept along the back of the property. In front of him, a sentry shuffled impatiently. Youngblood. Marcus killed the young vampire as easily as he had killed the eight others. Still, he had woefully underestimated the Lightbearers' resources. They had to have marshaled every soldier at their disposal. And this had to be recent. Constance hadn't mentioned anything about this.

Menkaure must have rattled Zagesi terribly. But now it was going to work against them. Instead of facing an Ancient and a dozen or so oldblood bodyguards, which would have been bad enough, they were attacking a hardened compound of more than a score of oldbloods, and easily an equal number of youngbloods and humans.

Marcus had considered going back and warning Menkaure and the others. He thought better of it. That would have accomplished nothing. They would have insisted on bringing reinforcements, which would have only meant more deaths. Already, Roeland's people weren't going to make it out. Marcus weighed his own odds and gave himself less than a fifty percent chance. If he killed Zagesi, it would be worth it. But then, he had Menkaure on his side, and the Lightbearers would not know, could not know, what they were up against. He added twenty percent to their odds of success.

Marcus approached the house from beneath a second-story window and leapt, powerful vampiric fingers finding purchase where there was none for a normal human. A moment's scant effort pried the window open, the sound of it much too loud for his taste, and like a breath of wind, he was inside.

His feet slid along the hardwood floor as he glided forward. The wood chirped quietly as he moved his weight along it. It wasn't a sound anyone but a vampire would hear. For an instant, he wondered if Zagesi had been so paranoid as to have installed a nightingale floor. Marcus sprung lightly upward and clung to the ceiling just in case. He made his way to the doorway and climbed over the lip into the hallway.

He crawled along the ceiling toward the sound of muted voices he could not recognize. He needed to get closer.

He avoided a light sconce and slid toward the open doorway.

Lelith murmured something. Someone else. A woman. It couldn't be. But it was. Constance's measured tones met his ears. This would complicate things.

"Come down from there. You look silly."

Marcus froze. He spun and Lugal Zagesi stood at the other end of the hallway smiling at him.

At the sound of Zagesi's voice, Lelith and Constance stepped out of the room. Marcus was scarcely aware of them. His focus was on Zagesi and how he'd managed to get behind him.

"Go back, my sweets," Zagesi said, addressing the women. Then his attention returned to Marcus. "Do get down. It is undignified for those of our station."

Marcus dropped from the ceiling, instincts at odds with each other. The vampire part of him wanted to flee even though his rational mind told him he wouldn't get far. Even now, his ears confirmed half a dozen men converging on his position. The Roman part, the knight commander of the Eternal Watch part, wanted to tear out Zagesi's throat and be done with it. He doubted he'd be fast enough.

Zagesi slipped past with vampiric speed and stood at the room's threshold. He held one arm outward, adopted a mock Hungarian accent, and invited Marcus in: "Enter freely, and of your own free will."

Keeping his eyes on Zagesi, Marcus squeezed past him, and entered a plush library with floor-to-ceiling cherrywood shelves populated with priceless volumes. On a tight reading couch no bigger than a love seat, Constance fussed over a bandage that covered half of Lelith's face. Lelith's arm was charred and she looked deathly pale, even for a vampire.

Zagesi entered behind him and walked past as if Marcus offered no threat at all. Zagesi moved to a decanter and poured several goblets of blood. He brought two of the chalices to the seated women. Constance drained hers in one go, sat back, and let her legs drape lewdly over Lelith's thighs. She closed her eyes, and her skin flushed red as the blood flooded her system.

"I believe you know the lieutenant. I'm afraid women are always drawn to power. You have to admit, Marcus, yours has been waning."

"A jab at my virility? I expected more from you, Zagesi. I am disappointed in Constance, but well, there's no accounting for taste."

Constance shot him a look that could have set the books in the room alight.

"You were only recently acquainted with Lelith. You'll have to forgive her, she isn't feeling well. That partner of yours is really quite singular. He gave us such a fright," Zagesi said.

"Did he?" Marcus said.

"Oh yes. Such excitement as I haven't felt in centuries. I was nearly afraid."

"No," Marcus said in mock disbelief.

Zagesi crossed the room and retrieved a goblet for himself. "Did you know he could speak Akkadian? Marvelous thing. Hadn't heard it in millennia and then there it was. Can you believe I didn't even understand it at first?"

What had Menkaure done? Had he revealed himself to Zagesi? No. Even at his most bullheaded, Menkaure was not that reckless.

"Well, he is quite the scholar," Marcus said.

"And yet he is dying. A pity to lose a mind such as his. Tell me, why have you not turned him?"

Marcus didn't answer. Let Zagesi form his own theory, damn him. Instead, he focused his attention on the goblet in Zagesi's hand.

Zagesi noticed.

"I'm terribly sorry, Marcus. I'm being rude. I didn't think to offer you any since you reacted so . . . poorly to the last batch."

Lelith and Constance laughed.

Outside the room, men stood at the ready. There were at least six.

"Tell me, how was that girl? Was that the first time you'd really taken one? After millennia on the prowl? Did your heart flutter at her death rattle?"

Despite himself, Marcus thought back to that poor girl. He'd been so deeply in the throes of the blood frenzy, he didn't remember any of it.

"Oh. You're thinking on it now. You're worried that maybe you've gotten a taste for it, like your former lover Constance here. A killer, through and through. There's no going back," Zagesi said.

"No. I am not like you. Not like her. I do not feed on the unwilling."

Zagesi laughed. He pounded his fist on the table and threatened to overturn the decanter. His laugh climbed in register until it was inaudible, but still his body shook with it. Finally, he was able to squeeze words out between fits of laughter.

"Romans. You're so legalistic. Quibbling. About degrees of rape." He forced himself to regain his composure. "Really, Marcus. You're too much. I'd forgotten."

Zagesi tilted the goblet back to drain its contents, and time froze. Marcus leapt across the room.

The goblet spun out of Zagesi's hand as Marcus snatched at his throat and smashed him into the splintering wooden shelves.

Zagesi, caught by surprise, tried to scramble back, his feet springing into the disintegrating shelves and pushing toward the opposite wall. His hands clawed into Marcus's.

Marcus nearly lost his grip when he smashed into the wall. His head snapped back and he saw flashes of red. And then Zagesi was prying his fingers from his throat. How had he gotten so strong?

The blood. The blood was the life.

Men charged into the room.

"Alive! I need him alive!" Zagesi rasped.

Marcus released him, spun away, smashed into one of the men and caught him unawares. He struck out with full force and the vampire crumpled, his chest a bloody ruin.

They hit him with something and his legs went into spasms.

A Taser, or a cattle prod, something like that.

Constance was screaming.

There were hands all over him. He couldn't move. Outside, he heard automatic weapons fire. Menkaure was coming.

Then they stuck something into him. His blood began to boil.

Academically, strangely disconnected from the situation, his mind identified the substance as silver.

Then his eyes felt as if they were burning in his skull.

41

Alex turned onto the main drive leading up to the gate, then floored it. Rhuna would catch up or escape as she saw fit. After seeing how she handled herself, he hoped she would catch up.

Within seconds, they were well inside the compound. Up ahead and to the left, the massive Haley House mansion loomed, its outer lights bright white-green in the night vision. He made the slight turn around the house and saw the outbuilding that was their target. One side door was open and there was a figure nearby doing something. Alex couldn't make it out.

Roeland called from the back. "There are heat signatures in the winery!"

Humans. Of course. There was no way they'd let vampires work on that meth blood. If there was some kind of accident, they'd have a blood frenzy on their hands. Good. Humans were easier to kill than vampires.

"I'm gonna pull up past the building," Alex shouted. "Get ready!"

He turned the truck. He fought the wheel and the mass of the vehicle and forced it over. Out of nowhere, he saw two figures standing right in front of him with weapons slung over their shoulders. They dived out of the way, faster than he would have thought possible.

His hand smashed at switches over his head. He heard the muffled pops of gas canisters as they deployed. He mentally chided himself for a brief second. If he'd foreseen the presence of humans, these could have been tear gas. Instead, it was just concentrated garlic. Too late. The second switch turned on the four banks of UV lights placed around the top of the truck. He slammed on the brakes.

"Go! Go! Go!"

Alex grabbed the shotgun, opened the driver's door, and was out into the night. One of the figures he'd almost hit was getting to his feet. Alex fired a slug into him. That knocked the figure back to the ground. Alex couldn't tell if it was human or vampire. The UV lights were playing hell with the night vision. He reached up to yank off the goggles. He had them halfway off and heard something behind him. He spun, but was momentarily blind, as his vision and cognizance switched from the night-vision view to the normal night strangely lit by UV.

He saw the source of the noise a second too late. He brought up the shotgun but his attacker swatted it out of his hands. Then he was fending off a vampire guard with his hands. He fell back on his old training. He grabbed the vampire, and briefly the two were locked in a struggle of pure strength. Alex surged and knocked the vampire back. He could see the look of shock on the creature's face. But then Alex had his machete out and swinging.

The weapon made a satisfying *ching* sound as it sliced through flesh and vertebrae. By the time the vampire's head hit the ground, Alex had already rounded on his companion. That vampire was still on the ground, writhing in pain from the shotgun slug that had blown out half its guts. Alex brought down the machete like a cleaver.

"Alex!" Roeland's voice called.

He snapped his gaze up and Roeland threw him one of the MP5s. Alex sprinted past Roeland and the others toward the side door.

"Stack on me!" he yelled as he neared the door. The man standing next to it had a dumb look on his face and a cigarette in his hand. Alex threw his machete. It had scarcely left his hand before he was reaching for one of the UV flash-bangs. The machete hit home with a meaty *chunk* before the man fell backward.

Someone tapped his arm twice. It had to be Roeland, using a signal for "ready" that was standard with entry teams almost everywhere. Using his pinky, Alex pulled the pin on the flash-bang and tossed it underhand into the building. He readjusted his grip on the MP5 in the seconds he waited for the grenade to go off.

He heard the loud bang and saw the flash momentarily light up the night through the door's opening. Then he was moving. Decades of experience took over. He moved to the left and double-tapped two men as he moved toward the corner. He swept the weapon to his right, saw more targets, and fired.

They were fish in a barrel. Most of them were doubled over, holding their eyes or standing dazed and disoriented. Alex reached the corner of the room and turned to face the inside of the building.

He saw that Roeland and the others had made short work of their targets.

"Clear left!"

Roeland called back, "Clear right!"

Holy shit. This might actually work.

"Light 'em up."

He and Roeland moved back into position to cover the door.

Arthur and John broke open some of the flares.

"It's not catching!"

Alex looked around. The floor was concrete, the building was steel, and the wine vats were steel. It looked like their old pal Murphy had tagged along for the ride.

"Shit!"

There were a dozen or so old wooden pallets stacked in the corners.

"Try those."

John moved across the room and applied the flare to the bottom pallet. After a moment, it started to smoke.

There was automatic weapons fire outside.

Alex looked at the vats. He hoped they were thin enough that the MP5s would penetrate. He fired a quick burst into the nearest vat near the bottom. Instantly, blood started pouring out through the holes.

Roeland saw what he was doing and started hitting the vats on his side.

"It's working here." John stood up. Behind him the pallets were quickly roaring into a respectable fire. Then John was thrown back against them as automatic fire rippled through his body.

Alex spun toward the main door. There was a vampire with a machine gun. Alex fired off several shots as he moved to cover. He saw the vampire fall, but there were lots more behind him.

"Cover!" He fired another round, but then the weapon was out of ammunition. His hand moved instinctively for another magazine, and his heart leapt into his mouth when he realized there wasn't one. He tossed the MP5 aside and drew his pistol.

He swore the vampire was smiling as it raised its weapon. Then it fell backward as well, its head a bloody ruin.

Alex turned to see his savior. Roeland was facing his way and changing magazines. A vampire came in through the side door. Roeland didn't see it.

Alex shouted a warning.

Roeland tried to jump backward, but the vampire swatted him hard and he sailed across the room. Alex ran back toward him, sidearm in hand. He took aim and was ready to let fly at the vampire near the side door when a stake materialized in the vampire's chest.

He snapped his gaze right. Arthur dropped another into the stake gun. Then Alex was at Roeland's side. Roeland wasn't unconscious, but he was coughing up blood. That strike had most likely broken a rib or two. Probably punctured a lung.

Alex grabbed the machete off Roeland's thigh.

"You ready to move?" he asked, and then shouted, "Get to the truck!"

They went out the side door but he could see a lot of vampires running up to their position. Where the hell were they all coming from?

It was dark now. The vampires had shot out the UV lights on the truck.

He heard bullets snap past them, but he moved off to the side away from the doorway and closer to the truck. Arthur wasn't so lucky. Rounds hit him as he came out of the door. Arthur cried out and fell.

The garlic gas was providing some cover, but not enough. Alex reached the truck and left Roeland. He turned back to Arthur just in time to see him trying to get to his feet and firing another stake out of the gun. It struck an oncoming vampire low, in the stomach. The creature made a moaning, gurgling sound and went down clutching the silver spike lodged in his belly.

"Come on!" Alex ran back toward Arthur. He had almost made it when a string of automatic weapons fire crashed into Arthur and he went down for good.

Alex whirled in the direction of the fire and saw six more vampires moving up. Their weapons rose tactically. He heard the shotgun blast from Roeland and one of them went down, but then Alex's left leg buckled out from under him and something hit him in the left side of his chest. He spun and went down.

He lost the grip on his pistol and tried to scramble back to his feet.

Everything sounded like it was underwater. Through the din, he heard Lelith shouting, "No! The master wants them alive!"

"Even better," Alex muttered to himself. He managed to get to his feet.

One of the vampires appeared about two feet from him. Alex

swung blindly with the machete and felt it hit something. Then it was just an insane melee.

He swung at anything he could. Hands and faces. He felt the impact from rifle butts and didn't know how long he could keep it up.

They were off him. Alex couldn't figure out why. Then he saw her.

Rhuna was a symphony of death. She jumped from one vampire to another, rending flesh with her bare hands from faces and necks and anywhere else exposed. The look on her face, the gore, and her white-blond hair made her seem like some nightmare demon come to life.

Alex charged in to help her. Before he could reach her, he saw a vampire smash into the back of her head with the butt of his machine gun and she went down. The vampire just kept pounding on her.

Then they were back on Alex. He swung madly. Desperately. Limbs growing stiff as he used up his energy. The machete left his grasp and he shouted in frustration as vampires swarmed him. He pulled the rip cord on the UV vest, heard the camera-flash whine as the capacitors charged and the LEDs activated. It bought him a second. He used his remaining strength to throw them from him. Their bodies sailed through the air. But it wasn't enough. The night had been too long and even he had his limits. They dragged him downward and something hard smashed into his head.

42

5:10 A.M.

Rhuna felt someone fixing a cold collar into place around her neck. She instinctively growled and tried to strike out, but they'd bound her hands and arms together behind her back at the wrists and elbows. She opened her eyes and stared balefully at the vampire af-fixing the collar. She kicked out feebly with her legs, but to no avail. They offered only a limited range of motion. They'd strapped her into some kind of bondage harness where she was bent over at the waist; her wrists pulled her arms straight up behind her pointed at the ceiling. She could only imagine what they had planned. She braced herself for the worst.

"Kitten's awake," the vampire said. Then he kicked her in the stomach. She gasped as he knocked the wind out of her. Tied up as she was, she could do little else.

She heard sounds of a struggle.

"Hold him. Damn it, hold him!"

She looked up. Blood ran freely down one of Marcus's cheeks and the flesh of his face hung loosely on one side where a terrible series of gashes ran down into his neck and chest. Something, someone, had clawed him horribly.

Four vampires manhandled him into shackles on the far wall. After securing him, two of the vampires beat him until they saw him slump.

Rhuna saw a red-haired woman enter the room through a large reinforced door. She might have been beautiful, but now it was hard to tell. She wore a bandage over one eye and the other side of her face was swollen and bruised. She spoke haltingly, her words slurred by her swollen mouth.

"The Lich King of Admah. The Dread Sovereign Lugal Zagesi."

The man that entered didn't look much better than Marcus. He had slashes and bruises over his body and he moved gingerly, obviously still in pain.

"Thropes and vampires working together." He said every word with disgust.

"Marcus. You should have run, Marcus. You should have known better. Do you know how much it pains me to have to remove an Ancient from the world? I am truly sorry. There are so few of us left. But examples need to be made from time to time in order to maintain discipline."

Marcus lifted his head and glared at him.

Zagesi nodded his head in the direction of the wall opposite Marcus. A luxuriously thick crimson curtain covered the entire wall. One of the other vampires stepped over to it and drew the curtains back.

It wasn't a wall at all. It was a large bay window.

"Strip him," Zagesi commanded.

The vampires ripped and tore at Marcus's clothes. Every single tug where the clothing would not give caused him tremendous pain.

"I told you earlier that I could have forgiven Acre. But that was before your partner destroyed my club and hundreds of my people. Some of them were actually innocent. And yet you still think you hold the moral high ground?"

Zagesi walked to the window. "Lelith had this window specially made, by my instruction. When the sun rises, your suffering will have just begun. An Ancient like yourself, even in your weakened state, won't perish from its rays. The pain you feel will be exquisite.

Take it from one who learned exactly what it felt like, after you left me chained to the outside of the Accursed Tower. You should learn to cherish it, for it is the least of what you will experience.

"As for you." He turned his gaze onto Rhuna. She shrank away from the ancient vampire the little she could in the bindings.

"You seem to have a body made for breeding, but too much spirit to make it truly pleasurable. You've maimed and killed many this night. You may take satisfaction in that, but it will be little consolation when I give you to their companions to use as they will."

He stepped back to admire them.

"I cannot tell, Lelith. Do I sense defiance or despair from them?"

"I do not know, Master."

"I think it may be defiance. Bring in their companions."

The other vampires left. In a few moments, they returned with Arthur's corpse and dropped it in the middle of the room. Puckered and discolored multiple gunshot wounds marred his upper body.

Next, they brought in John's corpse and dumped it unceremoniously on top of Arthur's. Despite herself, this drew a whimper from Rhuna. She could see some gunshot wounds, but John had been badly mauled afterward; the corpse was disfigured and nearly unrecognizable.

Next they brought in Roeland. He had been eviscerated. His intestines trailed after his body, tracking in a trail of blood and gore.

"Damned fools. Look at this mess. Lelith tried to make him eat his own intestines. She has yet to learn there is an art to such things."

Lelith looked down, ashamed.

"Oh, it's no trouble, my dear. You were understandably upset."

The last vampire brought in Alex's body and discarded it alongside the others. It was badly bruised and beaten. Rhuna could smell death coming from him even more than the others. One of his arms was broken and twisted in a gruesome unnatural manner. Puckered gunshot wounds dotted his exposed skin.

"And this one, he was too weak ever to have come along. I so wish he had survived, as I wanted to repay him properly for his audacity at the club."

Marcus laughed. One of the vampires cuffed him in the head.

"I am glad you are amused, Marcus. We will see if your mood matches your mirth this evening. Alas, the onset of daybreak is too near for further adventures this night. Rest well, the both of you. You will have much need of your strength in the coming hours."

Zagesi left with Lelith and the others. The last vampire tugged the door closed behind him, but had time to direct a lustful glance at Rhuna. He waggled his tongue at her between his fangs. Then the door closed with a clang.

A large lock snapped into place. Then there was silence and the sound of her own breathing.

Marcus spoke to her, his voice barely audible, sounding cracked and exhausted. "Can we expect help from your people?"

He knew more than she had thought. She shook her head.

Marcus's eyes swept around the room. He motioned toward the corner with his head, drawing her gaze to a small camera focused on the center of the room.

"What happened to you?" she asked.

"Zagesi got the better of me, I am ashamed to say. He had bodyguards, and I had just me. I sent many of them to the next world. Small consolation."

His head slumped down tiredly and he closed his eyes, exhaustion setting in.

His lips moved slightly and his voice, so faint that if not for her exceptional hearing she would have missed it, said, "Whatever you see, make no sound."

43

Rhuna woke to a low moan coming from Marcus. She didn't remember falling asleep. Sunlight bathed the room, but the direct rays had yet to touch him. They would be covering him in mere moments.

He strained against his restraints, every muscle and fiber stretched taut. Her own shoulders ached from the position of her arms, and her body felt stiff and sore. The bondage truss they had tied her in kept her in an awkward position. She couldn't move and they'd designed the thing to maximize discomfort. The collar chafed and choked her neck.

Suddenly Marcus screamed. It was a tortured howl of agony, and he bucked even harder against the restraints as direct sunlight struck him for the first time.

She wanted to say something. Anything encouraging. But she didn't know what to say. Part of her, the insensate animal within, enjoyed seeing Marcus in pain. He was just another vampire bastard, after all. Her thinking side knew better.

Over the sound of this, an electric motor whirred, and she looked for the source. The camera in the corner moved. Now its lens focused on Marcus. She should have known these bastards would want every moment recorded for posterity.

She watched with impotent compassion as the sun's rays crept down his face and his upper torso over the next few minutes. She could see his skin turn red and start to blister. The sunlight burned him horribly.

He stopped screaming only when his voice gave out on him. Even then, he gasped in misery, his breath coming in ragged wheezes.

The noise in the room changed again. She couldn't place it; it sounded like a shuffling, scratching sound. It was so low, she doubted that anyone but she or a vampire could hear it. She couldn't place the source. It seemed to be coming from the center of the room.

Finally, Marcus slumped in his bonds. She looked on with alarm, wondering if the sun had actually killed him. She couldn't tell.

She closed her eyes and tried to steel herself against despair. There had to be something she could do. Tonight, when they came for her, she would be ready. She would die well and let those vampire bastards know what it was to tangle with a member of the Pack.

Then, that scratching sound again. It nagged at her. It sounded as if countless insects were crawling over one another. Was this simply another torture the vampires had planned? Were they piping this sound in to toy with her sanity?

If she could somehow locate the source, it would make her feel better. She would at least be able to explain what it was. Her eyes swept the room again, searching desperately for a source. Everything was the same, except perhaps that it had grown slightly brighter, but even that could have been just in her mind.

Then she saw it. There was something out of place! She gasped, and then remembered Marcus's warning. Alex's arm, the one that had been shattered and twisted unnaturally, was no longer so. It lay alongside his body in a normal position.

This wasn't just a trick of her brain. She knew it had moved. She looked for signs of life. He wasn't breathing and her nose did not betray her. His scent was that of a corpse.

She stared at his body. The bruises seemed to be going away as well, though it was hard to tell, given his dark skin. She picked one bruise and studied it. She promised herself she wouldn't move her eyes from it until she could confirm whether it was changing.

She watched the bruise disappear.

Over the next hour, his skin became flawless. Then, just as the first direct ray of sunlight touched his body, his eyes flickered open. They stared at her. Unseeing. Almost imperceptibly, she saw his chest begin to rise and fall in shallow breaths.

In the face of this marvel, she had all but forgotten her own and Marcus's predicament. Alex blinked. Once. Twice. His eyes moved about and focused on her.

She nodded her head in the direction of the camera. It still pointed at Marcus. Alex moved his head slightly. She didn't know if he had seen it.

He looked back at her and winked.

She wanted to laugh. She fought to contain her emotions.

Alex started to move. He slid off the pile of corpses, carefully watching where his shadow fell. He removed his blood-soaked shirt. He moved like tar, no faster than the sunbeams crept across the room. The sunlight struck his dark skin, painting it gold. He lay there gasping, exhausted. She could see that somehow the sunlight was healing him, rebuilding his reserves of strength.

Another half hour went by without him making any movement. Then he began crawling toward her. At first he was on his belly, his arms outstretched toward her. He pulled his body forward, but it was almost as if the effort were too much. He slumped back down. A few ragged breaths. He was breathing hard, but trying to be quiet. Then he shook his head, and his breathing stopped.

He had died. Again?

He pulled his body forward. This time he didn't look as tired. Again. Then again. By the time he reached her, he was on all fours. He brought one finger to his lips. *Keep quiet.* He still wasn't breathing.

He reached up and undid her collar. The beast inside her recoiled

from whatever he was. She knew better. He tried to undo the restraints. From deep in his throat, she could hear the sound of his
straining. He stopped. Then lay back against the window. Held up
one finger.

Just a moment. Give me just a second. He mouthed the words.

She smiled back.

After several minutes, he shuffled back toward her. He grunted
slightly as he reached the restraints on her arm. They gave way with
pops and snaps. He fell back against the window and didn't move.
He closed his eyes. If she hadn't seen him get up earlier, she would
have thought he had died.

Died, again. The thought made her want to laugh.

His scent never changed.

He lay there a long time. His chest was still, with no sign of the
normal rise and fall. Just as she was beginning to think he would
never stir, he opened his eyes.

She tried to judge how much time had passed. The sun had shifted
position. It was near noon.

Alex stood. Now he didn't have to worry about his shadow being
cast on the far wall where the camera would pick it up. He stood in
front of the window, arms outstretched like da Vinci's Vitruvian
Man, intercepting as much sunlight as he could.

Rhuna sat in the corner and stretched her cramped limbs. Occasionally, Alex would look at her. Hours went by. She began to feel
safe. She was exhausted. She pantomimed going to sleep. Alex
nodded. If anything was going to happen, he would wake her up.

44

When she awoke, the sun was on the far side of the house. There wasn't much light coming in through the window. This whole side of the house was now in the shade. Alex sat with his back to the window. He was signing to Marcus. Marcus still looked unconscious, his skin blackened and burned, but she could see him looking at Alex through lidded eyes.

Alex saw she was awake and spoke very quietly.

"What you did to Marcus in the car. Can you do it again?"

She nodded.

"He's weak. We're going to need him to blood-frenzy."

She shook her head. That was a bad idea. He'd feed on anything, on anyone. Alex had to know that.

"Do it," he commanded.

That time, he didn't bother keeping his voice quiet.

The electric motor whirred again as Alex got to his feet. The camera swung around and stared directly at him.

Alex waved at it, then walked across the room and broke the shackles holding Marcus with a feat of casual strength that made Rhuna suck in her breath. Without the shackles to hold him up, Marcus slumped to the ground.

"The camera," Rhuna warned.

"I know." Alex turned toward it and gave it the middle finger.

"Rhuna. You're on."

"He'll feed on us."

"He won't feed on a thrope, not if given a choice."

"What about you?"

Alex shrugged. "You don't have to worry about me. Just do it. Quick as you can."

She turned her attention to releasing the pheromones she knew vampires responded to. It made her smell like the most delicious thing on the planet. They'd let their guards down and instantly enter the first stages of the blood frenzy.

She saw Marcus's head snap up and knew it was working. His eyes were taking on the bloodshot look, and his fangs were extending.

Outside, she could hear footsteps in the hallway.

"They're coming," she said.

"Counting on it."

Alex positioned himself astride the door. His fingers dug into the reinforced metal and it made a sharp creaking-grinding sound. He took a deep breath.

Rhuna heard someone on the other side of the door start to turn the lock. They never got the chance.

Alex grunted. The muscles in his back flexed and strained powerfully. He wrenched the door off its hinges. Half of the doorframe came with it. He tossed it aside and stared at the vampire on the other side, who was trying to shield his eyes from the sudden light with one hand. Alex yanked him into the room.

Marcus was on him before the vampire could cry out. Sinking his fangs into the other vampire, Marcus began to feed. Alex strode into the hall. Rhuna heard shouts and the sound of gunfire. Then screams.

Alex walked back into the room. Fresh blood and gore sloughed off his skin. Rhuna knew it was not his own. It stank of vampire. He had a gunshot wound in the center of his chest. He walked over to the window and pressed up against it.

"That hurt. A lot." He grimaced and wiped some of the gore from him.

Rhuna almost didn't want to ask. "Are you okay?"

Even as she spoke, she could see the wound closing back up. In a moment, it was a dull scar. Then the scar was gone.

Alex turned to Marcus. His skin was red but was looking almost normal. The blisters and blackening were gone. Dead cells fell away in flakes that looked like a bad sunburn.

"You finished?"

"No," Marcus answered, then added as an afterthought, "I am finished with *this* one."

"Good. Let's go."

Marcus dashed out of the room almost faster than she could see.

"What now?" Rhuna asked.

Alex stepped into the hallway and looked back over one shoulder at the corpses in the center of the room, then at her.

"Payback time."

45

5:20 P.M.

Menkaure strode down the hallway. There were six doors to his left, and beyond them the hallway ended in an elaborate dark mahogany stairway leading down. A handsome railing stretched away to his right, allowing the hall to overlook a great room on the ground floor. Long, expensive-looking drapes hung along the walls, separating historical banners and tapestries from one another. In each corner of the room, large bronze braziers contained hot coals and added an ancient ambience to the room. This was wasteful and dangerous. Was Zagesi so attached to the old ways, he still lit braziers? Apparently so. Every few feet there were cases and displays. From here, he could see artwork, vases, and relics—an impressive collection of antiquities even by Menkaure's high standards.

He stepped over the dismembered corpses of the vampires he'd torn into moments ago. He'd literally pulled them apart, ripping them limb from limb. All pretense of stealth or thought of surprise was gone. It was still daylight. They could catch half of these fuckers sleeping.

But he didn't want to. And neither did Marcus.

Marcus was already on the ground floor.

"Lugal Zagesi! Leader of the Confraternity of Admah. The so-called Lich King. Come out now, your time is at hand," he roared as only a vampire could.

344 ✦ MICHAEL F. HASPIL

A door to one of the rooms in the hallway opened and a half-dressed vampire ran out. Rhuna shouted when she saw him.

He turned toward her and Alex and charged. Alex sidestepped his clumsy attack easily and clotheslined him. The vampire crashed to the floor. Rhuna pounced.

"Breed me?" she screamed. Alex had no idea what she meant.

Her hands flew at the vampire's throat, and gore answered them. Alex caught a quick glimpse. Her fingers were no longer the fingers of a young woman. They looked like claws or talons of some kind.

She made short work of the vampire, and then stood, a feral grin on her face. She moved her hands sharply downward, splashing the floor with blood and viscera. Alex saw they were hands once more.

She caught him staring at her.

"What?"

"Pace yourself. There are *more*."

She laughed. It was the kind of laugh that didn't belong in a situation like this one, carefree and full of joy. It wasn't right.

Alex started down the stairs as Marcus kicked in the glass fronts of the display cases. He was trying to create as much noise and destruction as he could.

As Alex reached the ground floor, he heard more doors in the upper hallway opening up. He looked back and saw three vampires charge Rhuna. The largest one smashed into her and pulled her off her feet. She scratched and bit at him, making noises that should have sprung from some jungle panther. He raised her over his head and threw her over the railing down to the ground floor.

Alex saw her twist to right herself in midair like a cat and land on all fours. He had scarcely a second to admire her trick, because she was bounding past him and then back up the stairs, taking them three at a time.

A voice screamed at him, tearing his attention away from Rhuna and the carnage she was causing at the top of the stairs. He looked for the source.

And saw Lelith. Behind her, Constance stood, half dressed and clutching a robe tightly about her.

"You." Lelith spat at him.

"Me," Menkaure answered, and held his arms out wide. He had to admit, the day had been kind to Lelith. The bandages were gone and she almost looked her old self. Pity.

"Lieutenant, I'm going to kill Lelith here and then you're next."

Lelith leapt across the room at him, fangs out. Ready to make him feel her fury.

He timed his strike perfectly, thrusting out with his right arm as quickly and as hard as he could. She made a gurgling shocked moan as he knocked the wind from her. Alex flexed his hand, moving it, searching by touch alone for what he wanted. His eyes never left hers. He saw the look of perplexed terror enter her eyes as understanding dawned of exactly what was happening to her.

"Good-bye, Lelith," he whispered. Then pulled her heart out.

There was a loud crash to his right and he turned to see what was happening. Marcus and Lugal Zagesi wrestled one another in the final round of their ancient conflict. It was obvious there would be no quarter, no respite—only victor and vanquished. The two vampires knocked a brazier over, scattering the coals across the floor. Some of them reached the long drapes, which burst instantly into flame.

Menkaure turned his attention back to Constance. She was gone. He needed to go after her. There was no way she was going to get away with this.

The fire swept up into the high ceiling of the room; in a moment the heat would be blistering. They needed to get out now.

Alex looked up toward Rhuna. She finished the last of her assailants in an orgy of carnage and violence. She had only been passing as a human, but she was far from being one. He understood that now.

"Rhuna, this whole place is going to go up," Alex yelled. "Get out, as soon as you can." His thoughts turned to his own escape. How had Constance gotten out? Maybe he could catch up to her.

A pained cry drew his attention.

Marcus screamed as Zagesi pushed him backward. Marcus fell to one knee. It was clear that he needed Alex's help. Marcus was losing again, badly. In a few short moments, Zagesi would have the upper hand, and Alex didn't think Marcus had it in him to recover.

Alex raced toward the combat, but out of the corner of his eye, something caught his attention. He turned his head to regard the objects in the case and smiled. It was perfect. It was poetic.

Despite the fire, he had to do this.

In the case was a full panoply of Roman armor. Numerous objects shared the display; among them a pilum, a shield, and what looked to be a razor-sharp gladius. Alex shot a glance at the wall, which was now a raging inferno.

There was probably still time.

He smashed the case and grasped the gladius. Justice could be such a beautiful thing.

Zagesi had Marcus in a death grip. His fingers dug into Marcus's throat, and blood welled up from where they pressed. Zagesi's attention was so fixed on Marcus that he never even sensed Alex coming at him. Alex grabbed him with his left hand, his grip crushing the bones in Zagesi's shoulder. Zagesi screamed. Alex yanked him backward.

Zagesi stared stupidly at him as if wondering exactly what was going on. Then Alex threw him. The throw smashed Zagesi so hard into the far wall that the oak paneling of the old mansion shattered. Zagesi's impact put out a shock wave that shot glowing embers throughout the room and momentarily snuffed the flames in that part of the wall.

Marcus got to his feet, one hand clutching his bruised neck.

"You still know how to use one of these?" Alex tossed the gladius into Marcus's waiting hand.

"I'll manage." Marcus's voice was barely a croak.

Behind him, Rhuna loped up. She was a gory mess.

Alex spoke to her. "Watch our backs, will you?" Then to Marcus: "I'll hold him, you do the honors."

"With pleasure."

Zagesi was just beginning to recover from Alex's throw when Alex knelt over him and pinned him to the floor with one hand on his chest. He pressed down intentionally and felt things inside Zagesi give way. Telltale snaps and grinding sounds told of the wreckage he made of Zagesi's innards. Marcus knelt on the other side.

Zagesi's mouth moved. No sound came.

"Oh, he's trying to say something," Alex mocked. He let up the pressure slightly.

"How?" Zagesi asked.

Alex pinned him again.

"You're a fan of the Bard, so here's one for you: 'There are stranger things in heaven and earth than are dreamt of in your philosophy, Horatio.'" He nodded to Marcus.

Marcus drew back the sword. *"Vae Victis."*

He swung the gladius, and the Dread Sovereign Lugal Zagesi, the so-called Lich King of Admah, and the leader of the most dangerous conspiracy the world had yet known, was no more.

Alex relaxed.

Marcus chuckled. "I think you got that wrong."

"How's that?"

"'There are more things in heaven and earth, Horatio, than are dreamt of in your philosophy.'"

"Ah. We should probably get the hell out of here," Alex said. The fire wouldn't care who won or lost.

Alex looked at Rhuna. He pointed to the blood covering her nearly head to toe. "Any of that yours?"

"No," Rhuna answered.

"Come on then," Marcus said. "There's grim work to do if you're up for it."

EPILOGUE

They sat on the lawn in front of the mansion, looking at the blazing fire. The fire was so big now that people would notice. Emergency response vehicles were probably already on their way, if they weren't tied up in the city. There was no telling what had gone on over the last day. But now, with true night coming on, they needed to be gone.

"We made a pretty good team in there," Alex said.

"Some of them still escaped," Rhuna said.

"Yeah. Constance got away. That's the only one that bugs me," Alex said.

Marcus gave Alex a look.

"Oh come on, Marcus. You can't still be defending her. Not after all this. I can't believe we actually worked for her."

"I never did," Marcus said.

"How's that?" Alex asked.

"She works for me."

"Wait. Okay. At the risk of me feeling like a complete dullard, explain."

Marcus just smiled.

Alex started to figure it out. "The Order of the Eternal Watch? She's one of yours?"

Marcus nodded.

"And let me guess, Aguirre's source inside Haley House?"

Marcus nodded again. "Who do you think emptied out the Doral facility?"

"I thought Lelith did," Alex answered.

"Oh, I'm sure Lelith thought she did as well, but it was Constance who seeded the idea and then did some prodding for Lelith to pull the strings."

"Why not let me in on it? I could have killed her back there."

"Honestly, Alex, I thought you knew."

Alex shrugged. "And the others that got away?"

"They will speak of what happened here. The Confraternity will seek out everyone we know. They will try to find us. They cannot let us get away with what we have done."

"How much time do we have?" Rhuna asked.

"Twenty-four, maybe forty-eight hours. After that, consider the chase on. If you heed my advice, you will consider the chase on as of right now."

"So you're still for splitting up?"

"It gives us more of a chance."

"Fine. I'm beat. I'm used to pacing myself. I'm going to find somewhere to hole up and crash. Then, in the morning, I'm going home." Alex got to his feet.

"Menkaure, they'll come for you."

"I know, Marcus. But I'm not running. They'll be sending their goons after merely a cop as far as they know. Not after me. Besides, I've got a cat to feed and I just got the condo looking exactly how I wanted it."

"You know how to get in touch."

"Yep. Don't worry, I'll be going after this Confraternity, but I don't intend on doing it alone. I'll give you a yell as soon as I find out anything concrete. This last night has given me a couple of ideas."

"Like what?" Rhuna asked.

"Something our friend Aguirre said. That old quote about all that's needed for evil to triumph—"

"Is for good men to do nothing? It is one of his favorites. Alex, do not tell me he actually got to you?"

"I don't know, maybe. I'm feeling like we dodged a heavy bullet here and that maybe it wouldn't have been such a close thing if UMBRA had still been around. I'm thinking the world needs UMBRA, or something like it, now more than ever. If the govvies aren't going to do it, maybe someone else should."

"Someone like you?"

"Why not? What do you say, Marcus? How about getting the band back together? We can start with Trent, Stephanie, and Zorzi. We know where they are."

"Ask me in a month." Marcus rose and shook Alex's hand.

"One question," Rhuna said.

"Yeah?"

"How are you not dead? Even now, you smell like a corpse."

"That is a very long story that started a very long time ago. Before even Marcus or maybe even Zagesi was around. I might even get around to telling the whole thing someday. But not now."

Rhuna looked disappointed.

"A secret for a secret. What's the real deal with the Pack? Why can you change at will? Why are you not on a cycle like the other thropes?"

"Thropes are people most of the time and only become animals part of the time. We aren't thropes."

"How's that?"

"We're only people part of the time."

Alex chuckled and nodded. "So that's the Pack's big secret."

"Now your secret."

"I don't have one," Alex answered. He tapped his index finger along the side of his nose three times—the secret sign of Djehuty. "The nose knows."

"What?"

"Just tell her," Marcus said.

"I'm already dead, Rhuna. Technically, you can't kill the dead twice. Vampires think they have the market cornered on the undead, but I've got them beat. I'm undeader . . . that's not even a word." Alex chuckled. He rubbed his eyes in fatigue. His joints were seizing up and he was growing stiff; that fight had taken more out of him than he wanted to admit.

Rhuna looked even more puzzled.

"Explain it to her, Marcus. I'm not making sense anymore. I'll see you around. Don't get caught."

"Likewise."

Alex walked down the driveway, then turned and headed for the woods surrounding the burning estate. He bet no one would come looking for him in the trees. He planned to find a nice overhang with a good clear view of the sky and have himself a nice nap until morning. Already, his limbs were growing heavy and more corpse-like. He could hear Marcus talking to Rhuna as they walked to the hunter truck.

"You have had the esteemed privilege of meeting and fighting alongside the son of Khafre, son of Khufu. The Morning and the Evening Star. The Great Bull of Horus, Kha-khet. The king of the black land of Kemet. He who walks the Path of Osiris. The oncetime pharaoh Menkaure blessed or cursed to walk amidst the lands of the living once again."

Just like a Roman.

There was Marcus, using all the formal titles, when he could have just told her Alex was a reanimated mummy.